FOOTPRINTS ON THE HEART

Footprints on the Heart

a novel

JEAN NAGGAR

ISBN-13: 9781096415718
ISBN-10: 1096415712

Also by Jean Naggar

Sipping From the Nile, My Exodus From Egypt, a memoir

Life itself is an exile. The way home is not the way back.

Colin Wilson

….. when I am in one city, I am dreaming of the other. I am an exile; citizen of the country of longing.

Suketu Mehta

For my children,
Alan, David, Jennifer, with infinite love

CKNOWLEDGMENTS

My first thanks go to my agent, Harvey Klinger. Harvey held my feet to the fire again and again and would not accept anything but the best from me. With great kindness he told me what would not work and helped me to discover what would, and he never lost faith. No writer could have had a more wonderful agent.

Thanks beyond measure go to my husband, Serge, for always being there to support, advise, and encourage, and listen to me read whenever I needed to test something out. Thanks to my home team, my children David and Jennifer, who gave so generously of their time and advice. Huge thanks also to Edgar Berebi, who was kind enough to share his time and early experiences of exile from Egypt. Particular thanks to my sister Susan for her careful readings and invaluable comments as the novel took shape. Betty P., your friendship and invaluable advice have meant so much. I cannot thank you enough. Thanks to Benita, for her unwavering delight in the novel and for the many hours of insight she shared with me as she read its many iterations. My brother Jeff, Viviane B, Vivette, Helene, Lynne, and others too, read, commented and helped me to make the book better. I thank you all. It takes a village.

CONTENTS

PROLOGUE

THE MANGO HARVEST

Egypt 1956

Salwa, her expressive face sulky, trudged beside the sweep and glide of her mother's dark *abaya*. The day was sultry, a fierce sun shimmering and blazing. They had left the village well before dawn, her father perched on the donkey, balancing an array of straw baskets on either side, his sandaled feet turned out and bobbing as he went along; her mother balancing a pitcher of water on her head, drawn from the communal well the night before. Her brothers seeming not in the least affected by the heat and the long dusty walk, were leaping, fighting, laughing and tumbling alongside.

It was a very long walk to Cairo from their small cluster of mud huts on the borders of the Nile. Giza, a prosperous urban district sprawling between the bustling commercial center of Cairo and the pyramids, was also situated along the banks of the Nile, but where they were heading could not have differed more from where they lived. As they neared their destination, houseboats strung along the edge of the river, bounced and swayed as *feluccas* glided and motor boats roared past. A string of imposing mansions with luxuriant grounds faced the river across the broad street. Traffic swelled, donkeys and camels vying for road space with cars and people, horns blaring, dust flying.

Salwa and her family hurried along beside the river bank, trying not to be confused by the rising clamor of urban life. They clustered closer together as they headed toward the mansion they visited every year, where large mango trees in the gardens promised a fine harvest. Salwa's father knew the head gardener there, a sour individual whose family lived in their village. Salwa could never understand why the people who owned the trees and lived in the beautiful house took so little of the fruit for themselves.

Usually, Salwa looked forward to the day of the mango harvest. Her father and brothers, shaded from the punishing sun, thick ropes around their waists, shimmied up again and again into the canopies of huge leafy trees loosening the ripe fruit, while Salwa and her mother ran around in the heat below, managing to catch the shiny green globes in baskets as they fell, or grabbing them quickly off the ground.

Every year, the hawk-faced gardener, his white *galabiya* swirling about him, strode across the vast lawn toward them. As Salwa watched, her father immediately slid down from his tree, calling to his sons to continue their work. He bowed, grinned, and touched his forehead, "*Ya salaam, Effendi,*" he said, clearly pleased to visit with his old friend. The two men sat down together in a shady place, lit cigarettes, and resumed their yearly negotiations, bemoaning the cost of food, the price of mangoes, the exigencies of the *hawaga*, the growing unrest that was evident in Cairo, trading the latest politics for the latest gossip from back in the village. It was a game they both enjoyed and explored to the full with much stabbing of hands and harsh bursts of laughter, until agreement on a price for the current harvest was reached.

This year, however, Salwa had begged to be excused.

" I'm tired, *Oumi,*" she wailed to her mother. "It will be so hot. My feet hurt. I'd rather stay home and take care of the baby. Can't you take Nadia instead?"

But her mother was adamant. Thirteen-year-old Salwa would be far more help with the work than six-year-old Nadia, who could stay home and watch the baby.

The fragrance of rich ripe sweet fruit suffused the air around them as they worked. Every now and then they paused in their labors and peeled a mango with their knives, eating their fill as the day progressed. The sale of the harvest paid for food for Salwa's family for weeks.

No-one had ever seen anyone who lived in the mansion that dominated the center of the property. Last year, Salwa's brother Mahmoud had confided in her that he had tried his hardest to see into the tall windows when he was up in the tree, but filmy drapes at every window clouded everything inside. Disappointed, Mahmoud had not caught even a fleeting glimpse of the inhabitants.

Salwa sighed and wiped away the sweat on her face with a corner of her loose white robe. Looking around, she noticed that the harvesting had slowed. Her mother was slumped in a corner, exhausted, eyes closed. Her father was still smoking his cigarette under a palm. Her brothers had begun a game, swinging through the branches, shouting to each other, grabbing the last few mangoes they discovered hiding under the canopy of leaves. She wandered off by herself, gazing up at the thick red brick and grey stone walls of the house. Did people really live there? It was so different from her home. It looked so substantial, like a place where kings and princes might live.

She crept cautiously around the house until she found herself facing a small side door. It was ajar. Glancing around and seeing and hearing nothing, she took a deep breath and pushed at the door. To her surprise it swung open, revealing a spiral staircase. It was dark in the house and it took a moment for her eyes to adjust. She stepped inside, blinking, soaking in the welcome cool of high stone ceilings. A heavy silence spread about her, so that she could hear the pounding of her heart, the blood pounding in her ears. She stood still, listening.

The marble stairs that wound upward were stained and worn down in the center. She wondered whose feet had worn them down, and where they led. A strong desire to explore filled her, flooding out all caution. She put a hand on a banister smooth and shiny from use, and began a climb that was to resonate for the rest of her life.

The staircase opened out into a vast kitchen. Nobody was in the kitchen. Huge stoves, with roaring flames in their bellies, startled her. Cloths were spread out to dry on racks by an open window, fluttering slightly in the gentle breeze. An enormous box squatted to one side. She ran to it, glanced around, lifted the lid and stood on tiptoe to peer inside. The box held big blocks of ice. She put a hand on the ice and held it to her flushed face. It felt so good. She lifted the lid again and breathed in the icy air gratefully.

Glancing cautiously from side to side, she crept on past tall doors of dark carved wood, and found herself in a vast hall glittering in the late afternoon sun reflecting in mirrored doors, filtering from floor-to-ceiling windows through soft white curtains. She caught her breath, momentarily blinded by the light, enchanted by the sparkle and splendor, twisting her neck to stare above at gold and bronze designs scribbled on the borders of a high vaulted ceiling. Thick-piled bronze-colored carpet caressed her bare feet, and she shuddered with pleasure at the sensation, wiggling her toes, marveling at the size and opulence spread before her, dazzled by the jewel tones bordering the carpet and the fragile elegance of the sparse furnishings. A broad marble staircase led upstairs to a landing opening onto more tall windows. She could see that the staircase continued beyond her sight, winging upward on either side of the landing, leading even higher to another floor, gleaming brass banisters topping intricate ironwork.

Salwa stood still, arrested in her exploration by the magnificence that surrounded her. A slammed door upstairs startled her. She gasped, and stared, her hand on her heart, her eyes wide. Her heart beating fast, she ran back to the kitchen. To the left, the corridor was dark. There were several narrow doors on either side. She glanced through an open door and saw that the rooms were smaller, less intimidating. She listened, holding her breath, hearing only a thick pulsating silence. She pushed at one of the doors and stepped hesitantly inside. A bare mattress balanced on an iron frame in a corner, and shelves upon shelves lined the walls with books. A desk stood in another corner, thick with dust, and she approached, awed. Small as it was in proportion to the hall and the kitchen, this room was larger than her entire home. She crept hesitantly toward the desk and slowly reached out her hand to touch an extravagantly ornate gold frame that sat on the desk. It set off a faded daguerreotype of a young woman with slanted eyes and high cheekbones, wearing an elaborate lace dress, rows and rows of pearls cascading down onto her bosom, dark hair piled high, a fanciful hair-ornament of organdy, pearls and feathers perched among the curls. Salwa gasped. She had never seen anyone dressed like that. She had never seen anything so lovely. The woman's eyes held her gaze with an imperious power.

Mesmerized, Salwa drew even closer. She didn't hear steps approaching, but suddenly a deep voice right behind her scared her almost out of her wits.

"Hello, little sprite," said the voice, laughter in its depths, the guttural sound harsh in the quiet room, "And who are you?"

Salwa turned and gazed, terrified, at a lanky youth with dark eyes and a riot of dark curls, a half smile on his face. He grinned as he breathed in her mango scent and discerned the hint of a rounded figure under the grubby robe she wore. He took a step forward. She tried to speak but her voice stuck in her throat.

Seeing her alarm, the youth moved back. Then, never taking his eyes off her, he pointed at his chest and said, "Don't be frightened. I'm Sol. What's your name? Are you with the mango family?"

Salwa nodded. She contemplated making a run for it, but he stood squarely between her and the door. When he realized that she wasn't going to say anything, he moved over to the mattress, very slowly, careful not to startle her.

This was a totally unexpected beam of light entering his day. He didn't want to frighten her away. He wondered what to do next. She was small, with a neat brown face and big dark eyes shiny with alarm. He thought she seemed to be about his age. He had been feeling so bored, alone with his unspoken fears, with school closed and no-one to talk with.

Patting the mattress beside him, he said, "Like to sit down? You must be tired. It's so hot out there today. I only want to talk to you. My parents are out. My school in Heliopolis closed suddenly a few days ago, because of some sort of military operation to do with Port Said and the Suez Canal, and the servants are all having an extended siesta in the basement. I'm bored, and I'm lonely." He watched her hesitate and start to move toward him.

"Come, sit down and talk to me," he said. "tell me about yourself, your family, your life. I'd like some company." His dark eyes pleaded.

Salwa had never been bored. She didn't really know what the word meant. There was no time in her life for that, but she did know what it was to be lonely. She sidled slowly to the mattress and sat beside him, looking up at him shyly from under thick curling lashes. He did not look so different from her brothers, or from some of the youths in the village.

"You *live* here?" She asked in awe. He laughed. It was a full-throated engaging sound and a smile twitched at her lips in response.

"Where do you live when you're not harvesting our mangoes?" Sol asked, enchanted by her smile.

Salwa said "By the river. A small village."

"Any brothers or sisters?"

"Four brothers and two sisters," she said, smiling fully now.

"You are so lucky," said Sol soberly. "I'd love to have brothers and sisters. I'm the only child of my parents."

"Ah!" Salwa breathed. "Sometimes it must be nice to be the only one."

He laughed again, delighted by her response.

She was losing her wariness. Looking around, she asked "Do you sleep in this room?"

Sol laughed again. "No-one uses it," he said. "Our bedrooms are upstairs and the servants have rooms in the basement and up under the roof. I sometimes come here to read and think."

They chatted quietly, each learning with fascination about a life so different from their own, and soon the laughter and chatter became more animated. He was nice, thought Salwa, her fears and embarrassment fading fast. She had never had a friend like this, someone interested in her opinions, in her life. She thought about Sadik in the village, and the way he had of sneaking up on her and pulling her hair. Sadik was her friend even though he was a few years older. He was always seeking her out and delighted in teasing her, but he never seemed in the least interested in her opinions. He saved serious talk for the other boys.

The quiet and her exhaustion took over. The family had risen well before dawn to make their way to Cairo. It had been a very long arduous walk from the village, followed by relentless work with the mangoes. Her eyes fluttered and closed involuntarily and her head sank to rest on Sol's shoulder. Surprised and disarmed, he put a hand on her shoulder to steady her. Reaching over her head, he pulled down one of the dusty books from a shelf. Salwa roused herself and sat up, laughing, and they looked at pictures together, their heads almost touching.

"Can you read?" he asked.

She shook her head regretfully. His warm lips brushed her cheek and his hand reached tentatively for her breast, his eyes questioning. She looked deeply into his eyes and did not move away. She knew that upon their return to the village she would be forced to accept one of the two elderly suitors vying for her person and her life. She had seen their bald heads and large bellies and had shuddered at the heat in their eyes when they watched her walking about her chores in the village.

"So fussy," she heard her mother's disapproving voice, "I was married at twelve. You are late to marriage, Salwa. So fussy. The choice is not yours. Your father will decide on a husband for you when we get back from the mango harvest. This time, you will obey."

Salwa looked down at his hand. She sighed and shuddered with the power of her longing and the insistent call of her body. Here, beside her, was everything she had not dared to dream about. The sight and scent of this young man steeped her senses in wonder and delight. This was her opportunity to explore the mysteries of life that had been haunting her dreams and that crumbled to dust in the face of the reality awaiting her. Here, she was being given the opportunity to exercise her own will, to satisfy her own desires. She had always been defiant, and now her daring in entering the house in the first place had brought about this wondrous encounter. She knew in her heart that this was the way she wanted it. This would be a memory worth having. She moved closer.

Soon they were kissing more and more deeply, touching and exploring each other's bodies slowly, until her world spun and swept her away from everything. It was finer and sweeter than anything she had ever dreamed of. He smelled of lemon and jasmine, and his lips were full and soft on hers. She knew she should pull away, but instead she turned to him and reached up to touch his hair. He pulled her close, caressing her face and hair, his hand moving lower as they lay curled into one another, eyes closed, drifting in an unexpected whirlwind of senses and delight.

Lifting her head, she turned toward Sol and guided his hand to move under the robe. She wore nothing underneath. Her body smelled of ripe fruit, of sweat and sun. He gasped and pulled her closer, his hand making her legs feel weak. His hand caressed her until the ripples of pleasure that filled her became a roaring tide, and she felt her desire rise like a huge unstoppable wave to meet his.

She understood where it would lead, and she didn't care. This was so insistent, so overwhelming, her body trembled and responded. She liked how she felt and she liked that her touch seemed to fill the handsome youth at her side with a similar delight. She wondered at the silky heat of his skin in her hand, as Sol led her gently into the dance of the senses, the ebb and flow, the crescendo, touch and counter-touch, meeting desire with desire, and daring at last to venture all, until they were breathless and spent, replete in the afterglow and locked in an intimacy that neither had expected and that both treasured as the gift of a chance encounter of youth, circumstance and destiny.

As she fully embraced the fact that there was no going back from what had happened, Salwa was aware in the shaken depths of her being that this moment was unique, that this strange mixture of exquisite pleasure and pain was a terrifying secret she would take to her grave, a secret that would be hers to savor, one that would illuminate the hurried gropings of her life to come. It was the finest moment of her life.

They slept for a time, their breathing deep and synchronized. Time slowed and hours passed. Doors began to slam and distant voices and the sudden thud of feet rammed into their consciousness.

"I think you may want to go, now, if you don't want to be seen," said Sol, lifting his head, a wave of melancholy overpowering him, "The servants are starting dinner, and my parents will be home soon. My mother ordered some dresses from Paris, and she went to the dressmaker for a fitting." He sighed, and his eyes anxiously searched her face. "Are you alright?" He asked.

Salwa had no idea what he was talking about. She looked up at him, tears trembling on her eyelids. It was what she had wanted, but it was over. She had no words for this. She knew it would never happen again. She knew she would never forget it. She lifted her face for his last kiss, smoothed her robe, pushed past his outstretched arms and fled.

Outside, her mother said crossly, "Salwa, where have you been? I had to finish up the baskets by myself. You've been no help at all."

She did not notice the dazed expression on her daughter's face, or the faint aura of lemon and jasmine that surrounded her. Salwa didn't answer. She busied herself loading baskets on the donkey, and soon they were making their way out of city streets crowded with camels and cars, noise blaring around them. They trudged along the banks of the Nile, silent, without a second glance passing tall iron railings shielding the gardens of magnificent mansions, leaving behind houseboats and traffic, until they were alone on the narrow strips of dusty green that stretched on granite cliffs between the heavy Nile waters and the vastness of the desert. Peace and twilight stole over their tired faces and bodies, and they finally arrived at their village as night fell.

PART I

$\mathscr{C}$HAPTER ONE

Cairo, Egypt 1956
SOL MIZRAHI

Another day. Heat. Nothing to do.

Sol wandered restlessly around the house, upstairs and downstairs. It was too hot and sticky to go outside. Trundle, his father's elderly dog padded over to join him, gazing expectantly up at him with liquid brown eyes. Sol fondled the German shepherd's silky ears absent-mindedly, his thoughts returning to the charmed time he had spent with the little mango girl the day before. He realized with distress that he didn't even know her name. He felt an overwhelming sadness that the transcendental moment they had shared would never be repeated. It was highly unlikely that their paths would ever cross again. Clearly, it was to be a beautiful memory with no past and no future.

Now, he was bored and lonely again. The day stretched before him with no boundaries and no promise. His classes were supposed to have begun a few days earlier, but there had been a notice from the school that classes were postponed until further notice.

"Can I meet up with Hassan or Youssef this afternoon? We could go to the Gezira Club for tennis?" he asked his mother hopefully, adding, "could Ahmad drive us? Perhaps he could give me a driving lesson?"

But she answered "Not the moment for those things, Solly. Try to understand," her face troubled and her thoughts leaping from one thing to another as she tried to shake the unfamiliar situation into something resembling order. He waited, but she offered no other clarification, lost in her own reflections.

Sol set off to find his book, but he was feeling more and more confused as yet another day continued without the normal framework that held the hours together between dawn and dusk. Many of his school friends seemed not to have returned from their summer vacations. He had tried to talk to his best friend, Hassan, to set up something with him, but he was not often allowed to use the phone, which sat squat and black on the sideboard in the dining room, with an extension also in solitary splendor in a corner of the upstairs hallway.

The past few days, whenever he was able to dial Hassan's number Hassan's mother always answered at the other end, and she always said he was not at home. If only school would start up again, he and Hassan could walk to the bus together, sharing their jokes and confidences on their way to school as they had done for years. He missed Hassan. He missed the freedom to run and jump along the way to the bus stop, reaching for low-lying branches and trying out their strength on each other, hitting at each other with their satchels, laughing, grumbling about the latest homework, and talking about girls. He wanted so much to tell Hassan about his incredible afternoon with the mango harvest girl. He was almost starting to think it had all been an amazing dream.

Come to think of it, there had been a strange atmosphere around the house and in the town, as if everything were collectively holding its breath. Sol had become aware of the tension in the air, the sensation that unseen forces were gathering around him, preparing to take possession of everything he had known so far, but he pushed the knowledge deep down into his psyche, where he would not have to recognize that it was there. Meanwhile, he meandered uneasily through the days, trapped in a solitude of teenage *angst*, spinning wheels, waiting for his life to kick back in.

Aldo, his father, had taken to leaving for work earlier and earlier every morning, returning each day for lunch and his siesta with an increasingly solemn expression. He hardly spoke. In the evenings, after a grumpy appearance at the dinner table, he moved stoop-shouldered across the center hall, followed by Trundle, and shut himself alone in the library where he fiddled with the dials of the old brown radio, emerging every now and then to shake his head despairingly in his wife's direction, and to head for the crystal decanters in the dining room for a liqueur to cushion his anxieties.

Sol's mother, Eliane, sat with Sol in the living room every evening after dinner, slim legs elegantly crossed, fingers flying, focused on her embroidery. She was making an exquisite dinner set, a large linen tablecloth and twelve napkins embroidered with an autumnal pattern of orange and rust, her glasses perched on the end of her nose and her hands delicately placing each stitch in perfect harmony.

"What's going on, Papi?" Sol asked, a disturbed urgency in his voice, but his father only looked bemused, shrugged his shoulders, and turned away without answering.

"Everything's going to be fine, Solly dear, don't you worry," his mother said, her voice soothing, giving him a distracted kiss and an abstracted smile, as she hurried off to discuss the next day's menus with the cook. Sol sighed. It seemed that he was expected to ignore all signs of an impending disturbance and behave as if all were as it should be.

Sol walked slowly into the hush of the library. The brown wooden shutters at the tall windows had been hooked closed against the fierceness of the midday sun. He turned the light on and looked around until he found the book he had been reading a couple of days earlier. He ambled into the large drawing room, the book dangling from his hand. The light was better there. Sounds of a Chopin waltz drifted in and out of his thoughts as Sol, with a fine disregard for the pedigree of his grandmother's furniture, edged himself into a more comfortable position on a sofa, his long legs finding a good spot over the top while he slouched lower, one eye on his book and the other on the antique ormolu clock ticking the minutes away on the Louis XV table next to him. His mother's piano practice was progressing as it did every morning, scales, Chopin, lunch. Eliane Mizrahi was a creature of habit. Nothing new there.

Sol knew that Ahmad would glide in soon through the door behind him, carefully averting his eyes from the young man's careless posture, and he would announce lunch. Tantalizing smells were starting to drift through the heavy doors from the kitchen area. He tried to ignore his growling stomach. He was well aware that Ahmad, who had known him from the day he was born, disapproved of his flippant ways but loved him anyway, with a fierce and unquestioning love reserved for his own family.

At fifteen, Sol was often bored, and always hungry. The book he was trying to read was only minimally interesting. He sighed, wishing his mother would stop playing the piano in the music room, she was messing with his concentration.

"Oh God! I need to get out of here," he muttered to himself through clenched teeth, for the tenth time in the past hour, "I need my life back," somehow aware that the life he had known so far would never come back, but pretending even to himself that his uneasiness had no basis in reality. He had indulged in the usual teenage grumbles about school, but now he would have given anything to sit fidgeting through a math class with his friends all around him. He could feel the huge beautifully appointed house and its implicit demands on his future closing in on him. He was desperate to understand what was happening to the future he had always taken for granted, but his parents were becoming increasingly unavailable. His restlessness filled him with an unexpressed anguish that disguised itself as nonchalance. He wanted, and didn't want to know what was happening around him.

For the past weeks, Sol had lived in a constant broth of conflicting emotions, connecting fearfully with the pressures closing in on the world around him, feeling electric moments of mind-numbing terror that his future might be on the cusp of resounding change, and yet continuing to experience the softness and ease that his world had once seemed to promise would last forever.

He had understood that threat hung over his family because they were Jewish, but he had always considered himself Egyptian, perhaps more Egyptian than Ahmad, who had left three wives and a bevy of children in the Sudan to find work in Cairo, whereas Sol's family had lived in Cairo for many generations, even if they had originated in Spain and moved to Egypt from Turkey. None of it made any sense to him.

He was desperate to talk to someone about it all, but he was under strict orders from his parents to avoid any comment to anyone regarding the consequences of President Gamal Abdel Nasser's bold annexation of the Suez Canal, regarding the role of the new young State of Israel in the few days of battle that had shut down his school, or regarding the fact of being Jewish at all. They had insisted that one false word on his part in the explosive atmosphere that surrounded the apparent normalcy they lived in could result in prison, or worse. He was not sure he believed that, but he had no intention of trying it out. His way of dealing with it was to close himself off from it all.

A crash of dissonant chords surprised him and he looked up from his book and his musings, and sighed, taking his legs down from the top of the carved gilt frame of the sofa just as the door behind him swung open and Ahmad's gravelly voice echoed through the large hall,

"*Hawaga* Solly, *il Sitte* Mama waits for you."

Sol became aware that the music had not started up again. He bounded to his feet, and made for the dining-room.

Lunch was delicious, as usual, and he ate heartily. Nonetheless, a heavy pall of silence hung over the meal. Sol's father had not come home for his usual lunch and siesta. They were already sitting at the dining table when he phoned to say that he would be stopping by the *muski,* the bazaar, and Sol watched with growing unease as his mother paled, her slim fingers tipped in a pale pink polish, white-knuckled, as she clutched the phone, nodding vigorously and making little gasping sounds. He could not hear what his father was saying, but as soon as Eliane put the phone down he asked,

"What was all that about?"

Eliane shook her head without looking up, put a finger to her lips, and he understood that whatever it was must not be discussed in front of the three servants who glided smoothly about the dining room, bringing hot dishes from the kitchen, refilling heavy crystal glasses with iced water, and seeing to their every need with well-trained efficiency.

The day had started out without signaling that it would be any different from any other day. It was a day like any other. Except that it was not.

After Ahmad had produced fruit plates and finger bowls, each with a rose petal floating in the warmed lemon-scented water, and he had pulled back the heavy dining room chair so that Eliane could leave the table when she so desired, he bowed and left mother and son to themselves.

Eliane jumped up from her chair and stood at the window, staring out over a profusion of purple morning glory covering the roof outside the dining-room. The sun shone down on the back lawn glittering rich and green, as the gardener's apprentice, a small boy, wielded a large garden hose to help it along. He saw her at the window and grinned up at her, gap-toothed. Sol watched with alarm as fat tears rolled silently down his mother's face, and he felt icy fingers of fear invade his stomach.

"Solly, stop standing about," his mother said at last, wearily, wiping at her tears, irritated with herself, "Go up to your room this minute and put together your most precious treasures and some very warm clothes." She turned away from the window and added "Papi will be coming home with suitcases. We may have a few days or weeks to prepare and get things together, but we may have to leave tomorrow. I heard that they will take our Egyptian passports at the airport and make us sign a paper that we will never return to Egypt. They are saying that people are only allowed to take with them the clothes they are wearing, but perhaps a suitcase or two…?" Her words trailed off into a stunned silence. The words rang in Sol's ears but only compounded the unreality of the situation.

"Leave for where?" He asked, afraid to understand what she was implying, "we just came home. Leave, why?" He paused, "you mean - *leave Egypt?*" His voice cracked as he tried to envision such an unimaginable possibility. Thinking back, he recognized that deep fissures had been opening in his secure world for some time. He had noticed the servants putting up blue paper at the windows that faced the Nile. He had heard distant gunfire, but some sort of agitation was always going on in Cairo, it was a city of loud noises, vivid colors and sudden altercations. There were often demonstrations in the center of town, and by and large his parents had seemed unperturbed. Four years ago Sol remembered that there had been violence and fury loosed against Jewish businesses, but that had to do with Israel, it had nothing to do with him, and it had passed. It had only caused a temporary blip in Sol's life.

Now, there was obviously some strong new disturbance going on somewhere about something, but his mind deliberately skirted examining the matter too closely. When his parents deflected his questions he had not pushed hard enough for answers. Now, understanding had suddenly descended in a crushing blow. While he had been bemoaning his isolation from his schoolmates, and wallowing in his boredom, something much more terrifying had invaded his life and was threatening to wrench him from it. Why, he wondered, had his parents shielded him from what was going on? He had repeatedly tried to obtain clarity from them, to share in whatever crisis they were anticipating. The stress in the air created invisible waves that eddied about him in unrevealed tumult. He was not a child. Why had they kept their concerns from him?

He looked about him at the thick walls and sumptuous surroundings that had cradled his grandmother's youth, his mother's childhood, and his own fifteen years so far. His mother's voice seemed far away. There was a ringing in his ears.

"How can you be so oblivious to what has been going on around you?" His mother continued, unfair in her exasperation, forgetting that she had not wanted to alarm him with her own fears by sharing the full situation with him, unaware of where her son's thoughts had taken him. "Papi and I have tried to explain to you that many friends of ours have been gradually leaving Egypt, and sending out their young people to get educated elsewhere. Remember the demonstrations, the terrible fires, the riots in town in 1948 and in 1952? Remember how your father's cousin, Zaki, left for Paris in '48? Zaki knew what would happen. As soon as Israel was officially recognized as an independent state, he came over to talk to your father. '*Now*,' he said, 'don't put this off, Aldo, you need to leave *now*. The other Arab countries will never recognize that the Jews have any claim to that land. They will back the Arabs from Palestine to the hilt. This is war, Aldo, war … you are no longer living in the Jew-tolerant Ottoman empire. Can't you see that as Jews, we are at grave risk? At the very least, try to get some money out of the country.'

He told us again and again that we should sell the house. He told us the writing was on the wall and that we should make our plans to go elsewhere, but your father and I couldn't believe it. This is our home. We are Egyptian. Why would we leave because a tiny Jewish island has been carved out of a vast ocean of Arab lands? What had that to do with us? Why would our Egyptian brothers turn on us?"

Eliane's usually gentle voice burst from her in a hoarse bark, startling her son, who was trying to make sense of what she was saying.

"Oh Sol! Zaki was so right. Just do as I say. We need to move fast. Your father and I had planned a code word between us that would indicate that events are accelerating faster. He must know something, because he used that word. Now I know what we need to do. I have a list of things that have to be done before he gets home." She looked at her son and was aghast at the blank expression on his handsome face, not recognizing the effort he was making to keep his fears to himself.

"Solly, surely you must have realized that this Suez Canal thing was serious?" She asked anxiously. "Israeli troops joined the British and French to try to recapture the Suez Canal after Nasser nationalized it. Now they have their excuse to kick out the Jews. We were in a dream world of denial. Zaki was right. We have become the enemy in our own country. It will not be the first time." She turned away, adding "Papi said they have already arrested Andre Harari."

"Who…?" began Sol, but his mother cut in, "You *know* who, Solly, think! Our neighbor from that big villa down the road, your father's bridge partner with the white hair and the carnation in his buttonhole." Her voice came out in a sob, "They've *arrested* him. What could he possibly have done? Your father says he has already been taken to prison and no-one knows exactly where he is. Imagine, he has probably been thrown into a cell somewhere with thieves and murderers." She looked at her son and burst out "We could be next." Hiding her face in her hands, she ran out of the dining room.

Sol got to his feet slowly. The world he knew had begun to shift under him, and he felt heavy and full of fear. He followed his mother and asked "What about Trundle? What will happen to him?"

"Papi is coming to take him to the vet," said Eliane. "He's very old. It may be kinder to put him down rather than to leave him to strangers."

Sol gulped down tears. "Couldn't we ask Ahmad to keep him?" He asked in a strangled voice, but his mother had already bustled out of the room.

In his room, Sol looked around, unable to focus on what might be his most treasured possessions, trying to grasp the fact that whatever he did not pack, he would never see again. He moved slowly around his room, picking up sports trophies, framed photos, mementos and books in his hands, staring at them, and putting them down again. Too heavy. Too big. Not significant enough. Trundle had followed him upstairs and every time the dog's soft nose nuzzled his hand, his throat closed up and his eyes teared. How could this be happening?

The next two days passed in a blur of panic as Aldo Mizrahi rushed to various government offices to try to obtain a stay of the expulsion notice he had received. His efforts were in vain. Departure was certain and imminent. Eliane and Sol spun in circles of confusion. They could take one suitcase. No, they could take one suitcase each. They could take as many suitcases as they needed. No, no suitcases would be allowed ... They packed, unpacked, and re-packed, before arriving at last at the Cairo airport, disheveled, bleary-eyed from fatigue and sadness, with one large brown leather suitcase each into which they had done their best to cram survival necessities for an unknown future, together with vestiges of the past of many generations.

Before leaving, Eliane walked slowly through all the rooms, passing her hand lovingly over ornaments and furnishings that she had always taken for granted and that she would be leaving to an uncertain fate. She had managed to fit some photos of her wedding, of her parents, and of Sol when he was a baby into her suitcase. As she moved through the back rooms, she picked up the small gold frame that held the portrait of her grandmother.

"I'm taking this," she said, looking defiantly at Aldo, who shrugged, shaking his head. "This will be for you, one day, Solly," she said to her son, "wherever you find yourself in the world, you should keep some ties to your past. Grandma Elena will help to bind your children to their past and their future. Make sure to pass it on to your oldest child one day." She wrapped the frame carefully in a warm scarf and tucked it into the side of her suitcase.

"I can't quite close it," she called out to her son who was on his way to his room, "come over here and sit on it. Ahmad says he will drive us to the airport. He says he'll keep an eye on the house while we are gone, in case we ever come back. I've explained to him that they'll take our passports and our right to ever return, but he simply refuses to believe it."

In his room, Sol stood still and looked about him as he tried to imagine a future where he might belong somewhere again, a future where he would never again belong here, in this room, in this house. Who, he wondered with a stab of pain, would sleep in the bed he had slept in since he was three years old? Yesterday he had still been able to imagine that the world might right itself, but today was shining a light so bright on his capsizing world that his eyes hurt. He shook his head in distress and continued to rummage ineffectually through his clothes and stare with deepening melancholy at the shelves of beloved books he would have to leave behind. He wondered what had become of his schoolmates.

"Can I say goodbye to Hassan?" He asked his mother anxiously, later, following her around, concerned that his closest friend would not know what had happened to him, but no-one paid attention and he was carried along on a fast-moving current of echoing calls and feverish activity as departure loomed.

The pain and chaos had escalated to such an extent that they were almost eager to leave, to enter a less threatening world and begin their new lives. Eliane wept silently as she pulled the heavy door closed behind her. This was the house into which she and her mother had been born. Memories of her beloved grandmother were always with her, like a delicate perfume hovering in the background. Her daily scales and Chopin etudes tinkled faintly in her head as she bent her head to climb into the car. She wondered if she would ever be able to play the piano again. They were silent, each wrapped in their own thoughts as the car headed toward the airport.

"Look!" said Aldo, "There's the museum. I remember when I was a boy ..." his voice trailed off, "my office is just down that side street ..." No-one responded. Ahmad did not say a word as he drove them out of his life. Tears were not an option. He was certain they would return.

Soon, they entered the frantic atmosphere of the Cairo airport where the decibel level maintained fever pitch. Ahmad hesitated, and then embraced each of them with solemnity.

"*Hawaga Aldo*, what shall I do with the car?" he asked in his deep voice, his dark face creased with bewilderment and concern. Aldo shrugged impatiently, "Keep it, Ahmad," he said, his attention on the suitcases and the crowds swarming about them, "it's yours."

"I will keep it safe for when you return," said Ahmad firmly as he left them. Aldo rolled his eyes in disbelief.

Sol's ears buzzed with fear and noise overload. He watched Ahmad hurry away, tears stinging his eyes. He felt nauseous, encased in the bizarre unreality of the reality he was living. They dragged their suitcases toward the crowd gathered around long trestle tables where customs officials were shouting and waving their arms about, opening luggage, grabbing distraught passengers and hustling them into back quarters. Movements accelerated into a frenzy as they were jostled and pushed through the final moments of departure. Then, suddenly, it was over, and there was only the monotonous hum of the plane's engines as they sat huddled in their seats. They had left Egypt forever. Their future stretched as amorphous and dark as the night outside the plane's windows.

They were gone. Egypt was gone.

Ahmad drove slowly back to the house where he had lived his life for so many years. He had taken such good care of his people, and they had taken such good care of him. Every now and then he sighed and shook his head in distress. What would become of him now? He did not quite believe that the Mizrahis would not return, but what would he do if they never came back? What would he tell his wives and children in the Sudan, who reveled in the status of his job as well as in the food and clothing it provided.

He muttered to himself as he swerved to avoid a clamorous clattering conglomeration of camels and donkeys and the shouting gesticulating men who were trying to keep them in check. His head ached as he tried to make sense of it all. He had watched Sol grow up more intimately than he had watched his own children. He loved the boy with all his heart. What would become of this family without him to watch over them? His thin dark face shiny with stress, he carefully parked the car at the back of the house in the garage and went inside. He looked around. It dawned on him slowly that he was alone in the house. The other servants had gone. The house weighed on him. There was no-one else about. Its silence filled his heart with terror. He walked from room to room, and realization came to him at last. He knew the Mizrahis would never return.

$\mathscr{C}$HAPTER TWO

THE HOTEL VICTOIRE

Sol was still feeling queasy when the plane came to a bumpy halt at Le Bourget airport. He knew that his father's cousin, Zaki, would be at the airport to meet them, but he also knew that they could only stay at the apartment on Avenue Mozart for three weeks, because Zaki and Pam were expecting their daughter and her family from Australia to occupy the rooms they had temporarily allocated to the Mizrahis. Stepping out of the airport building felt like stepping off firm ground into a bottomless void. There were no landmarks ahead, nothing recognizable to grab hold of. The wind blew sleet into his eyes and he winced. His stomach lurched. He turned to speak to his mother, but he saw that she was hunched over, her eyes watering.

"This will be a very different life," she said somberly as she caught his eye, her hand tightly clutching at her stylish hat as they stepped out into a gray world, buffeted by a raw wind laced with sleet.

His father looked anxiously around and caught sight of Zaki, and the two men rushed toward each other, hugging, calling out *"Ahlan wusahlan, ahlan bic,"* slapping each other's hands and thumping each other on the back in a happy ritualized greeting dating back to their boyhood in Alexandria, as they dragged the old leather suitcases that still smelled of the *muski* to Zaki's small car. They wrestled themselves and the suitcases into the car, and threaded their way through traffic to the bustling center of Paris. Sol and his parents stumbled across the cobbles of an interior courtyard with their luggage, as Zaki left them to find a parking space for the car. They were looking forward to relaxing into the welcoming peace of a lovely apartment. Indeed, fragrances of a festive meal laced the air as they stepped out of the tiny elevator.

Zaki's wife, Pam, stood in the doorway, her face wreathed in smiles, watching as the elevator cranked its way up and down the stairwell outside her door, transporting groupings of the Mizrahis and their luggage wedged into the narrow space, up four flights to their temporary lodgings. They crowded uncomfortably into the small foyer, and Pam hustled them off to wash their hands in the tiny guest bathroom and then led them straight to the dining room, her eyes bright with unshed tears as she took in their bedraggled appearance and heavy suitcases.

"We'll need to see what work we can find for you," said Zaki later, as they sat in the glow of a delicious dinner, a worried frown on his face as Aldo began to talk about looking for work. "but I'm not sure you'll want to stay in Paris. The HIAS will take over when you leave us, and they'll help you to settle, or to go elsewhere. Have you given some thought as to where you might like to go?"

"We had talked about America," said Aldo hesitantly, "It would be good for Sol's studies, too. He was at the English School, so there would be no language problem. By the way, what exactly is H.I.A.S?" Eliane stopped sipping her coffee and looked up, interested.

"It's an American charitable organization that began in the late 19th century to help relocate Jewish immigrants from Russia," said Zaki. "The acronym stands for Hebrew Immigrant Aid Society. They've now expanded their scope to helping Jews to relocate wherever and whenever it's necessary. Here, in Paris, they are working with a flood of Egyptian refugees uneasily inhabiting a limbo between the life that was, and the life to be."

Aldo nodded thoughtfully.

"Were you able to bring *anything* out?" Pam asked Eliane as the two women stood in the kitchen, washing and drying the dinner dishes. Eliane opened her mouth to answer, but no words followed. She shook her head and burst into tears. Solly, charged with bringing the dishes from the dining room, watched from the doorway with growing consternation. He had never seen his mother weep so often. When she had regained her composure, she glanced around, stepped closer to Pam, and said in an undertone "I sewed my jewelry into the lining of the hat I was wearing when we arrived. I didn't dare even to tell Aldo. Don't say anything to Zaki. I knew Aldo wouldn't have approved. He was sure we would be marched straight to some horrible jail if we were caught trying to slip anything of value past the customs officials. They were stopping so many people and rushing them off to prison or worse. People were resisting frantically, sobbing and screaming. It was dreadful. Actually, I thought I would faint with fear when we got to the head of the line, but they were focussed on the man ahead of us who was caught with money in his suitcase. They were all gathered around him yelling, pushing each other, and gesticulating, and they grabbed his arms and took him out, struggling, and they just waved us on through as soon as we had signed the papers and handed over our passports. It isn't much, but it could help us get a start in America when we get there."

Solly stared at his mother in amazement. He had not suspected anything.

"Don't worry," Pam added soothingly as she put an arm around her friend's shoulders. "I won't say a word. You're so brave. Zaki and I want to help as much as we can."

Three weeks later the Mizrahis found themselves staring up at a dark archway leading through a narrow alley. They had reached the Hotel Victoire, at #36, Rue du Faubourg Poissonniere, the stone walls on both sides of the alley permanently blackened from years of heavy pollution. Zaki struggled to unload the three leather suitcases, and drove off quickly, waving as he navigated traffic. Aldo gestured to the porter, who stood immobile by the entrance to the hotel, arms crossed, glaring at them, muttering to himself, "*encore des sales Juifs.*"

"How about a helping hand here?" burst out Aldo, furious, his chest burning with the rebuttal he did not dare to express, but the porter continued to stare insolently, lounging by the entrance, making a sarcastic gesture inviting them in. A petite lady in a tight skirt and very high heels came bustling out as they started to bring in their own suitcases. Sensing a certain tension in the air, she nodded toward the sour-faced porter,

"Don't pay attention to Etienne," she said briskly, "he's been at the Hotel Victoire for forty years or more. He remembers better days when the hotel was in its heyday. Filled with a better class of customer, I might add."

As Aldo blinked at the implied insult she carefully peeled off her brown suede gloves, and pulled half-heartedly at the handle of one of the suitcases Eliane was struggling with.

"I'm Madame Meurice, and you must be the Mizrahis," she said over her shoulder, with a bright smile that never reached her eyes, "You are expected. I'll take you to your room."

They climbed the stairs in silence, pushing the suitcases ahead of them as she led them to a room on the second floor of the hotel. There was an odor of mildew, old sweat, and stagnant air, and something else, unpleasant and unidentifiable. A small night table with a cracked marble top and a lamp with a faded fringed Victorian shade separated twin beds covered in threadbare blankets. Everything was bleached of color, dingy. An old sink stood in one corner. Sol found himself staring at a fireplace in the other corner. He had never actually seen a real fireplace.

"Look, Papi, there's a fireplace," he said eagerly to his father. "Do you think it really works?"

"Oh, no! My goodness, no!" interjected Madame Meurice with a laugh before Aldo could reply, "it hasn't been in working order for years." She fished about in her tiny bag and produced a sheaf of tickets.

"These are for your meals at the Richer down the road," she said briskly, handing them to Aldo, "there's no restaurant in the hotel, so don't lose them, whatever you do. These will get you your meals for a week, seven francs per adult and three francs per child. "

She turned, catching sight of Eliane's troubled face. "Toilet's down the hall," she said, pointing, and started down the stairs, her heels clicking a determined rhythm on the stone steps.

"Wait," called Eliane, "Where's my son's room?"

"You're in it!" said Madame Meurice, "One room to a family."

"But there are only two twin beds," Eliane protested, looking around at the floorspace, already crowded with their suitcases.

"Best we could do for you, dear," Madame Meurice said firmly. "This hotel is full and so are two others in the neighborhood. We had to get you in within walking distance of the Richer, for your meals." She looked back at Eliane, "Egyptian refugees have been pouring into Paris for some time," her voice took on a steely tone as she disappeared around the curve of the stairs, "we are not a tourist bureau, you know."

And just like that, she was gone, and they were left staring at each other in consternation across the narrow room.

The Hotel Victoire, built in the early 1900s, retained a few faint remnants of its former elegance. Silk drapes faded beyond recognition hung in tattered splendor at some windows. Wooden moldings, their gilding brown and chipped, were nailed haphazardly on the walls. Faded paintings immortalizing moments of ancient splendor hung here and there. Everything seemed covered in a faint film of grime. Incongruously, polished brass bannisters and doorknobs shone with a gleaming luster over the threadbare carpeting.

"Zaki said this used to be a good Jewish neighborhood," Aldo said at last into the stunned silence. "Why don't we unpack and then walk to the restaurant for dinner, and get a look at the area."

They walked into the gathering twilight and found the Richer. Expecting a bustling brasserie, they were disappointed to discover that it was a workmens' cafeteria housed in a basement. Metal rails led to a window, and a line formed and straggled forward, to where a large red-faced woman gathered the coupons as they were handed to her, stamped them without a word, and exchanged them for plates of food.

"What is this?" asked Eliane in consternation as she stared at the anonymous food congealing on her plate.

"Shhh!" said Aldo nervously, "There's no choice. We can't afford to go to a restaurant. We have to eat whatever they give us."

Behind them, a tall blonde woman in a stylish broad-shouldered beige cashmere coat began to weep, burying her head in her husband's shoulder. "A bread line," she sobbed, "Who would have thought we would be reduced to this?"

"Lady," said the burly man behind her impatiently, "Just be thankful we have any food at all."

Her sobs grew louder as she took the plate that was handed to her and moved off to a table in a corner, where her distraught husband patted her hand, and dabbed at her eyes with his handkerchief, all the while encouraging her to try a mouthful or two of the food in front of them.

Sol walked behind his parents as they made their way back to the hotel.

"Look," said Eliane, suddenly delighted, pointing to a poster outside a movie theater, "The Ten Commandments! It must be a Jewish movie!"

Aldo laughed. Suddenly, they stopped, aghast, and Sol looked to where his parents were staring at a young couple feverishly kissing and petting in a doorway, tugging at each others' clothes in a vain effort to reach hidden places.

"What?" he demanded, embarrassed, "Why are you staring? They're just kissing."

"I never saw anyone doing that in public," whispered his mother, her face red with embarrassment, "what sort of people are these, anyway? Your grandfather would be turning in his grave. When we were engaged," she glanced up at Aldo, "remember? He would watch us carefully, and if we got too close he would say '*moosh odam el nas*, not where others can see!'"

The next night was Friday night, and they noticed several of the women gathered in the downstairs hallway after dinner. Curious, Eliane went across to join them and see what they were whispering about.

"New here? You'll need a gas stove," said one of the women, smiling at Eliane, "I'm Miriam Levy and I can tell you where to get one, but whatever you do, don't let the management see it. It's forbidden to cook in the rooms." Eliane felt a prickle of panic.

"What happens if they find it?" She asked.

"Oh, don't worry too much," said another woman, laughing, "I can tell that you just left Egypt. They won't throw you into jail here. The worst they could do is take it from you."

Next day, all the windows of the Hotel Victoire were kept wide open, releasing the stench of cooked fish into the alley below. Local fishmongers reduced their prices after midnight on Fridays, after all the Catholics had eaten their fish meals. That was when the resourceful residents of the Hotel Victoire splurged for a good meal of fresh fish with which to welcome the Sabbath.

Aldo had taken to congregating at a corner cafe every day, with two or three friends, other Jews from Egypt who were housed at the Victoire or surrounding hotels. Poring over newspapers, a small cup of coffee in front of each of them, they spent long hours studying the stock markets, bemoaning the recent past, sitting under grey Parisian skies dreaming of Egypt and sunlight, united in an all-encompassing nostalgia for the lives they would never experience again. It was a community of exile, and it allowed them to forget the urgencies and needs of the present in recollections of the past. Eliane watched him anxiously. Miriam Levy had been very helpful, and she was beginning to make friends with some of the other women, too. She wondered why their lives seemed stuck in this forlorn place, struggling to see what she could do to move them forward. When she ventured a remark to Aldo, he gave full vent to his own insecurities, shouting her down, oblivious to her mortification at the listening ears of the other residents.

"Do you think we meet for fun?" he shouted, guilt flooding his reason, "We are all trying to find ways to get our families out of here, to where we can be respected members of a society and where we can find work. We advise each other about ways to navigate this stifling bureaucracy that has entangled our lives and is suffocating us to death. That's what I'm doing while you busy yourself messing with clothes and gossiping with the other women."

An ancient telephone was attached to the wall in the hallway outside their room. Zaki phoned to say that his assistant had taken pregnancy leave. He wondered if Eliane might be able to fill in at the financial firm where he worked until a replacement could be found. Eliane jumped at the opportunity of getting out of the depressing atmosphere of the Hotel Victoire, eager for the possibility of earning some money.

"What will you need from me?" she asked nervously, "I've never worked in an office."

"If memory serves me well," said Zaki, "you play the piano very well indeed. That should help you to pick up typing skills quickly. You might also check with the HIAS people if they could get you into a crash typing course. I've heard they are willing to send the refugees to schools for re-training."

"I'll try to catch Madame Meurice this afternoon," said Eliane, her spirits lifting.

"Good," said Zaki, laughing, "Other than that, I know that you have an elegant presence and a quick mind. I feel sure you'll be able to handle the job."

"But what about Aldo?" asked Eliane, frowning.

"Nothing yet," said Zaki. "I've reached out to business contacts and I hope something may turn up soon, but it's much harder to find something for him. At least this could relieve some financial pressures for you all, while you're waiting to settle yourselves into a new life."

Through the long cold winter months, Sol trudged to the school assigned to him, shivering in his thin coat, shunned by schoolmates and teachers alike. Like most of the refugees from Egypt, he had spoken many languages at home, echoing the diversity of the Egypt that had shaped his consciousness from his youngest years. His French was acceptable, but his high school years had been at the English School in Heliopolis. He felt alienated from the lycee culture. Even some of his Egyptian-French vocabulary caused sniggers and whispers as he moved among his classmates. Their mockery at his awkwardnesses left him feeling as if he were drowning in an endless grey ocean. He missed the Egyptian sun and the uplifting quality of light that he had always taken for granted. He missed the indolence and comfort of a life where he was known and cherished. He missed the friends he would never see again. He recognized that the pain he felt would never go away, whatever the future held, and wherever they might end up.

A few months into the school year, he was trudging back to the Victoire, his book bag laden and sagging with homework, his loneliness enveloping him like a faint dark cloud about his shoulders. If he was lucky, he might be able to appropriate one of the rickety desks in the downstairs lounge to do his homework. He hoped the lounge would not be teeming with other residents, careless with their noise and laughter. The light there was better than in the cramped bedroom he shared with his parents.

A group of younger girls not far behind him, were whispering, and chatting as they walked, pleated skirts swinging against slim legs. He looked back, thinking longingly of friendship, and of Hassan, and of the fun they used to have on their way to and from school, and he noticed one of the girls detach herself from the group and heard her say, "I'll ask him."

Her friends, giggling, called out "*Vas y Catherine*," as the girl, a couple of years his junior, ran ahead to walk beside him as he headed for the Victoire. He glanced at her, wondering what she wanted. She was a pretty girl, trim and composed in a very French way. They had never spoken before.

"Why are you here?" she asked, her eyes sharp, "We were all wondering why you had to leave your country? Did your family do something wrong?"

Sol sighed. "Nothing like that," he said, "It's because of the Suez Canal military operation last autumn. Didn't you hear about that? Last autumn, when the French joined the British to take back the Suez Canal?"

The girl nodded. Her small face still showing puzzlement. "Why did they want the canal?" she asked. "Who were they taking it back from?"

"The Suez Canal was an important international passageway for all countries," Sol explained, "but Gamal Abdel Nasser, who is president of Egypt, wanted to keep all the Canal revenues for Egypt. It's a valuable passage for ships and cargo, you see, so he nationalized it and made it belong only to Egypt."

"He could just do that?" she asked, surprised.

Sol nodded.

"But I still don't get it," she said, stumbling a little, tucking a stray strand of flaxen hair into her braids as she tried to keep up with his long strides, "You're Egyptian. They said so in class. Why did you come here? My parents know some French people who had to leave Egypt last autumn and come back to France, but why did *you* have to leave, if you're Egyptian?"

Sol glanced at her uncomfortably. "You know I'm Jewish?" he asked. Seeing her look of dismay, he added, a slight edge creeping into his voice, "It's a religion. Like you're Catholic. I'm Jewish. So when Israel joined the British and the French, Egypt decided to kick out its Jews, whatever their nationality, and my family had to leave their home and everything they owned and find a place to live somewhere else."

"Jewish?" she stared at him. "The Jews killed Christ," she said slowly. "Our priest said so in church last Sunday."

Sol stopped in his tracks. "Look," he said wearily, "We don't have to be friends. We didn't kill Christ, or anyone else. My family and I just want to live in peace, and for our home to be real, and forever."

He searched for words to contain his pain, his alienation from the self he had known all his life. " Anyway, don't worry," he said stiffly, "we're not staying in France. The HIAS are trying to help us get to America."

She continued to stare at him, disconcerted, then wheeled around without another word, and ran off in the opposite direction.

No surprises there, thought Sol sadly. No friends here. He thought of his years at the English School in Heliopolis, the camaraderie that took him at his face value and asked nothing of his background, the joining in the swelling clamor of the lunch room amid the variety and diversity of his schoolmates, the friendly competing in sports. He had not understood that it could end this way. His book bag felt heavier and heavier. His feet dragged. A lump in his throat was making it difficult to breathe. He trudged on, his heart heaviest of all.

There were other children at the Hotel Victoire, but they were all younger, roaming in packs through the neighborhood, or standing mesmerized in front of a shop with flickering television sets in the window. The kindly owner often took pity on them and turned up the volume so that they could enjoy the full experience.

Sol watched with concern as his father became increasingly morose. Days became weeks and weeks became months. Aldo spent day after day sitting at the cafe with his other expatriate friends, or navigating consulates and bureaucracies, wearing through the thin soles of his shoes looking for work, looking for visas that would take them to the Americas. Some families had already left the Hotel Victoire for Brazil, where visas were not required, exhilarated, but terrified to leave the doubtful comfort of the Hotel Victoire, wrenched once again from new friends and reassuring habits to plunge into another unknown. Aldo had requested North America for himself and his family, destination city, New York. But a year and a half later, when the desired papers came through, they were for an unknown town, Phoenix Arizona. He hurried to the consulate primed for battle.

The consul smiled anxiously. "But Mr. Mizrahi, we thought you and your family would be pleased. Phoenix is in a desert. The climate..."

"New York," shouted Aldo shaking his finger in the face of the startled bureaucrat, his apoplectic fury alarming the mild-mannered consul. "What is this Phoenix? I need to be in New York. My contacts are all in New York. How can I find work in the desert?"

After a few weeks of increasingly heated argument and many sleepless nights of discussion and frustration in the small room in the Hotel Victoire, agreement was reached that their destination city would be changed from Phoenix Arizona to New York City.

In the meantime, Eliane had been doing well at Zaki's firm. She really liked the world of finance and surprised Zaki on numerous occasions with her flair and acumen for the business. The admiring, appreciative response to her work and to her presence at Zaki's office gave her a self-confidence she had never dreamed could be hers. Nonetheless, she viewed their imminent change apprehensively. Her English was not as good as Aldo's and she was leery about finding herself, in America, an unknown and unwanted quantity in an unfamiliar environment, a woman in a man's world. She was, however, determined to make a success of whatever challenges awaited them across the ocean. Zaki, who had many business contacts in America, had promised to furnish her with references and contacts in New York.

Somewhere deep in his heart, Sol knew that the Hotel Victoire had left its imprint on them all. He knew that he would never leave the stench of the experience behind him. Unseen by others, it would trail him forever. It had etched deep scars on his soul. His childhood lay behind him in tatters. His parents, the giants of his youth, had dwindled to insecure creatures, constantly bickering about everything, desperate and ineffectual in the new roles into which their exile had cast them.

CHAPTER THREE

Egypt 1969
JAMILA

Fringed by tall palms and caught in the glare of a relentless sun, the village by the Nile had settled into a late afternoon torpor. Jamila's mother, Salwa, was anxious to enlist her twelve-year-old daughter to watch the cluster of squabbling squealing little ones tumbling in and around their mud hut, so that she could take a moment's nap. Little remained of the charming carefree girl she had once been. That had ended years earlier, in 1957, soon after the last mango harvest. Now it seemed she was always pregnant and nursing, rarely moving out from the confines of her hut and its tiny vegetable garden. An exhausted embittered woman now resided in Salwa's aching body. She snaked a sudden hand out to grab a slim brown arm, but Jamila sped out of her reach like a startled gazelle, graceful and fleet of foot, running until she stood still to catch her breath under a group of tall date palms swaying in the gentle breeze.

Jamila watched cautiously as a dusty taxi hurtled to a stop beside her. Few visitors ever came to her village. The driver of the taxi stuck his head out of the window, smiling broadly, his gold front tooth gleaming in the light, his unwinding turban catching and flapping in the breeze.

"*Ismah, ya bint,* tell my brother Dahab that I have brought a fine lady to our village today," he shouted to the girl, smiling broadly. "She asked to see a typical Nile village, so I brought her all the way here, to my own village." He laughed, delighted with his own wit, "Now I shall spend the day with my brother, Dahab, while she spends her good American dollars in our village." He winked at Jamila.

She nodded and stood silent, keeping in the shadows as a woman slowly unstuck herself from the cracked upholstery, stepped out under a sweltering sun, and began to wander toward the cotton fields that bordered the village, snapping pictures again and again. She headed uncertainly for a cluster of brown river mud huts, some of them colored in faded pastel shades of pale yellow and orange, crude openings carved from the walls for windows. Groves of tall swaying date palms delineated the borders of the small village, surrounding formless clumps of huts rising out of the ground like mud playthings of a monstrous child. Beyond the village, the Nile river swallowed gleams of the blue of a cloudless sky into sluggish grey waters swirling toward Cairo and the chaos of urban metropolis.

"American," said the taxi driver, jerking his head toward his passenger and winking again, his dark eyes twinkling. He nodded at the girl as he pulled his head in and drove off at breakneck speed toward his brother's hut on the outskirts of the village. Jamila edged closer to the woman, fascinated, reaching out to touch her shirt. She had never seen such lovely shiny fabric, fabric that floated with a life of its own as the woman walked, camera in hand.

Suddenly noticing a hand on her arm, the woman pulled away in shock, exclaiming "Take your hands off me!" Her gaze softened as she saw the young girl startle and poise for flight. She glanced down at her.

"My word, this kid has unusual eyes," she muttered to herself.

Jamila stayed where she was, mesmerized by the beautiful floating fabric.

The woman looked at her thoughtfully. She would need someone to show her around the village now that her taxi driver had disappeared.

"I wonder, could you show me around your village, *ya bint?*" she asked, coming to a decision and smiling down at the girl, "My name is Malvina."

She hefted her large bag onto her shoulder and pointed toward the mud huts scattered among the palms. Jamila understood the vocabulary of gesture far better than the distorted Arabic she was hearing or the few words of English she had learned in her twelve years. It had proved an essential survival tool in her world, where everything appeared simple but where undercurrents so often swirled just outside her comprehension. Her face brightened. This would be fun. She had no wish to help her mother with the care of her younger brothers and sisters, chores that she knew would be awaiting her were she to go back home. There was a hot, still feel to the day, and she had been waiting for something of note to happen. She took the woman's hand, grinned up at her, and began to lead her through dusty fields where men labored at the cotton plants, along a muddy path to the small group of huts.

They walked together toward one of the mud huts, where motley objects hung in colorful bunches from hooks haphazardly clustered outside. Jamila drew the woman's attention to it, the closest to a store that the village could offer. Malvina, who had been chatting animatedly oblivious to the fact that Jamila understood little of what she was saying, glanced up at the display of gaudy plastic, jumbled objects, and bright colors, and shook her head in disappointment. This was not at all what she had come to see, fearing for life and limb as the intrepid Arab taxi driver who had offered to be her guide raced his way through Cairo's impenetrable traffic, ignoring traffic lights and the shrill whistles of the traffic police. They had passed several small clusters of huts and palms on their way out of the metropolis, but her driver kept shaking his head and insisting "We find better. More better place," until they had arrived at this spot. It had looked much the same as the others to Malvina, but she was relieved when he pulled up, happy to be out in the air, stretching her legs at last.

Undaunted, Jamila swiveled, pulling at her hand, and led her past an open area where worn carpets had been spread on the dust, the generous limbs and leaves of a large mango tree rustling overhead. A bunch of small children sat in neat rows reciting verses from the Koran in unison, swaying from side to side, giggling and nudging each other as a dog and then a goat galloped among them and skittered away. A small man, supremely conscious of his responsibilities and the superiority of his literacy, rotund and pompous in his black *galabeya,* seemed in a constant state of apoplexy, waving his arms and screaming at the wide-eyed children, leading them in their loud recitation. Some chickens scrabbled nearby. Jamila glanced around for her brother, Ali, who liked to climb the trees and play in the area, but he was nowhere to be seen.

The woman and the girl walked slowly on through the village, Malvina pausing occasionally to point at something that piqued her interest, Jamila kept up a rapid patter in a jumbled mixture of Arabic, gesture, and the few words of English she had picked up from the occasional British visitor to the village. Outside one of the huts, an old man in a white *galabeya*, a white skullcap ringed with black embroidery on his head, sat hunched on a stool, deeply concentrated, polishing a tiny piece of bone, a wooden table in front of him, the top partly decorated in an ancient pattern of geometric shapes. An elderly donkey grazed nearby.

"Hamid," said Jamila, pointing.

"Wait," commanded Malvina, peering at the man deeply engrossed in his task. "Great picture." She nodded at Jamila, pleased, "Local craftsman at work." She positioned her camera, but Hamid looked up and before she could focus the camera, he had disappeared like a shadow into the dark hut. Malvina started to follow, but Jamila grabbed her hand and pulled back, shaking her head vehemently. She knew that some of the men hated to be photographed. Hamid was an official for the district and guarded his privacy. Sometimes she had noticed men from other villages coming to his hut for meetings, cloths pulled over their features and only fierce dark eyes showing as they slid quietly into the hut, and vanished as discreetly as they had come.

Her father, Sadik, also belonged to the Muslim Brotherhood, as did most of the men in the village. He prayed as required five times a day, facing Mecca, and laying down his frayed prayer carpet wherever he happened to be, but he took a laid-back approach to the dictates of the Koran's more radical tenets, as he did with most things.

Jamila knew that Sadik did not like confrontation. If things got sticky he either moved away, a confused look on his face, or flew into a violent rage, summoning energies casual acquaintances could never have imagined that he possessed. His easygoing ways had earned him many friends, and the smartest prettiest girl in the village for a wife. He was still amazed that Salwa had accepted his modest offer, thirteen years ago. She had returned from the mango harvest in Cairo determined to marry Sadik and no-one else, despite offers her father had received from more desirable prospects. Sadik knew she would have had an easier life with one of the older, more prosperous suitors, and it never ceased to amaze him that he had landed such a prize. Startled into a grateful monogamy, he never considered taking a second wife as so many of his friends had done, after frequent pregnancies and a hardscrabble life took their toll of the young women they had once so desired.

Jamila had learned early to manipulate his good nature to her advantage and to sense when his violent outbursts were about to erupt and shake her world. She had long ago fashioned a hidden burrow in a patch of overgrown weeds close to her home, and she hid there whenever she sensed that Sadik was about to have one of his explosions. Ali, her younger brother, on the other hand, had never learned to let well enough alone. He met his father's erratic outbursts with a mirrored rage, and only Jamila's protective presence and good advice kept him from bodily harm as he tried to launch his wiry small boy person at his father, almost airborne with a fury that far exceeded his size. At such times, Jamila could only occasionally count on her mother to run interference, for Salwa was often hard to rouse from her lactating apathy as year after year went by, as she nursed baby after baby, crouched in her hut, her features thickening with the years, wrapped in a voluminous black *abaya*, a finely filigreed gold ornament pinning her headscarf to the enveloping gown, the latest baby a bulge in her arms, another a growing bulge beneath.

Her mother seemed to Jamila to drift through the years in a perpetual haze of pregnancy and birth. She rarely went anywhere. She never spoke of her feelings or expressed interest in anyone else's. Meals appeared for the family at the appropriate hours although the cooking happened almost invisibly, without fuss or chaos. She seemed oblivious to the comings and goings of her older children. She was unavailable for real conversation. Her communication with them consisted of issuing orders, or commenting sourly on their behavior as she moved ponderously among them, taking care of the bodily needs of her younger brood. Consequently, Jamila and Ali had formed a close bond, filling in for each other the significant interaction they could not find elsewhere.

By now, Malvina had decided that the village was too ordinary after all, to warrant more photography. She looked impatiently at the girl waiting at her side and stabbed a finger back the way she had come.

"Taxi's probably waiting," she said, smiling, handing Jamila a crumpled bill. "Thanks." She put a scarlet-tipped finger under Jamila's chin and lifted her brown face to the light.

"Really, you do have the most lovely eyes, dear," she said, smiling down at her, and then, "Hm. Yes. Quite extraordinary." Something in the girl's expression went right to her heart and she gasped. Stepping back, she pointed at a particularly tall palm beside the path, and asked, "Will I find you here tomorrow?"

Jamila scuffed at the stones at her feet as she reluctantly made her way back to her mother. Her face lit up as she heard a guttural cry of "AAH! AAH!" and saw her friend, Walid, skinny as a whip, flicking his switch at a herd of scrawny *gamoose*, shouting as he guided them down the path. He grinned widely and waved a cheery greeting when he saw her and her heart tightened under her grubby white robe. His smile sprang straight from her heart to her abdomen and lodged there, creating a sensation not quite pleasure, not quite pain. She waved back and hurried home.

To Jamila's delight, Malvina did appear again by the tall palm next day, and again for several days after that. She greeted Jamila cheerfully.

"Never got your name," she said, laughing, "I'm glad you're waiting here. Sorry I couldn't get here sooner. Had some business to take care of at the consulate. What is your name, by the way?" She pointed at Jamila's chest.

Jamila understood. "Jamila," she said with a big grin.

"Real pretty name," said Malvina, smiling.

Not sure whether her American friend would turn up again, each day Jamila loitered about the village from early in the morning, neglecting her chores and fending off Ali's demands for her to play with him. After clowning and tugging at her, he realized that she was neither going to laugh with him nor respond. Frustrated, he eventually ran off in a huff to join a group of boys clambering about the large mango tree that dominated the open air *madrassa*, hurling laughter and mangoes at each other to the distress of the teacher and the squeals and giggles of delight of his pupils. Ali counted on Jamila. He and she had formed a close-knit unit from the moment when he had begun to crawl around the hut, and he hated it when her attention was deflected elsewhere.

It was late afternoon when the taxi finally appeared in a welter of screeching tires and clouds of dust, the driver's grin stretching from ear to ear in his dark face as he jerked to a stop. He winked at Jamila as she sidled up to Malvina, smiling hesitantly. She noticed immediately that the American woman was not wearing the floaty fabric she had so admired. She looked very different, in a wilting white blouse and black pants streaked with dust. Her hair was plastered to her head from the sweat and heat, and a huge purse was slung over one shoulder. She climbed out of the taxi, her hand on her heart, clearly disoriented from the wild ride, taking a moment to find her balance.

"What shall we do today?" she asked Jamila, smiling down at her. Jamila had given some thought as to what they might do. She took Malvina's hand confidently in her slim brown fingers and led her along a muddy path to a far field, where Walid was watching the *gamoose* feeding on sparse clumps of vegetation. Jamila stopped, called out to catch his attention, and waved to him. He waved back and watched as she and Malvina started to climb a steep incline on the banks of the Nile. Jamila skipped ahead with the agility of the goats that were everywhere underfoot. When they reached the top of the bank, they looked around. She glanced at Malvina expectantly. Below them lay the Nile river in all its majesty. As they watched from their perch at the top of tall granite cliffs, graceful white-winged *faloukas* swooped along muddy grey waters.

Men, barefoot and agile in white *galabiyas* scurried back and forth on the decks, shouting to each other as they adjusted sails and boom to make the most of the hot wind at their backs, settling finally into a monotonous rowing rhythm, harsh voices joining in some sort of primal song mingling with the wind and the squeak of the sails. Across the river, flecks of granite sparkled in the sun. Jamila, always exhilarated by this view, turned to see Malvina's reaction. Malvina had a broad smile on her face, and her camera out.

"Good girl," Malvina said happily. "This is exactly what I hoped for."

Behind them, an elderly *gamoosa*, gray with dust, trudged despondently around and around a well, harnessed to a pulley and a bucket, drawing water, paying no attention to the wrinkled old man who flicked his switch half-heartedly at her hide, his face so corrugated that his eyes almost disappeared. Other men grabbed the overflowing buckets as they came up, attaching them to both sides of a yoke on their shoulders, hurrying off to take water to fields still baking in the setting sun. A few women graceful in their *abayas* walked by the well, doughnuts of colored cloth on their heads, elegantly balancing pitchers and bundles as they walked.

Malvina slipped her camera back into her purse and looked around, reveling in the exotic atmosphere that surrounded her. She sighed with satisfaction. A retired fashion model of some repute, she was the founder of a select, highly respected model agency in New York City. Nonetheless, despite a full life and a successful one, there was a sealed look in her dark eyes. Few things gave her pleasure since the tragedy that had stolen her small daughter from her. Tim, her husband, despaired of ever again finding traces in the wife she had become of the exuberant girl who had captured his heart years ago. Silent with pain, he watched Malvina go through the motions of life, year after year, hoping that something would somehow find its way through the barrier and break the spell of her overwhelming sadness.

She had once mentioned in passing, a childhood wish to see the pyramids and ride on a camel, and her trip to Egypt had been a generous birthday gift from him. He had surprised and delighted her with the gift of these few days in the land of the Pharaohs, a splendid splash of fantasy before she grasped the inevitability of middle age and settled back into the pressures of her New York life. She had traveled widely throughout the States and Europe for her work, but had never been this far afield. He watched her as she reacted to his gift, and was rewarded to see sparks light her eyes. She laughed with surprised delight.

"When do we go?" she said, a hint of real happiness in her face.

"No, I won't be coming with you," he had said in answer to her question, "I'll be waiting when you get back. See it for both of us, and take plenty of photographs. I'll paint from them when you come home. An Egyptian series. The gallery will love that. The agency is running smoothly, and I'll keep an eye on things while you're gone. Climb the pyramids, greet the Sphinx, ride a camel into the desert, and have the time of your life. I want to see it all through your eyes. Take care. I'll look forward to getting you back, safe and sound."

Malvina had stared at the plane tickets in her hand with wonder. "How did you know...?" She began, but he ushered her off to pack her case, secure in the knowledge that he had found the right gift. She planned to make the most of it. Having, with customary energy, exhausted all the iconic experiences that Cairo offered tourists, she was determined to seek out some less familiar experiences for her few remaining days. It had been a marvelous break and had at last begun the process of healing in her soul.

Turning to Jamila, Malvina said, "Those women move so gracefully. It takes a lot of training back home to get our models to walk with such ease. Is one of them your mother, by any chance?"

Jamila shook her head.

Malvina pulled a floppy green hat from her purse and set it on her head, somehow with a practiced hand setting it at a fetching angle. Jamila stared, and grinned. She had no hat, but her wiry brown hair, thick, rich and abundant, was braided into the only protection she needed.

An outrageous idea was beginning to take root in Malvina's mind. Her travels had taken her all over the United States and Europe to scout for talent for her model agency. She had learned to trust her instinct, the success of her agency proof that she knew what she was about. Her instinct was stirring in her now. She was discovering that this delightful girl had unexpected grace and intelligence as well as the promise of great beauty. She was intriguingly different from the young women she usually encountered, very different from the models who stalked the runways in New York in cookie-cutter perfection.

Seduced more and more by Jamila's charm and the possibilities it could present professionally, she asked, "I'd really like to meet your mother. Where do you live? Can you take me to her now?" Jamila hesitated, then nodded and led her back down the steep incline.

They walked together to a hut on the outskirts of the village, where Jamila's mother sat on a small stool nursing the baby, one hand stirring a glutinous green soup that simmered on the stove, a pungent smell of garlic perfuming the air. Malvina glanced about, her eyes on the ragged clothing that festooned the back of an old chair. It was dark in the hut. A small boy with huge dark eyes crept close and stared at her. A little girl, hair matted around her face, crouched beside her mother sucking a very dirty thumb. Another boy was making mud pies in a corner of the hut, his diaper full and sagging. She had noticed other children playing in the dirt outside. She was hungry after her climb, but there was no way she was going to eat in this place. She looked around with distaste and sighed. Salwa, intent on the *meloukhia* soup and the contented baby, barely looked up.

"Your daughter is a good girl, *kwayessa awi*," Malvina said at last into the silence. The nursing woman lifted large dark eyes and stared at her, uncomprehending. Malvina's smile faded. She nodded toward Jamila, who was standing awkwardly on one leg, looking faintly embarrassed.

Watching her, Malvina's heart lurched with remembered pain. She stared at Jamila. The girl was the age Teresa would have been had she survived. So many years, and still the pain overwhelmed her. She struggled to regain control of her emotions. Her eyes went from Jamila to her mother. Malvina had been helpless to save her daughter then, but perhaps she could save this burdened mother's daughter now. Perhaps her unresolved grief could help her to give this girl a better life. Something about Jamila was stirring feelings she had buried for years. She knew there was so much she would be able to do for the girl, but the thought also suddenly swept through her that there was so much this child could do for her bereft heart. The flow of warmth made her flush. She wondered briefly what Tim would make of it. This was surely not what he had in mind when he handed her the ticket to Egypt. Disconcerted by the continuing silence in the hut, and used to making rapid decisions, Malvina decided to take a plunge.

"I was thinking that I would like to take Jamila away with me," she said, moving toward Jamila and putting her arm around the girl's shoulders. "Could you spare her? It may take some time to organize the formalities, but I think I can obtain a student visa for her quite quickly, and we can take it from there. She would live with me in my house. I will send her to school and she can learn to be a fashion model. What do you think?" She smiled, looking at Jamila, and asked, "What's your mother's name?"

" *Oumi* Salwa," said Jamila.

Malvina, relieved that Jamila's limited grasp of English nonetheless seemed to help her enough to understand some of what she was saying, was unsure if Salwa had understood any of it. She knew her own Arabic vocabulary was not up to the task. She had spoken in English with the odd Arabic word inserted here and there, hoping that she could somehow convey her meaning through gesture and expression. But whether or not Salwa had understood, it looked as if Jamila had some-how grasped some of the gist of the conversation. She looked alarmed, gasped, stepped back, and almost fell. Her mother looked up, startled.

"*Eh?*" she asked, followed by a rapid stream of Arabic that left Malvina lurching to try to catch the odd word she might understand. Intent now on expressing her purpose, she pulled some large bills from the purse on her shoulder. "I will pay you whatever you think is right, and of course if Jamila is not happy with us, I will make sure that she gets back to you, safe and sound." She hesitated over the words. How could she promise anyone "safe and sound" when she had failed so dismally to save her own daughter? She pushed the thought aside, sighed deeply, and continued, trying with gestures and the few Arabic words she knew to explain again that she was prepared to obtain all necessary visas for Jamila to return to America with her.

"She's very bright and has the beginnings of an unusual beauty," she said, and added hesitantly, "she will be like a daughter to me," her eyes glistening with unshed tears as she said the word. She glanced away from Salwa.

Jamila's mother stared at her in horror, her gaze moving in confusion past the American woman in her fancy clothes to her eldest daughter, never at a loss for words, standing in stunned silence. What could this strange American want the girl for? Salwa had heard of bizarre sexual practices in America. No way would she accept money for her daughter to be used as a sex slave by this woman. Jamila was special. Besides, there was still the marriage proposal to consider. Salwa lowered her eyes to her suckling baby, and shook her head vehemently.

Malvina gasped impatiently. She saw that she was not getting her message across. Catching sight of a soiled beauty magazine used as wrapping for some vegetables, Malvina shook the vegetables out onto the seat of a chair, ignoring Salwa's cries of distress, jabbing a finger at the image of the glamorous woman on the cover.

"*Ashan di*," she said earnestly, the words clumsy in her mouth. "I want to take her for this. I can make her into this."

She waited, then saw that Salwa was still staring at her, weary dark eyes ringed with kohl. She had not understood at all. Salwa was wondering why this strange American woman thought she could walk into her hut and throw her carefully harvested vegetables onto the chair, why she was shaking a piece of paper at her. She shook her head in bewilderment.

Malvina threw the magazine onto the chair with the vegetables and tried another tack.

"Mod-el," she said, moving closer to Salwa, emphasizing the word with jabs at the picture on the magazine. She pointed at her own eyes. "Her eyes and her cheekbones are exceptional. Nice little figure, too. I'd like to send her to school, *madrassa*. I can teach her to be a fashion model. I could help her to have a good life. What do you say?"

Salwa was watching her warily, but with growing interest. Malvina turned and rummaged around in her bag, pulling out a rumpled piece of paper. Smoothing it carefully, and moving slowly so as not to startle her, she showed it to Salwa. It was a photo of Malvina in a garden, surrounded by a bunch of laughing girls in beautiful flowing gowns, each gorgeous in her own way.

"Mod-els", she said, speaking slowly and loudly, as if volume would somehow make up for her deficiencies in communicating with words, "My models. My school. *Madrassa*. This is what I want for Jamila." she smiled at Jamila who was following the exchange with puzzled interest.

"Will you let me take her to America? I know this is all happening very fast, but I leave in a few days, and spending this time with Jamila has convinced me that this could work out well for both of us. I feel she and I will get along very well indeed, and I will take good care of her, I promise you. I can pay whatever you feel is fair."

"*Jamila?*" said the woman on the stool slowly, still puzzled, "*Awaz Jamila?*"

This odd woman's insistence and intensity made no sense to her, but she had understood two words, "America," and "school," and she was beginning to comprehend that this might be an unimaginable opportunity for her eldest child. Jamila had always been different. She was the only girl in the village with slanting green eyes that glowed like stars when she was happy. Salwa knew all too well that life often held moments that could change a life forever.

She sighed, shifted the baby to the other breast, and resolved to discuss the matter with Sadik. He would be home soon, wanting his evening meal. Loud, boisterous and cheerful. She hoped he would not be in one of his bad moods. She knew he would not like this. He had been so delighted by the offer of marriage for Jamila that he had received from Mustafa. He longed for the status that a relationship with Mustafa would bring him. Sadik had never felt secure, she had watched his insecurity affect his life in so many ways. A relationship with Mustafa would propel him into the circle of movers and shakers of the village. Salwa kept her own counsel, as the American woman stood there, watching her silently weighing the benefits for both husband and daughter.

Malvina was still staring at Salwa anxiously, trying to interpret her silence.

"She's a sweet kid" she said at last into the heavy silence, sighing, "but those eyes are what I find particularly arresting, that's why I ask that you entrust her to me and to my model agency. I know she will make her mark in the fashion world with those eyes. I really want to give her this opportunity."

She leaned forward and awkwardly patted Salwa on the shoulder. "She has a very engaging personality," she said, "I truly think I could make something special of her in the world of fashion." She added, "I promise you that Jamila will have a much better life in the States than she could ever have here." She straightened, shifted the wallet from hand to hand, and waited.

"This enough? *Biziada*?" She asked again, starting to feel exasperated by the lack of any visible reaction, taking two more soiled bills from her wallet and waving them about. But Salwa did not smile. Her gaze remained impenetrable. She turned her head away and continued to focus her attention on the nursing baby.

After a long uncomfortable silence, she lifted her head and saw that Malvina had not moved.

"*Bukra*," she said decisively, nodding, "tomorrow," having arrived at the decision to approach Sadik with this revolutionary new idea as soon as he came in. Ali sidled into the hut, tired and hungry, hoping to catch Jamila's attention, but his mother unleashed a torrent of angry words in his direction, the sound like an avalanche of harsh consonants to Malvina's ear, sound with no meaning. Ali glanced at his sister and darted out immediately, determined not to be caught into helping out with the small brothers and sisters, secure that his mother would save some food for his return.

Neither Salwa nor Sadik knew how to read or write. They had both learned to recite passages from the Koran at the village *madrassa* where the schoolmaster served more as a conductor than an educator. He carried a large stick which he wielded whenever anyone's attention flagged, so they all made sure that they sang lustily along, but Salwa knew that the world held much more from which she was forever excluded, because she had never learned to read. Jamila did not know how to read or write either. The dreams of Salwa's youth had sagged and crumbled under the weight of the circumstances of her life. Perhaps this woman could give Jamila a better life. She studied Malvina. She saw suffering and heart in her eyes. This woman had strong feelings. Perhaps she needed to be a mother to Jamila. Pain began to seep into Salwa's heart.

"*Bukra*," she said again.

Disappointed, Malvina understood. "I guess you need some time to think it over," she said.

She turned to Jamila. "Okay," she said, almost to herself, "I'll try again later. Let's move on. Is there anywhere to eat around here?" pointing at her mouth and rubbing her stomach, hunger outweighing prudence. They walked together to the center of the village where a cart rickety on its wheels stood leaning to one side. A man carrying a barrel on his back passed them, clinking two brass cups with a rhythmic tinkling sound, offering water to drink. A young boy was holding up sticks of sugar cane for sale. A small girl stood beside him, chewing on a peeled stick of cane, sucking away intently as the sweet sap ran down her chin. An old man offered them a toothless grin as he ladled something hot and fragrant onto a flat bread. With amazing dexterity he piled on crisp brown balls, lettuce and sauce, folding them into the bread and handing the breads out to a line of hungry men who threw clinking coins into an old tin on the cart, in return.

Malvina recognized *falafel* with relief. This was a street food that could also be found on the streets of Manhattan, where she lived.

"Yesss!," she said with great satisfaction, throwing caution to the winds. "We'll have some of this and then we'll decide what to do next."

As they walked away together, both munching on the hot food, Jamila glanced up at her. She had understood both the gist of Malvina's question as well as her mother's hesitation. Just two days earlier, her father had told her that Mustafa had talked to him about taking Jamila as a wife. Granted, she would only be a second wife, she had no dowry, and Mustafa had an important job. He was a major-domo in a big palatial house in Cairo, working for a relative of Gamal Abdel Nasser himself. All the house staff reported to him. It was said that he organized important gatherings, some of which President Gamal Abdel Nasser himself attended. Mustafa knew how to read and write, and had much knowledge of the Koran.

It was a much better offer than she could ever have expected. His first wife had the biggest hut in the village and she lived comfortably there with their six small children, but Mustafa had promised that he would take Jamila with him to Cairo, to live with him and help the laundrywomen at the big house. Seeing her father's hesitation he had agreed to wait until she had her first bleeding. That would come soon. Her breasts had begun to swell under her ragged caftan and when she noticed Mustafa's eyes narrow and gleam as he stared at them as he was making his stately way toward the car that waited at the edge of the village to take him back to Cairo, a shudder ran through her. She had turned away and hurried to her Aunt Nadia's hut nearby. She had not really understood why she felt so uncomfortable.

Aunt Nadia, her mother's younger sister, had no children of her own and could be counted on for a listening ear and a wealth of information on many subjects that were not discussed in Jamila's hut. Salwa and Sadik were all about survival and dealing with the day to day. Nadia, Salwa's younger sister, had married a taciturn older man who spoke little but enjoyed provoking his wife to her easy hearty laughter that pealed out in gasps and waves as her entire small person shook with mirth. As she headed toward her aunt's hut, Jamila reflected sadly that she could not remember when she had last seen Salwa laugh. Visiting Aunt Nadia always lifted her spirits.

Aunt Nadia loved nothing better than a good gossip. She listened intently to Jamila's concerns and leaned back thoughtfully.

"Things change," she said slowly. " Times change. Sometimes Allah opens a path we do not expect. I would miss your visits if you went to live in Cairo, but still…" She paused and sighed "to be able to leave this village and live in a fine house in the big city…"

Her eyes had a faraway look Jamila had never seen before. "*Habibti*," Aunt Nadia said, "You must consider the matter very carefully. This is an important decision. None of us has ever had such an opportunity. I, myself, wanted so much to see Cairo. Did I ever tell you about how it was in the old days when once a year our family used to walk all the way to Cairo to harvest mangoes at a big house by the Nile?" Jamila shook her head.

"I so wanted to go," said Aunt Nadia wistfully, "but I never got to have my turn, although my mother promised that I would go the next time." A bitter edge crept into her voice.

"Salwa went that last time to help with the harvest, but I had to stay and look after the baby. There was never a next time after that. We learned through the head gardener at the big house who had family in our village and who was a friend of our *abou*, that the people who lived in that mansion were Jewish, and that they had been forced to leave their house and leave Egypt for good."

Aunt Nadia shook her head sighing deeply, her narrowed eyes meanwhile taking in the fascinated interest of her audience of one.

"Those were hard times." She paused, remembering. "The head gardener there lost his job, you know," she went on, "everyone who worked there found themselves without work. He never came back to our village, so I don't know what became of him."

She stopped, and eyed her niece.

"So, that was the end of the mango harvest for us." she sighed deeply. "I missed my turn. After that we went through some difficult times without that money coming in every year."

She was silent, unusually thoughtful, watching as Jamila pondered all this new information.

"Salwa married soon after that," Nadia added, "and then you were born. No-one speaks of any of it any more. She had a baby every year after that, with Sadik."

She hesitated, and then went on, "Come to think of it, Salwa was never quite the same after she came back from that last mango harvest. She told me a big secret and I swore never to tell of it, but there is a time to be silent and a time to speak. She told me she had slipped into the big house by herself, and how huge and grand it was. I should so have liked to see that, too. She went on and on about how she would never forget the experience. She said it was one of the most wonderful moments of her life." She sighed again, launched her substantial bosom and heaved herself off the stool, wagging her finger at her niece as she added,

"But you take my advice, Jamila, if you have a chance at work in a big mansion in Cairo you should grab it, even if Mustafa comes with it." Seeing Jamila's bewildered expression, Nadia sat back down on her stool and laughed. "You'll get used to it, believe me."

Jamila's father had been so excited when he told her of the offer. He pulled her close and she smelled his cigarette breath and the sweetish smell of his sweat as he told her that she would live in a palace and send money home every week to help her family. She tried hard not to think of Walid, Mustafa's eldest son, skinny as the cattle he herded for the village, whose dark eyes stirred such fire in her abdomen whenever she caught his gaze. Mustafa had a prosperous man's girth. She had seen him in his magnificent major-domo clothes, the finely tailored royal blue *galabiya* with real gold trim and the broad gold and blue sash that wrapped around his protruding belly. He had arrived unexpectedly for a village council meeting with no time to change his clothes, and had impressed the entire village with his obvious importance and prosperity as he strode majestically into the council meeting and took part in the discussion. Mustafa had promised her father that there would be fine clothes and good company awaiting her among the laundrywomen, and that he would take very good care of her.

As darkness began to fall, the American woman's taxi drove her away, her hand with its red nails and jangling bangles waving to Jamila out of the taxi window as the taxi hurtled and bounced its way back toward Cairo.

Jamila slowly made her way home, her bare feet navigating dust and rocks with the ease of familiarity. Her stomach hurt and she could feel tears pressing against the back of her lids. She had not completely understood the exchange between her mother and the American woman, but she knew it involved her, and she knew that it meant something momentous. She suddenly felt as if the world she had always known was about to tilt and slide her off into another life. A part of her never wanted to leave this village, but somewhere deep inside her, along with red-hot fear, came tiny prickles of excitement at the thought of what might lie ahead.

Ali came running toward her and walked back home with her, his deep dark eyes serious and reflective. He was her junior by a year, but taller by a head, the best friend she had in the world.

"So what's going on?" he asked anxiously. "*Oumi* is having a big discussion about you with our father. I never heard her yell like that before. Are they sending you away? Have you done something bad?"

Tears seeped down Jamila's face. "I don't think I've done anything bad," she said, "I don't really understand what's happening. *Oumi* seems to want me to go away, and I don't even know why. She never really talks to me, she just goes her own way and makes me follow."

She looked around and whispered to her brother, who bent his head to hear what she was saying. "*Abou* told me that Mustafa made an offer to our father, and it means I would go and live in Cairo, and Aunt Nadia says I should go, but the American woman was saying something about America to *Oumi*, and I didn't really understand what she was saying, or what it all means."

She gazed up at him with haunted eyes. He put an arm around her shoulders and held her close. "I don't want you to leave, or to go anywhere," he said, his voice thick with fear. "I'll take care of you when I grow up. Just tell them you won't go." But Jamila was no longer listening, her attention caught by the clamor of agitated voices.

They had arrived at the door of their hut and a fierce exchange exploded out at them as they pushed open the door and stepped in. Sadik was waving his arms frantically at his angry wife, whose *abaya* had been pushed to one side, and whose face was fast turning an alarming shade of red.

"What will I tell Mustafa?" He shouted, "*Eh? Walahi,* I don't know my own wife. How can you think of sending our daughter to America? You will lose her forever. If she becomes Mustafa's wife she will come and visit us from Cairo. She will bring us her babies. She will bring us great honor. She will still be a part of our family. What do you know of this American woman? She will give you money, yes, but she will steal our daughter forever."

Salwa's face had set in a mulish expression. She took a breath and opened her mouth to shout an angry retort, but the baby in her arms woke up and started to scream, red face and tiny limbs wiggling furiously. Sadik leaned forward, and took the crying baby from his wife. He sighed deeply, patting the baby on his shoulder, shaking his head. This was clearly not going away. He had never seen Salwa so furious. She was pregnant again, of course, although she had not told him yet. Perhaps that was why she was coming up with this ridiculous proposal. On the other hand, he had given Mustafa his word. Honor was at stake.

"She's not going," he said at last, in a tone that brooked no argument, "she's marrying Mustafa."

Salwa broke into hysterical sobs and ran out of the hut. So many secrets. So much she could never tell.

The call to prayer echoed from a nearby minaret and the men headed to the mosque for evening prayer. Salwa wrapped herself more closely in her *abaya* and made her way out of the village. The long Nile twilight had begun, and she hurried on, a dark shadow among the shadows. She slipped into a field of tall sugar cane and found what she was looking for, the secret place she had fashioned for herself many years ago. She crouched down, drew her robe over her eyes and gave way to deep sobs and wails. There was no-one to hear. Pain and anger echoed around her, disappearing into the rustling stands of sugar cane. The baby in her belly stirred.

Her mind drifted to the day long ago when the elderly *daya,* the local midwife, had called on mothers of marriageable daughters in the village to be sure to visit her hut for their daughters "to be made women," and become good and faithful wives.

" I won't do it. I won't go," Salwa had screamed at her mother, when soon after the day of the mango harvest, her mother had come to Salwa early in the morning, pulling her out of bed with slaps and cries, pulling her out of a deep sleep. Salwa had screamed and cried, struggled, and tried to run away, but her mother was stronger, filled with the righteousness of her purpose. Before Salwa had realized what was happening, her mother had dragged her across the village to the *daya*'s hut and forced her inside, throwing her into a vortex of unimaginable violation and agony at the cold bony hands of the *daya*.

It had been so dark inside the hut. Before Salwa had fully grasped what was about to happen, the *daya* had grabbed her with an iron grip and thrown her down hard on a mat on the floor, tying her legs to two posts and pushing her mother out of the hut. Muttering and murmuring in a monotonous sing-song, the *daya* ignored her shrieks of pain and terror and Salwa was left for the rest of her life with the searing memory of a fearsome toothless leer as the old woman leaned over her, parted her night shift, lifted her knife, and proceeded with her task. Her mother had turned up again outside the hut when at last the *daya* had finished her ministrations, and directed by the *daya* she helped a sobbing Salwa to her feet. She bowed her respect and handed the woman her payment wrapped in a piece of cloth. Salwa cried herself out and great shudders and sobs still shook her as her mother half carried her back home. Nothing had ever been the same for her since. Her birthright of pleasure had been traded for a lifetime of pain. Salwa's mind flashed to Jamila's hopeful face and she knew that she could not subject her to the same mutilation. But she feared that Sadik would never agree with her, for without it no man would want to take their daughter to wife.

Jamila, the stubborn, independent child of her heart. What could she do? She had understood something of Malvina's promise of a better life. It would break her heart to lose her daughter, but she wanted that better life for her. She wanted it with all the suppressed passion of her own youth. She wanted her never to feel the horror of the knife mutilating her most intimate parts. She wanted Jamila's green eyes always to sparkle with delight in the world. If Jamila married Mustafa she would lose her in a different way. The promise that was Jamila would drown in pain, in tears, in dust and babies, struggle and apathy. It could never be retrieved. She, of all people, was aware of that.

A mangy cat slunk toward her through the rustling stalks. She shooed it away. She knew what she would do. She got to her feet and padded back to the village.

CHAPTER FOUR

1969 Leaving Egypt
MALVINA

To the delight of the enterprising taxi driver, Malvina came back to the village again and again, day after day. She had let Tim know that she would have to stay in Egypt a little longer than originally planned, but she kept to herself her interest in bringing Jamila home with her. It would be a surprise, and knowing Tim, it would be a surprise he would delight in. He had often suggested that they adopt a child after the loss of Teresa, when it became clear that Malvina would not be pregnant again. Tim, clear-eyed generous Tim, had never stopped hoping that they might somehow be a family again, that Malvina might overcome the caul of sadness that held her prisoner. She knew her surprise would please him as much as his had pleased her.

Jamila liked spending time with Malvina. She felt important, walking the American woman around, nodding to the neighbors as they strolled past, showing her more of the village and the surrounding desert with each visit. She was relaxing comfortably into the relationship, enjoying Malvina's companionship, and looking forward to being relieved of her family chores whenever the American woman turned up.

But the day came when the situation suddenly took on the quality of a strange nightmare. Before she quite realized it, she was clambering into Malvina's taxi with her, clutching a small bag of her belongings, heading for Cairo and the airport. She had never been out of her village, and the explosion of sights and sounds thrust her into a state of frozen terror. She opened her mouth to say something, but all that came out was a faint terrified whimper. Colors assumed an almost psychedelic intensity as she tried to absorb the sight of hordes of people crowded together, milling about in some sort of organized chaos, among magnificent structures taller than she had ever seen, bright lights blinking on and off, while cars, goats, sheep, camels donkeys and mangy stray dogs jostled in the streets, the taxi threading its way among them.

Jamila had suspected that something of the kind might be going to happen to her. She had understood that her life was teetering precariously on the edge of monumental change. Either the American woman or Mustafa would be lifting her out of the only environment she knew, and precipitating her into something unimaginably different. She had confronted this with a mixture of terror and excitement. She had tried to explain it to Ali, but he didn't want to hear what she was saying. She understood that he was deeply hurt and puzzled by her sudden involvement with the American woman, an involvement that seemed to exclude him, but she could find no words to express the conflicting emotions that warred in her psyche, or the vastness of the possibilities she intuited, and her attempt at explaining herself to him had left him as bewildered as she.

The world she knew was dropping away from her grasp and plunging her, unprepared, into the unknown.

"Listen, dear," Malvina said, later, turning to the girl crouched beside her in her airplane seat. "I was wondering, how do you like the name Jasmine? I think we should forget about Jamila. I think Jasmine is the perfect professional name for you. Your name should be Jasmine from now on. It has an exotic ring to it, but not too much. I think you'll find it will go down much better in the States, and will be easier for you to interact with your schoolmates. How do you like it?"

Jamila stared at her, her heart in her eyes, her eyes swimming with unshed tears. Grasping a little of the fear and disorientation that Jamila was experiencing, Malvina sighed and looked away, gesturing to the stewardess. A few moments later, the stewardess was leaning over Jamila, her eyes kind.

"Here you are, honey," she said, handing her a book and some crayons. "Have fun with these. They'll help to pass the time."

Malvina had fallen asleep. The twist of fear gnawing at Jamila's stomach had become a raging force. She was starting to feel terrified. Who was she? She wasn't even Jamila anymore. She was this strange person, Jasmine. Where was she going? Why had her mother thrown her out without a word. She had never been in a plane before. She had felt a momentary thrill of anticipation as she followed Malvina down a long ramp and up a flight of metal stairs into the narrow body of the plane, her bag of meager possessions clutched in her hands. She looked around her, fascinated by the scale and texture of the interior of this metal camel that would carry her out of desert sands into a new world. She tried out the different buttons on the panel above her head, moving her seat back and forward while Malvina watched and smiled, but when the plane took off with a bone-rattling roar she yelled in terror, clutching Malvina and burying her head on the American woman's bony chest, wanting Salwa's warmth and cosy familiarity so badly that she thought her heart would burst right out of her body.

When Malvina had come to take her away, she had panicked and run to her mother, but to her horror, instead of protecting her, her mother had pushed her away, pushed her hard toward the American woman.

"*Yallah*, go, Jamila," she said coldly, and turned back into the hut without a further word. Sadik followed her inside, defeated, shaking his head and clutching the money Malvina had brought. That had been the last she had seen of them, the last she would ever see. She did not see Salwa fall into Sadik's arms, weeping uncontrollably. The pain and confusion of the parting, which had felt so sudden because she had been unable to understand everything that had preceded it, began to excavate a deep wound in Jamila's heart as she took in her strange surroundings.

Huddled in her seat by the window of the plane, she stared out at fields of cloud, wondering about them. She caught sight of a gleaming silver snake far below. Was that her beautiful Nile? It looked so tiny, receding farther and farther away. On the other hand, the fluffy clouds outside the small oval window were huge, shaped just like the puffy clouds of cotton in the fields of home. Were there cotton fields in the sky? Were these the fields she would see when she was in America? Everything in America would be big, she knew that. Everyone knew that, but these cotton clouds were enormous. She reached up and touched the window pane with cautious fingers, wondering if the clouds outside were as soft to the touch as the cotton she knew, but something told her that they could not have been more different. She sighed deeply, troubled and afraid, totally unable to understand. The buzz of the aircraft at last lulled her to sleep and she awoke to the rasp of the captain's voice announcing the imminent landing at Idlewild Airport.

She was in America. Her new life had begun.

Malvina's home was in Manhattan, a tall brown house with living space on the upper floors and offices in the basement. Pots of bright pink geraniums and impatiens surrounded the perimeter of a tiny garden space, ivy trailing onto the steps leading to the basement door. A larger garden opened off the back of the house, and held a couple of ornamental rocks and tiled pathways bordered with low clipped hedges, the effect, minimalist and sculptural. Malvina made her way down the steps, opened the door, and led Jamila into the garden. Two young women in silk kimono wrappers sat on a wrought iron bench, impossibly long legs stretched out to the sun, short cropped hair fluffed around tired faces. Jamila followed behind Malvina and the two women sat up straight and stared at her.

"Hey, Malvina," said the brunette, "You're back." She glanced at Jamila and added, "what on earth did you bring home from your vacation?" Her laugh was not entirely pleasant. Jamila did not understand the words, but she understood the hostility and hung her head, embarrassed.

"This is Jasmine," said Malvina, putting an arm around Jamila's shoulders and patting her head, smoothing the wiry hair that puffed out around her small face. "She's come here to go to school, gym classes and ballet school, and she'll learn

English and learn how to be a model. She's going to live with me, here," and she added, "Beatrice, no need to get snarky. She's going to be one of the best. Mark my words."

Beatrice made no comment, and sighing Malvina added "Okay, tell me, how did this morning's shoot go?"

Beatrice glanced at her friend and muttered "Frank kept me for hours. I'm exhausted."

Malvina shot her a sardonic look, took Jamila's hand and led her back into the house and up some carpeted stairs. She glanced at Jamila's dazed expression and smiled.

"Until we get you settled," she said, "This is your own room. This is where you sleep." She accompanied her words with gestures, and Jamila looked around. She could not quite believe the comfort the tiny room promised. It seemed she was to have it all to herself. She had never had a room or even a bed to herself. She stood still and turned to take it all in, an expression of intense wonder crossing her face. The room was clean and bright with crisp flowered sheets and a tall narrow window that faced the street.

"Okay?" said Malvina, watching her, "You can wash up in there" she pointed to a door, "and I'll come and get you at dinner time and show you the rest of the house. I want you to meet Tim. I wrote to Tim and told him all about you. Tim is my husband." She pointed at the gold ring on her finger. Seeing Jamila's puzzled expression she added, "Next week we'll get you a tutor and work at your English before we do anything else."

She smiled at Jamila, and noting the forlorn look in her green eyes, she gave her a quick hug.

"I don't usually start my girls so young," she said, a little anxiously, "but that's why I have you here in the house with me." She knew that Jamila hardly understood anything she said, but she went on, "I really enjoyed the way you showed me your world. Now it's my turn to show you mine." She waited for a reaction, but there was none. She sighed, hoping it would not take too long for the girl to learn English. Smiling at Jamila's bewildered face, she added "I'm hoping we'll get along, and I hope you'll settle down comfortably," and she walked out of the room and closed the door.

Jamila stood still for some time, afraid to touch anything in the beautiful room. Then she moved cautiously to a mirrored door and opened it to find a closet, metal hangers jangling as she jerked back in alarm at the noise. Not knowing what they were for, she took her bag and stuffed it into the bottom of the closet. Another door yielded a small bathroom with a shower and she stared, puzzled, at the shiny faucets and mysterious buttons in the wall. Tentatively she turned a faucet and watched with awe as clean water gushed out. She was so tired and bewildered. She put her head under the water and washed her hair and face as best she could. She kept sniffing the soap, entranced by the pleasant fragrance it provided. Clean white towels hung on a handrail and she stroked one, amazed at the softness, and then decided that they must be meant for drying. When Malvina came to get her, she found a small girl curled on top of the bedclothes, lost in a very sound sleep.

CHAPTER FIVE

New York 1970
BECOMING JASMINE

As the weeks sped by, bristling with challenges, strange new experiences, and so much to be learned, Jamila's watchful eyes missed nothing of the world opening out ahead of her. She struggled to understand the way things worked, inside the townhouse and out. She followed Malvina around, a small silent shadow as they moved together throughout the day, absorbing words and their meanings, until patterns began to take shape for her and she saw what they meant. She sat beside Malvina in a corner of her office and watched her at work.

Her heart ached for those she had left behind, most of all for Ali. She tried to imagine how he was navigating the days without her there, to smooth his path. From his earliest days she had been his anchor. Ali's turbulent nature brought him constantly into conflict with his environment. His parents left him largely to himself, except where shattering clashes erupted between father and son. As she listened to the unfamiliar sounds that surrounded her, Jamila wondered how he would manage on his own, and if she would ever see him again. But while her heart ached, her mind hummed. She was starting to understand.

As days and months streamed by, the challenges increased. School had proved to be an ordeal, but Malvina complemented schooling with a strict round of tutoring at home, and Jamila was soon able to find ways of making herself understood. She had found herself initially in a kindergarten class, with special tutoring in reading, but she still had to interact with kids her own age during breaks and playtimes. Unused to navigating a competitive gaggle of peers, her friendly overtures in a tangled rush of mangled and mingled languages attracted suspicion and withdrawal from the other kids, who thought her definitely weird. Her strangely accented attempts at American speech and her unusual appearance made her an instant pariah at the local public school. She belonged neither to the groups of dominant blondes, nor with other ethnic groupings, nor with the misfits. She had somehow managed to be a misfit among the misfits, welcomed only by a few of the teachers, who saw past her thorny beginnings to the keen intelligence beneath. She shrank back into herself and set herself to learning everything as fast as she could, in order to drag her way up the grades. It was so hard.

Despite all the difficulties, Jasmine loved her new surroundings. She marveled every time a faucet spewed water when she needed it, or when her bare feet met the softness of the carpet by her bed. She came to rely on the warmth she found in Malvina's hugs, and to appreciate her kindnesses. Once, she had opened a drawer in the kitchen and had found a picture of a younger happier Malvina, her arms around a small dark girl who looked very much like her.

"Who is this?" She asked.

Malvina had taken the frame from her and put it carefully back in the drawer, face down. Tears glittered in her eyes and her austere face lost its edges, blurring in pain.

"That was my little girl," she said at last, her voice breaking as Jasmine stared at her with anxious eyes. "She was very very sick, and she died."

Jasmine nodded. She knew about death. Children in her village often did not survive the early years. She put her arms around Malvina and hugged her as tightly as she could.

"I am your girl now," she said.

Much as she liked where she lived and who she lived with, she continued to dread school. She had not had many friends in her village, and she understood that friendship would not come easily in this new life. Still smarting from what she perceived as her mother's rejection, Jasmine hid her new wounds and cloaked her vulnerability with a surface impassivity and a fierce concentration on her schoolwork, struggling to find intellectual footing and the words with which to speak her mind. She had an innate ability for languages, and she made the verbal leap into her new world with hardly a stumble.

"She's bright as a button," Malvina said to her husband in amazement, beaming. "Soaks up everything we put in her reach. I knew she had the face for it, but the intelligence is a bonus. I am really enjoying watching her blossom into everything that life here offers. Our life is so very different from anything she has ever known. I am loving having her around. How about you? Think she's happy?"

Tim pulled at his beard and studied his wife's face, noting that it had come alive once again with love and excitement. Jamila had released her back into life. He sighed with relief and smiled at Malvina.

"She hasn't tried to contact her people back home has she?" He asked at last. "I do notice that those amazing eyes light up whenever there's something new for her to learn. Looks happy to me. She's a good kid, and she has the face, the guts, and the ambition. I suspect she's settling in nicely."

Malvina smiled. She had ceased to fight her growing love for this girl who asked for nothing, but noticed everything, responding to everything Malvina asked of her with a touching confidence. Jamila had crept quietly into Malvina's heart and lodged there in a way she had not expected.

Before the start of agency business, having seen Jasmine off to school, she sat at breakfast with Tim who was getting ready to go to his studio, a faded paint-stained orange backpack on the chair beside him.

"I want to keep Jasmine out of the limelight as much as possible until she's ready for the major runways," Malvina said thoughtfully, adding milk to her cereal, "I don't want to send her around for whatever commercials and photo shoots just happen to come up. I plan to pick and choose. I want to try to shield her from the competition and jealousies out there. I want her never to regret having come here to live with us. That's how I see it. I know I've never done it this way before, but she's such a wild little thing, running around the house barefoot with that corona of wiry hair around her face. She tries so hard at everything she does. She still needs a lot of grooming, and polishing, without taking away that unusual exotic edge. She has exceptional eyes and bones, not to mention an outsize personality, and I want her to enjoy the pay-off of success after all the hard work she's putting in."

She looked up at her husband, "What do you think, Tim?"

Tim had his mouth full of cereal, but he nodded. He had been watching the walls of pain and anger that Malvina had built between them dissolving with every week that passed. She was slowly returning to the woman he had married, before the terrible trauma of Teresa's loss had swept each of them into their own private circle of hell. He had hoped that his idea of a trip to Egypt would jolt Malvina into a different frame of mind, but his hopes had never dared extend to her finding a girl she could love with all the wasted mother love that lay stagnating in her heart. Jasmine had released her back into life, back into a proud and yearning motherhood.

Malvina had been finding potential young models for years, traveling around the country, scouring Europe as well as traveling the US, but none of the young women whose modeling skills had built the sterling reputation of the premier Malvina agency over the years had the indefinable combination of innocence and poise that Jasmine wore without effort. She was like a very subtle perfume, tangy and lingering, but light as a butterfly's kiss.

"She's got the charm alright," he mused as he pushed back his chair, looking back as he grabbed his backpack and headed for the kitchen door, his eyes serious, "I think you're right. Just give her time to understand the opportunities she'll have. You shouldn't rush anything. She's still struggling to catch up with school."

After school hours, Malvina had organized a grueling schedule for her every day, with an intricate web of music and dance classes, style management lessons, swim classes and poise instruction, interspersed with practice sessions and speech therapy. It was hard to fit in the homework from school, but Jasmine took great pride in her visible progress and somehow always managed to complete the work. She was so tired by the time she got to bed that she fell asleep as soon as her head hit the pillow.

Malvina and Tim went together to the nearby church every Sunday.

"Should we try to find a mosque for her to attend?" worried Malvina.

"Ask her," Tim advised.

Jasmine was surprised at the question. She shook her head. "I am American now," she said firmly, "no Egypt. No Muslim. No Arabic. I am American like you."

"Well then, do you want to come to our church with us?" asked Malvina.

She watched anxiously as Jasmine pondered the question.

Jasmine had a sharp mind but felt no existential need for religious observance. Since she had arrived in New York she had never once felt the need to fall to her knees and pray. *Madrassa*, as it had been when she was a child in a Nile village, was long over. Had she remained in her village she knew she might never have learned to read or write. Reading was far and away the most exciting thing she had discovered in America so far. She had recently begun to devour books with amazement and she plunged into the tales they unlocked for her, with passion.

Had she remained in the village she knew that she would have had to undergo some sort of mysterious rite in order to become marriageable. Her mother had never discussed it with her. Young village women disappeared for some days to a distant hut and never talked about what went on there. They reappeared later, eyes dull, their walk ungainly, their bitter response to anxious questions, "You'll find out soon enough. You'll be made a woman too."

Marriage to Mustafa would have required that. But that life would not now be hers. In this new life wrapping itself around her, she determined to set her own rules and to follow where her destiny led. It had amazed her once. No doubt it held other surprises, and she was not about to add a baggage she did not fully understand. She had observed that in America women walked freely, dressed freely, and intermingled freely with men. They wore scarves to keep warm, and for no other reason. She had no wish to lay claim to a metaphorical *abaya*, no wish to hamper herself with a new set of obligations, even if she rejected the old. No need for that. She smiled at Malvina and shook her head.

Malvina did not insist. Young as she was, Jasmine gave off a strong sense of presence and personality, and seemed to have no need to identify with her past. Clearly, she had turned her back on the past and expected to embrace her present without compromise. She was mature beyond her years, and the aura of otherness she carried about her was the key to her magnetism.

As she went about the business of the everyday running of her agency, Malvina found herself unexpectedly thinking about Jasmine, making plans for how she would manage this unusual girl's career even as she spent hectic days interviewing potential models, seeking out new venues, pairing each venue skilfully with the perfect young person for their needs, monitoring jealousies and disagreements among the chaperones, the bookers, and the clients. It was an intense, demanding life, but one she loved. She sped headlong through her day, a phone in one hand and a calendar in the other.

She wanted to make so many good things happen for this engaging creature it had been her good fortune to meet. She wanted to be sure that the trusting girl, Jasmine, would be entirely fulfilled by the abrupt change in her life's trajectory. She knew what it was like to have to adapt to a new environment. For her, it had been again and again. She wanted Jasmine to find her happiness in the differences. She suspected it had been a cruelly wrenching change, but Jasmine had never complained, or exhibited in any way the trauma and struggle that must have been going on inside her.

Although Malvina was eager for Jasmine to burst into the world of high fashion with mystery and glamor, she wanted to make certain that it would only be when the time was right. The way Malvina saw it, her slight accent would be indefinable. Her demeanor and presence would hint at secrets and keep secrets, and all of that would add to her charm. Until then, there was so much for her to learn.

"For why I do this?" Jasmine had asked in the early days as she trudged back to the townhouse, exhausted, amazed at the fierceness of winter in this distant land, tasting snow on her tongue with wonder. Malvina always gave the same answer, "Because I want you to have all the tools you need to have a wonderful life here, to be the very best, without effort. I know you can do it. I want that for you."

Jasmine listened, and absorbed the message. She, too, had grown fond of Malvina and Tim and she felt it incumbent on her to match up to their expectations. She pushed herself into each challenging requirement with vigor, hoping that she would somehow learn how to be Jasmine, how to be able to navigate her new world with the ease with which she had raced the goats on the cliffside banks of the Nile. She thought often of Ali, and wished there was a way she could tell him that she was fine, even happy. She hoped he had not been too distraught at her departure. She hoped he had recovered enough to find his own footing in a life of his choosing.

She was sometimes homesick for the gentle air and blue skies of her childhood, but very rarely felt pangs of real homesickness. Although her resentment of the way that Salwa had pushed for her departure had cut deep into her heart, she had also begun to understand something of the future that her present challenges offered, and she marched into that future with courage and dedication.

Jasmine watched Malvina phone for takeout one evening, as she sat at the kitchen table with her homework. Malvina never cooked. "My dear," she said, when Jasmine asked why the state-of-the art kitchen in the townhouse saw so little use, "Take-out menus have everything we need, accessibility, variety, instant gratification, you name it. They leave me free to take care of my agency, and Tim free to paint until all hours without having to rush home for dinner if he's in a good creative space. That's very important for an artist." She smiled.

She had taken Jasmine to visit Tim's studio early on, and Jasmine had stared, dumbfounded, at the canvases stacked against the wall, smeared and daubed with color. It all looked a complete mess to her. She had no comprehension of this kind of art. The paintings did not show any relationship to reality. She was sure that she could have thrown paint at the canvas and done them herself. Looking around, disappointed, she noticed a small painting of a horse and pointed at it with delight. There, at last, was something she could recognize and admire. Malvina and Tim, understanding what was happening, grinned at each other as Tim solemnly offered her the small painting for her room.

For a moment, as she watched Malvina open the door to the delivery boy and return to the table with paper bags containing dinner, a wave of nostalgia enveloped Jasmine. She remembered the warmth of the mud hut spilling babies and confusion. She remembered her mother's deft brown fingers making patties, stirring soup, constantly producing food with one hand, while balancing the newest baby on her hip. For the quick stab of a moment come and gone, she missed Salwa.

But the moment passed and left no residue of pain. She reveled in the freedom of conversation and chatter she had discovered in her new life. Salwa had never had time to discuss ideas or laugh about the illogic of the world around her, but Malvina, although she projected an aura of stern professionalism, was always ready to listen and respond. Jasmine's agile mind blossomed in the relationship, and the more she relaxed and allowed her intelligence and playfulness to emerge, the more she felt at home with the kind people who had taken her to their hearts and had introduced her to a much larger world than she had ever imagined possible.

The first time she had gone outside alone to do an errand for Malvina, she had been stunned almost immobile by the sight of the milling crowds and strident cars racing past her on Manhattan's upper east side. Her taxi ride through Cairo had prepared her for tall buildings, but these seemed to reach up to claw at the sky. She had spent her childhood in an indolent sun-drenched progress through a small village of mud huts under a vast canopy of blue sky, where she knew everyone by name. Her mind almost came to a halt as she tried to fathom how there could be so many people scurrying about their lives in the huge hive of interdependence that was New York City. She had been prepared to live a larger life as Mustafa's wife, in a big villa on the outskirts of Cairo, but the stirring scrambling stunning variety and warp speed of the life she observed around her plunged her psyche into shock and deflected her energies for several weeks. She managed to maintain a certain equilibrium until her mind caught up with her body, until she could embrace the splendor of this gritty new world that was hers for the taking.

"I have a new friend at school," she told Malvina one day, with pride.

Malvina looked interested. "What is she like?" she asked.

"She is a boy," said Jasmine with a grin. Malvina groaned. "There are some things I need to discuss with you," she said, anxiously, realizing that the many months of good food and comfort had added a voluptuous dimension to Jasmine's neat figure. "You are a very beautiful girl, but..."

Jasmine interrupted, shaking her head, "no, no." she said in all seriousness, "he does not want to marry me, he like to help me with my homework and to fight with Bettina and the others."

"Bettina?" asked Malvina, confused by the turn the conversation was taking.

"Bettina not likes me. She trips me to make me fall all the time, and makes everyone to laugh at me," explained Jasmine, who had experienced great difficulty adapting to the wearing of shoes every day and everywhere. She had held her head high and pretended not to care as her schoolmates made fun of her and excluded her from their whispered secrets and games. She glanced at Malvina and added fiercely, "But I don't care, you know, I make them to laugh at *her*."

Malvina saw her mouth droop and realized that what she had imagined was a smooth transition had been far more complex than she had thought. Clearly, it had been an awkward and painful one. Jasmine had not looked to her for help or sympathy. She had fought her own battles. The girl had courage and independence.

Malvina sighed, filled with regret that she had not grasped the extent of the challenges Jasmine had faced in stoic silence. "I'm sorry you've had such a hard time settling in, dear," she said, "I promise you, it will get easier." Jasmine looked at her quizzically and said nothing, her eyes darkening.

Malvina hesitated. Then she said, "When you begin to earn money, you will first have to pay off the money the agency expended on your behalf, I know you understand that? But that will soon be done after we get you on the circuit. I am getting excellent reports from the style and dance teachers." She smiled at her.

"And then I expect you will probably want to send some of your earnings home to your people," she added. "However, there's a real problem there. I spoke to my bank manager about how we could organize some transfers and he told me that would not be possible unless your family lived in one of the cities or had contacts there. Your village is so small and has no bank, and you told me your mother and father don't leave it at all. So I decided that the best thing would be to arrange a college savings account for you, and if you later find a way to get money to your family, it will be up to you."

She waited for an answer, but Jasmine fidgeted uneasily, her gaze opaque. At last, she looked up and said, "Thank you. I am happy to go to college one day, and maybe when I learn more I will find a way to send money to them.

CHAPTER SIX

1970 New York City
THE MICHNIKS

Summer in Manhattan. The heat waves had come and gone. Jasmine's demanding schedule had lightened but not altogether given way to indolence. She had gone to a nearby swimming pool to do her daily workout. Malvina was standing by her window, waiting for Jasmine to come home, gazing absently toward the most attractive brownstone on the block, the one with rough-cut wooden window-boxes spilling over with a riot of color, rich purple petunias, bright pink fuschia, sprays of tiny blue lobelia flowers scattered among straggling variegated ivy and bold geraniums. It was eye-catching and excessive, as only Marcel and Irina Michnik could be. She smiled to herself, remembering the day long ago, when she and Tim, walking home from church on a brisk fall day, had noticed a flamboyant Russian couple deep in vociferous argument, their hands moving in expressive accompaniment to their voices, both staring up at a dilapidated property on the block, a house that had long seemed on the verge of crumbling into dust and debris if a strong wind blew.

"Who would want to buy such a horribly neglected old wreck?" She remembered saying to Tim in disbelief when the FOR SALE sign first went up. "I keep waiting for the city to condemn it."

But the Russian couple across the street seemed to have resolved their argument as they stared up at the peeling facade, their hands and voices stilled, their smiles radiating hope and dreams. Then and there, as Tim and Malvina watched in fascination, Marcel and Irina hugged each other, eagerly shook hands with the real estate agent who had just arrived, and took possession of the house, which was to become not only their home, but also, it turned out, the cornerstone of what was to form the nucleus of Marcel's lucrative business. Malvina still found it amazing that Marcel had brought about such an extraordinary change in the tired old house. She and Tim watched as the months rolled by and squatters were summarily evicted. They watched construction workers with strange accents swarming all over the property, Marcel leaping about the scaffolding, shouting, directing everything at high volume, and they watched in amazed admiration as with time, the fine bones of the house became visible.

The evening the Russian couple moved in, Malvina and Tim decided to take a neighborly welcome dinner over to the new inhabitants of their block.

"What is this?" Irina had asked in surprise, arriving flushed and breathing heavily at the door, eyeing the cartons from the nearby Chinese restaurant that Malvina held out to her.

"I remember how hard it was to move in, so we just thought you might like some food for this first evening in your new home," said Malvina, proffering the shopping bags and adding

"We wanted to congratulate you, you have made the old lady look so fine." She laughed.

"What old lady?" Irina asked suspiciously, making no move to take possession of the bags Malvina had brought.

"The house, of course!" said Malvina, as she and Tim burst out laughing. Irina roared with laughter along with them, although she had not really understood the joke, and in that moment, friendship was born.

"Come. I cook." announced Irina firmly, holding the door open wider and pulling them inside. "You come, see my house, and eat with us."

Later, as they were leaving, Malvina noticed her Chinese dinner cartons lying untouched in the garbage, but this was some hours after Marcel had joined Irina in the foyer, arms wide, roaring a magnanimous welcome, crushing Malvina in a bear hug and pounding Tim on the back. The two young couples chatted deep into the night.

"How ever did you manage this?" asked Malvina in amazement, as she helped Irina take dirty dishes down to the basement, to the enormous state-of-the-art kitchen that still wooed her sated appetite with fragrant reminders of the meal they had just eaten. "This is the most well-equipped kitchen I have ever seen, and the meal ... the meal ..." words rarely failed Malvina, but she was lost in admiration for someone who could instantly craft such delicious food the day after moving house.

"Are you a chef? Do you work in a restaurant?" She asked, interested.

Irina shrugged, shook her head, and laughed a hearty laugh. "My mother she teach me," she said happily. "She love to cook. I love to cook."

Her accent thickened as her eyes lost their light. "She have to stay in Russia."

"Oh! I'm so sorry," said Malvina, "you must miss her."

"Your mother, she teach you?" Asked Irina, eyeing Malvina's slender figure dubiously.

Malvina hesitated. She rarely spoke to anyone about her childhood. The two women climbed the stairs and sat facing each other on a comfortable couch in the expansive living room, carefully placed solar lights illuminating the small garden beyond floor to ceiling windows, a huge silver samovar in need of a polish on the table in front of them and steaming cups of strong tea in their hands. Tim and Marcel were watching sports in the library. Guffaws and shouts of glee and disappointment echoed faintly into the living room.

Looking into Irina's broad candid face, and seeing only acceptance and interest there, Malvina found herself saying, almost in a whisper, "I never knew my mother. She left me at the church door in a market crate, and the minister found me there, wrapped in a beautiful hand-knitted blue blanket with a note that said '*This is Malvina. Take good care of her.*' I know, I know! It's like something out of a book, but it really happened. They tried to find out who had left me there, but no-one was ever able to find any trace of her." She saw Irina's stunned expression and added "I do sometimes wonder about her, what it must have been like for her to make such a decision. She must have been very young, and very frightened, I think. So she left me in the safest place she could think of. I hope her life turned out alright. Mine has."

Irina's face lit up with relief, "Ah! So all was good then, no?"

Malvina paused. "It wasn't all good," she said slowly, "but it could have been a whole lot worse. The minister had no wife, so the ladies of the congregation took over, and members of the congregation helped social services place me in a series of foster homes connected to the church. They sent me to school, and made sure I was clothed and fed. They were very kind, but they took care of me out of a sense of duty and they made sure I never forgot it. There was never any love. There was always that unspoken shadow over my existence. I never felt a part of their families. She paused and added with a chuckle, "and I never learned to cook." Irina was shaking her head and clicking her tongue in distress.

Watching her, Malvina hesitated, and then continued, "When I was fourteen years old a man followed me home from the grocery store, pushed his way into the house, and told my foster father that he would take me off their hands and I could learn to become a model. My foster mother heard and leapt at the opportunity. I think she had noticed that her husband had become a little too interested in my new shapely figure. So I became a model. That's how my dream life began, and here I am." She struggled to contain the tears that were so unexpectedly rising unbidden to her eyes. Only Tim knew all her story, and here she was, talking about it to a total stranger, even though Irina did not feel like a stranger.

Irina put a robust arm around Malvina's shoulders. It felt warm and comforting. She looked at Malvina with slate grey eyes that had become huge pools of compassion. She said firmly, "We will be good friends, no? We will be family. And I will teach you to cook, and you will teach me to be American."

Malvina laughed and shook her head. "No cooking for me," she said ruefully, "It's too late for that. I'm addicted to take-out. But it's never too late for friendship. I'll be happy to help with becoming American, and with anything else you need, and you can count on Tim and me to come over and eat your delicious food, any time."

The friendship had taken firm root.

PART II

CHAPTER SEVEN

1968 Egypt
HAMID

The small village clustered on the banks of the Nile was still cloaked in the silence of deep night, except for the occasional cry of a child having a nightmare, or the distant grunt of a predator stalking the night. It was dark in the mud hut. Hamid had arisen just before dawn. He reached up and took down the brass *kanaka* from its shelf above the wood stove, and made himself a small cup of bitter coffee. Ignoring the pain in his arthritic fingers, he saddled his elderly donkey, soothing its distress with pats and whispered words as it jerked its head in protest and prepared to bray.

"Shhhhh," he said urgently, as he slid the worn saddle onto the donkey's back, anxious to slip away before the village erupted into the sound and motion of a new day, "shhhhh." The donkey eyed him balefully, but stayed silent.

Placing two bulging sacks on either side of the saddle, he tested them carefully to make sure that the weight was evenly distributed. The village had barely begun to stir as he urged his donkey beyond the cluster of palms and mud huts toward the river path that would take him to Cairo. He had worked long and hard to complete enough inlaid boxes and small tables to warrant the tedious journey to the big city.

Rumors of political turmoil had reached probing fingers into the quiet village on the banks of the Nile, where he lived. It was essential that he connect with the men he knew in Cairo, who inhabited the shadowy political underworld of the Muslim Brotherhood. As the years fanned out behind him in an ever-spreading wake, Hamid had learned early how to tread carefully, gradually muting the passionate political activism of his youth as crises flared and faded, power changed hands, and the mood of the country shifted around him. As a young man in the 1930s, he had been drawn to the Muslim Brotherhood when the aim of the brotherhood in its earliest days was to provide a counterbalance to colonialism by returning to the precepts of the Koran. Their goal, then, had been to peaceably bring about a healthy modern Islamic society.

As the years succeeded each other, World War II came and went. Colonialism waxed and waned as the French and then the British brought their language, their culture, and their ambitions to Egypt.

Hamid had seen many changes in his life. He had watched many dreams blaze briefly, fade, and die. Hamid never forgot the day in 1938 when his mother had woken him before dawn to take her young son with her to join milling crowds converging on Cairo for the royal wedding of the young King Farouk and his lovely bride, Farida. He never forgot the wild excitement of the crowds, and the pomp and circumstance heralding the wedding of the beautiful young royal couple. It seemed an epic moment of glamor, joy, and hope, captured in the image of a dark beauty climbing the marble steps of the Kubbe Palace in her shining silver gown to meet her prince. The boy was enraptured.

Later, Hamid often thought about the ephemeral nature of such moments. Obesity and debauchery vanquished the golden glow of the young king as the years went by. By 1949, the marriage was over. In 1952, a military coup brought an end to the last of the royal Turkish line of Fouad and Farouk and brought in the military rule of President Naguib, followed by the election of Gamal Abdel Nasser.

Through it all, Hamid grew older. His eyesight was still keen, but his back had begun to bend from the weight of his years. He sat outside his hut day after day, polishing and placing chips of ivory and mother-of-pearl in age-old patterns into wooden surfaces, with infinite patience. He watched, and he waited. He continued his solitary life in the village and his occasional travels to the metropolis to sell his wares. He was close-mouthed, and careful. It was good to live long. He had no need to brandish his disappointments, his shattered dreams, or the comrades he met with from time to time, for any and all to see. His love for Egypt kept him in contact with those he hoped might eventually effect change for the better.

As the sun rose and the day lightened around him, he trudged steadily along the borders of the Nile toward the distant metropolis, lost in thought. There was always danger in Cairo, but more danger in remaining ignorant of the situation building at the turbulent center of political power. He knew that the village elders counted on him to warn them of any new crackdowns against the Muslim Brotherhood. He sighed deeply, hoping that no more of his long-time comrades had lost their lives or their freedom since his last visit.

Hamid urged his donkey along as he made his way toward the teeming market where he would settle in his accustomed place to display his wares for sale, and where he would signal the hidden Brotherhood through his unobtrusive presence in their midst. The word of his arrival always spread quickly. He had no idea how. It was safer not to know.

Cairo was seething with unrest. He could sense the tension building and building as he advanced steadily into the urban confusion.

Change was again at hand. Change was inevitable. Hamid had lived long enough to accept that. He viewed change with guarded optimism, always hoping it would be for the better. As he walked along, head down, ruminating on his memories of the past, and the possibilities he envisioned opening out before him, he was suddenly accosted by a large group of men in military uniform, guns at the ready, blocking his way.

"Where so fast, *Effendi*?" one of them shouted, waving his gun in Hamid's face. "*Eh?*".

Hamid, looked up, startled, and then pointed to the two large sacks on the back of his donkey.

"*Muski*," he said dryly.

Wondering why he had been singled out from the crowds surging around him in clamorous disorder, he glanced warily up at the soldier, muttering under his breath that he was just a peasant from one of the Nile villages hoping to make a few *piasters* selling his wares at the bazaar. The soldier continued to challenge him.

Along with many others, Hamid would not have been sorry to see the end of the strong military dictatorship of Gamal Abdel Nasser, the general who had forced the abdication and exile to Italy of the unabashedly corrupt and flamboyant King Farouk and his family in 1952, and who, throughout his presidency, cracked down mightily on the Muslim Brotherhood. Nasser's nationalization of the Suez Canal in 1956 had resulted in an international crisis, with French and British troops parachuting in to the Port Said area, joining forces with Israeli troops from across the desert, to march toward Cairo to take back the canal. Although world political interference had aborted the invasion, the military threat provoked a furious Nasser to order an immediate expulsion of the French, the British, and the descendents of many generations of Jews who had formed a solid part of the country's infrastructure for generations.

Hamid sighed and shook his head as he reflected on the disastrous effect that had been inflicted on the infrastructure of his country through the simultaneous loss of such a formidable cluster of highly functioning individuals exiled from Egypt, never to return. He had been observing with growing concern, year after year, as the nation tried to reposition civic, social, and educational systems into the vacuum it had created, unable to extricate itself from the ensuing chaos and unrest.

Hamid had perfected the art of keeping a very low profile, but some of his more fiery friends had ended up imprisoned for years, kept in prisons and concentration camps where they were tortured for information and barred from any contact with the outside world as the regime attempted to forestall any opposition to its dictatorship.

He was still committed to the brotherhood he had joined in his youth, but he watched fearfully as the Muslim Brotherhood, so committed to peaceful social undertakings in its early days, shifted far from its origins over the years, seeking shelter in a clandestine underground existence as it resorted to more and more violent and destructive forays onto the national political scene.

Hamid, on his way to the *muski*, was well aware of the explosive possibilities of his unexpected encounter with the military. He carefully kept his head down, his hand gently patting his donkey, quieting him, as traffic and a cacophony of car horns built up behind them.

"I go to the *muski*," he kept repeating, keeping his voice low, humble, his eyes downcast.

The young soldier who had accosted him, his eyes fierce, and a luxuriant black mustache hiding a mouthful of stained, wildly irregular teeth, eyed him suspiciously as a motley collection of vehicles, livestock, and cars built up behind him. The noise level increased as they faced each other. The group of soldiers yelled at the gathering crowd and waved them back. An old banged up truck jerked back against a cart carrying precariously balanced crates of chickens. The driver of the cart yelled in panic as some of the crates flew open, disgorging a pandemonium of squawking birds as they fled from the crates, banging against windshields and scuttling between pedestrians and traffic. They ran in terrified freedom in different directions, pursued by their shrieking owner, the blaring of car horns, and angry screams from the crowd, creating a mind-numbing explosion of sound.

"Did you not know that there are major demonstrations planned for today, *ya agouz?* old man?" Shouted one of the soldiers, waving his gun about in exasperation, his rotund form pushing at the seams of his ill-fitting uniform. He leapt to one side, dropped his gun, and captured a squawking bird mid-flight, a surprised grin spreading over his face.

"Of course I knew all about that," said Hamid, mildly, his presence a tiny oasis of calm in the growing chaos spreading behind him, "I just didn't know it would be today."

He added quietly, "Either way, the *muski* will be open. Can I move on? I have to sell my wares and get back to my village before dark."

Tried beyond measure, the soldiers waved him on and turned their attention to attempting to organize the braying, grunting, squawking livestock, the shouting gesticulating crowd, and the pile-up of frustrated drivers into some sort of order.

Hamid wove his way quietly through the city, skirting the many celebratory demonstrations, and took up his accustomed place at the market. He nodded at the thin-faced man who often occupied the stall beside him. Mahmoud's elegant designs on brass always seemed to draw a crowd, as he sat crouched over his table, intent on etching intricate patterns onto a magnificent tray of glowing beaten brass. Tourists were standing around his work table, intently watching him conjure to life interconnected scenes and ancient patterns with a sure hand. He looked up as his young son brought him coffee and he gestured to Hamid to join him. Hamid smiled and bowed, hand on head and heart, shook his head, and laid out his wares. He had lost valuable time. He was already tired. Looking about him, he saw large garishly colored portraits of Gamal Abdel Nasser everywhere and in every stall, some ringed with flashing neon lights, others nestled in black velvet and heavy gold. He sighed. The day stretched endlessly. People came and went, and he learned what he had come to learn. Goods and money changed hands and fireworks lit up the evening sky. The crowds dispersed.

Hamid made his way back to the village earlier than usual, weary and footsore. He brushed down his donkey, made sure he had water, and led him to a small patch of grass near his hut. The donkey flung back his head gratefully before stretching his neck down to the stubbly grass. Hamid gave him a last affectionate pat on the rump and walked slowly to his hut. He knew that many of his neighbors, intent on their own concerns, would not even have noticed that he had not been sitting at his work table outside his hut all day, puffing on his *hookah*.

$\mathcal{C}$HAPTER EIGHT

1973 Egypt
ALI

"Hey, Ali," mocked a band of young men in the village as Ali stepped out of his hut, "heard from that pretty sister of yours, Jamila? Is she giving it to all the men in America?"

Ali shook his fist at them, red with rage. He had not heard anything from Jamila for years. At first he had waited patiently for her to come back. He had gone to the outskirts of the village day after day, scanning every vehicle that rattled past in a cloud of dust. He asked his mother what had happened, how long Jamila would be gone, but Salwa only looked at him vaguely and deflected his questions. She had no answers. She could not even begin to imagine the life Jamila might be leading. She was certain she would never return, and her only comfort was to know, deep in her heart that she had opened the door for her daughter to have a larger life than her own had been. It had been a wrenching decision but she did not regret it, and had only impatience for this tortured son who could not let go. She had tried to involve him more in the care of his other brothers and sisters, but Jamila had always been his lodestone. He had never been able to count on anyone else in his short life. He was lost and lonely without her and a deep pit of anxiety lodged in his heart, turning everything around him sour. No-one any longer stood between him and the corrosive anger that often took possession of his spirit. Nothing made sense. Why had she not explained? Why had she not returned?

Time passed, and more time passed.

Four years after his sister's disappearance, he still spent much of his time slinking about the village, sulky and morose. He had been tall before Jamila left, and had grown again. He was now a full foot taller than his father. Unused to his height, he slouched his lanky body, unsure what to do with himself, since school held no further interest for him and the possibility of a job had receded from reality. Jobs had always been scarce. They were now almost nonexistent.

Jamila's departure had wrenched her from him without explanation and his failure to understand it four years earlier had left scar tissue in his spirit. He could not even begin to process the loss. He could not understand why there had been no word from her since the day she and Malvina had departed for Cairo, rocketing away in a taxi, his parents leaving her to the American woman without a word, and then his father yelling, his mother weeping inconsolably, the babies wailing, the place in an uproar, and Jamila gone. He could not forget the sight of Jamila, pale and determined, never looking his way, her mouth set and her eyes dry, clutching a small bag of treasured possessions. He had run into the cotton fields to hide his tears. No-one came to comfort him. No-one even noticed. No-one cared how he felt.

He hated doing the chores and jobs he and Jamila had always done together.

His friends had eventually tired of listening to his grumbles and no longer sought him out. He could hear their excited voices on the dusty path as they ran, swooped, leapt and shouted, pummeling each other in companionship, passing a tattered football among themselves, looking for girls they could harass. He was no longer one of them. And he was no longer Jamila's brother. She had vanished from his life as completely as if she had died.

His mother, locked into her own pain, begged him to help her with his gaggle of younger brothers and sisters, or to tend the tiny vegetable patch at the back of the hut, but he ignored her, ignored all of them, slamming out of the hut and out of her sight as soon as he had wolfed down the breakfast she had prepared. When Salwa called after him in distress, "*Ibni, ya Ibni,*" her voice almost a sob, he stared straight ahead and shouted her down. He used his hoarse unmodulated voice to distance himself from her, convincing himself he did not need to do the biddings of womenfolk any more. He was fifteen now. A man.

So much had changed in his life and in his world in the past four years. There had been fighting, bombs striking and flaring in the distance where Cairo lay, tangled in its morass of contradictions. His father met with the other men in the village, some of whom had reached out to other villages where they had family connections, and they reported at home that men in the city demonstrated daily in swelling yelling crowds, pouring into public spaces in a turbulent sea of billowing white, egging each other on to destruction and violence, setting fires, throwing stones at mansions and temples that had once belonged to foreigners and Jews, breaking glass, scrambling over iron railings into manicured gardens, letting loose fury and venom with no restraints. The police had been conspicuously absent. The distant popping of guns could be heard at night, and villagers along the Nile hunkered into their huts, wondering when the full force of the violence would reach them.

Walid stopped Ali one day as he wandered aimlessly about the village. The little goatherd had grown tall and robust, but his merry eyes were solemn as he looked at Jamila's brother.

"Any word from Jamila?" He asked hesitantly, already anticipating the response. Then he added urgently into the silence, "Ali, you're not the only one who misses her. I need to know. Do you know anything new?"

Ali grunted and kicked at a stone. He did not dignify the painful question with an answer.

"See, it's like this, I'm leaving the village tomorrow," said Walid anxiously, "I will be leaving for good. My father has sent for me to join him in Cairo. We are to look for work together. I don't think I will ever come back here. I just wanted to say goodbye before I left."

He reached his hand toward Ali, who raised his eyes and saw that the youth was no longer barefoot, no longer dressed in his grubby goatherd robe tied with fraying rope, but wore a clean striped *galabiyeh* and leather sandals on his feet. Ali had grown increasingly careless about his own appearance, but he noticed that Walid looked polished and bright as a new-minted coin.

"So you are going too," he said bitterly, pushing away the outstretched hand. "Nice to have a famous father in the big city."

Walid grinned. "An out-of-work father, you mean," he said cheerfully. "Look, I just wanted to ask you to be sure to let Jamila know where I am, if you ever hear from her." He waited a moment, but seeing that Ali had no intention of responding, he shrugged his shoulders, turned away, and walked back toward his mother's hut. Ali stared after him, pain and jealousy fighting for possession of his heart.

Like Hamid, many of the village elders had been drawn to the Muslim Brotherhood in its early days, attracted by its doctrine of non-violence. In the 1930s, the Brotherhood had provided a return to traditional Islam, offering a welcome nationalistic counter-balance to British colonialism. Its emphasis, then, had been on religious and educational programs, and social services. The Brotherhood had spawned a huge response and saw its membership grow in numbers and power. But ten years later, caught up in the global inferno of World War ll, the organization had become increasingly politicized, and an offshoot had developed, sponsoring violence, bombings, arson and assassinations despite its commitment to a peaceful Islamic rebirth. In 1952, the series of incendiary explosions of arson throughout the city and the shocking destruction of many of Cairo's iconic hotels, restaurants, night clubs and theaters were squarely laid at the door of the Muslim Brotherhood. Arrests, imprisonments, torture and assassinations followed. The swelling civic turbulence drove the Brotherhood underground, where their activities remained largely clandestine.

Hamid, a fervent supporter in his idealistic youth, had enthusiastically recruited many of his village neighbors and had begun to create a network with other villages, their energy fueled by patriotic and Islamic ideals. But he watched with growing concern as the movement turned more and more into militant Islamism, and he gradually retreated into a silence that was broken only in the shadows of night, as a few anonymous figures slid into his hut to shake hoary heads over the virulently anti-Western doctrines that were filling the void left by the deposition of the monarchy and the erosion of British colonialism.

Yes, they would sigh, puffing at their *hookah*s and nodding to each other, the country they loved was going to the dogs. But what to do? What to do? And they looked despairingly to Hamid, hoping he would bring them some hope that all was not lost to chaos.

As the years passed, Hamid's expeditions to Cairo to sell his wares brought him into periodic contact with a larger world, where he met with his old friend, the *Imam* who ruled over the mosque behind the old city, and together they plotted and prayed and watched regimes rise and fall, year in and year out. Many of the village men hovered anxiously around his hut whenever he returned, hoping for news, but he puffed away on his *hookah* and maintained a close-mouthed distance, focusing his attention on the tiny pieces of bone and mother-of-pearl he used to create his exquisite and intricate designs. He knew that he could at least exert control in his demanding craftsmanship, if not on a violent chaotic world where nothing made any sense.

Everyone was aware that there were no jobs to be had. Cotton fields lay largely unharvested because there were no ways to access markets for the crop. A hard-scrabble life became even harder, but there were still the *gamouse* to be driven daily to pasture along the banks of the river. They gave milk and cheese and there were a few scrawny vegetables in patches here and there. The sun shone, fierce and predictable. Beyond the village lay miles of undulating sands, the desert. Only a thin strip of green along the banks of the Nile indicated the presence of habitable land.

Sadik, always skinny, had become the essence of himself, brown skin tight on his bones. He smiled less and yelled at Salwa more. He often sat despondently outside the mud hut, puffing on a *hookah*, glancing at the distant fields where a small boy watched the village goats, calling to them and wielding his staff, puffed up with the importance of his new responsibility.

It was said in the village that Mustafa had found himself without his prestigious job marshaling staff in the big house when Gamal Abdel Nasser's relative fell out of favor, and was marched off to prison between two hard-faced military guards. Screaming and crying, his wife and children had also left the house under escort and had never returned. No-one knew what had become of them. The possessions they had taken over from the foreign people who had disappeared following the Suez crisis sat silent in the silent rooms. The other servants had vanished as soon as it was obvious that their employers had fallen out of favor. Mustafa hung around the big house for a while, at a loss, wandering the deserted premises, dignified and dispossessed, uncertain if anyone would appear to pay his wages. Eventually he sent for Walid, his eldest son, and the two of them searched for work together, continuing to sleep in the deserted house.

In the months that followed, engineers had arrived at the villages that bordered the Nile, and surveyors set up scopes and yellow tape as they went about their work, milling about in ill-fitting suits, sweating profusely under the unforgiving sun, and treating the villagers with disdain. Ugly concrete structures rose rapidly, low-ceilinged apartments with glass windows that glittered in the sun, refracting heat into the small rooms. It seemed people were now to live on top of each other in airless apartments with dubious ventilation. Many saw this as progress and hurried to sell their small plots of land, letting their huts be razed to the ground, but Sadik and Salwa viewed the change with suspicion and had not embraced it.

Hamid, too, still sat at the entrance to his mud hut, puffing on his *hookah*, watching all the comings and goings with a sardonic eye, challenging himself to create ever more intricate geometric designs in bone, mother-of-pearl, and ivory. Every so often, he continued to set out for Cairo with his wares and seemed to sell everything he made, for he always returned empty-handed and tight-lipped a couple of days later.

As he often did, Ali walked slowly past Hamid's hut. The man ignored him, and the more he ignored him, the more he intrigued him. He talked to no-one but worked away outside his hut, day after day, as the village he knew withered away and tall structures rose around him. Ali knew that Sadik thought highly of Hamid, and that many still sought advice and leadership from him. He wanted often to open communication with him, but had not found his way into a conversation. Ali frequently found only rage to offer where discourse should have been.

The cabinet maker was sitting outside as usual, hunched over as he worked on two unusual chairs, bow-backed, the sun glinting off the back spindles delicately inlaid with mother-of-pearl and ivory. Ali kicked at a stone, setting off a cloud of dust, and Hamid looked up.

His sharp black eyes took in the barely controlled anger and frustration that hung like a disturbed aura around the boy. He took in the dark stubble on Ali's face, the torn and grubby *galabeya,* the disproportionate features that sat clumsily at the top of his lanky frame. His wise old eyes could see that the boy's features would blend into shape with time and make him a handsome man. Hamid had seen countless youths come and go. He had watched them tumbling like puppies, gradually defining themselves into the men they became. This one was different. The times were different. Hamid had seen many years and his bones ached as the days grew colder. Perhaps this boy's energy and anger could be put to good use.

He sighed, coughed, and without looking up, said mildly "What is it you want, Ali? I see you often around here, but you never tell me why you hang around my hut?"

Ali stopped in his tracks, surprised, and glared at him. A thought came to him suddenly.

"I want you to teach me your trade," Ali said, surprising himself, "I want to learn everything you know. I want to go to the big city, to Cairo. "

"Why?" said Hamid, his eyes on the boy's face. "You could get lost there. Cairo is a big loud city. There are many people and few jobs. There is much anger and turbulence in the city. Can you not find something of value to do here? Why all this anger?"

Ali hesitated. He could not find the words to encompass the enormity of his pain. He could hardly say "I'm angry because Jamila left me and has vanished. No-one knows what has become of her. My heart is sick because I meant nothing to her. I'm angry because she has gone to America and the American woman said she is going to be famous, but I will be nothing if I stay here. Nothing. I am nothing now."

Instead, he said gruffly " Well, can you teach me? I'll be a good apprentice and I'll work hard for you. I'm strong. I can help you carry your wares to Cairo every month, old man."

When the older man didn't answer, he added, his voice rising, breaking, "So, can you do it? Will you teach me?"

Hamid puffed on the brass and copper *hookah* that always stood near his chair. He fingered the skull cap that covered his head. His face thoughtful, he took his time. At last he said, "Are you sure you want this? I need someone who can work cleanly and precisely. There is more to my work than the making and selling of wooden objects. I have many friends in many places and I will expect you to be a part of it all. If you decide to work with me, I will expect you to come wherever I go without question, and to keep your mouth shut about whatever you see and hear. I will expect you to show up every day in clean clothes." He paused and looked at the boy.

"Can you do that?"

Ali's eyes lit up. This was the first interesting thing to happen to him in four years. He nodded eagerly, intrigued.

"I'll talk to Sadik, then," said Hamid, shaking his head and sighing, "I suppose you're not much use to anyone the way you are. Perhaps we can get you involved in something other than yourself and make a man of you." He glanced up and added, "You'll have to be prepared to do everything I tell you. True, there are no jobs, but there is much work for those who know where to find it."

He left the boy to decipher his cryptic statement. He did not smile at him, but swiveled in his chair, his back to Ali, and bent over his work again. Disconcerted, Ali waited, but seeing that nothing else was forthcoming, he started for home, out of habit scuffing at dirt and swatting at flies as he went.

CHAPTER NINE

1975 Cairo, Egypt
ALI'S NEW LIFE

"When do we start for Cairo?" Ali asked, his voice losing its anchor to manhood, see-sawing high and low in his excitement. He had worked with Hamid for two long years, but Hamid had never taken him to Cairo before. He had learned how to cut and buff the tiny irregularly shaped chips of bone and ivory, and he loved inserting them in patterns in the wooden slats of chairs or the polished wood of inlaid boxes.

This day was different. He had worked hard, strapping Hamid's work and tools to the donkey, who brayed loudly and kicked out sideways at this violation of his personal space. It was hot work as the sun started its rise. Hamid had grown more hunched as the months went by, stepping more slowly. He had aged. He watched Ali, but did not help.

"As soon as everything is ready," Hamid answered patiently.

As they approached the outskirts of the city at last, noise and traffic hurtled around them, sheep, goats, camels and cars vying for space on the roads and on the pavements. Faded trams rattled along rails in the center of the city, with crowds of white-robed men hanging onto the outside of the tram doors like bulbous bunches of grapes, sometimes letting go and darting into the street, barefoot, their laughter raucous, their *galabeyas* billowing around them. Veiled women slid cautiously, weaving through the shadows, gliding about their business, dark ghosts with watchful eyes. Outside the food markets their light voices rose in laughter and in argument as they bargained relentlessly for food for their families, fingering vegetables wilting in the sun, palpating fruit with expertize, putting their purchases into straw baskets to carry home as they wandered the stalls, indistinguishable from one another in their enveloping *abayas*. Colorful posters and huge portraits of Anwar Sadat hung side by side amid a confusion of neon signs that flickered on and off despite the bright daylight. It was a disconcerting turbulence of audial and visual stimulae, and Ali's eyes darted everywhere in his eagerness to take it all in.

A boy about his age wove his way through the crowds, fleet of foot, an enormous tray balanced on his head with a tower of puffy breads piled high. It seemed impossible that he would not stumble and scatter his breads, but he was as nimble as the mountain goats from the village, and was soon out of sight. Ali gazed after him. He was hungry. He turned, and tried to persuade Hamid to stop at one of the roadside carts selling a brown bean stew, *foul madammas,* drawn to their pots of steaming beans, the fragrance of the hot food plunging right into the hollow space in his stomach. But Hamid shook his head, and with a huge sigh, Ali tore his gaze away.

It was a difficult struggle to thread themselves in and out of the chaotic traffic to get themselves and their heavily laden donkey out of the center of Cairo into the crowded bazaar where Ali discovered that Hamid owned a small space next to a dark cafe etched far into the depths of the *muski.* Two men sat hunched at a round hammered brass table outside the entrance to the cafe, silent as the eye of a storm, intent on their backgammon game, *hookahs* by their sides, and tiny cups of rich dark Turkish coffee in front of them, oblivious to the hordes of pedestrians swarming about them. Hamid glanced about for Mahmoud, the brass craftsman, but he was nowhere to be seen. On the other side of Hamid's space was a narrow stall with brilliantly colored slippers and leather goods dangling in bunches like exotic fruit. Next to that, a *maquagi* plied his trade, his foot steering a heavy red-hot iron over a spotless shirt as he sucked in water and sprayed it onto the shirt as he ironed. Intent on his work, he never looked up.

Ali stared, mesmerized and fascinated by the constant overload of color and sound, as he and Hamid set up the boxes and chairs they had brought, tethered the donkey, and put up Hamid's table together, jostled by crowds of tourists streaming through the narrow passage, cameras dangling from their necks. Around them, aggravated shopkeepers burst out of their narrow stalls into the alley in frothing *galabeyas,* shaking angry fists at escaping customers in an intense ballet of negotiation, weaving in and out of bemused tourists, dark eyes fierce. Looking about him, Ali wondered how anyone ever found their way in this web of narrow alleyways, offshoots spreading and connected like branches of a huge tree, crammed with so much color, sound, motion, people, and drama.

The day wore on. Money changed hands and many of the finer pieces of Hamid's work left in the possession of delighted buyers. Soon the sparkle of the sun on the glittering merchandise began to fade and the crowds began to thin. Hamid packed up his tools and untethered the donkey. The wail of the *muezzin* broadcasting the call to prayer wrapped the night in mystery.

"Follow me," he said to Ali, and the two of them made their way deeper and deeper into the *muski*, into a warren of deserted passages, to where hard-faced men glanced at them with furtive looks, vanishing behind beaded curtains into a hidden world.

Looking up, Ali gradually became aware of the eyes of women staring at them from behind intricately carved and fretworked panels enclosing the balconies that jutted from ancient twisted buildings. The minarets of distant mosques rose in the distance, the call of the *muezzin* floating through the gathering twilight.

"Where are we going? Where will we sleep?" Ali could not contain himself. This was the great adventure he had dreamed of for so long.

Hamid turned and skewered him with an impatient gaze. "Didn't I tell you not to ask questions?" he said.

Ali nodded reluctantly.

"You'll know when we get there, and why."

Hamid walked slowly ahead, wary of stumbling, and Ali, downcast, followed behind with the donkey.

Suddenly, Hamid stood still, waiting, and a shadowy figure ahead turned, beckoned, and led them into one of the buildings. A dim path opened into a courtyard where brightly colored pillows and chairs were scattered throughout the space, faded rugs carpeting the floor, a fountain burbling in the center, men of all ages lounging about, laughing quietly among themselves, the click of dice on many backgammon boards punctuating every moment. They seemed to know Hamid, *salaaming* respectfully as he passed, smiling, and acknowledging his passage.

Hamid turned to Ali.

"Tomorrow," he said, "You will start to attend the *madrassa*. I will myself take you to meet the *Imam*. He is an old friend of mine. You will learn to read and to write. You will live here, and I will come and visit you whenever I come to Cairo."

"But I thought ...?" began Ali.

Hamid placed a stubby finger on the boy's lips and hushed him with a glance.

"You promised to obey without question. So, no questions. This is what you wanted, is it not? I have your future in mind. The last months of working together have shown me your potential. You are a careful workman but you lack the creativity to coax the most out of the ancient inlay patterns I have taught you. That kind of work is not where your future lies. I believe you may have an important role to play, but you have much to learn here before you are ready to meet your destiny."

Thoroughly puzzled, Ali glanced around and sighed. He would do as Hamid said. He liked and trusted the man. Besides, what destiny would he have in the village.

He thought wistfully of Leila, his little sister Nevine's best friend. Not many would miss him, but she would wonder where he was. He had often tried to persuade her away from her giggling friends, attracted to the curvaceous body alluringly promised under her robe, the sway of fleshy hips as she walked, the glitter of her eyes, black and shiny as polished jet, as she surveyed him through thick lashes. He liked to imagine how she would look naked, her voluptuous body enveloped in the rich mane of hair she kept tamed into a thick rope all the way down her back. He sighed deeply.

"What about my father and my mother?" He asked at last, cautiously.

"They know the plan, and they are content," said Hamid. "Now take our bed rolls, find a good quiet space, and lay them out. Here is some money to buy us some food from the kitchens inside. They may even have some of that *foul madammas* you were hankering after. Better get some sleep. There will be much to do tomorrow."

They made their way to the mosque at dawn next day. After the conclusion of the morning prayer, Hamid sent Ali back to the courtyard to feed the donkey and wait for him there.

"You are right, he's very intelligent," the *Imam* told Hamid, "I could see that immediately, but his anger will push him into troubled waters." He shook his head and sighed. "I will do my best. That is all anyone can do."

The two men were standing facing each other in the vast space of the mosque, faded carpets covering the floor between stone pillars. Hamid nodded thoughtfully.

"The boy has such promise," he said wistfully, "If you can teach him and keep an eye on him, he may yet serve the Brotherhood and Egypt well."

The *Imam's* penetrating eyes took in the anxiety he saw in his friend's face. Hamid continued, "I am very sick, my friend. I do not know how long I will be able to watch over him. He does not know this." He looked into his friend's eyes and added,

"I took him on as an apprentice on a whim, but I have grown to care for him. One day he will outgrow the spiny casing of his youth and will be a fine man. He is the son of my heart. I need to leave him in your care."

The *Imam* sighed deeply. Only Allah knew what would become of this restless boy. He put an arm about Hamid's shoulders and the two men walked out into the street, deep in conversation.

CHAPTER TEN

1962–1965 New York
THE MIZRAHIS

Winter had been brutal. The warm clothes they had brought with them had not been nearly warm enough, and although Eliane had contacted a reputable jeweler friend of Zaki's as soon as they arrived, and sold her huge star sapphire engagement ring to get them into a small apartment in Queens and out of the dreary hotel where the NYANA (New York Association for New Americans) had parked them on arrival, there was barely enough money for food and rent, and none for new coats. So they layered their clothes as best they could, trudging out like ridiculous human bundles and then sweltering in the fierce heating as soon as they were indoors or on the subway. They had never imagined adapting to a new country would be so hard. Nonetheless, they coped, until the snows came.

After the first blizzard of the winter, Eliane sold her diamond bracelet. They had been chilled throughout the winter in Paris, but this was a ravenous cold that ate into their souls and bit into their bones. The bitter winds funneling through the streets had made short shrift of their cloth coats and leather shoes. Thanks to Eliane's bracelet, they bought parkas, boots, wool hats and scarves. She had also located a small furnished apartment on the lower East side through a woman who befriended her on the subway, and they moved to Manhattan so that she would not have such a long commute to work. The apartment was basically a one-bedroom with an alcove, a tiny kitchenette and a bathroom, but she found some bamboo screens discarded on the pavement and she and Sol hauled them up the stairs. Now Sol had his own room. The radiators and steam pipes in the apartment introduced them to an entire vocabulary of hissing and clanking, which kept them all awake at night until they began to learn to find the occasional hiss of steam and the metallic clatter of the radiators a comforting assurance that all was well. Whatever difficulties they had to overcome, they were united in their relief at having left Paris and the Hotel Victoire behind them forever.

Immediately on arrival, Eliane had made some calls to Zaki's business contacts and with Zaki's stellar recommendation in hand, she soon landed a job as an office manager at an established investment firm. The salary was modest, but it would help them for a while. They could pay the rent and have food on the table. She was aglow with triumph. She had been given to understand that with time, she might be permitted to develop her own clients and rise in the organization. Her pleasure in this success was shadowed by her growing concern for Aldo. He seemed to have no idea what he wanted to do, and no concept as to how he might go about accessing the many possibilities that surged and eddied around them.

Spring finally arrived, heralded by smoky skies laced with fast-moving clouds, and thunderstorms. On the first mild day, Aldo walked slowly along a path beside the East River. Every now and then, a cyclist zipped past, intent on his own agenda, alternating with a few scattered runners, young and dedicated, or older and out of breath. Aldo no longer knew where to turn, or who to turn to. He hardly noticed the crisp blue sky reflected among sparkles glinting in the waters of the East River. It was a day to fill the soul with light, but he was totally oblivious to the activity and beauty around him, focused inward, reflecting, with growing concern, about the continuing deconstruction of his life and his world. What had he become?

What little energy the move to New York had initially provided had seeped slowly out of him as he tried to find his footing in a swiftly flowing unfamiliar world of commerce and opportunity. He could not begin to understand the flood of energy that seemed to have engulfed his wife and son, freed at last of the misery of the Hotel Victoire, rushing eagerly out into a world that opened itself to both of them. Sol, who had never evinced much enthusiasm for his studies at the English School in Heliopolis or at the Paris lycee, seemed to have done a complete turnabout.

His eagerness had instantly charmed Tamara, the flamboyant Russian social worker assigned to the Mizrahis through the agency that had taken responsibility for them and had replaced the HIAS.

Tamara seemed increasingly confused, however, as to how to help Aldo. She first suggested that he join a nearby Jewish congregation. "You will find friends there," she said brightly, "you will find people who can help you find work." Not wanting to offend her, he took the ticket she offered, thanked her politely, and attended services there one Saturday. But rather than finding a common thread and a congenial communi- ty, he had been so confused by the incomprehensible accents and unfamiliar tunes, and had found himself so uncomfort- able with the many differences from the Sephardic services he had infrequently attended in Egypt, that he never went back. When Tamara asked him how it had been, and whether he had met anyone interesting there, he said dismissively, "*That* was a Jewish service? The rabbi looked more like a priest. I couldn't understand a word they were saying." Tamara rolled her eyes in despair and gave up.

Aldo was adrift. He seemed unable to find a key to moving ahead and to envision where he might fit into this new envi- ronment. No-one in New York seemed to have time to linger over coffees. There were no outdoor cafes where men gathered in groups to shake their heads over the complications of the world around them, and to dwell on the glories of the past. Aldo's few friends from the past were too busy to take time with him, facing their own adaptation problems at work and at home. Aldo spent days alone in the tiny apartment, poring over the job section of the New York Times. When Eliane came home, he laughed bit- terly as he showed her the jobs he had encircled in black marker.

"Can you imagine me doing this?... or that?" he would ask, inviting her to join him in mockery, his eyes bleak.

"Come on, Aldo," she said, pleading, " This is the land of opportunity. I'm settled and working hard. Now it's your turn. You have to reach out. This is where you wanted to be. Go out there and talk to people. You're a good, intelligent man. There's certain to be work out there, waiting for you. You just have to get yourself out there and find it. In this town, without work, there is nothing. "

Tamara admired Eliane's resilience and efficiency and was awed that she had so quickly settled into this new culture, and landed a good job, too. She had seen too many of the recent refugees from Arab countries floundering and drowning in the alien environment of America in the early sixties. Yet, here was a woman who was somehow managing to make her own luck. Tamara found it exhilarating.

She had seen so many refugees from a hostile world struggling to adapt to their new country, where the Cuban missile crisis ballooned around them. She watched as the political crisis, growing in intensity, fed directly into their worst fears, exacerbating the trauma of their recent expulsions. Had they been welcomed into America only to find themselves swallowed up in a new war? Tamara watched their struggles as the following year, the charismatic young American president, John Kennedy, was assassinated. Other assassinations followed. The appalled refugees from conflict in their native lands encountered a virulent racism struggling to redefine itself where they had hoped for peace. To many of them, this new world into which they had been catapulted against their will began to seem a calamity rather than an opportunity. Tamara felt for them, but she knew she could only do the best she could, to help them to adapt to their new circumstances.

Every morning early, Aldo shuffled into the little kitchenette and made coffee for Eliane and Sol. He had brought a battered brass *kanaka* with him, tucked into his brown leather suitcase from the *muski*, and he found a shop near where they lived that sold Turkish coffee. It was expensive, but he could not abide the American coffee, which he complained looked and tasted like colored water. Eliane prepared cereal or eggs for the three of them, and then she and Sol left to follow their separate paths to the American dream.

"What will you do today?" She asked her husband anxiously every morning, as she stood at the door adjusting her clothes and peering into the crackled mirror that hung in the foyer. Giving her hair a final pat, she turned back to look at him.

"Aldo, I was asking", she said, unable to keep the impatience out of her voice, " what are your plans for the day?"

"I'll keep looking," he said dolefully, knowing what she wanted to hear, waiting for the door to close behind his wife and listening for the click clack of her high heels descending the stone steps.

When the apartment was truly empty, with heavy sighs he searched out the beloved burgundy silk robe he had always worn in the mornings in Cairo. He had almost left it behind, but had managed to squeeze it into his suitcase at the last minute. It helped him to feel that all was not lost, that he was somehow still himself, as he settled down full-length on the couch, newspaper in one hand, the aroma of Turkish coffee permeating the room. He made sure to circle some of the offers in the job section and to make a point of discussing them with his wife when she returned.

He had tried interview upon interview for managerial jobs, but time after time, he left empty-handed. Early on, before she had given up on him, Tamara had suggested firmly that perhaps he could fill in for a while as a cashier in the nearby supermarket until something better came along, or he could apply for a teaching position in one of the language

schools, since he spoke so beautifully and knew many languages. Aldo just looked at her with sad eyes and shook his
head. He would not know where to begin, he said. He was a
mild-mannered man, unused to the strident noise and rapid
acceleration of New York City. Harsh voices burst out in the
streets outside their apartment, seeming to threaten with an
urgency and impatience that translated into violent anger in
his mind, accustomed as he was to a quiet home surrounded
by the tranquility of gardens and river. It pierced him, scram-
bled his thoughts, and left imperceptible wounds. People
spoke fast, moved fast, and expected him to do the same. As
the days succeeded each other, he saw more and more clearly
that he would never be able to adjust.

The job recruiting office to which Tamara finally sent him
was a rejection in itself. The walls were a slubbed dirty green,
a bulletin board with old yellowing job ads torn from various
papers pinned to the cork. Behind a metal desk far too large for
the cramped room, a spectacularly obese woman sat chewing
on a yellow pencil, her fingers twirling an enormous rolodex,
a file open in front of her. A squat black telephone sat on the
desk. Behind her was an ink-stained table with a grey metal
typewriter, neat piles of paper and blue-black carbon paper beside it. She looked up warily as Aldo hesitantly pushed open the
door and stepped inside.

"Needajob?" She asked, the words falling out of her mouth
like ashes from a cigarette.

"You the fella the NYANA called about?" Taking the pencil
out of her mouth, she stared at him. When he didn't answer,
she gestured to a chair opposite the desk and motioned for him
to sit. He dusted it off with his hand and sat, and then remem-

bering his carefully crafted resume, opened his brief case and took it out. She put out a hand heavy with be-ringed fingers and took it from him, bracelets rattling as she placed it in front of her. She read it carefully, and sighed.

"Nothing much here," she muttered, glancing up at him. "They always expect me to work miracles." Shaking her head and holding up the resume, she added "How about a job as a shoe salesman? You look like a shoe salesman to me, and it seems you speak decent English, which is more than I can say for most of the people who come through that door." She shuffled through the papers in the file in front of her and pulled out a sheet. "I got an opening for a shoe salesman a coupla blocks from here." She peered at Aldo and waved the sheet at him.

"Want to give it a try?"

Aldo had not said a word. He felt paralyzed. A shoe salesman? His father and grandfather, courtly gentlemen both, would be turning in their graves in the land of his birth, the Egypt that had vomited him out like bad food. His throat constricted and he could not get the words out.

He could see that she was waiting, so he tried to clear his mind and come up with an acceptable response. At last, he asked, "Do you have anything else to suggest? Surely there must be work for someone like me? I am a cultured man. I managed a very flourishing business in Egypt. Many people worked for me."

"That's what they all say," She sighed and gave a laugh like a neigh, "Don't like feet, then?" and she went back to her file, shuffling the papers, twirling the rolodex, shaking her head and wagging her chewed pencil in the air. "I see who you *think* you are," she said at last, looking at him, not unkindly, "but the question is, what can you *do*? Do you type? Ever worked as a waiter? Know the grocery business? Know the hotel business? Ever worked in a factory? Ever drive a taxi? You don't look like a very strong candidate for a white collar job, to me. In America it matters little who you *were*. The woman who cleans the floors in your building may well have been a Russian princess, once. Nobody cares. The question is, what are you willing to *do*?"

That was the question Aldo asked himself like a persistent resounding drumbeat every minute of every day. He had no college degrees. He had no obvious skills other than a charming smile and a well-turned vocabulary. He knew nothing about doing business in America. His few contacts who had known him in Egypt had taken him to lunch when he arrived, with much back-slapping and jovial assurances that they would keep him in mind should anything come to their attention.

"Eh, Mizrahi, give it time. Give it time," they called out as they hurried off to their work and their homes. "You'll soon find your way." He never heard back from any of them.

"You call them back right now, and *insist*," Eliane urged him, over and over again, her exasperation ballooning beyond the bounds of her patience, but he only looked at her gravely and muttered "*Ca n' se fait pas*, Eliane, *je ne suis pas un mendiant, quand meme*. I'm not a beggar. That's not the way to do things. I must wait for them to call me."

Now, looking up at the large woman's inquiring gaze, he shifted uncomfortably in his seat.

"I could go and see them, I suppose," he said at last, doubtfully, reaching out his hand to take the paper, thinking that perhaps if he went there, they might actually consider him for a managerial position.

"That's the spirit," said the woman, nodding approvingly and handing him her card. She held out her hand, "Meryl Mc-Dermott. That's me. Address for the job is on the sheet I gave you. You get back to me if you get that job, okay? Good luck."

She gestured to the door and went back to chewing on her pencil, her hand absent-mindedly continuing to rotate the wheel of the large rolodex with its mysterious promises.

Aldo glanced at the address on the paper and reluctantly made his way to a bright clean shoe store, long and narrow, with a seating area down the center. There were For Sale signs in the window. A few customers stood about inside with shoes in their hands, looking around, waiting to be helped. Thinking that he could have used a new pair of shoes himself, he went in and walked to the cash register at the back of the store, where he found a small elderly man sitting on a high stool, staring through half-moon reading glasses at an invoice.

"Are you the manager?" Aldo asked hesitantly. "They sent me here to apply for the salesman job."

The manager stared at him, and a look of doubt crossed his face.

"You?" he said, "Meryl sent you? Well, I do need help." He gestured at the bunches of assorted customers who were standing hesitantly about, drawn in by the For Sale signs in the window.

"Tell you what," he said suddenly, "I'll pay you for the day and we'll both try it out, shall we? Something tells me you've never done this before?" He peered over his reading glasses at Aldo and gave him an unexpectedly warm smile.

"Tell me what to do," said Aldo. "I'll be happy to help you out."

It was an uneasy fit, but it lasted for six months, and Aldo got his paycheck and his new shoes. His back ached from bending, and his feet hurt from racing up and down a narrow back staircase balancing boxes at the requests of customers who often tried everything on and left without making a purchase. The store was struggling, and the gnome-like manager, kind as he was, finally had to let Aldo go. He needed someone younger and more agile, with a real interest in the job.

Eliane offered solace, night after night, as Aldo limped his way home, groaning, his body in protest.

"Don't take it so badly," she said sorrowfully, deeply saddened to see how hard it all was for him and trying to help him make the best of it, "Just think, you may make a good contact there that could lead you to the job of your dreams."

Aldo glared at her, speechless. "There is no 'job of my dreams'," he said at last, pain and bitterness spilling from his words, "my dreams are shattered. They will never recover."

Eliane's day had seemed interminable. It was a hot muggy day and there was a problem with the air-conditioning in the building where she worked. The pace all day had been brutal. Eliane's back ached, a nasty nagging pain, her feet ached, and her head ached. She allowed herself to stoop a little as she headed for home, her shoulders hunched and her mind teeming with all the things she would have to do when she got home. If only there could be dinner waiting for her at home. If only Aldo would greet her with a smile and the welcome news that he had found a job. His disappointment made it all the harder to bear the responsibilities that sat so heavily on her shoulders.

"Eliane?"

She stopped at the sound of her name.

"Eliane Mizrahi?"

The intonation was unmistakeable. This was a woman from Egypt. It must be someone who had known her in her other life. Eliane shuddered, wishing she had given a little more care to her appearance before she left the office. She turned around. A small rotund woman was hurrying toward her, waving her arms and calling her name.

Eliane sighed. "Margot?" she said, and managed to summon up a smile.

Margot slowed her pace as she came closer. "We haven't seen you and Aldo for so long," she said, out of breath and gasping a little, her hand to her chest.

"How are things going for you? Do you hear anything from anyone in Egypt? Are you still working? Has Aldo found work?" She paused briefly to catch her breath.

"Funny, Joseph was just wondering about Aldo the other day. He said 'we haven't heard anything from the Mizrahis.' He said, 'I wonder if Mr. Mizrahi found work?'" The questions continued, thick and fast.

Margot's husband, Joseph, had been an assistant manager at one of the Mizrahi stores in the old days. They had sometimes socialized, but Eliane had always found Margot annoying, and Joseph something of a sycophant. Painfully conscious of her shabby shoes and worn clothes, she registered the carefully coiffed hairdo and manicured nails, the designer dress and elegant heels on the woman in front of her.

"Aldo is still looking," she said at last, uncomfortably. "How is Joseph doing? I know that Aldo and Joseph talked a while back, when we first got here."

Margot sighed, then beamed. "Joe has done so well, so well," she said, her hand waving five fingers back and forth to push away the evil eye of envy.

"I had to leave my job. He won't hear of my working. Doesn't want me tired, he says." She winked and giggled. "He got that job at Macy's soon after we arrived in New York, and two promotions later, he was able to move us into a better apartment." She looked expectantly at Eliane and added "We get wonderful health insurance, and we have been able to furnish our apartment at a fraction the cost because we also get a generous employee discount off anything we buy at Macy's."

She looked down at her designer dress and smiled.

"America has been very good to us."

She looked up and her voice faded as her sharp eyes took in the bleak look in Eliane's eyes, and the tired slump of her shoulders. She hesitated, and then added,

"Do you think that perhaps Aldo might consider a job at Macy's over the holiday season? I'm sure Joseph could get him in. He has a friend in personnel. They hire all sorts of part-time people to deal with the added holiday crush. Even though it's certainly not the kind of thing he was used to, he might be able to parlay it into a better permanent job when the holiday season is over? Shall I talk to Joseph?" She peered anxiously up at Eliane.

"That would be so kind of you," said Eliane, sighing. "He needs to get out more. He tried a couple of things, but they weren't right for him. Something at Macy's sounds like a real possibility. This is so nice of you."

"Give me your phone number," said Margot decisively, "I'll call you tomorrow." She hunted around in her purse for paper, and not finding any, she shrugged, grinned at Eliane and scribbled the number on the back of her hand. "Old habits die hard," she said, "remember how we used to do this at school?" Impulsively, she hugged Eliane before trotting off down a side street, her plump figure wavering a little on her high heels.

Eliane felt a swell of hope. She hurried the rest of the way home and found Aldo slumped in front of the TV, eyes half closed, barely acknowledging her appearance.

"Aldo," she said, trying to keep the rising excitement out of her voice. "Guess who I ran into on the way home?"

Margot phoned next morning, her voice shrill with delight.

"Eliane, it was so nice meeting you like that, yesterday. Joe is talking to his boss today. He thinks he may have something for Aldo in the china and crystal department. It seems they're short-handed there for the holiday season. I'll call as soon as we know for sure and then I expect Aldo will have to go in for an interview."

"Thank you, Margot," said Eliane, her voice cracking, regretting all the unkind thoughts she had ever had about her, "this means so much to us. You cannot imagine..."

Margot giggled nervously, "We exiles must stick together," she said.

Aldo got the job to cover the holiday season. Optimism came flooding back, and Eliane begged him to try to make it work so that they would want to keep him on. "You are such an elegant man," she said, smiling proudly, "they'll see how lucky they are to get you." She flung her arms around him and hugged him, not seeing the strain in his eyes.

Although he tried to temper his excitement, Aldo was delighted with the job. When his first paycheck came in after the first two weeks, he insisted on taking Eliane out to dinner to her favorite sushi restaurant.

Smiling, he said "and the best of it is that I really enjoy interacting with the customers. I know the merchandise. I know what they want. They aren't into heavy holiday shopping yet. Most of them are looking for wedding gifts, or setting up wedding lists of their own. We chat a little, and then I get a good sense of the sort of things they like, and I have usually been able to find the right thing for them and make the sale."

Eliane noted that he was a changed man. He left for work each day with a jaunty step, his cap at an angle on his head. But as the weeks passed, he began to come home looking drawn and tired.

Aldo could not identify when exactly things began to sour at work. He knew he was doing a good job. He took his time and rang up sales with satisfying regularity. His customers left the department looking happy. He steered clear of Danisha, the manager, who seemed to be constantly steaming with barely controlled anger. He began to identify with the department and to look at the displays of merchandise with an eye to more effective use of the display space. In an effort to effect some improvements, he pointed out to his churlish boss, Danisha, that there were insufficient displays of the finer brands of china. "My customers are looking for the best," he said, "They want the Limoges, the Bernardaux, the Waterford, the Meissen, the Villeroy and Bosch, but all of those are displayed on a back shelf instead of out on the floor. Don't you think we should change that?"

Danisha, a squat woman with outsize features and a loud unmodulated voice, stared at him with amazement and open dislike.

"*Your* customers?" she boomed, sarcasm spilling from her words, "And who are you to make such choices? You're just temporary here. I'm manager of this department. I make the decisions." Her voice rose as she went on, "and just get on with your work, Mr. Aldo Mizrahi. You need to speed things up. Keep your views to yourself." She started to move away and then turned back,

"What sort of name is Mizrahi anyway?" she said aggressively.

"It's Middle Eastern," said Aldo, a little confused by the tack the exchange was taking, but pleased that she seemed to be taking an interest in him. He explained, "I was Egyptian, but Egypt threw all the Jews out after the Suez Canal crisis." He shrugged apologetically, and oblivious to Danisha's baleful glare he would have continued, but she cut in scornfully, "That's not a Jew name. As far as I'm concerned, you're Aldo while you're working here."

From then on, it seemed to Aldo that her voice was always yelling his name in various degrees of exasperation.

"Move faster, Aldo. Where are you Aldo? Your customer will die of old age before you get her the crystal bowl she asked you for. Aldo? Aldo.? Aldo ..."

"I don't know why she has taken such a dislike to me," he said helplessly to Eliane in the evening. "From the moment I was introduced to her as a new salesman for her department, she has been pushing and needling me. I do my best, but instead of getting better, it keeps getting worse."

"Did Joseph bring you in that first time? Did she think you were hired because of some sort of nepotism?" Asked Eliane.

"No, there were three of us that day, and the girl from personnel took us to the department and said 'Danisha, here are the three extra pairs of hands you requested.' That's all she said."

Although he did not want to believe it, he said to Eliane, "Do you think it's because I am a Jew? Is it possible that the craziness that ejected us from Egypt has followed us here?"

Eliane sighed and put her arms around him. "Whatever it is, you'll have to work around it," she said sadly.

Aldo began to feel more and more belittled every time Danisha spoke to him. It was the way she spat out his name like an insult, or yelled it from the other side of the floor so that everyone turned around to stare at him. She shadowed him, listening in on his interchanges with customers, questioning his every move, surrounding him with angry sound. It was making him profoundly insecure. He was tired all the time, now. He had to drag himself up and out in the mornings, and Eliane watched the change in him with growing concern.

The other temporary salesman on the floor, Harry Rubenstein, was a cheerful college kid on Christmas break, his hair swept to a peak on his head, ready with a wide smile at the drop of a hat. It amused Aldo to see him moving jauntily across the floor, humming loudly, eyes on the alert for a customer.

"You should ignore the anti-semitic old bat," Harry whispered to Aldo, "You do such a great job, Mizrahi, and you know so much. She's really lucky to have you here."

Aldo tried to tone down any initiative that might occur to him and to keep out of her way as much as possible, but he continued to be the exclusive butt of her tirades. He tried his best to stay on message. He tried to close her out and keep his mind on the customers, but all the joy had leached out of the job. Danisha never let up. She seemed to enjoy humiliating him. Her constant proximity and hostility awoke fears and insecurities he had not felt since leaving Egypt. He grew anxious and awkward around her.

The pace on the floor picked up as the weeks went by and holiday panic began. The floor became crowded with eager shoppers, and more and more displays were set up, piled high with tempting wares, and set off with scarlet ribbons and glittering tinsel, while Christmas songs blared from loudspeakers throughout the store. He had enjoyed helping with the occasional gift, and working with young couples to put together wedding lists, but now Aldo found himself hastening from customer to customer without pause. People streamed into the store armed with long lists, and left burdened with bulging shopping bags. There was an air of frenetic urgency surrounding every transaction. It was dark early, outside. Herald Square intensified the colors, flashing lights, and crowds, as November headed for December.

It was a week before Thanksgiving. The pace had challenged him earlier, and now he was really rushed off his feet. As he finished a sales slip and turned to look around, a tall young couple headed in his direction.

"Are you free?" the woman asked with a charming smile.

Aldo glanced around and saw that Danisha was engaged with another customer.

"Can I help you?" he asked, looking from one to the other.

The couple smiled at each other. "We do need help," said the man. "We got married a month ago in LA, and we're just back from our honeymoon. In a moment of unreality we asked both our families to join us in our new home for Thanksgiving dinner…" the wife chimed in "and we realized that our wedding presents are still in storage and anyway, not appropriate for the holiday. Can you help us to put together everything we'll need for a gorgeous Thanksgiving dinner with twenty hyper-critical people?" She laughed, "We need entire settings, silverware, platters, wine glasses," she glanced around, "and linens, but I guess that's from another department." She smiled at Aldo and added "It's our first married holiday party and we are determined to pass the test with flying colors and impress them all!"

Aldo was delighted. This was the kind of thing he loved to pull together.

"What exactly does this holiday require that's special and particular to a Thanksgiving dinner?" he asked, smiling.

Just then, Danisha, who had noticed them talking and had caught his last few words, barreled up to him pushing him aside so roughly that he almost fell, and shouted "Aldo, what do you think you're doing? Go in the back room right now, and sweep up in there. Someone broke a vase there this morning." As he stood, stunned and mortified, she grabbed his arm and shoved him toward the back room, steering the customers away, full of apologies to them as she led them to another part of the floor. The young couple, bewildered, glanced back at him anxiously, and later he noticed them leaving, empty-handed.

Danisha came up behind him. "Have you cleaned up in the back room yet?" she asked belligerently, "My god! I cannot believe that you don't even know what Thanksgiving is. How can you be so stupid? How can you live in America and not know about the most important holiday on the calendar?"

Aldo paled, rage and indignation rising in him like a tornado. He moved away, but she followed him.

"You put on your airs and sashay about the floor as if you are better than everyone, but you don't know anything at all," she said. She was shaking with rage.

Shaking, himself, but determined that he would not add fuel to her fire, Aldo tried to explain calmly that he had meant that he did not know what *particular* details were needed for celebrating this feast.

Eyes popping with fury, Danisha yelled "I know! I know! You Jews only know your Jewish festivals. Nothing else counts."

Rubenstein, who had been listening, rolled his eyes at Aldo in sympathy, but he didn't say a word. Aldo knew he was counting on the job to help with his college tuition fees. He did not expect him to voice any support. He could feel all of his hard won self-confidence draining away. He felt demeaned and disrespected, and for no reason other than that he was Jewish. He turned away so that he would not give Danisha the satisfaction of seeing how profoundly she had affected him. His spirit slid slowly back into the pain and disempowerment of the departure from Egypt."

More and more exhausted as the days went by, the humiliation of having to put up with Danisha's constant harping was making him unusually clumsy. Searching for a particular pitcher he had in mind, he almost tripped as he held it out to the customers he was serving. He caught himself at the last moment as the couple stared at him in panic. Embarrassed, he managed to retain his balance and his dignity. He completed wrapping their purchase and handed them the sales slip, his hands shaking. They headed for the escalator, thanking him for finding them exactly the pitcher they wanted, the husband slapping him good-naturedly on the shoulder. But his stumble had not missed Danisha's gimlet eye.

"One more like that, and you're out," she said grimly.

Eliane commiserated with him as they talked over dinner, knowing that he lacked the spiritual armor that had helped her to navigate unobtrusively through the rough waters of the early days in her job.

"No use dwelling on it, you'll get the hang of it," she said, sighing, "you'll see. They'll want to keep you on. Perhaps they could move you to another department after the holiday season? You know how to recognize and handle fine things. You lived with them all your life. They'll appreciate the class and dignity you bring to the job. They'll notice how much you are selling, and how much the customers like you. I know they will."

"You haven't met Danisha," he said bitterly, as she brought him ice to bind around the sore ankle he had banged against a step as he stumbled.

The crowds massed more and more feverishly as Thanksgiving passed and Christmas beckoned. Hurrying to escape Danisha's relentless eye and maneuvering his way with difficulty through the noise and the glitter, Aldo caught his foot in the dangling corner of a tablecloth, bumped into one of the laden display tables, and with Christmas music blaring in his ears, he fell heavily, an entire pyramid of artfully displayed crystal splintering and crashing to the floor beside him. Aghast as he tried to disentangle himself from the tablecloth, Aldo cried out in despair, blundering around in a desperate effort to regain his balance and get to his feet. He reached for a handhold, and grabbed at the closest display table, creating a domino effect and sending other nearby tables collapsing and crashing into each other, china shattering as it hit the ground. Customers froze in place, arrested by the sight of so much destruction. Some moved hurriedly away from the scene, stopping, turning back, and staring in horror. A little girl in her mother's arms gave an ear-splitting scream and began to howl with fright. Everyone seemed to be shouting things and rushing about, stepping on crunching porcelain and crystal, and Aldo felt faint as the nightmarish scenario unfolded around him and as he began to come to a full realization of what had just happened. He tried repeatedly to get up, but his leg was still entangled in the tablecloth and he fell back, unable to catch hold of anything to help himself to his feet and horribly aware of the scene of devastation evolving around him. His face and hands were cut and bleeding from the broken glass. Harry Rubenstein who was working the floor with him came rushing over, pale with distress, pushing concerned customers to the side.

"Mizrahi, my god, did you hurt yourself?" he asked anxiously as he helped Aldo to his feet and dabbed at the scratches on his face. "Are you alright? They should never have left that corner of cloth dangling like that."

Danisha bore down on the scene, arms flailing as she pushed people out of her way. Furious, self-righteous rage oozing from her, she sputtered, "Have you any idea how much those glasses and dishes cost? They're the top of the line. I knew you would never work out here. Too full of yourself for your own good."

She stood, arms akimbo, and glared at him. Then she shook her head. "No use, Aldo," she said, sibilant with barely controlled fury. " Get out of my sight. I'll see that your paycheck covers the breakages, but I don't want to see you anywhere near this department tomorrow. Collect your things. Go home, and don't bother ever coming back."

Aldo limped home. He had badly sprained his sore ankle in the fall. He was deeply mortified to think that Joseph would learn about the incident, and would know that his old boss, Aldo Mizrahi, had been summarily fired for incompetence. He wondered how he could break it to Eliane when she got home from work. She had been so delighted about the job, so sure that he had found a wonderful opportunity to move ahead with his life. He had time to wash up and wash the blood off the cuts on his face before she got home, but his leg was excruciatingly painful, and he could barely limp to the bed to lie down on it, the world whirling around him, his vision blurring.

Eliane stared at him in horror. "How could they fire you like that?" she gasped, despair breaking through her control as she gave way to unconsolable sobs just as Sol burst through the door, his face alight with excitement.

"I got in!" he shouted, "Tamara called. I got into City College. I'll be starting there in the fall of next year." His voice faded as he saw the state his parents were in. He sighed heavily and went to put his arm around Eliane, who was still sobbing hopelessly, while Aldo, his face contorted with pain, hobbled into the living room.

"What happened here? Sorry I burst in like that," he said apologetically, looking from one to the other. "I couldn't wait to tell you both my good news," He waited until his parents were sitting on the couch, his mother smiling through her tears.

"So, they can't take me in January, but they've offered me a paying job in a cafeteria close by from the first of the year for as long as I want it." He looked at his weary parents. "Come on," he said encouragingly, "Let's go to dinner on the first paycheck I haven't yet earned." He grinned, and Eliane and Aldo smiled weakly and followed him to the door.

CHAPTER ELEVEN

1965 City College, New York
SOL

Tamara had instantly taken to Sol. "Cuuuute," she had said drawing out the word in her gravelly voice, her dark eyes half closed as she appraised him the first day they met, heavy eyebrows raised, and Sol blushed fiercely as his parents laughed.

But following her advice, Sol had plunged into the intricacies of qualifying for a college undergraduate program with a boundless energy that left no room for setbacks. He was ecstatic to find himself in an embracing anglo-phonic environment, and Tamara, whose cynicism usually spilled off her like a sharp perfume, redoubled her efforts to help him, carried along in the slipstream of his delight. To their mutual amazement, she had been able to obtain everything that was needed for him to begin studies at City College. He was not sure what that would be like, but he couldn't wait to find out. His excitement flowed out from him like a magical essence that Aldo did not possess, had never possessed.

Wherever he went, Sol drew smiles and laughter in his wake. He saw an open world where Aldo faced closed doors. This was New York, this was America, and Sol welcomed the opportunity to work at creating the life he had always sensed might be out there for him, somewhere. He was almost ready to jettison the past and plunge into a challenging present, however much it demanded of him. He barely noticed the peeling paint on the walls of the tiny apartment his mother had found. He felt confident that he would change all that. He felt strong and powerful. He was seventeen. Youth and hope infused him with an energy that spilled out into the world around him.

It seemed like an eternity to Sol as he waited for the fall. The thick green of summer began to fade, and soon a few early leaves turned yellow and rust, clinging to the trees. At last, it was time. He set off for his first day at college.

Sol checked the slip of paper with directions as he emerged from the subway heading for Shepard Hall, anxious to see what City College would be like. He picked up his pace, fascinated by the imposing structure taking shape ahead of him as he drew near. He had never imagined that a free college in this new world would be so extraordinary. As he walked, he noticed that he was gradually becoming engulfed in a stream of people, all intent on reaching the same destination, each wrapped up in their own agendas. He stood still and let the waves of assorted humanity wash past him, staring in amazement at the tall narrow mullioned windows, marveling at the unabashedly neo-gothic arches, and the graceful gables. The weathered grey stone seemed edged in white lace. Gargoyles leered at him from cornices as he stared at the huge magnificent structure, crenellated towers and turrets reaching upward into a cloudless sky. It looked to him like a true palace of learning, and he felt a thrill of anticipation that he would be spending much of the next four years exploring this august institution.

To one side, a rich green lawn caught his eye, students scattered about, notebooks open, sitting alone or in groups, studying or engaged in serious discussions. A crisp blue sky stretched overhead and a brisk fall breeze blew at the few fallen leaves and spun them into a whirling dance.

Jostled by the growing crowd of students hurrying past him up the wide driveway, packs of books bouncing at their sides, he began to move forward again, part of the eager tide of freshmen surging toward the doors.

"This is amazing!" he exclaimed, unaware that he had spoken out loud until a small girl with long brown hair turned and grinned cheerfully as she sped past him despite her heavy briefcase.

"Fabulous, isn't it?" She said, "They call it Harvard on the Hudson, or the poor man's Harvard. Good luck with registration. See you inside." And she waved, merged into the massing crowd ahead of him, and disappeared.

As he learned his way around in the weeks that followed, gazing in awe at the mural at the very end of the Great Hall, sitting with hundreds in the packed auditorium, or hurrying down the Lincoln corridor marveling at the expansive width and the stone arches bordering both sides, he could hardly believe his good fortune. He was determined to make the most of it.

He liked his job at the cafeteria, and enjoyed the unlimited hot food that went with it. His days were filled with books to read, papers to write, and friends to discover. At the onset of winter, Sol felt an undercurrent of icy confusion spill into his heart as the sustained rush of adrenaline and the exhilaration of finding himself in an atmosphere so much more inviting than the Victoire began to fade. He realized that it was not enough to have escaped the crushing tentacles of Paris and the Hotel Victoire, he could not rid himself of terrifying moments of a churning black anguish. He was getting the hang of his classes at City College, but as he trudged to school every day, up and down grimy subway steps in the slush and frigid air of a New York winter, slipping on hard packed dirty ice bordering streets and avenues, his eyes stung and he longed for the friendship and acceptance, the ease and beauty, the warmth and light, the rituals and boundaries that he had found so stifling before, in his life in Egypt.

Here, food seemed almost incidental, not the ritualized companionable mealtimes of his childhood. The ways people greeted each other seemed offhand and insincere, "You take care, now," strangers said, "have a great day," their eyes fixed beyond him as they spoke, moving on to the next person, the next question, the next challenge, the words empty noises that meant nothing to him, as he pocketed the tip and cleared the table for the next customers. After the first rush of the novelty of being a college freshman, he found himself wondering how he would ever feel at home in this huge hive of relentless activity.

There had been some problem with the subway, and Sol, never a stickler for punctuality, was late for class. He hurried deep into the bowels of the college, along narrow corridors with green tiled walls, passing a board covered with notices about everything from jobs, housing, cafeteria specials, to reading lists, lecture calendars, and test results. The fact that there was not a soul in sight magnified his anxiety, and as he pushed open the heavy double doors to the lecture hall, he realized with a sinking heart that class had already begun. Professor Swerdlow stood at the podium, glancing about the room, his black sweater bunching about him like the ruffled feathers of a gaunt old crow. He had clearly already launched into a discussion of the economy, and a board behind him was covered in graphs and charts. He glared at Sol from under bushy black brows as Sol edged cautiously into his seat and took his notebook out of his briefcase. The professor waited until the whispers and shuffling of papers, the coughs and sudden bursts of subdued laughter had calmed down before turning to the board again and beginning to talk.

The energy and pace of the city challenged Sol constantly. He thought often of Hassan and his school friends and wondered with sudden waves of longing if he would ever see any of them again. He understood that he would never again find an environment where he would be accepted without explanation. When he answered questions about his background, he drew stares and disbelief, and he felt he had to justify himself again and again to his classmates, and explain himself in all social situations.

Following his first euphoric embrace of the opportunities he saw ahead of him, Sol was slowly coming to the realization that he had lost access to his former self forever. He was in a new life that was permanently severed from the old. Even his parents had become needy, deeply flawed and changed by the process of exile and reinvention. He hardly recognized them. His mother had always been the purveyor of calm nurture, a symbol of comfort and stability at home, and he had admired his father's elegant personality, always gravely competent, always greeted everywhere with recognition and respect. Now he observed that his mother was firmly taking command of herself and their future, a steely veneer deflecting all emotions, while his father, without the context of a recognizable life, was clearly falling to pieces. The cushioned protective environment that the teenage Sol had scorned and pushed against had vanished along with his childhood, and as he struggled to rebuild himself in this new context, he looked back with a residue of deep pain and loss at a world no-one around him understood or could even imagine, a world he knew was gone and would never return. Fighting to keep aloft in the torrent of emotions and experiences that threatened to drown him, he realized he would have to let go of the past before he could discern the full shape of the future, hurling himself into the swift-moving river with a steely determination to make it to the other side.

He had been daydreaming and came to with a shock as he realized that Professor Swerdlow had called his name, "Mizrahi," he barked, his voice resounding harshly throughout the hall, "you there, in the back row. Taking the parameters we just discussed into consideration, where do you think you might see the economy, five years from now?" Everyone turned to look at him. Amazed that the professor knew his name, he gulped as he tried to reconstruct the question and come up with a plausible answer.

"I ... er ... everything changes, doesn't it, and five years is a long time ..." he bumbled along desperately, trying to sound as if he knew what he was talking about, to the stifled amusement of his peers and the exasperation of his professor.

"Obviously, Mizrahi has not been paying attention," said Professor Swerdlow coldly "I hope I am not *boring* you, Mr. Mizrahi? Heaven forbid that I should *bore* my students? I take it you are here because you want to learn?" Nervous laughter rippled through the room following his comment and all eyes again turned to Sol, who blushed to the roots of his hair, wishing himself anywhere but where he was, and resolving to pay better attention in future.

Despite his wariness as he navigated among the other students, he soon made friends, almost in spite of himself. Carlton, a lanky African American was the first to make overtures of friendship, clapping him on the back as they walked toward class.

"Hey, man," he said jovially, his voice as rich and deep as the color of his skin. "Noticed you before. Why the gloom? Pretty good gig we have here, right? Want to grab a coffee?" Glancing at Sol he added, "How do you like that economics professor? He really caught you out last week, eh?" And he laughed a booming laugh as they walked along side by side.

Sol glanced up, eyeing him with suspicion, but seeing only good humor and eagerness in his face, he decided to go along. On the way to coffee, the intrepid Carlton also collected three freshman girls who had been wandering around looking lost, and a large guy with glasses. Things had begun to look up. This was not the uncomplicated give and take of his high school friendships with Hassan and his friends from the English School in Cairo, but after the first hesitant introductions, he realized that his fellow students were all prepared to accept each other for their differences rather than in spite of them, and that rather than feeding off the differences among them, the diversity of their backgrounds created a unique bond as they moved together into the unknown geography of college life.

Carlton organized impromptu basketball games and dragged a somewhat reluctant Sol to join in. "You're not a complete washout," he teased Sol, "but you do need work."

"My game was tennis," said Sol ruefully, remembering the ocher-colored courts at the Gezira Sporting Club, where he had spent so many happy hours. "I never played baseball or basketball before."

They shared homework and kept seats for each other. They hailed each other in the halls and relaxed together over coffee, plunging into far-reaching conversations about life and death and everything in between with a group of other friends who gathered and dispersed around them. They were all working hard at various jobs when they were not studying. As the year sped past, Sol found it increasingly difficult to leave the free and easy interchange with his friends for the anxiety ridden confines of his home.

"Can I ask my friends over?" He asked his mother hesitantly. She looked around the small cluttered living room. Aldo lounged on the couch across from the perpetually active television, a pile of suitcases covered with a piece of ornamental cloth from the *muski* serving as a coffee table in front of the couch. The clank and clatter of the radiators periodically drowned out all conversation.

"Are you sure that's a good idea?" Asked Eliane dubiously. Sol looked around, seeing the place through her eyes, and shook his head with a sigh. "I'll get together with my friends elsewhere," he said.

He was a pleasant looking young man, and his personal charm won the day, dragging him away from the sheltered boy he had been and thrusting him into a vision of the man he might become. Although the struggle was proving far harder than he had anticipated, he grew less wary of trusting his new friends and more aware that his differences were also his strengths. He knew he could not rely on Eliane and Aldo to reach out a hand to help, or even to notice that he needed help. His parents were too mired in their own struggles to perceive the destructive influence their fragilities were having on their son.

Sol came to the conclusion that he had to get away from his parents if he were to fully embrace the possibilities of this new present he was living. He tentatively broached the subject of housing and rent and Carlton immediately clapped him on the shoulder and offered up a spare room in his Harlem apartment.

"I'm not sure I can afford it," said Sol, "and my parents will be furious, it's just that they're so wrapped up in their own problems, and I have to say, being with you guys is a real relief."

"I should warn you that I live on the edge of Harlem," added Carlton, grinning, "so although you will still find glimmers of white here and there in the mix, you'll need to get used to being in the minority on the streets."

"I don't think that'll be a problem," said Sol, laughing.

"Oh, do take the room," exclaimed Claudia, reddening, "it would make everything so much easier." He looked at her in astonishment. She was a small Asian girl with an oval face and a tiny perfect figure, her straight black hair pulled back with a rubber band, no trace of accent in her speech. Sol was fascinated by the paradox of her doll-like countenance and the pragmatic steel she exhibited in every encounter. Time and again in class she dazzled him with her poise and understanding of complicated concepts. While he floundered, she swam unfamiliar waters with ease and grace. He had not thought she would give him the time of day, but here she was, urging him on to independence, and he read a subtle invitation to further intimacies in her comment.

"College is about starting to break away and creating our own lives, don't you think?" Claudia continued, "You will have to explain to your parents that this will make it easier for us to study together and for you to get good grades." She gazed up at him with slanted glistening black eyes and a timid smile that held promise and clinched the deal.

"I hope you don't mind," he announced to his parents that night, "I've taken an extra part-time job in the library, and a room closer to college. It will help me to study, I can study with friends, and it won't disturb you. I can pay for it myself with the money from my jobs, so it shouldn't add to your burdens. It's a furnished room, so I won't need to take much with me, I'll just need bed linens and a pillow, and I'm hoping to move in there next week."

Eliane looked up from the papers she was studying and smiled at him, deep circles under her eyes, her eyes unfocused. "Come and see us often," she said. "I am so proud that you are strong enough to push out on your own. I know you will succeed." She got up wearily and hugged him. "Let me know if you ever need anything."

"Do you really have to do this?" Asked Aldo, tears in his eyes as he, too, hugged his son, "how can we manage without you?" He added, "How will you ever be able to manage on your own?"

Sol felt his father's fears and insecurities tugging at him, pulling him down into an abyss. "I won't be going far, Papi," he said, pulling away, sadness washing over him, drowning his courage in fear, "and I'll be here if you need anything at all."

He added with a grin, "anyway, you can't get rid of me that easily. I'll be home for dinner most Friday nights." His father smiled.

Leaving his parents cast Sol into a new dimension. He gave himself entirely and with energy to embracing his new life. He shouldered his responsibilities with growing ease. He knew at last with certainty that he would emerge from the past and find his way into the future. New York was teeming with people like himself, people who had plunged bravely into a future they hardly understood and had carved success from the tattered remnants of an exiled life.

He and Claudia shared many of the same classes. As their freshman year passed, and they watched another flood of new students fill the halls in the fall, they spent more and more time together. He learned that her parents were third generation Japanese. Her grandparents had been interned during the second world war, but her parents had raised their children with all of the freedoms and entitlements of the American born. Claudia was totally at ease with herself and her surroundings. Mired in his own complicated brew, Sol admired her absolute focus and her assumption that she could demand what she wanted and discard what she did not like without a backward glance.

She, in turn, was equally fascinated by his exotic origins, so different from her own. She never tired of hearing about the life of ease and privilege that had been irredeemably shattered, the broken pieces cast into exile in a distant land. She admired his determination to glue the pieces back together and find his own path to success and acceptance in his new life. When tests approached, they studied together late into the night in Sol's room, turning up the music on his radio to drown out the sounds of the street and the wail of ambulances, and soon enough, the study sessions ended with kisses and cuddles on the narrow bed in Sol's little room in Harlem, and then, why not spend the night together? It would not be safe for Claudia to head for home so late. As she had predicted, his independence and the room in Carlton's apartment made everything easier.

"Don't your parents mind?" He asked anxiously. She laughed, and he lost his concerns in contemplation of her exquisite mouth and the way she put her hand up to shield it, as if her laughter might be viewed as unseemly when she had been exploring his body with that same mouth with ravenous intensity moments earlier. She was a creature of delight and paradox, and he ceased to question any of it, happy in the moment.

Many of his new friends viewed his old life with admiration and respect. They had not known that Jewish families in the Middle East had enjoyed such privileged lives. They did not hold it against him. As he felt less need to hide parts of himself, he learned to find ways to integrate the past seamlessly into the present he was creating.

Other students dropped by to watch or participate in the basketball games that Carlton continued to organize, and soon Sol and Claudia became inseparable from the group. Sol found the studies easier as the months flowed past, and he enjoyed the companionship of Carlton and their group of friends, and the promise of the carefree girls who crossed his path whenever they could, each determined to be the one who would erase the sadness from his dark eyes. When his mother asked him curiously what college life was like, he told her it was like a candy store filled with varied and wonderful delights. He enjoyed the freedom of earning his own money. He liked the contrast of the hushed focus of the library and the urgent clamor of the cafeteria. Life and hope began to glow again, and the glow allowed his charm and charisma to open doors and lead the way into happiness.

"We're going to line up for seats real early tomorrow, at Shakespeare in the Park, at the Delacorte Theater," Amir called to him as he was about to leave the campus, "can you spell me in the line?"

"What's Shakespeare in the Park?" Asked Sol, "what line?"

Claudia who had come up behind him clapped her hands with excitement. "Oh my god, it's so great," she said, "You'll love it. You have to come, Sol. They're doing The Taming of the Shrew in Central Park this summer, and it's absolutely free. We usually take blankets and a picnic and stand in line for hours for tickets, and then we sit out in the open theater and watch the play. We all take turns and replace each other standing in line. It's so worth it. You'll see." She jumped up and down, her eyes sparkling with anticipation and he whirled her around, lifted her high in the air and kissed her.

Later, sitting in the open theater, his arm around Claudia's shoulders, the rich Shakespearian dialogue resounding in his ears, a rough blanket over their knees, he glanced up at the night sky behind the tower of the Delacorte Theater. The sun was setting, wisps of cloud turning to shades of pink and purple as the sky darkened. A huge harvest moon pierced the growing dark. A light breeze circled them.

"Another sandwich?" Asked Claudia, delving into the basket she had brought. He nodded, and sighed his deep content. This was his new world, and he had found his place in it. This was happiness beyond his hopes.

Claudia snuggled up to him. "I think I'm going to try to get into medical school," she said thoughtfully, "What do you think?"

The months came and went, and suddenly it seemed as if the adventure of college that had only just begun had plunged into fast forward. Claudia had changed her major and was directing her fierce ambitions and energy toward medical school. She left Shepard Hall, and forged ahead into the future of her choice. Sol missed having her close by, but they managed to get together now and then, despite their heavy workloads and schedules.

Gradually, the accelerating pressures of Sol's intense commitments to work and studies carved an even deeper divide. They found fewer and fewer ways to coordinate their demanding schedules to make room for time together.

Claudia was waiting for him as he hurried to their usual meeting place, and he thought blissfully of the weekend ahead, hoping she had no tests to study for. But Claudia seemed tense and she kept looking around uneasily. At last she said, "We really need to talk, Sol, neither of us can keep this up. I'm sure you feel the way I do. It has been such a strain to try to keep up a relationship in these circumstances." Eminently practical, she looked sorrowfully into his eyes.

"Let it go, Sol," she said, gently, "Let's be friends, always. We must both let it go. We've had a wonderful time together, but now the time has come for each of us to move on."

"What do you mean?" said Sol, his heart sinking.

"I've met someone, a doctor," said Claudia after a long uneasy silence, her face flushing. "I didn't want this to happen, but it just did. He's a few years older than we are, and he and I discovered that we have so much that we share, so much in common. He wants to get married soon and have a family, and so do I."

She looked anxiously at Sol's devastated face. "Don't do this to me, Sol," she pleaded. "What we had was great, but it's time to face reality. You aren't ready to have a wife. Akito wants me to continue my studies after we marry and he is planning for us to work toward a shared practice."

"He's Japanese, then," muttered Sol gloomily.

Claudia smiled and took his face in her hands. "He's older," she said, pointedly, "He has a house and a fine career ahead of him, and I will be able to live the life I dreamed of. I'll never forget you, but he's a man, and you are still a boy. You will make some lucky girl so happy one day." Her eyes filled with tears. She reached up and kissed him on the cheek before gathering her coat and her bag and hurrying away. Sol sat in stunned silence, not realizing that tears were running down his face.

Sol mourned their relationship for a time in the loneliness of his little room in Harlem. She left him with fond memories of a butterfly of brilliant colors, a creature of strength and beauty who had fluttered through his life for a while and had now fluttered out of his reach. He had liked her parents, whose old-fashioned courtesy and free American ways demonstrated the best of blended cultures.

After Claudia left, he let himself drift into brief flirtations and out again, but nothing touched him as Claudia had. He joined other groups, and was emerging as a leader by the time his sophomore year was drawing to a close. A new self-image was starting to come into focus, and he entered his senior year with his heart firmly set on the goal of a prestigious financial graduate program. He studied the requirements for scholarship aid, and set his sights on Wharton, and his energies on developing a resume that might take him where he wanted to go.

"You must find a way to get a graduate degree," his mother insisted one Friday night, reveling in the good grades he had brought with him. "There are decisions to be made. You will soon have finished with college, hard to believe it, but you are in your senior year." She smiled at him. Dinner was over, although the fragrance of roast chicken still lingered in the small living room and candles still flickered in brass candlesticks on the table. "Are you planning to go into law?" She asked, "Medicine? What do you think you will want to do?"

"How will he pay for it?" Aldo asked anxiously. "Shouldn't he get a job and work his way up?"

Sol laughed at his mother's concerned face. "I like the world *you* navigate in," he said, grinning at her. "I want to head for a graduate degree in finance, and then a comfortable future."

Eliane stared at him. "Never comfortable," she said dubiously. "One can never be comfortable. But a good degree should mean that you will not have to scrabble for a job." She looked closely at her son and noticed how much his shoulders had filled out. He must be finding time for sports, she thought. His gaze was clear and untroubled. No trace of his Egyptian background crept into his speech. She got up and hugged him.

"Come and help me clear the dishes," she said, sighing as she made her way to the kitchen, "and let's plan together for your future. America is bursting with possibilities. You are young, and will be able to make your way in this country without the burdens your father and I carry." She turned back and glanced at him, adding, "I hope you know that I will help you in whatever you choose to do?"

Sol glanced at her, surprised. She had seemed so absent for so long, drowning all emotion in the overwhelming need to trudge along the slow path, eyes to the ground, steadily advancing to build it into a fast track. Now she was clearly offering to help set his feet on the fast track from the start. He had tears in his eyes as he hugged her in return and whispered, "Thank you, Maman. Thank you for everything."

"Here," she said, disentangling herself and turning her head away as she handed him a cup and saucer. "Take your father his Turkish coffee."

CHAPTER TWELVE

1969 New York City
ELIANE

Hurrying to catch the train that had come roaring into the station like some violent ravenous monster just as she was coming down the stairs onto the platform, Eliane elbowed and pushed her way through the doors and wedged herself into what little standing space she could find. Her daily commute was the part she liked the least about her New York life. She sometimes sighed, thinking of how her life had changed, thinking back to the careful ministrations of Ahmad to make sure that she was comfortable in the back seat of the car, as he drove her wherever she needed to go. That was all gone now. She rarely allowed herself to waste energy remembering.

Over the past seven years, she had adjusted well to her work at the investment firm. Today, she was running late for the monthly meeting at the firm, and she was sad that her staunchest supporter at the firm, kind, elderly Massimo Taglioni, would be announcing his retirement at the meeting.

Many were already seated as she hurried into the conference room.

A dull murmur buzzed around her as the assembled money managers waited for everyone to be seated and for the meeting to begin. They sat around a huge magnificent gleaming mahogany table, glasses of water at each place, sharpened pencils and fresh pads of paper beside them. She saw that Massimo had saved her a place, and she slid gratefully into the seat beside him.

She had only recently been given the privilege of attending the monthly meetings as a junior money manager, rather than organizing them as the office manager she had been. The only other woman at the table sat at the other end. She was much disliked and much admired. Cristina Falti never looked anyone directly in the eye. Predatory, lean and hungry, eyes heavily made up, she constantly shifted her gaze to make sure that she did not miss something important going on just over the shoulder of the person she was talking to. She was credited with being the company's biggest rainmaker, but as the only woman on the board, she guarded her position with the intensity of a Cerberus at the gates of hell. She had fought her way through business school in an environment that was almost entirely male, and she knew that the eyes around the table regarded her success with an envy that was close to hatred. The look she gave Eliane Mizrahi as she took her place at the table bordered on blistering contempt. Eliane ignored it.

Eliane had quickly understood the politics of the situation and had always been careful to maintain the low profile of someone at the bottom of the food chain. Thanks to Zaki's recommendation, she had been hired almost as soon as they had arrived from Paris. She was well aware of the politics and hostilities that sizzled around her, and she knew that she had no academic qualifications to rival those of the other money managers. She needed the job and the income and took great care not to rock the boat. She kept her eyes open and her mouth shut. Her quick mind absorbed everything about the fast-paced aggressive new world she had been fortunate enough to enter. She kept away from the alliances she observed around her, and focused on doing her job as well and as unobtrusively as possible.

She had been handed the job of assistant to younger and younger hires as they came into the firm, increasingly valued for her knowledge of the world they were entering as years passed and they made their way through the ranks. She had eventually been promoted to office manager, and recently, to junior money manager. A few years after her arrival at the investment firm, she had come to the attention of one of the founders, Massimo Taglioni. He had grown deeply appreciative of her uncomplicated attitude, her lack of pretension, her sound advice and her attention to detail. Valuing her contribution to the smooth running of the firm, he had generously handed over to her a couple of his less important clients in the clothing and grocery business, Cremona Lingerie and the Tea for Two grocery group.

"Here," he said, handing her the files one day, "Let's see what you can do with these. Clothes and groceries should interest you, eh?"

Eliane, thrilled to have been given this opportunity, met with the principals of both businesses and dispensed careful nurture and attention, gently guiding them to develop their businesses where her instincts and financial acumen led her.

She saw that Sol seemed to be finding stability and happiness in the life he was designing for himself, but she despaired of Aldo finding a new life in America. Their survival as a family lay heavily on her shoulders.

She knew that Massimo was about to announce his retirement, and sitting beside him at the meeting, she was drifting into thoughts of Sol and his new apartment when she realized that Massimo had the floor and was talking about her.

"So I wish you all well," he was saying, smiling, having clearly announced his departure while she was day-dreaming. "Be good to my clients. And I also want to commend Eliane Mizrahi here, for the great work she has been doing with Cremona Lingerie, and also the Tea for Two grocery line. I have some totally astonishing results to leave with you." He patted a file in front of him and continued "She has increased their income considerably in the past years, exceeding most of your results this year, and has also been guiding the two companies surprisingly successfully in growth and visibility. I must confess that I, myself, never saw this sort of potential when they first came to me."

He smiled warmly at Eliane, who flushed, looked down, and clasped her hands tightly under the table to keep them from shaking. The firm was very much a dog eat dog culture and she was unused to public praise. "I think the firm would be well advised to encourage her along this path," he added, "so perhaps you will remember her when you are dividing up the spoils from my departure?" He gave a deep guffaw as he looked at the intense faces around the table. He got up slowly and beckoned them all over to his office to look through his files.

Sharp glances were exchanged around the table. Cristina licked her lips, her dark eyes narrowed, almost reptilian, her arm outstretched. It was clear that no-one would be eager to share.

But Eliane was flying high on the words of appreciation and praise she had heard from a man she deeply admired. Massimo thought her capable of bigger and better things. Perhaps he was right. The other money managers would never share with her, she knew that, even if Massimo didn't, but she would make her own way until they were obliged to acknowledge her. She would cast about for other clients, and she would make the most of everything that came her way.

At home that night, she tried not to show her excitement to Aldo, whose gloomy face warned her that he was in no mood to hear how well she was doing. She threw her briefcase onto the couch with a sigh and hurried to the kitchen to start dinner.

Eliane had been surprised and thrilled when Massimo had handed her the two small accounts to manage. She was determined to give the projects her best advice. She had hurried home after work, the two thin files tucked into her bag, and as soon as dinner was over and Aldo had sunk into his customary somnolent stupor in front of the television, she laid the papers from the two files on the kitchen table and began to study them. She was surprised, as she familiarized herself with the two companies, that the firm even handled such insignificant accounts. Cremona Lingerie had already been in business for five years but was showing no growth at all. She got out her calculator, and worked deep into the night, long after a surprised Aldo had stumbled off to bed.

Next day, she called Lillian Cremona and suggested that they meet for lunch. She found herself sitting opposite a pale mousy looking woman with a hesitant smile, and a faint stammer.

"Did you bring the list of your inventory?" She asked, as they sat down and each disappeared behind the enormous menus handed to them.

Lillian Cremona opened a stuffed briefcase and pulled out a crumpled sheaf of papers, some covered in figures, others with designs. "Don't you think we should do all this back at the office?" She asked timidly. "No-one ever asked to see anything before. Do you have time to come back to the office and see some of the stock and some of my new designs? You could meet my manager, Estelle. She and I have been thinking of developing a line for large sizes. What do you think about that? Perhaps we can have lunch and then go back to my office? It's not far." She smiled engagingly at Eliane.

Eliane hesitated. She wanted to appear very professional, very knowledgeable and in control, and she did not think that money managers usually took a look at the stock that produced the money they managed. But she had taken a liking to Lillian Cremona as they ate and talked, and she learned that this unassuming woman was a single mother who had sunk every penny she had into backing the lingerie designs she loved to create. By the time they had finished lunch, they had moved into a different level of discourse. She went back with Lillian to the small dark rooms where the stock was housed, boxes squashed together and stuffed onto cramped shelves. Estelle came out of a back room where she had been working on the books. She smiled nervously at Eliane and retreated back into her work.

"These are truly exquisite!" Eliane exclaimed, holding up a delicate pair of panties and a bra. She glanced at a hanging rack tucked into a corner of the space and walked over to it. "My god! These are gorgeous, Lillian," she said, pulling out and inspecting a white lawn nightgown with delicate lace ruffles at the neck, on the shoulders, and at the hem. "Is that really vintage handmade lace? Where on earth did you find it? It's lovely." She picked up a very pale lilac georgette ensemble, lost in admiration.

"Where do you advertize? I've never seen anything like these. The quality and workmanship are impressive. What stores are carrying these?" She asked.

Seeing Lillian's blush, she realized that little was being done to publicize merchandise that she understood immediately was unusual and very high-end. She called in to her office and said she was at a meeting with a client and would not be in all afternoon. Then she sat down and began to pore over Lillian's designs.

By the end of the day, she had a whirlwind of ideas buzzing in her mind.

"Let me give all of this some thought," she said, smiling at Lillian. " Of course we also need to check the investments that have been made on your behalf over the past few years, but I think we should get together again next week and consider ways you might be able to maximize your wonderful talent and the truly exceptional workmanship you produce."

Lillian's eyes shone with excitement. "You really like my work? You really think we can grow the company?" she asked, and clapped her hands in delight when Eliane nodded.

They were simple enough ideas, really. When she first came to America, Eliane had been fascinated to learn about the Tupperware parties that had catapulted the sales of Tupperware into the stratosphere. She thought about ways in which Lillian might develop a community of society women who could both purchase her lovely lingerie, earn a small commission by throwing select parties to publicize and sell things themselves, and boast about it to their friends who would want in on the secret, and would network out to their select groups of friends in their turn.

Several months later, she had developed a detailed plan involving a very small financial outlay, and introducing a series of selective gatherings offering canapes and champagne, where young models would show off the company's exquisite wares to a chosen few. Eliane knew that there were few things as seductive as being let in on an exclusive event, and she counted on that element to create the word of mouth that could be fanned into something much more impressive in the long run.

Her perspicacity proved accurate. Over the next few months, Lillian saw stores like Bergdorf and Bendel courting her assiduously, desperate to carry her wares. She actually had an excellent business sense but had been totally paralyzed by the fact that she had little money for development, no deep pocket investors, and no idea how to go about finding them. Eliane's energy and strength released her innate creativity and entrepreneurial flair, and she grabbed the reins with both hands, hired more workers, and as she watched her tiny business become a stellar enterprise, she thanked her lucky stars that her account had landed in the capable hands of this woman, Eliane Mizrahi.

CHAPTER THIRTEEN

1973 New York City
JASMINE'S CHALLENGE

While the Mizrahi family struggled to overcome obstacles and consolidate its hold on a new life in America, a girl from a Nile village engaged in her own struggles. Only Malvina recognized the Herculean effort it had taken for Jasmine to scramble her way up the ladder of learning to find herself at last in the company of her peers in the sophomore year of high school. She was sixteen, and while there were still huge gaps in her grasp of her studies, the passion for reading that had consumed her from the start continued to furnish her mind and heart far beyond what anyone had expected. She had adjusted to the speed and intensity of her new life. She had come to care deeply for Malvina and Tim, and as she saw more of life and understood more of the diversity around her, she recognized with profound gratitude that they had offered her an unimaginable opportunity to spread her wings and fly as far and as fast as she was able.

Sometimes in the deep of night, she woke up, disoriented, and thought she was back in her village curled up with her brother in the dark hut. Then, she shed bitter tears that she was not able to share all of this with Ali, but she had resigned herself that there was truly no way that she could reach back to her past to lift any of them into the life she was living. She could only stretch forward to the future. She could only hope that his life, whatever it was turning out to be, would give him the happiness that she had found in hers.

Gradually, Malvina introduced Jasmine to the ways in which she could make good use of the many skills she was learning. As time went by, she watched and monitored carefully, waiting for the moment when she felt that Jasmine was ready to try herself out in the fashion world that would become hers. She by-passed the other bookers in the office and made Jasmine's introductory bookings herself, despite the constant flurry of phone calls and parading models that surrounded her, the rivalries and crises of the staff, and the heavy demands on her time and patience. Choosing with great care, she sent Jasmine out to a few appointments, clutching her comp sheet, always accompanied by one of the agency chaperones.

Jasmine was proud and excited to be able to try out her wings at last. She was heading to midtown, her chaperone in tow. Her first assignment was for a line of designer outerwear. She walked nervously into a cavernous space filled with movement and echoing voices, to where clothes racks were being readied. Cloth, leather and fur coats, and jackets of all sizes, styles and colors were being sized at an impressive rate by a small staff working at warp speed, jamming them into the appropriate racks, the racks slung about the room faster than their clunky appearance would seem to allow. Just when they seemed about to careen out of control, they were stopped short by a buzzing swarm of assistants, who managed to catch them at exactly the right moment to settle them into the designated gap against the wall, before moving on to the next one. Jasmine stood still at the entrance and stared, fascinated by the superbly orchestrated chaos.

A young woman rushed over to her, a wide smile on her face, make-up brushes stuck in her hair, her green shirt smeared with mascara and foundation. She took Jasmine's comp sheet, looked through it, and unceremoniously held Jasmine's face up to the light.

"I'll do this one," she called over her shoulder, and hurried Jasmine and the chaperone to an area at the back, where there was a row of mirrored cubicles where other young women were having their hair or faces styled.

"I'm Beth," said the woman, as she gave Jasmine a pink wrapper to put on over her clothes. "Now, let's see. We want to emphasize the eyes and cheekbones, don't we?" She smiled at Jasmine's eager gaze, pulled a brush from her hair, and began to wield the bewildering array of brushes and pots laid out beside her, with skill and aplomb.

When Beth was done, Jasmine stared into the mirror, hardly believing what she was seeing. She was herself, and not herself. Her eyes stared back at her, huge and sultry under a thicket of false eyelashes. The pale glow on her lips and creamy foundation pushed all attention to the eyes. Beth smiled complacently as she made way for the hairdresser.

"Nice, eh?" she said to Jasmine's face in the mirror. She winked, and was off to the next one. Meanwhile, the man now standing behind her chair was pulling and twisting her thick hair this way and that.

He said doubtfully, "Everyone's in love with the Vidal Sassoon smooth cap look, but I don't think it would do anything for you. Whatever can I do with this wiry thatch? I'll see what Paul thinks."

Paul, a tall guy as gaunt and bent as a wire coat hanger, was summoned. He cast a cold eye over the proceedings and ran a disdainful hand through Jasmine's hair.

"Nothing you can do here, except go with it," he said, "Don't try to tame it into something else."

The young man behind Jasmine's chair nodded as Paul loped off to another consultation.

Her hair pulled tight above her forehead and then teased out to a wide corona around her small tan face cast an interesting play of light and shadow, and gave an exotic contrast to her exquisitely detailed makeup. The head of the studio came over and nodded approvingly.

"This the new Malvina girl?" He asked. "Interesting. Great face." He glanced at her measurements on the sheet. "Still got some growing to do, I see." He smiled at her. "She's a little short for the runway, needs to grow a couple of inches, but let's have her try on the Dorcas line, and I'd like to see her runway walk. I think we'll definitely want to use her."

A warm glow spread outward from Jasmine's abdomen and added a faint flush to her face. She had made it. The assignment was hers. Malvina would be so pleased.

Despite the care Malvina took to monitor the many assignments that came flooding in for the various young models she represented, the volume and intensity of the business called for quick decisions and the ability to provide immediate response. There were many agencies out there poised to fill the jobs, but Malvina knew her girls well and her venues even better, and matched them at lightening speed.

So Jasmine found herself one day hurrying out of the rain into a huge bare basement, fluorescent ceiling lights stark along its length, a heavy metal gate clanging shut behind her. Two other girls were already there. A formidable woman with short black hair and a voice that echoed in the cavernous space swiftly ushered the bewildered chaperone into a small side room where she installed her in a comfortable armchair in front of a television set with a cup of hot coffee.

The two other girls were wispy blondes, with hard eyes and scornful mouths.

"Is it still raining? How old are you?" The taller of the two asked, "Why do you have that woman with you?" As Jasmine was about to answer, the door at the other end of the studio opened and a motley collection of men straggled toward them.

"These the girls?" One of them asked, "Get rid of them blondes. The only good one is that one." He pointed straight at Jasmine, and swaggered over to her, chucking her under the chin and then saying jovially, "Take off your shirt honey, let's see what you got."

"No," said Jasmine, simply. "You have all my measurements on the comp sheet. I was told that you wanted me to model some sportswear for a sports magazine?" She glanced about her, "Where will I find the clothes?"

One of the blondes gasped and the other gave a shriek, ending in a high-pitched nervous giggle.

"Sure," said the man, "I'll take you there, all the way." he winked, and the men all laughed, "but first, as I said, let's see what you got," and he advanced toward her, his hand outstretched toward her breast.

Jasmine ducked under his arm and ran to the small room where her chaperone had succumbed to the charms of a soap opera, pulled her up from her seat, and was out of the door before anyone fully realized she was gone. Tears burning at her eyes, she stepped into Malvina's office and told her what had happened. "I'm so sorry I lost the assignment," she said hesitantly, "but I really didn't like them at all."

"Oh my God!" said Malvina, outraged, "you did absolutely the right thing. I can hardly believe it." She leafed angrily through the rolodex on her desk and called the chaperone to her office. When the woman stepped in, she ignored her defiant rationalizations.

"Don't even bother," she said coldly. "It was your job to know what was going on and to protect the young woman in your charge. You failed to do that, and no thanks to you, Jasmine took over and got you both out of there. But I can never trust you again. Get out of my sight." And she shooed the distraught woman out of her office.

Then she called the editor of the magazine and told her in no uncertain terms that she shouldn't bother trying to book any of the Malvina girls ever again.

"You should know class when you see it, Emilia," she raged, "I'll be spreading the word about you in the fashion industry.

You'll only get to see the sort of girls you deserve, from now on. Don't come looking for any of mine."

"Hard to believe, but Jasmine, young as she is, has a presence and a class that some of my older girls never learn," she said to Tim as they sat companionably in the living room, Tim disappearing behind the newspaper.

"She's learned it from you," said Tim complacently, peering from the side of the paper and smiling at his wife.

"Well, I don't know about that," said Malvina, embarrassed, "I blame myself. I realize I had no idea what I was sending her into, today. My research showed that magazine to be perfectly legit, and I've met Emilia, the editor, several times. It looked like a good opportunity for Jasmine, but clearly they are using the magazine as a front for other things. I feel so bad about it, but at least I have the comfort of knowing now that she's not going to fall for any of that kind of nonsense. I really did think that Emilia had a better sense of the Malvina agency than to try that sort of thing with any of my girls. I thought I was vetting everything quite obsessively, and by now the industry knows how careful I am with my models, but you can be pretty damn sure I'll vet my venues much more carefully from now on." Tim patted her shoulder consolingly and went back to his newspaper.

Malvina looked down, studying a sheaf of photos in front of her on her desk. "This is a terrific portfolio," she said, pleased. "Do you know," she looked up at Tim, "Jasmine actually told me today that she didn't want to have to deal with any nudity. I asked her how she felt about lingerie ads and swimwear, and she looked every which way and then spoke so softly I could hardly hear her. She said reluctantly that she had no objection to modeling clothes that were revealing, but would prefer not to audition for lingerie. I think I understand. Even though she has not pursued her Muslim faith, some of the teachings about modesty in the way she grew up must have been very hard for her to discard, don't you think?"

"I think this fashion world she has plunged into may have been something of a shock at first," said Tim thoughtfully, "but you notice she never said anything to either of us. I suspect that now she knows exactly what she is comfortable doing, and what is outside that range."

He smiled. "I could have told you she would know how to look after herself," he added, "timid little Jamila has disappeared. Jasmine has grown tall and gorgeous, and has absorbed everything you've taught her. She knows who she is, she knows who she can be, and she holds her head high. I'm glad she found the courage to tell you where she wants to draw the line. She is so much in awe of you that I was afraid she would not say anything that might contradict what she sees as your goals and aspirations for her."

"My greatest aspiration is for her to be happy," said Malvina, thoughtfully, "and I also want her to know that she has the tools to have a great profession if she wants it."

She stood up abruptly, suddenly all business, "but her runway walk still needs serious work. I watched her the other day and she seems to have mislaid the wonderful grace and glide she used to have. Now she lifts her legs so high she looks like a horse showing off its paces. Carlos always emphasizes that particular element of the runway walk in his classes, but he hasn't realized how much more effective Jasmine's walk could be with the addition of her natural grace. I think I'll take a little time with her, myself, tomorrow."

Tim folded the newspaper and leaned back in his chair. He slapped his knee, and roared with laughter. "She doesn't look like any horse I've ever seen," he said between gasps of mirth, "But you go ahead and take care of that walk, my dear. Don't worry about a thing. That girl will never disappoint you. You found a rare gem there. A rare gem. I am so happy for you both."

CHAPTER FOURTEEN

1974 New York
JASMINE: NEXT STEP

Toward the end of her sixteenth year, Malvina revealed to Jasmine that she would be moving her out of the townhouse into an apartment owned by the agency in a ramshackle building in the thirties on Third Avenue. Another young woman was already living there.

"Who is she?" Asked Jasmine, apprehensive, well aware that relationships with other girls had not always come easily for her.

"Have I ever met her?"

"I don't think you've met Drenka," said Malvina, "But I know you'll like her, and it will be very good for you to be with other young women, other models. You need some good friends around your own age, and there is much you can learn from them."

Jasmine took a deep breath. She was ready to take it all in stride. This was a new adventure and she was eager to confront it. She knew she would always be welcome in Malvina and Tim's home, even if she was living elsewhere.

"So," Malvina said, as she and Jasmine looked around the small room in the townhouse, now empty of Jasmine's books and clothes, a light patch on one wall where Jasmine had hung the horse painting that Tim had given her. A touch of sadness tinged her voice, "now is the time for you to take the next step." She looked up at Jasmine's eager face and added "I know you're ready, but I want us to continue to take it slowly and monitor any assignments that present themselves. You know Monica and Claire, the two best bookers in the agency? They will keep you in mind and let me know when and where your next assignment might be, but I will continue to take it from there. Have you decided what you want to do with your earnings? You've been out on several assignments this year, and your account will soon put you over the top of the loans you had to pay back to the agency. You'll be sharing the apartment and expenses with Drenka, who is also a Malvina model. She's a little older than you, but she's working nicely and steadily. I'm quite certain you'll like her."

"I'm excited," said Jasmine, trying to ignore the mild feeling of panic in her stomach as they trudged together up the subway steps, "I promise I won't let you down."

" Of course you won't," said Malvina, giving her a hug, and they both looked down and smiled a little tearily, the deep affection they had developed for each other evident in their faces. Together, they climbed the steps of the stoop and paused outside the door. Jasmine had grown tall in the past four years, and was now taller than Malvina. She walked with a suppleness that combined the easy grace of her native background with a classic sense of style she had absorbed from her American teachers. The many dance and style classes she had attended over the past few years had taught her that her body was at her service, and she had an effortless distinctive elegance in all her movements.

Malvina fumbled with a set of keys and opened the door. She was forty-four years old and while she still walked with the assured elegance of a successful former model, she occasionally had to stop to catch her breath as she followed Jasmine's rapid ascent up the flights of stairs. She continued talking as she and Jasmine climbed the stairwell to the fourth floor. The naked bulbs dangling above their heads cast a dim yellow light on the stained stone of the stairs.

"We'll start you out with interviews with some of the smaller designers," she said, stopping to catch her breath as they climbed, "and you'll still always have a chaperone with you. But before we move you into all of that, I'll be setting you up with an important photo shoot. I want Kevin Bates to weigh in on your potential. Kevin has an ego the size of the Empire State Building, but he is the most talented and best regarded fashion photographer I know. When people see his name on your comp, they'll expect the best. You'll need to have a very fine comp sheet to take with you when you meet with the accounts I have in mind. I'm not sending you out on random cattle calls. I want you to put together a well-chosen impressive portfolio. We'll try some of the magazines, but we must get the right sort of buzz out about you to feed the media. I plan to pick and choose who sees you until we're completely ready for the big time."

Jasmine wasn't really listening. She put down her small suitcase with her clothes and few possessions and looked around as Malvina opened the door to the apartment that would be her home. The building was a dreary walk-up on the outside, fire-escapes rusting and listing, paint peeling, but inside the apartment itself, the fourth floor apartment, freshly painted, gleamed in light pouring from tall windows. She ran to a window and saw a splendid view across the river. The large living room was furnished with a cozy décor of comfortable couches, and boasted a huge television set bulging into the living room from a deep alcove carved into one white wall. To the side was a small dining area with a round oak table and four chairs with spindle backs and rust-colored seat cushions. There was an air of shabby chic about the place, comfortable and unsophisticated. She loved it immediately.

"Kitchen's over here," said Malvina, opening a louvered door in a corner of the room and grinning at Jasmine as she displayed the small efficient space. "You'll have to learn how to make your own food from now on. Take-out gets expensive now that you are spending your own money."

"Will I have my own room?" Jasmine asked hesitantly. Having her own room was her favorite thing since she had arrived in New York.

Malvina smiled. "Of course," she said, opening a door to a small room with a single bed, a small rug with bright geometric patterns beside the bed, a desk with a typewriter, and a chair. The window frames were rusty, painted over with thick white paint, and the window glass opaque, spattered with rust stains and splatter, but a soft white curtain billowed in a draft, the clunky radiator gave off comforting warmth, and a freshly ironed gingham duvet bedcover gave the space charm.

Jasmine smiled. She was still awed by the fact that the entire townhouse where Malvina and Tim lived was home to only two people. She rarely thought now of her life in Egypt, with Salwa and Sadik and the mud hut in the village teeming with babies and small children, pungent with smells of garlic and spices, the close quarters of too many people, washed clothes hanging like rags on a pole outside the door. Looking around at the room that was to be hers, she reflected that perhaps her mother had not rejected her after all. Perhaps she had had her daughter's welfare in mind all along, when she insisted on her going with a stranger across vast distances, alone and afraid, to plunge into a terrifying new life. Perhaps Salwa had somehow intuited that this world existed, this world so different from anything she had ever known. Perhaps she had wanted her daughter to have a chance at a better life than hers. The thought gave Jasmine comfort and made her smile.

"I'll be leaving now," said Malvina reluctantly, knowing full well how much she and Tim would miss Jasmine's daily presence in their lives, certainly far more than Jasmine, on the cusp of a brilliant new life, would miss them. Something about Jasmine had touched Malvina more profoundly than she had ever intended. Jasmine had become deeply embedded in her heart. She had become family. She herself had always lived on the fringes of one foster family after another. She had never known her own family, nor would she ever know anything about them, and the loss of her own daughter had devastated her. Jasmine had settled into a void in her heart that she had not even realized was there. She had welcomed Jasmine into her heart and she basked in Jasmine's affection in return. It had never happened before that her professional and personal worlds would cross so fortuitously, and she knew it would not occur again. This was the daughter destiny had given her. This was the child her heart had embraced.

"The phone's over there on the wall, if you need us," she said, watching Jasmine's pleasure in the place, adding "you'll be pleased to hear that there will be no more school. Middle school and high school are socially challenging. I know you never grew to like it there even though you did so well with your studies."

She added, "But I hope you'll think about college one day. You'll find a very different attitude there. Meanwhile, you'll be home-tutored here, between the modeling sessions. I have the paperwork all signed and approved. You'll even be able to graduate with your class when the time comes. Drenka is already a high school graduate. She should be home soon. I'm sure you'll get along." she smiled as she picked up her briefcase and turned to leave, "I'll leave the two of you to get acquainted," she said. She opened the door and stepped outside.

Jasmine ran to her. "Thank you, thank you, Malvina," she said, flinging her arms around Malvina's spare frame and hugging her, "Thank you for all you've done and all you are doing for me. I'll do my best not to disappoint you."

The door closed behind Malvina, and Jasmine was alone. She thought about what she would like to do with her earnings. College? She loved to learn new things. She had struggled with the social aspect of school, but try as hard as she did, she was never able to fit in. On the other hand she had reveled in the intellectual challenges, and she would need a new career to see her through when she was no longer the fresh new face in town. She had tried several times to see if she could send money to her village, but the bank had not been able to suggest a way of handling it, and she did not know how else to get it to her family. She had kept up with news about the political upheavals in Egypt, and the bank manager had told her that much had changed along the banks of the Nile in the past few years. He had heard that many rural families had moved away from the Nile villages. She wondered if her family had moved on to places unknown. She had not spoken Arabic in four years, but the music of the language of her childhood still echoed faintly in her heart.

She reflected that she would like to make enough money to be able to get some sort of college degree that would help her prepare for a life after modeling. She had come to view modeling as a step toward her real life as an adult, a means to an end, not the driving force that it had been for Malvina all her life. She understood that youth was a huge asset in the modeling world and youth would not last forever.

Living as a model was a make-believe life, she explained to Malvina. After college, she wanted to open herself to a life of reality. So many possibilities. Malvina and Tim had made her aware that there was little she would not be able to do if she put her mind to it. Her head full of complicated thoughts of an unknowable future, she unpacked her possessions in her bedroom, found a book, and sat down on one of the comfortable couches waiting to hear the key in the door that would herald the arrival of her apartment-mate and the beginning of a new stage of her life.

That evening, the upper East side townhouse distressingly empty without Jasmine's lively presence, Malvina put her feet up on the couch with a sigh.

"It's been an exhausting day," she exclaimed as Tim walked in, surprised to find her resting. The Michniks want us to go for dinner tomorrow night. Interested?"

"Sure," said Tim. "Love to."

He was a big fan of Irina's cooking, and he enjoyed Marcel's larger than life personality. It did not hurt that Marcel loved Tim's art and had it on his walls."

After the aborted welcome wagon attempt years earlier, they had cemented a very close friendship with the Michniks over the years. Marcel Michnik was a Russian Jew with a nose for business that was making him a considerable fortune and was propelling him into the upper echelons of New York society. His wife, Irina, salt of the earth, was resisting with all her might. She had no interest in achieving the visibility on the society pages that her husband craved. She had little patience for the niceties of polite society and the doubtful pleasures of celebrity.

Tim and Malvina had been dubious of the wisdom of the Michniks' choice when they had first bought the dilapidated brownstone three doors down from the Malvina Model Agency. But pulling himself up by his bootstraps was nothing new for Marcel. He had vision, he had tenacity, and he had Irina. Marcel had worked hard at renovating the old hulk into a princely residence, putting together motley crews of sinister looking construction workers and closely supervising all the work himself, as the ramshackle building slowly lost its down-at-heels look and began to gleam with recovered elegance. With a visionary sense of which neglected areas of the city were on the verge of change, he had expanded his experience with renovation into an immensely lucrative business, buying up run-down buildings and transforming them into hugely desirable residences. He was now desperate to continue his upward climb into the rarified circles he aspired to, and where his money was opening doors and leading the way.

During their decorating period he and Irina had visited Tim's studio and bought several of Tim's paintings. Malvina, essentially a very private person, had opened up to Irina's warmth and uncomplicated affection. She and Tim loved their new neighbors, admiringly watching them bristle with ambition as they described to their new American friends how they had radiated out from Brighton Beach daily to different neighborhoods in Manhattan in search of a dilapidated house they could afford to buy and renovate.

Enticing dinner smells greeted Malvina and Tim as the grim-faced butler Marcel had hired opened the door, took their coats, and ushered them into the large living room. Malvina walked over to the windows, to admire the beautifully landscaped garden. Tim glanced approvingly at his paintings on the walls, interspersed with a de Kooning, a Calder, a Magritte and a small Chagall. Marcel liked what he liked, and bought and displayed what he liked, any way that pleased him.

Irina had steadfastly refused to hire a cook, despite Marcel's urgings. She was a superb cook herself and could have done honor to the kitchen of any of the best restaurants in Manhattan, but she took pride and pleasure in her huge state-of-the-art basement kitchen and in Marcel's loud grunts of appreciation as he dug into her day's labor. She rose from her chair as Tim and Malvina walked in, her arms outstretched in welcome.

She and Marcel lived in a state of perpetual drama, loud and explosive, whether deep in argument or in equally extravagant gusts of laughter, but they were devoted to one another and their one sorrow was that they had not been able to have children.

"Come in, come in," she said, her face flushed from her kitchen activities, a large loose orange caftan swirling about her ample person, as Marcel ushered Tim to the bar along the side wall.

"Do you want to eat in the dining room, or shall we go to the kitchen? It's too warm really for a fire in here, don't you think?" She put an arm around Malvina's shoulders.

"Kitchen sounds great," said Malvina, ignoring the disappointed look on Marcel's face.

After dinner, they climbed the stairs to the living room. The butler reemerged with coffee and tea.

"I have an idea," Irina said quietly to Malvina as the two couples sat in comfortable couches in the large living room, the wood furniture gleaming with abundant gold ornamentation.

"Tell me I'm crrrrazy!" She rolled her r's dramatically and struck herself on the chest, "You know how Marcel pesters me day and night to go with him to this party and that gala now that his business is expanding? Well, I refuse. No way. Not for me." Irina shook her head vehemently. She was a big-boned, striking-looking woman, her dyed red hair thick around a broad face with high cheekbones, eyes the color of polished steel.

Seeing that she had Malvina's full attention, she went on "I am thinking, Malvina, you have young model in your house, the little Jasmine? She needs visibility too. What you think if she makes escort with Marcel? What you think, eh? He is like big old uncle for her? Yes? Yes? He can show her off in all the big galas and events. It can help her career too. What you think?"

She laughed loudly, punching Malvina on the shoulder to emphasize her point and winking at her husband who was deep in political conversation with Tim.

Malvina was startled and intrigued by the idea. She knew that Irina was savvy enough to have concerns about what could develop if Marcel was always alone at every major social function. Marcel was an extrovert. He had a rough bad-boy charm, and an irresistible smile, and he had amassed a considerable fortune and liked to let the world know it. Irina was well aware what that meant. She was savvy and suspicious, and while she trusted Marcel, she trusted none of the women he would be meeting at these events.

Jasmine was about to start being seen around town and she was indeed very young, and in some ways startlingly naive. She did need someone with her who could discourage the wrong sort of attention. Malvina knew that Marcel was totally devoted to his Irina and indeed had always behaved like a protective uncle to Jasmine. This could be a very smart idea for everyone. She would talk it over with Tim when they were home.

"And," confided Irina edging closer to her friend, her voice lowering several decibels, "I need your help with another matter, Malvina. who else can I ask? Listen to me. Marcel was with money manager, but the man takes his money and treats him like dirt. Do you know anyone else he could work with? I tell him he must leave the man."

Malvina thought for a moment. She sighed, thinking that she knew few people in the financial arena. Suddenly, her eyes lit up and she exclaimed, "Irina, I don't know anyone, but I actually happen to know someone who very well might. I know just the person to ask. Estelle, my contact at Cremona Lingerie was booking some of my best models yesterday for a major show they are doing in one of the department stores, and we somehow got onto the subject of how well their business was going. She raved about the woman who takes care of their accounts. She lays their success at her door, says she has multiplied their income and shown them ways of diversifying and growing the business beyond anything they had imagined. I can't remember the woman's name, but I'll call Estelle tomorrow and get the name for you."

Irina clapped her hands, delighted. "I knew you would know someone," she said, beaming.

Malvina phoned her next morning. "Estelle says her name is Eliane Mizrahi. She's a fairly recent immigrant from somewhere in the Middle East, low on the totem pole at the firm she works with, but Estelle raves about her. She says she is truly extraordinary."

CHAPTER FIFTEEN

LARA

Sol landed a demanding job in an investment company impressed by his resume and Wharton degree. He was energized by all the possibilities ahead, and by the goal of starting his own financial firm in time. He felt comfortably in charge of his life, and was actually making the time to look around him to reach out and take in more of the abundant cultural life of the city.

As usual, he was running late for a lecture he was eager to attend. He disliked wearing a watch, and had developed a breezy attitude to the boundaries and requirements of time, his eyes searching out the various city clocks as he hurried about his days. For too long, he had been too caught up in the heady world of finance he was navigating to take advantage of the many wonderful cultural events the city had to offer, but a friend had recently strongly recommended a book by the woman who was giving the lecture, and Sol, intrigued by the subject, seeing that the author was giving a series of talks based on her research, had carved out the time and signed up for the series.

The lecturer, a tall blonde with striking features and a formidable presence, had written a groundbreaking analysis of the effect of body language on important business decisions. Sol had found the subject disappointingly marginal in the opening lecture, but he was mesmerized by the statuesque sexuality of the lecturer, whose body language was having a definite effect on his decisions as to how to spend his free time. He committed to the series.

Halfway to the lecture hall he found he had forgotten his pass. He thought it must be in the library. Muttering angrily to himself as he negotiated the icy temperatures outside the protection of the building, he ran back, clouds of breath following his path.

Bounding up the steps to the library, Sol brushed past a young woman bundled to within an inch of her life against the penetrating cold. She was small, and as she clutched at the bannister to keep from falling, her backpack slid off her shoulder, so that in passing he knocked it down and it burst open and disgorged its contents. She gave a wail of distress and he turned back and apologized, helping her to collect her scattered possessions and continue into the warmth of the library building. They stood awkwardly facing each other, stamping their feet, shaking numb hands, and gradually peeling off layers of clothing. She pulled her hat off last and shook out a head of thick rust-colored hair. She tried to pat it into submission, but it seemed to have a life of its own. Her expression was angry and uncompromising.

"You should be more careful," she said, glaring at him.

"I'm so sorry," said Sol, flustered and contrite. He was about to move on, but he turned, "Can I offer you a cup of coffee to make up for it?" He reached out a hand. "My name is Sol Mizrahi, by the way."

She hesitated and then put a small hand into his. "I'm Lara," she said, "Lara Feldman. Coffee is a great idea. Is there really somewhere around here where we could go to get coffee? I'm frozen to the bone. I really need something hot to drink."

They gathered up their clothing and headed for the cafeteria. The coffee appeared to thaw more than their cold hands. Lara's tense posture relaxed and Sol found himself unexpectedly seduced by the enchanting face across the table, and the clear gaze of deep blue eyes as Lara lost her reticence and spiced the conversation with humor and warmth.

Two hours later, Lara looked at her watch and gasped. Sol stared up at the clock on the wall in amazement. They had each missed the reason they had come to the library for, in the first place, but she had learned that he hoped for a career in high finance and he had learned that she was fascinated by the study of genetics and planned to go into research. Destiny, they felt, had played a part in the moment, when it turned out that her father and his mother worked in the same financial management firm and probably knew each other.

They struggled back into the many layers of clothing that a New York winter demanded. Sol swung her heavy backpack onto his shoulder, and they walked to the subway station together, looking forward to their next encounter – a planned one this time. Sol walked home in a state of ecstasy. He knew with total certainty that this was the girl he would marry.

CHAPTER SIXTEEN

1974 New York
ELIANE AND ALDO

The years followed one another in a relentless flow. Eliane kept hoping that Aldo would find a handhold in the accelerating chaos that surrounded him. Gradually, all her hard work paid off. Her happy clients were recommending her to friends and business associates. She began to be accepted into exclusive social circles where her business acumen blended well with her dignified appearance and classy style, leading her to more and more lucrative and demanding contacts. Sol had long ago left his college room on the borders of Harlem and had settled into an attractive apartment on the upper east side. She had tried to interest Aldo in researching real estate and orchestrating a move for the two of them to a better neighborhood, but he stared at her blankly.

"Why should we move?" he asked. "Now that Solly has gone, there is plenty of room here for the two of us."

He would not involve himself in the upward climb that had begun to consume Eliane. It was no longer a matter of his resentment at her successes, the gulf that had begun to open between them in the Paris days at the Victoire spread exponentially and deepened, becoming a steep ravine that neither of them could cross. They could hardly see each other across the divide. Their voices reached each other faintly, across great distances, incomprehensible.

Year after year, Eliane moved slowly and steadily upward, and Aldo watched from the safe haven of their apartment. Now and then he took care of a few household chores, but he had stopped circling job offers in the newspaper and lost all interest in socializing or trying to keep up with friends, even with Eliane. The distance between them deepened. When Eliane once again proposed that he try to involve himself in an interesting start-up that had come to her attention, he shook her by the shoulders and shouted,

"Drop it, Eliane. Not another word. I will never try anything again. Even if you can't accept it, I have accepted that I will never work again. Face it, Eliane, we don't need the money thanks to your amazing success. Never talk to me about working again. I'm done."

A deep well of bitterness began to take over Eliane's heart. She could neither understand nor accept Aldo's defeat. She could not accept that he was unwilling to make any effort to join her in the new worlds she was exploring. She could not accept that he could not share her life with her and no longer had any intention of attempting to do so.

At last, she gave up hope that he would interest himself in bettering their lives. She hired a competent real estate agent and engineered the move on her own, but a corrosive bitterness was beginning to eat away at her heart. She liked where these

New York years had led her. She reveled in the hard won respect she had earned from colleagues and clients. Most important of all, she had at last lost the secret numbing fear that had curled hidden in her psyche since they had been expelled from their home and country, the fear she had refused to acknowledge, as she buried its fangs in work and more work.

Now, she knew she would survive, no matter what. She felt safe again at last.

As new vistas opened out for Eliane, she recognized that she needed to move more forcefully into the world that was now hers. She had matured into an elegant, attractive woman, and as her financial concerns eased and her business flourished, she began to dress with flair, discarding the image she had earlier cultivated in the firm of someone hardworking and invisible. The world of high finance she was entering demanded certainty and a compelling presence. Her colleagues admired her achievements, but more visibility made her more of a target for the mens' vulgarity and intrusive actions aimed to throw her off-balance. She was competing with hard-nosed business men whose focus was success at any price. It was war. She began to adopt some of their vocabulary and attitude as she moved deeper into the social circles of New York's elite, rubbing shoulders with every aspect of the culture, attracting attention wherever she went, as much for her presence as for her achievements. She reveled in her new-found ease and had little patience with anything that stood in her way.

Sitting at her desk in the office one day, her eyes glued to her computer screen, she sensed a presence behind her. Turning, she was startled to see a heavy-set man with twinkling eyes, his brown wool suit barely covering a substantial paunch, waving a worn, bulging briefcase at her.

"Who are you?" She asked, puzzled and somewhat disconcerted, knowing she had no appointments scheduled for the day, "What do you want?" She wondered uneasily how he had slipped past her assistant.

"I'm Marcel Michnik," said the man in a deep rich voice, a disarming smile creeping over his face. "You are Eliane Mizrahi? You will manage my money for me, yes?"

"Did you have an appointment with me?" She asked, surprised, switching off her computer and getting to her feet. He shook his head, his enthusiasm somewhat deflated.

"You can see me, yes?"

"Well, let me see if I can get us into a conference room, Mr. Michnik," said Eliane, amused at his directness and optimism, and motioning an assistant to search out an appropriate venue for conversation. Settling into one of the smaller conference rooms, she sighed. She had no idea what this man's unorthodox appearance and heavy Russian accent presaged, but she was ready to listen. He was clearly a fairly recent immigrant, and she still remembered what that felt like. She would try to be of help.

They sat down facing each other, and Marcel pulled out a sheaf of papers, placing them carefully in front of her. Elaine looked down, blinked, and looked again. She could not believe her eyes.

"What business did you say you were in, Sir?" She said, her voice wobbling.

"I am contractor-developer," said Marcel proudly, "and a woman from Carmona Lingerie she tell my wife, Irina, that you will take care of my money. Yes?" He sat back and gave her another disarming smile. Eliane stared down at the figures in front of her. The man did not seem to realize what a windfall he was offering. Here was the lucky break she had hoped might happen someday. Someday was today. She smiled at Marcel and sat back in her chair.

"Of course, I'll be happy to take care of your affairs for you," she said, "Tell me more about your business and how you would like us to proceed. And Mr. Michnik, if you have no other engagement, would you let me take you to lunch? It's almost one o'clock. I was just about to go out and grab a bite myself. Let me get my assistant to make a reservation at the Four Seasons?" She left the room.

Marcel's smile widened. He liked food, and he liked this woman. The money manager he had left had barely made time to see him at all, and had certainly never offered to take him to lunch and to explore what he wanted to do with his money. He had felt diminished by emanations of the man's disdain whenever he spoke to him. Irina had been right. He rose as Eliane returned, and they walked companionably to the elevator.

Eliane's work began to fulfill her wildest dreams as time went by. The quiet contentment of her life in Egypt had gradually been replaced by a churning excitement. The growing realization of how much she was capable of in this brash new world gave her a purpose that had been missing in her young years. A sense of excitement and possibility shone from her, and Aldo watched her move forward with amazement as the years went by. Aldo had been a well-dressed man of means in his life in Egypt, but as the years crawled past for him, he discarded anything that demanded effort, refusing to accompany his concerned wife into the social world of cultural intelligentsia and financial splendor to which she had aspired, at first from need and then from a growing addiction to the heady atmosphere it provided. They continued to grow further and further apart. Eliane stepped with grace and agility into everything her new role demanded of her, focusing her energies outward, finding challenge and satisfaction in her work.

Eventually, she stopped asking Aldo's opinion. She no longer felt sorry for him. She forged deeper and deeper into the opportunities and demands that stretched before her, less and less willing to reach back and find Aldo's hand to lead him along the path with her. Aldo had gone from being a disappointment to being an encumbrance she could no longer tolerate. Her heart sank whenever she caught sight of his lugubrious face, so incongruous in the glittering life she had carefully created around herself. The handsome debonair *bon vivant* she had fallen in love with had vanished. In his place, a tired graying old man shuffled, often unshaven, always gloomy.

He insisted on wearing threadbare suits, claiming that they could not afford new clothes. He no longer read the newspaper in the mornings or circled the job entries. He no longer made any effort to accompany her into the social life she was leading. His conversation had dwindled to commonalities. Eliane suspected that he was sinking into a depression, but he refused to get help.

"Let me be," he muttered, "Eliane, what do you want of me? You have everything you want, everything you need. Let me be."

She was dressing to go to a gala at the Pierre. He watched her, his eyes sad.

"What charity are you supporting this time?" he asked list-lessly, pulling his old silk robe more closely around his shoulders. It had faded with the years, and gathered some stains that refused to come out. Sometimes he felt that it was a metaphor for his life. The life he had once lived and loved was faded and stained, useless to anyone except himself.

Eliane stared at him. She wanted to believe that there was still time to salvage their marriage. She wanted to believe that in the husk of the man she had married, there still existed some vestige of the man she had loved with all her heart.

"Won't you change into your tux and come with me?" She asked suddenly. She looked at him hopefully, but when he failed to respond she realized that her heart was not in it. She realized that she no longer wanted to have to worry about his clothes, his lack of conversation, his lack of effort to walk beside her along the path her life had taken. It had been a long road to this point, but Eliane recognized it for what it was. She suddenly knew that she could no longer tolerate a situation that had no upside, that merely continued to slide downhill at every turn in the road.

Aldo did not even bother to answer. He shrugged, and turned away heading for the couch, clutching the old burgundy silk robe. Eliane felt all the suppressed rage of the past few years rise in her and spill away, leaving only emptiness and a huge sense of relief. She knew what she had to do. She turned toward Aldo.

"I'm asking you to leave," she said, her breath catching in her throat as the harsh words fell from her lips. She was standing in their bedroom, in the sumptuous white and steel environment she had created at great expense in their new Fifth Avenue condo. A rare white Steinway gleamed in a corner of the living room, although she found little time to play her Chopin waltzes any more.

Every day, Eliane glanced about her with intense satisfaction. She had worked hard and she had found her footing and her calling in the challenging world of New York's financial circles so often dominated by men. This dazzling apartment in the heart of Manhattan was her reward. It was all hers. It reflected back to her the new life she had created since her arrival in New York. It could not have been further from the seasoned traditional mansion she had left behind in Egypt. Her life could not have been more different from the leisurely life she had enjoyed there. To her own surprise, she had come vibrantly alive in New York City, feeding off the energy around her, reveling in the skills and intuition that fueled her success. She missed nothing of her past. All she had taken with her from her gracious home in Egypt besides her music, was an ornate gold frame containing the portrait of her grandmother, whose Victorian taste for beautiful antiques and elaborate settings had created the surroundings of her youth.

She registered the lack of response from her husband, and looked up, exasperated.

"Don't you understand?" she said at last, despair in her voice. "I've truly had enough, Aldo. I've tried to help in every way I could. I've tried to understand what has happened to you, what has happened between us, but you're not the man I married, the man I loved for so many years. You're so profoundly changed. We have both so profoundly changed. The loss of the life we had in Egypt has made you lose your deepest self. I realize that we are still suffering from the trauma of having had to leave everything we knew overnight, everything we felt we had belonged to for generations, everything that gave texture and context to our lives. I recognize that for some reason it has been harder for you than it has been for me. I'm sorry it had to be this way for you, but I truly don't know who you are anymore." A hint of bitterness seeped through her tone.

Aldo still stared at her without saying a word.

She continued with a sudden flare of real anger. " Let's come to terms with the reality we live. I am saddened, of course, to have to put this into words, and to have to acknowledge that our marriage has come to an end. I know Solly will not take it well, but I suspect that it will not come as a complete surprise to him. He knows how far we have drifted from each other and from our old life. Thankfully, he's fully launched in his own life, and his ship is sailing to safe harbor."

Aldo opened his mouth to interrupt, but she went on, speeding into the uncomfortable void, her voice rising, "The establishment of his own financial management firm last year has moved him clearly into his own space. He, at least, knows how to work and how to make the best of everything this country has to offer. He and Lara Feldman are talking of living together now, Aldo, did you know?" She glanced anxiously at her watch, pulled out a tissue and peered into the mirror, wiping a hint of lipstick off her teeth. Turning back to Aldo, she added,

"Yes, I know, not what we were used to. In our day, marriage came first. But none of us are who we once were. This is how the young people go about it these days. I feel certain that marriage will follow, and I could not be happier with his choice. I know you like her, too."

She paused and continued more quietly, "it's a good thing our parents are not alive to see us separate, but I think you will agree that we can no longer live together. We are no longer living together on any level of our lives. There's truly nothing left between you and me, Aldo, except Solly, and our memories of a world we thought was ours forever, a world that no longer exists."

She waited for him to respond and when he kept silent, she went on, pain and bitterness clouding her voice, "you have decided to drown in those memories, but while you were drowning, I found us a raft. Only you let it slip through your fingers and the waters closed over your head. I have finally come to realize and accept that I am alone on the raft."

She waited for Aldo to speak, and when he remained silent she continued, "We never talk. We share the same bed, but we never touch, we never make love. I try to involve you in decisions about our life here, about our home, about our future, but you don't seem to care about any of it. I can no longer go on this way. I need to feel free of the bitterness of the past and free of the sadness and encumbrance of our failed marriage."

Her voice was shaking as she added, "I will always love you for the Aldo you were, but that man is no more than a memory now. It is no longer my reality. There is no longer anywhere that we come together, and no - there's no other man. I don't need any man." She sighed and turned to leave the room. "I have learned at last how to stand on my own two feet," she said. Eliane's eyes teared. She shrugged, and left the room.

He watched her slight figure, elegant in a pearl-colored Armani suit, her greying hair short and sculpted to her head. Dove gray shoes perched on high slim heels, the soles edged with a thin red line, took her on her way with clipped staccato accompaniment. He thought back to the sumptuous harmonies of the Chopin waltzes she had once so loved to play, and a bitter smile curled his lips. His voice came to her faintly as she headed for the door, "You have grown so hard, Eliane. I am not the only one who has changed."

Aldo was far from surprised. He had been expecting this as the months went by and he watched Eliane stepping into heady financial circles in New York City with grace and ease, leading the way for Sol to find footing in this new world their exile had forced upon them. He knew she was right. She did not need him any more. She was indeed standing very firmly on her own two feet. The huge Michnik account had established her as a significant mover and shaker in financial circles. Others had followed and opened the way for her to become more and more in demand, more and more the celebrated rainmaker of her firm. Cristina Falti, finding herself outclassed, had stalked out of the office one day and left for a rival firm, taking her clients with her. Her departure left Eliane to settle into her position as the only reigning woman in the firm, and together with Leon Feldman and two younger partners, she now ran the company. It was as if her growing empowerment drained whatever energy his battered spirit still held. Little was left of the gentle musician he had fallen in love with so many years ago, the woman who sat placidly beside him in the evenings, creating beauty with tiny delicate stitches, the woman whose world had revolved around him and their small boy. His parents and hers had rejoiced in their marriage, and he had loved living in the gracious mansion her grandmother had deeded to them as a wedding gift. That was a home. This New York apartment was a stage-set to celebrate

Eliane's dominance over the world around her. He would not mind leaving it.

Work, to Aldo, had always translated into an enjoyable round of social meetings sweetened with cups of rich Turkish coffee, surrounded by impeccable service and every luxury. Beyond work, in Egypt he came home every day to a wife he loved who ran a beautiful home seamlessly, diligently practiced her piano all morning, and lived for his daily return to the comfortable social life that surrounded them both. Money was always there. It did not have to be made.

He was gradually coming to the realization that he had slipped so smoothly into the position his father had vacated because the seat awaiting him had already been broken in. There was little need for effort or innovation. He merely had to follow paths laid out by others. He had taken respect and acceptance from those around him as his due until now, when it had become obvious to him that it had all come to him not because of any particular skill of his, not because of what he did, but because of who he was within a known context. He was respected as his father had been, because he was his father's son. He reflected, with clear-eyed sadness, that his father had also flown on the wings of his father before him. Neither he nor his father had inherited any of his grandfather's entrepreneurial spirit. They had inherited what he had built and had kept it afloat with a minimum of effort. Cast into a different world, he had lost his anchor and was drifting untethered in a vast ocean of the unknown, no land in sight.

Without the trappings of a secure life, he realized that he could not function. Old friends had found new lives and new energy in themselves in order to build something for their families in this new brash world of the Americas. They reveled in the challenge. They stood taller, spoke louder, and plunged with vigor into new experiences. He had found nothing in himself but despair. The exile from Egypt had galvanized Eliane to discover a much richer self, but it had reduced Aldo to an ineffectual shadow. This ending had been a long time coming.

He moved to his closet without a word, and took down a suitcase.

CHAPTER SEVENTEEN

1974 New York A Lunch
SOL AND ELIANE

Sol wondered why his mother had requested his presence at her favorite restaurant for lunch. She rarely had time for him these days. Since their dreary arrival in New York fourteen years earlier, he had watched her transformation from gentle mouse to roaring lion with amazement and growing pride. He understood that she alone had held them afloat through sheer strength of will after the expulsion from Egypt, and even though he missed the mother who had always had time to listen to his concerns and tease him out of them, the formidable business woman she had become had earned his gratitude and admiration. By her example, she had given him permission to move past the trauma of their losses and recreate himself in this new world, as she had.

He loved his father, but despaired of galvanizing him into any sort of action. He knew that Aldo was proud of his son's achievements, but they found less and less to talk about as the years went by, and the gulf between them widened as Aldo continued to abdicate from serious interaction with the world around him.

Sol sat down at the table and noted with pride that Eliane looked the very essence of sophistication. She had aged well, he thought, she had navigated the years with dignity.

"Hello, Maman," he said, leaning over to kiss her on both cheeks. He noticed that she was not smiling. "It's not your birthday, or mine. What warrants this break in routine?" She rewarded his effort at humor with a reluctant smile.

When they were sitting companionably with coffee and desserts, she leaned toward him.

"Solly," she said, "this will not surprise you, but Papi and I have decided to live separately from now on. I found him a good studio nearby, with a spectacular view, and he has moved in. I arranged for Carmen to go in to clean for him once a week. He seems to have settled in very comfortably." She smiled sadly. "He has his burgundy silk robe and his Turkish coffee. He spends his days reading and listening to the radio, and his evenings asleep in front of the television, and time passes." She sighed.

Sol nodded. He had been expecting something like this for some time. He knew his father had never been comfortable with the aggressively stylish new apartment Eliane had moved them into. His mother handed him a card with his father's new address. She seemed anxious, and a little hesitant. He had not seen her like that for some years.

"Is there something more the matter? What is it?" He asked.

"I would like you to check in on him as often as you can," she said at last, her expression bleak. "There is a health problem that he refuses to discuss with me. I know he saw the doctor and has been having tests, Carmen let it slip last time I saw her, but he brushes me off when I try to find out more. He may be more forthcoming with you. I am concerned. He never willingly consulted doctors. There must be something serious. He is not well."

Sol felt a rise of anger fueled by panic. He pushed his plate away and stood up. "I'll go over this weekend," he said, glaring at his mother. "Poor Papi, alone and sick. Why didn't you tell me all this sooner? Why wouldn't he tell you?"

Eliane studied a crease in the tablecloth. At last, she raised eyes clouded with pain. "There is much between us that you will never understand," she said at last. "Marriage is complicated, some more so than others. We still have love for each other, but we can no longer trust that the other understands and reflects our individual needs and fears. The expulsion from Egypt shaped us into puzzle pieces that no longer fit together. He will talk to you as he no longer talks to me. I will have to count on you to let me know what you discover. I do still love your father, but I can no longer carry the burden of his pain. It will sink me too. I so wish things could have been different."

"I promise," said Sol, sad to realize that at the very moment when he was moving into a joyous vision of love and marriage, his parents had accepted that their own marriage had irretrievably disintegrated in the churning waters of disempowerment and exile that had begun with the traumatic expulsion from the country of their birth. He hugged his mother and stood up.

"I'll go over to Papi right away, I won't wait for the weekend," he said, "and I'll let you know what I find out."

She smiled, and sighed.

They left the table together, stood silently outside the restaurant a moment, hugged and kissed, and went their separate ways.

Some months later, Sol and Lara met again outside the library doors on a bright clear spring day. They had taken to meeting there regularly once a week, to plan her move into his apartment. Their engagement was now official, and there were wedding plans to consider. She had earned her PhD and was starting her work as a researcher in genetics. She was filled with buoyant excitement about her work.

"Do you realize how much my work could make a difference?" She said, hugging herself, jumping up and down and breathing in the spring air. "I mean, your work makes a difference to the lives of the people you help with their financial needs, of course, but my work could actually shape the future of humanity." She grinned at him.

"OK, Einstein," said Sol, smiling back. He loved her enthusiasm, her integrity and intelligence. He could hardly believe his luck in having found this exceptional person with whom to share his life. They hurried to the cafeteria where they had first met, and pulled out notebooks.

"Let's get this show on the road, then," said Sol leaning over to kiss her. "What part of our wedding are we planning today?"

"Actually, I was wondering how your father is doing?" Lara said. "He seemed pleased when we announced our engagement, but he looked so sad when we told him the wedding date we had in mind. I wish we could have the wedding sooner. I think he is afraid he won't be able to make it."

"You know it's not possible to change that date," said Sol, his exuberance dimmed. "It was so hard to find a date that worked for everything and everyone, I don't want us to start out with a huge debt, and we need the time to get things organized. Everything seems to take such a long time. It was so hard to find the right date in the first place. Reserving the reception hall, the caterer and the synagogue for the same day was more of a challenge than anything I face at work." He laughed.

Then his face turned serious. "The doctor seems to say that the chemo is working well, and that he should have many years ahead of him, but I do know what you mean. He doesn't look well at all. He seems to be slipping quietly out of all demands of life. The world he inhabits now is a monotone gray world, and even your charm," he held her hand to his lips, kissed it, and smiled at her, "isn't enough to pull him out of it into the light."

They were silent a while, and then turned to their wedding lists and the more manageable exigencies of their calendars and their world.

CHAPTER EIGHTEEN

1975 New York
JASMINE, COMING INTO HER OWN

Jasmine was uncharacteristically nervous as she made her way to the day's photo shoot. She knew that Kevin Bates was the photographer who could make or break a career. This was her big test. Malvina had told her so in no uncertain terms.

She let him move her this way and that until he was satisfied with the angle of the shot. She was wearing a black gauzy caftan shot through with silver thread, the cleavage plunging down to her navel so that the ripe mounds of her breasts showed almost to the nipple. A slight breeze rippled the light material, molding her body beneath. Her eyes slanted at a sexy angle, glowing green as if from an inner light, and her full mouth pouted, covering teeth Malvina had paid to have expertly capped and whitened. The pout had developed from years of hiding the bad dentistry of her childhood, and she was unaware of how provocative it made her look. She was desperately tired and her back ached, but she kept her pose until he had finished with her. She had learned well, she had been standing immobile in her pose for quite some time. The ache in her muscles began to flood her consciousness.

"Can I go now?" She asked at last,

"Yes, yes!" Kevin said impatiently, "Tell Malvina it went really well and I'll be sending the report and the sheets to her as agreed." He turned away abruptly, swiveled back, and added "It's all good, but we may want you back for a few more shots."

Jasmine dressed slowly, her dark skin flushed from the heat in the tiny cubicle tucked behind the landscaped garden setting they had used for the photo shoot. Little Jamila with her crooked teeth and timid smile crouched in a corner of her mind, invisible to the world. She wondered, not for the first time, why Malvina had insisted on changing her name to Jasmine. She was Jasmine now and forever, her real name lost behind a barrage of lights and fancy clothes.

Kevin pushed aside the drape and thrust his head into the cubicle. "Malvina wants you in her office right away," he said, and disappeared.

Back at the Malvina townhouse Malvina was busy at her desk in the basement office, wielding two phones and sorting through a pile of papers at the same time. Two other bookers, Monica and Claire, sat at desks behind her, talking spiritedly into phones, laughing, miming despair at each other as they negotiated and exuded charm into the phone, shuffling shots and comps on their desks as the deals took shape.

Three young women auditioning with the agency that day wilted despondently in the waiting room and stared enviously as Jasmine passed them. Malvina peered at Jasmine over the rims of her half-moon reading glasses.

"Ah, here you are!" She said, smiling with satisfaction, "They do want you back. I knew they would, but Kevin wants us to pay some attention to that rear end of yours. It has a sexy swing when you're walking, he says, but you need some reduction there, for the best runway modeling. I'll talk to Carlos about some targeted exercising."

Jasmine flushed and looked at her feet. She loved Malvina, but she was spare and angular with a bony nose and no rear end to speak of. Her age was starting to show, and what had once been a rounded smooth slimness was slowly cascading into a gaunt look honeycombed with very fine lines. Did they want her to look like that? She was aware that she looked very different from many of the other models she had met. She had not yet decided if that was an asset or a disadvantage. She was starting to understand that she could not conform, and therefore must try to leverage her differences into something desirable.

"Did you find the photo shoot difficult?" Asked Malvina, unaware of where Jasmine's thoughts had been taking her.

"Not at all," said Jasmine, "Although I do feel tired now. My muscles ache. If you have nothing else set up for me this afternoon, I think I'll go back to the apartment and lie down."

Malvina peered at her. "You're looking a little down at the mouth," she said, concerned, "anything wrong?"

Jasmine shook her head and smiled. "Just tired," she said.

Malvina and Tim had been so good to her. She had no intention of mentioning that of late, flashbacks to her childhood, her family, and the sunny little village by the Nile had begun to creep into vacant moments when she least expected it, a strange counterpoint to the world of sophistication and celebrity she was entering.

She left the townhouse and headed for the subway, her thoughts in a jumble. Confused images of Ali, and of her parents, Salwa and Sadik, threaded in and out of thoughts of Kevin and the beautiful gown she had worn for the photo shoot. The floating fabric of the gown had reminded her of the beautiful floating shirt that had so caught her attention the first time that Malvina had arrived at the village by the Nile.

The intriguing possibilities developing in her modeling career receded into the background as she tried, yet again, to summon up the face of her brother, Ali. She wondered how he was getting along without her help. He had been a smooth-faced wide-eyed boy of eleven when she went away. He must be bearded now, she thought, and he must be even taller. She tried to construct a new image of him in her mind, but she could not conjure up any image at all, although she thought she heard his voice, deeper now, calling her name, calling for Jamila. She missed having him to talk to. She missed being able to tell him about all the extraordinary things that had come to pass for her since the day she left the village in the taxi with Malvina. Would he understand any of it, she wondered? Would he have changed? They had been so close. What had become of him? If only she could think of a way of letting him know that she was happy in her new life. There was no way she could reach any of them. They couldn't read, so she couldn't write to them, the village had no telephone accessibility, so there was no way to hear their voices.

She had kept her memories of the Nile village locked away her first few years in America, as she raced through the days, trying to learn everything, striving with every fiber of her being to fit in. Now that she had more of a foothold on the life she had been plunged into, a little more time to reflect, she realized that her past was lost to her forever, hidden behind a barrier she could not scale. The small babies tumbling about the mud hut must be big children now. They would not remember their oldest sister.

She peered at her reflection in a grimy shop window as she walked past; small tanned face, high cheekbones, slanty green eyes, a full mouth, and an untamed head of dark hair like a halo. Could she really be considered beautiful? Bad food and unforgiving elements usually left the women of the Nile with pitted complexions, but here in America, she had skin as smooth as tawny silk. Why was she suddenly thinking these thoughts? Why did her heart hurt?

She blinked away tears through long lashes and started down the subway steps. She was no longer Jamila. She was Jasmine, an American girl. Her mother had not wanted her to stay in Egypt. Her mother had pushed her away, closed her out of her life and her heart. She would not think about the past. She would make her way through the present with her heart firmly focused on the future.

She had no way of knowing that Salwa had come across a discarded Vogue magazine half buried in mud, with a cover photo of Jasmine standing on some steps in a landscaped area, among a handful of other young rising stars of the fashion world. Salwa had made sure that no-one was watching, and then in one swift motion she picked it up and hid it under her *abaya*. She had carried it home and lovingly washed it and dried it out in the sun. She kept it under her thin mattress, where she could feel it and hear the soft crackle of the pages as she lay awake at night, imagining her daughter close. It was nightly evidence that her painful decision had been the right one. She could see that Jamila had grown and become very beautiful, and that she had found a good life with the American woman. She looked happy. It had been worth the agonizing decision to push her away.

Unaware of her mother's thoughts and loving sacrifice, Jasmine skipped down the steps to the subway, her mind filled with the clatter, the grime and rumble of New York as she sank into a vacant seat, looking forward to sharing her recent experience with Drenka.

Upstairs in the apartment on Third Avenue, Drenka had her arms full of laundry. The machine was in the basement, and they took the laundry and cooking chores in turns every week. She looked up when she heard Jasmine's key in the door, and opened her arms dramatically, turning herself into a giant question mark and dropping the laundry on the floor.

"Weeeeeeelllllllllllll?" she said, her head with its silky red mane cocked engagingly to one side. "How was it, Jas?"

"Fine," said Jasmine, her gloom lifting, "And how was your interview for the nail polish commercial?"

"Didn't get it," said Drenka ruefully, tossing her head, "They said my fingers weren't slim or long enough." She sighed, examining her hands anxiously. "But you know what," she added with a wide grin, glancing up at her tall friend, "the guy who set up the interview was super hot. I slipped him our phone number when no-one was looking and he winked at me. He had the craziest black eyes." She paused and added "I think he'll call."

Jasmine giggled.

The young women had become an excellent support system for each other as they moved gingerly through the choppy waters of the modeling world. Men lusted after their youth and innocence, irresistibly drawn in by the magnetism of their beauty and rising celebrity. They were each making a steady income, and the pressures that attended their daily lives were hard to manage. Drugs and sex beckoned to them from every corner, but Malvina's iron clad rules followed them in every facet of their lives. She was like a stern and demanding parent, making sure they were trailed everywhere by the chaperones imposed on them by the Malvina agency. She was well aware that the sheltered circumstances of their lives before modeling gave them few tools with which to navigate the urgent call of their nascent sexuality and the heady environments their modeling career exposed them to every day.

Deeply conscious of her responsibility to shape young lives, Malvina had warned them to be wary, that their looks and their profession might pull them into shady waters, where promises of instant glory could bring about ruin. "Men prey on girls like you," she said darkly, "which is why you will go nowhere without your chaperone. Listen to me, girls! Many a promising career has fallen by the wayside into porn and prostitution because a girl was too adventurous or too trusting. That is why you have us. Keep your focus on the work, and I promise you will have fun, make money, and become a celebrity besides." The girls had giggled and nodded obediently.

CHAPTER NINETEEN

1975 New York
SOL'S WEDDING

Despite their initial efforts to keep things modest, Sol's wedding was a grand affair. Eliane had developed an impressive roster of deep pocket clients, many of whom had also become friends. Lara was passionately interested in her genetic research and was already on her way to making a name for herself in the scientific community. She was also an elegant young woman with a sunny disposition, and Eliane's pride and delight knew no bounds. This resplendent life moment brought tears to her eyes, as she stood beside her tall son and his petite bride, beaming at the crowd of fashionably dressed guests swirling around them, the women, every now and then, honing in with shrieks of delight to plant an obligatory air-kiss on her cheek.

The service was held at Temple Emmanuel in Manhattan, the *chuppah* and temple awash in a cascading abundance of dazzling white flowers. For a moment she felt a stab at her heart, wishing that Aldo could have been beside her under the *chuppah* witnessing their handsome son's marriage, the Aldo she had married, the man she had loved with all her heart. But the moment passed as she stood regally in the receiving line beside her son in the grand ballroom at the Pierre Hotel, greeting their guests as they arrived. A sumptuous buffet was spread across the room behind them, and a small table stood to one side with an exquisite wedding cake, delicate wreaths of tiny sugar roses climbing up layer upon layer of glistening white icing to end in an extravagant display of spun-sugar flowers, leaves and tendrils twisting their way downward. Eliane reflected that she had been right to leave so much of the arrangements to Lara and her mother. They both had excellent taste.

She watched the guests as they circled past her, her gaze settling on a tall young woman, her face turned away, gliding by on the arm of a balding man, his paunch visibly straining at his well-cut suit. Eliane was pleased and gratified to see that her friend and most valued client, Marcel Michnik, had made it to her son's wedding. He turned his head, smiled, and bowed to her with old-world charm, and she smiled back. The woman he was with was clearly very young and extraordinarily beautiful. Heads turned as she sailed past, seemingly oblivious to the stir she was creating, although the gleam in the eye of her escort made it clear that he was not. She reached out to take a glass of champagne from the tray of a passing waiter. She was wearing a Halston original, Eliane noticed at once, diaphanous dark green silk caught up by a gold braided rope at the waist and shot through with gold thread. It glinted in the light as she walked past. She looked electric, iridescent. She glanced up as she passed and Eliane was instantly captivated by the flash of brilliant green eyes framed by thick dark lashes.

Beside Eliane, Sol turned to see what she was looking at, and was immediately distracted by the emerald ring on the young woman's finger as she took the champagne glass from the tray. Having himself so recently shopped gemstones for Lara's engagement ring, he was intrigued. This stone was a deep color, not very big, but obviously of a very fine quality. He had wanted an emerald for Lara, but she had preferred a square sapphire between two small round diamonds.

"Who is that?" he asked his mother, pointing to the young woman, "Isn't she with your Marcel Michnik? She has the kind of ring I was originally looking at for Lara."

"Yes," said Eliane, "I just noticed her too. She's one of the up and coming young models of the day. I think her name is Jasmine. Unusual looking, isn't she? That's a Halston original she's wearing. Quite the woman of mystery, so young, and so hot. No-one knows where she sprang from, but she is suddenly everywhere, in ads, on the cover of Vogue, and every other major woman's magazine, and on the runways. She has instantly become the model of the hour, the one everyone wants to hire to endorse their highest styles."

She laughed ruefully, and added, "A client of mine lost out recently when he tried to get her for his luxury line of lingerie. I understand she comes with a mighty price tag. I've met her before. I was introduced to her at the Met gala. I don't know her well, but it's great that she's here, because where she goes, the *paparazzi* follow. Thanks to her, your wedding will probably be featured in all the major newspapers tomorrow with a photo of her and her escort. Marcel's wife, Irina, never accompanies him to social events. I'm very fond of him. He's a little rough around the edges, but a really nice guy. It's thanks to his great success that my portfolio became what it is, and led to my current position in the firm."

Eliane turned her attention to the hugs and congratulations that continued to flow into the hall. Turning back to Sol, she added "Marcel's originally from Russia, you know. Unbelievably wealthy – by the way, I hear the girl with him is a lot more than the usual arm candy for a billionaire to bring to a party. They say she's very intelligent." Her gaze followed the couple as they moved about the room.

"Incidentally" she said, turning again to her son, " did you notice her eyes? They're exactly the color of that emerald you liked. The only other person I have ever seen with eyes like that was my grandmother, Elena. Do you remember her? You were such a little boy when she died." A brief shadow crossed Eliane's face as she thought of her young days, her grandmother, her wedding to Aldo, the life they had lived and lost in Egypt. She wondered what her grandmother would have thought of the paths she had taken. A sudden wave of nostalgia flooded her, eclipsing her joy in the moment and bringing unexpected tears to her eyes. So much had been lost. But she instantly reminded herself that so much had been found.

Sol's attention had already shifted to Zaki and Pam who had flown in from Paris for the wedding and had just entered the crowded ballroom. Pam was nervously fussing with her hair and the folds of her delicate chiffon dress, looking overwhelmed, when Zaki caught sight of Sol. He pulled her into the room and they hurried over to envelop Sol in their exuberant delight.

"Sad about your father," said Zaki, his smile turning to concern. "I wish he could have been here to see you married, and to the lovely Lara. He should have been a part of this beautiful wedding. It would have meant so much to him. He was always so proud of you."

Sol shifted awkwardly. He fought the lump in his throat. "I so wish he could have been here," he said at last, "I do miss him. He was never the same after our months at the Victoire." He paused and took out a handkerchief to wipe his eyes. "Maman and I were with him to the end," he said, his voice catching in his throat. He looked down at Zaki's kind face that reminded him so much of his father.

He said, "They really loved each other, you know. But the year at the Victoire set them on widely differing paths. Papi could neither understand nor adapt, while Maman pushed herself into becoming a hard-nosed businesswoman. She made herself into an image that spelled success to this new world she was living in, and she grew to love the life she created. Took to it like a duck to water."

He blinked away tears. "When Papi died, we thought of postponing the wedding, but the rabbis insisted that once the year of mourning was past, we must not change the date we originally set, and that we could and should have music and dancing. They told us weddings and joyous occasions should never be postponed. It's been good for Maman, too, helping us to plan everything. Papi's death hit her much harder than I would have anticipated." He paused and looked around. "Lara has been the most wonderful support through it all," he said, "I am so happy that you and Pam will finally get to meet her."

He added quietly, "We made sure that Papi had the very best medical care and that he was not in pain. That was all we could do. When we knew what he was facing, we never left him. I'm sure the cancer that took him was brought on by the stress of leaving Egypt. Of course I know that the doctors don't believe in that sort of thing..." He paused and added in a low voice, "He didn't even try to fight it, you know. He didn't want to live." His voice faltered.

Zaki nodded, tears in his eyes. "You're a good son, Solly," he said. "I feel so bad about it. I tried so hard to suggest contacts and work that would be appropriate for him, but it was as if he was being sucked under by quicksand from the moment he left Egypt, until the Aldo I grew up with disappeared completely. He just couldn't adjust."

"I know," said Sol. "It wasn't your fault."

The band had begun a spirited hora, guests were making their way to the dance floor from all corners of the room, arms outstretched, to clasp each other and form a whirling circle of joy and motion. Lara came running across the room to Sol, her dress floating like a cloud behind her. She grabbed his hand, laughing, her face aglow with happiness.

"Come on!" She said, "They're going to want to lift us up on chairs soon and bounce us around. Look at all the young men gathering on the dance floor with shifty expressions. Mother's hiding. She said she wouldn't do it, and swore they'd never find her." She giggled as she pulled him along, "It's an old Jewish custom, you know. I think it dates way back to the handkerchief bridal dance in the Polish *shtetls*. The bride and groom were each given one end of a handkerchief to hold and were carried on chairs like royalty, and danced above the heads of the hoi poloi. King and queen of the moment. I think that's the origin of the custom. I know it wasn't the custom in Egypt, Eliane told me." She grinned invitingly, her eyes sparkling with joy, her wedding dress filmy as angel wings around her tiny person. "Come on, Let's do it!"

Sol followed her to the dance floor, a slightly sheepish expression on his face as he looked back at Zaki.

CHAPTER TWENTY

1975 New York
FAME

Malvina's phone rang and she grabbed the receiver, intrigued to learn that Lois Moffat was on the line.

"Malvina, haven't spoken in a while," said Lois, " I'm interested in that exotic young model you have there. I was just talking to Kevin Bates and he tells me Jasmine is exactly the fresh talent and sexy elegance I need for my big spring issue. He says she will be an immediate contrast to all the extreme youth that flirts with us from every magazine fashion section." Lois waited, but Malvina stayed silent.

"How old is she?" Lois asked, "Eighteen? Twenty? Time to develop polish and still have looks, and I hear that her looks and style are exotic and exceptional. I have Brad under contract for the photography, Olga for makeup. Can I tempt you? When can you bring her in? I promise you, the clothes are drop dead gorgeous. You'll love them. She'll love them."

Malvina took a deep breath and prepared to respond when Lois added

"Please be a love, send her in tomorrow, and name your price."

Malvina let out her breath. She had not realized she had been holding it.

"I'll bring her in myself, tomorrow," she said, "what time did you want her?"

And just like that, Jasmine burst on the world of high fashion. Her magnificent eyes were the talk of the town. Young girls everywhere teased their hair and tried to achieve the halo effect that was Jasmine's signature. She was twenty years old, dramatic and elegant, poised and professional, and to the amazement of a culture dazzled by baby faces and wraithlike youth, she took the world of New York fashionistas by storm.

"I always knew she had it in her," Malvina confided to Tim that night. "I just wasn't sure I could pull off my part in the scenario. I didn't want to rush it. I wanted to be sure that she was on steady ground, and I wanted to be sure that she wanted it. I have never had a call like that from Lois. I couldn't breathe. I was just happy that I could get words out to agree."

Tim laughed, happy to see his normally controlled wife almost giddy with excitement. "Well done, Malvina," he said, "The combination of you and Jasmine is unbeatable. I hope you both enjoy every minute of this. You both deserve it. Jasmine is remarkably clear-eyed about the ephemeral nature of it all. She constantly surprises me with her down-to-earth common sense. She knows that the media feeds on youth, and youth does not last forever. She and I have talked about this. She likes the work, and she likes to succeed, but she has other plans for the future. She has an extraordinarily pragmatic view of it all."

Jasmine was an instant hit at the magazine. Used to the prima donna type, they appreciated her understated professionalism, and the way she studied the clothes, poses, and backdrops, and then gave the concept an individual twist that put it over the top. She was a delight to work with. She was thrilled with the assignment and she watched in astonishment as the fallout from the big spring issue vaulted her into more and more prestigious venues. She was working every day, and every day she dazzled herself and everyone around her. It was her moment. When Versace approached Malvina to request Jasmine exclusively as his top model, Malvina knew she had realized the plan that had flashed through her mind years earlier, in a remote Nile village. Captivated by the haunting intensity of glittering green eyes at a slant in a small brown face with high cheekbones, and the enchanting personality of a girl on the cusp of womanhood, she had found a daughter, and she had helped her to the pinnacle of success. This was as good as it would ever get.

"Another two years like this, and I'll be able to quit modeling altogether and use that college degree," Jasmine told her with glee. "It was so hard to work at it between bookings, and until I can use it, it's just a piece of paper."

"You might miss the celebrity," Malvina said, somewhat wistfully, "but the world is yours to claim. You've earned your place in the sun. I am so proud of you," and she took Jasmine in her arms and hugged her.

Jasmine continued her conquest of the world of high fashion. She disliked clubbing in general, but her work demanded that she be a part of the New York scene, and she visited Studio 54 two or three times a week in the company of friends or on the arm of Marcel, showing off sumptuous clothes she had presented on the runways. With adept grace, she side-stepped the allure of bountiful free alcohol and the menace of a pervasive drug presence in the feverish drug culture that surrounded her, and she kept her wits about her.

"Make way, out of the way," the bouncers declared night after night to the disappointed lines of hopefuls, pushing, shoving at the door, and turning to usher her in like royalty to the groans and cries from those still waiting in line.

She never bought in to the club culture, but she loved to dance. She was a fiery dancer, flinging her arms and legs about with abandon, eyes ablaze with pleasure, her head thrown back, and her hair like a crown. It was precisely the difference between her public and private selves that gave her the aura of mystery that the public found irresistible. Her presence added *cachet* to any club. Designers vied with each other to offer her clothes to wear to the events she attended. Jewelers were happy to lend her their best pieces to match the glow in her green eyes. Magazines wrote feature articles about her and about the Malvina agency, and TV hosts vied for the privilege of interviewing her on their shows. She had made it to the big time. Everyone knew her name. Everyone sought her presence and wangled her participation in gala events and fashion extravaganzas.

Malvina's careful curation of all things Jasmine at first succeeded in fielding the rabid attention of the press, focussing their interest on her unusual looks and her soaring success, her astounding green eyes and quiet elegance, rather than more personal matters. But the spring fashion edition that signaled her exotic appearance to an international public avid for new fodder for the gossip mills confirmed her celebrity and flushed out a whole new flock of *paparazzi* flashing bulbs at her and hurling questions about her love life, her childhood, the exotic origins of her unusual beauty, and her relationship with the Malvina agency.

Jasmine was careful to stay on message. Malvina, she said, again and again, was known for scouting out her models at a young age. She had taken a trip to the Middle East some years ago, and had found a barefoot girl in a remote village and brought her back to the States, where she had introduced her to the magnificent opportunities possible in America, had guided her studies and her life as a model, and had helped her to fame and fortune. Jasmine had long lost all contact with her family and with the Middle East. So much had changed in that region. She had no way of knowing what had happened to her family. She insisted that she had no interest in returning to the Middle East or seeking out her past.

As political events in Egypt gained more and more traction in the press, questions became more pointed and pointed more feverishly toward that particular location.

Finally an article came out in a prominent womens magazine, linking Jasmine to a small village along the Nile, where people thought they recalled a girl called Jamila who had been spirited away many years ago by an American woman. No-one seemed to know for sure what had happened to her, or to her family, but the subterranean buzz continued to plague Jasmine like a bothersome fly.

"Why won't they leave it alone?" she complained to Malvina, who laughed and said "It was bound to happen sometime. Get over it, Jasmine, it's the price of fame."

" Are you in favor of Israel? What do you think about the Palestinian question?" shouted a snub-nosed stocky young man, aggressively elbowing his way to the front of the grouped journalists and waving his microphone in her face as she left Studio 54 one night.

"I don't think about it at all," said Jasmine, flashing him such a radiant smile that he lost his footing and almost fell. "I can tell you what I think of the new bell-bottoms, and I can tell you the color of the new black this winter, but I know nothing about politics." She turned and was immediately swallowed up by the waiting limo before he could regain his equilibrium.

But the questions persisted. Had she been kidnapped? Was Malvina an Ugly American, taking advantage of an illiterate peasant girl and snatching her up for her own benefit? Did Jasmine miss her family? When did she plan to return?

With nothing concrete to attach themselves to, television hosts and magazine editors nonetheless continued to float the idea of photographing a return of the young woman and her fame to the exotic background they had imagined for her. Jasmine smiled politely, listened to their proposals, and kept her own council.

Journalists descended on several Nile villages in the hope of digging up a juicy story, but came away empty-handed. So much had changed in Egypt. No-one was sure what had happened to the girl, or whether Jamila and Jasmine were indeed one and the same. So the probing shifted to her love-life, to their great consternation exposing the personal lives of her escorts, one by one. Jasmine felt beleaguered. Finally she agreed to a featured interview, but only if the questions would focus primarily on fashion.

"I have been far too busy to have a love-life," she announced to her incredulous interviewer, carefully positioning herself with professional poise for the photographer as she spoke. As the gossip press continued to dig and to posit false positives with flamboyant conviction, she learned to laugh it all off and to keep her private self secure from the limelight into which her glamor had plunged her.

"Are you sure you don't want to go back to your village for a visit?" Asked Malvina, worried that all the interest in Jasmine's past might have released a homesickness she had not perceived, "just say the word and I'll have twenty venues offering to pay your way. You could personally deliver a financial helping hand to your family. What do you think?"

Jasmine hugged her, once more the small girl who had captivated Malvina's heart years ago.

"They don't need me, I did make enquiries," she said sadly, "but it seems my family may have moved away. No-one was sure of anything. It has all changed so much in such a short time. I was always going to be sent away, you know, if not to America, to another life in Cairo. I do often wonder what they are doing and how they are, and I miss the village of my childhood. I suppose I will always be a child of the Nile, but I have come to accept that I will probably never see them again. Losing my brother, Ali, and perhaps never knowing what has become of him is the hardest to accept."

She smiled at Malvina, "I have my life here," she insisted, seeing the concern clouding Malvina's eyes, "you and Tim are my family. I belong here. I love the life you have given me."

CHAPTER TWENTY-ONE

1976
RETURN TO EGYPT

Nonetheless, the thought of returning to Egypt and finding her family again had wormed its way into her mind and would not let go. What if she could share some of the good fortune that had been hers? What if they were still living in the mud hut in the village, and what if she could take gifts and money to them and help her younger brothers and sisters find an education and a better life? She began to imagine exchanging stories and experiences with Ali. She grew excited at the thought. The more she thought about it, the more the idea of seeing her family again took hold. It was the only way she could get money to them and have them share in some way in the fine life she was leading

Malvina, too, continued to suggest that she needed a change, and that it might be a very beneficial thing for her to make contact with the self she had left behind.

"I'll come with you if you want me to," she said, "I have such wonderful memories of your village, the Nile, the desert, I would be happy to help reconnect you to your past. Remember,

Jasmine, I will never be able to find my own past. My parents are a dream I never lived. They never had substance aside from the fact that they made me. You have the amazing privilege of knowing who you are and where you came from. There has never been anything for me to search, and that is a deep wound in my soul that will never heal."

The more Jasmine toyed with the idea, the more she began to want to make it a reality. She wondered if anyone would recognize her. So much time had passed. She was no longer Jamila. But even as fears and doubts began to surface through the excitement, she cleared her schedule and made plans to take a week's vacation from work and clear her calendar of all work assignments.

"Thank you for offering to come with me, Malvina" she said, as they ate dinner together in a peaceful Indian restaurant close to her apartment, "but much as I would have enjoyed sharing this with you, I think it's something I must do on my own. I hope you understand. In so many ways, you and Tim are my true parents. I love you with all my heart and always will, but I need to try to get money to Salwa and Sadik and the little ones, and this seems to be the only possible way. And I guess I do need to connect with my family one more time, to let them know what became of my life, and to catch up on theirs. Once that is done, there will be nothing more to draw me back to Egypt."

Feeling a rising excitement, she bought gifts for her mother and father, for Ali, for Aunt Nadia, for her younger siblings. She chose soft creams and fragrant soaps, silk scarves and gold earrings for her mother and Aunt Nadia, and toys and games for the children. For her father she chose a cashmere sweater, and for Ali, a pair of real American jeans and the latest song hits with a player that worked on battery, with a large pack of spare batteries to give him music for a very long time. She smiled as she packed it, imagining his delight. She arranged for funds that she could retrieve in Cairo and take with her to the village. Malvina alone was privy to her plans, and was sworn to secrecy.

When she landed in Cairo, walking on the tarmac from the plane to the terminal she felt the hot air of a *hamseen* on her face, and her heartbeat suddenly raced, in an intense explosion of memory. She remembered the mingled smells of dust and sun-drenched plants, of camel dung and petrol, and the singular fragrance of jasmine released by the heat. She remembered the confusion and chaos of Cairo, and the comforting sound of the language of her childhood.

Malvina had arranged for a car and driver to pick her up at the airport and take her to a hotel, where she was to stay for a couple of nights to get her bearings. Then she was to take a taxi to the village she had left years earlier, a small, scared girl, facing an unknown future.

Tears filled her eyes as she stepped into the cool of the vast hotel lobby and checked in, following the bellboy to her room. She remembered who she had been before she became who she was, and she mourned the girl child with bare feet and wild hair who had left the desert village for a world of sophistication and celebrity far away.

She tipped the bellboy with a generosity that caused him to bow to the ground and then bow himself out of the room, repeating his thanks over and over again. She went to the window and pushed the slatted wooden shutters to the side, and there it was, far below, the Nile, her beloved river, now glutted with speedboats and *feluccas*, lined with a multitude of bouncing houseboats, not the serene river she had loved to watch from the top of the granite cliffs of her village.

She dined alone in the hotel dining room and went up early to her bed in the large beautifully appointed room. She thought she would be unable to sleep, but sleep mercifully felled her the moment her head hit the pillow. She decided next morning that she would not linger in Cairo, but leave next day for the villages of the upper Nile. Now that she was so close, she could not wait to see her family. Her mind buzzed with all the things she planned to tell and ask them, and she imagined the look of dazed admiration on her mother's face when she opened the gifts and saw the money, and the way she would run her fingers over the softness of the silk scarves. She wondered why she had waited so long, and why she had dreaded this return.

They drove along the banks of the Nile for some time, past several agglomerations of old and new dwellings, mud huts squatting uncomfortably between concrete apartment buildings, tall swaying date palms interspersed with cars. So much had changed. Apprehension began to rise in her.

"Are you sure this is the place?" She asked the driver uneasily, as he swerved into a rutted lane and stopped. She was bewildered by the squat blocks of flats that stood where the mud huts she remembered had clustered. The cotton fields still stretched lazily under the hot sun and she could see a small boy in the distance, wielding a switch to the lone *gamousa* who had ventured away from the rest. A couple of stray dogs rushed her, yapping at her heels. There was no-one else about.

"*Aywa, ya sit,*" the driver responded, nodding and grinning, throwing his arms open wide. She got out of the taxi slowly and moved toward the center of the buildings, and she saw with a thrill of delight that the big old mango tree still held its own in the open area. A few small children scampered about, chasing two goats and squealing with excitement. She saw the faded carpet under the tree, but it was the middle of the day and the village was asleep. She had half expected to see the schoolmaster and to hear the singsong of children at the *madrassa*, but there was no-one. A hot wind blew through the palms and rustled the branches. She searched and found the tall skinny palm tree where she had waited for Malvina so many years ago.

Finally, as she moved further into the village, she caught sight of a skinny older man sitting motionless on his haunches, dozing in front of one of the mud huts that still remained, his face polished ebony. She walked over to him and asked if he knew where she could find Salwa, Sadik and their family. The Arabic spilled from her without effort. She could not see her home where it had once stood, or Aunt Nadia's hut, or anything familiar to her. The village had clearly undergone a huge transformation. The man shook his head, and gestured that they were gone.

"Where?" She asked, her anticipation plummeting, "Where did they go?" He did not know. He spat into the sand at his feet and closed his eyes. Disheartened, she turned, almost bumping into a bent old woman with a cane moving slowly toward her. She looked, and looked again. It was Mustafa's first wife, Nabila. As she approached, Jasmine saw that her eyes were covered with a white film, and she realized that she was blind, struck by *bilhartzia*, the river blindness. She moved toward Nabila and took her hand. Tears in her eyes, she said, "I'm Jamila, remember me?"

"Eh?" said the woman, craning her head toward her "Eh?"

Jasmine sighed. "Do you know where Mustafa and Walid are now?" She asked.

"Gone to Cairo," the woman said, shaking her head in sorrow and flicking her fingers. "Cairo. Gone."

The pounding heat and scorching sun were making Jasmine feel dizzy. Clearly, she was not going to find her family. As she had at first suspected, they must have moved on and left no trace.

She looked back and saw her driver gesturing that it was time to leave. In a last burst of hope, she asked, "Aunt Nadia?" but Mustafa's wife shook her head again, a puzzled look on her face.

"Who are you?" Nabila asked, her hands lightly touching Jasmine's face and hair. "Do I know you? You are American?" By now, Jasmine was crying, deep ugly gulps of pain and loss. She nodded, then realized that the woman could not see. "Yes," she said through her tears. "Yes, American." On impulse she delved into the bag she had brought and pulled out the gifts and money she had intended for her family.

"Here," she said, pressing them into the surprised woman's hand. "Please keep these. They are for you," and before Nabila could react, she turned, ran back to the taxi, jumped in, and headed back to Cairo. At least Walid's mother would be better off because of her. The thought warmed her heart even as she came to grips with the fact that all she had left of her early life were her memories.

CHAPTER TWENTY-TWO

1976 New York
JASMINE'S CLOSE CALL

Malvina climbed the steps to the apartment on Third Avenue on a sleepy Saturday afternoon. Jasmine had just washed her hair and it sprang out around her face as she rubbed it dry. Malvina watched her anxiously. Since the return from Egypt, Jasmine had not been herself. She had entertained such hopes of seeing her family and reconnecting with her past, and now she knew with certainty that this could never happen. She was listless, going through the motions of her modeling assignments, but her natural *joie de vivre* was muted. Malvina knew all too well how it felt to be adrift in the world. Only she knew where Jasmine had been and what had happened.

"How are you doing?" Malvina asked. "We had dinner with Marcel and Irina last night, and they were asking about you. Marcel seems to have quieted down a little, and is less involved in rushing out to the latest gallery or gala. Do you miss those events?"

Jasmine smiled and shook her head. "It's all part of the visibility game," she said, "and having Marcel with me was so reassuring at first. But I don't mind doing a little less of the prancing about on his arm and being stared at enviously by a whole lot of women I don't know."

Marcel Michnik, still sometimes escorted Jasmine to social events. His wife, Irina, through the years, continued obstinately to resist being part of the social round as his success propelled him more and more into a social stratosphere.

Jasmine had become very fond of the Michniks. She had appreciated having an avuncular escort who was also something of a protective father figure. The relationship ensured that neither Marcel nor Jasmine were vulnerable to undesirable overtures.

Malvina settled on the couch with a cup of tea, and reviewed the past months' assignments as Jasmine finished drying her hair. "It's looking good," she said, pleased, "You seem to be managing to hold your own with the modeling assignments. Requests keep coming in. How are the studies going now?"

"Great," said Jasmine, smiling. "It's so exciting to do college level work."

They settled down to a comfortable talk about their lives.

Jasmine was on her way back home to the apartment on Third Avenue one afternoon, after a rigorous photo shoot for a group of talented young designers who had all been present at the shoot. She had enjoyed the unconventional pairings of their designs and their startling use of color, and had helped them to display their clothes to major advantage. But it had been quite exhausting.

She lifted her face to the lingering sunlight and sighed with relief that she would soon be home. As she rounded a corner she came upon an accident that had caused chaos and consternation on her block. A van had veered onto the pavement and struck some pedestrians. Startled, she saw a mess of ambulances and stretchers, police cordons and news crews, realizing that had she returned a few hours earlier she might have been among the wounded.

Horrified by the realization, and eager to avoid the news cameras she hurried into her building. Drenka was out at an assignment. She made herself a cup of tea with shaking hands, sat on the couch, and called Malvina.

She broke into sobs. "I never thought anything bad could happen to me," she wailed, her defenses down.

To Malvina's distressed exclamations, she added, "Yes, yes, I'm OK, just still very upset."

She learned on the evening news that the driver of the van had died in the crash. Jasmine was unable to put out of her mind the sense that death lurked one step behind the glamour of her lifestyle. The profound psychic shock she had experienced was far greater than the situation warranted. She had not fully absorbed the huge disappointment of her efforts to find her family.

CHAPTER TWENTY-THREE

1977 New York
CARL

A few weeks later, Drenka swept in through the door to the apartment in a flurry of elegant shopping bags and frigid air. Balancing on one foot she pulled the door closed with the other, shrugged her coat off, threw the bags onto the floor, and bounced onto the couch next to Jasmine, kicking off her shoes and bending over to massage her feet.

"Getting really cold out there," she said. "Jas, we need to talk.

I've been doing a lot of thinking since that horrible experience in that gruesome new club I insisted on trying out. I know, I know. I'm the one who suggested that we go there to take a look. It was not my finest moment. As you suggested at the time, we should just forget the whole nasty thing." She gave Jasmine a shame-faced grin.

"Listen," she said, "I have some good news to share. I wanted you to be the first to know that Tony asked me to marry him last night, 'For God's sake, make an honest man of me,' is what he said." She laughed. "It will come as no surprise to you that I've decided to accept."

She giggled again, pulled off her woolen hat and tossed her hair so that it spread out in a glossy burnished sweep down her back. Seeing Jasmine's startled expression, she added "I was never as focused as you are about fashion and modeling. Tony makes a good living, and I have quite a bit stashed away after all the activity I've been able to book these past few years. We can buy a really nice house in New Jersey, and have a family and a family life. I want that. I really *want* that."

She saw the disbelief in Jasmine's eyes and added, "I'm so tired of the clubbing, of being poked and prodded into different shapes all the time – the hair guy yesterday had his scissors out and was ready to cut my hair really short, *without asking*. He said he thought a Vidal Sassoon cap thing would look stupendous with the cape I was modeling, without even thinking that it would take forever for me to grow my hair back, and that at least half my bookings are because of my long red hair. I was just an object to him, not a person. I screamed before the scissors reached my hair, and almost killed him on the spot. Luckily, Cheryl the chaperone was right there and she let out a yell and grabbed the scissors out of his hand. Saved the day!

In the end, though, Jas, I've begun to feel there's no me, there is no 'me' left. There are only these illusions created by others. I want a *real* life, a life that is truly mine. I love Tony, and I want to have his babies. That's the life I want. There, I've said it!" She stared defiantly at her friend.

Jasmine said thoughtfully, "You know, I've never felt like that about modeling. I can let them do all that stuff on the outside, and sometimes I like it, and sometimes I don't, but I truly never feel that they reach or change the 'me' that matters. I always understood that ours was a make-believe life, and after all, don't all little girls want to be a princess when they grow up? When I was a little girl, I never even knew what a princess was, so in an odd sort of way, my entire life is really a little girl princess fantasy. The unreality of it never touched me deeply until I saw that accident on our block, and now I will never be able to enjoy the glamour without feeling the shadow behind it." She smiled ruefully at Drenka,

"I never realized how much the modeling bothered you." She added.

"Well, it's more than just that," said Drenka, "truthfully, Jasmine, the politics and the jealousies are really getting to me. Besides, I know I'll never make it past the mediocre level. I'll never be you."

She sat up and made a mock bow in Jasmine's direction.

"You know I love you, my friend," she said, her voice catching in her throat, "I'll miss you so much. We've had some great times together, haven't we? I want you to be my maid of honor at my wedding and godmother to my first child." She jumped off the bed and executed a pirouette in typical Drenka style, catching her foot in the side of the couch and ending up in a tangle on the floor.

Jasmine laughed, but she asked "Aren't you taking things a little far, a little soon?" adding, "I don't know, I feel marriage is such a huge commitment. I'll miss you so much, Drenka. You're the best friend I have ever had, except for my brother, Ali. Don't you want to use some of your earnings for college? That's what I'm doing. I really love the classes and the reading, and I've mostly been able to weave the courses in without sacrificing any modeling assignments. I suppose that's the 'me' I'm aiming for, and all the rest is a means to that end."

"I don't have those ambitions," said Drenka. "Tony's the man for me, and he is on board for me to laze around in a negligee all day looking beautiful," she tossed her red mane seductively, "and, of course, to be at his beck and call morning and night, until Junior turns up. I suppose I'll have to do some laundry and cooking every now and then, but we do that here, anyway, don't we?" She sighed happily, spread her arms out in her favorite snow angel pose and fell back on the bed, "sounds like the life for me, don't you think?" she said dreamily, and she smiled.

Jasmine held herself back from saying that she thought Drenka would soon be bored. She was sure she would miss the attention and the excitement, the satisfaction that came with the hard work, and the money. But if this was the life Drenka thought she wanted, she was happy she had found it.

Somewhere at the back of her mind, Jasmine had never forgotten the dull look clouding Salwa's eyes as yet another baby emerged to drain away her energies. She sometimes thought she remembered a more playful Salwa, a woman who laughed giddily, chasing them as Jasmine and Ali scampered outside the hut, a woman who ran circles around Sadik when he came home in the evenings until his scowl turned to laughter too, but she was not absolutely sure whether this was a memory, or a desire. The mother she remembered best never laughed and rarely smiled. For years, Jasmine and Ali had tried to resuscitate the Salwa of times past, clowning around together, doing their best to summon the fun and the laughter, to distract her, trying in every way they could think of to find ways to light a spark in her soul. Jasmine wondered if her mother had always been like that, a stranger to joy, or if her many pregnancies and the hard life of every day had leached the joy out of her, and robbed her of the promise of her youth.

"I truly don't want to rain on your parade," she said at last, hesitantly, looking down at Drenka sitting cross-legged on the floor, "I'm just a little concerned that you've chosen to make such a big life decision so young."

"Not that young, anymore, I'm twenty-two," said Drenka wistfully. "My best modeling days are over."

The Drenka she knew and loved was such a fireball of fierce hungers and energies. How would she keep all that in check in a quiet middle-class life? Jasmine sighed. Her own future lay ahead, but she envisioned it as a beckoning space welcoming her into a larger world. She could not imagine putting restrictions to that.

Drenka's wedding was a quiet affair in the pretty New Jersey church where she had been baptized as a baby. Her parents and her younger brother surrounded the young couple, Drenka radiant with happiness, her red hair flaming in the sunshine as she left the church on Tony's arm, her exquisite lace dress and her froth of veil lifting in the breeze, Malvina and Tim staying discreetly in the background. Watching the banter and love between brother and sister reminded Jasmine sharply of Ali and the strong relationship she had enjoyed with her own brother. Suddenly, the pain of not knowing what had become of him and of her family surfaced in a roaring tumult of feelings. Jasmine ached with sudden loss, her eyes stinging as she compared the simple continuity of Drenka's life with the complexities of her own.

Somewhere hidden under the polished facade of Jasmine, the sophisticated model, there still crouched a small girl from a remote village who had scampered over the dunes heading for the cliffs above the Nile river with her brother, Ali, and her goatherd friend, Walid, trying to find shade from a punishing sun. Friendship with the other village girls had not come easily to her. Now she felt secure in the life into which she had been thrust, and she reveled in friendships she trusted and valued. She was a lauded and beautiful fashion model, but she was barely twenty. She was also aware that there would always be a fault line in her life, visible to no-one but herself, a line that marked the disappearance of Jamila and the emergence of Jasmine. She felt certain that nothing would ever change that. She was almost content to accept it.

Drenka's younger brother, Carl, was a male version of her friend, spilling charisma and sexual magnetism from every pore. His head topped with bright red hair, he exuded vitality and laughter. He was eighteen years old, and lived in Los Angeles, where he worked in the film industry as a lighting consultant, and she knew from Drenka that he was a constant worry to their parents, who adored him.

"He's such fun to be with," Drenka said, her eyes clouding with concern, "but he's completely unreliable in so many significant ways, I don't think he'll ever grow up. And he's an inveterate flirt. He'll make a pass at you, Jas, you can be sure of that. Better watch out."

Carl's visits to his sister had been brief, few, and far between, and he and Jasmine had never met before his personality burst on her in all its incandescent splendor at the wedding.

Polished to within an inch of his life in a rented tuxedo tight across broad shoulders, a red carnation in his buttonhole, he was suitably solemn as Tony's best man at the intimate ceremony.

"Hey, Jas," he said, grinning, as he brought her a glass of champagne after the ceremony, "Drenka has told me so much about you. Do you have time to show me the New York scene? Drenka never had time. She was always such an older sister. She kept insisting I was too young for the clubs, parties, and all that? It would be such a kick to raid the New York celeb scene with you." He gazed at her with limpid eyes, "Anyone ever tell you how gorgeous you are?" He said it with feeling, and then added, embarrassed, "nah! just kidding."

"Sure, I'll show you the town," said Jasmine, laughing, a little confused by his rapid patter and vibrant person, but seduced by the sparkle in blue eyes so like Drenka's. "How long are you here for? Anywhere special you'd like to go?"

"Three days...and nights," he said.

Three days and nights Jasmine would never forget. She had carefully created a wall of thorns around her heart, determined that she would not invest her true self in the entire fragile construct of publicity and canned flirtation that surrounded her. She danced and smiled, wore revealing and dramatic clothing with panache as required, and kept herself aloof from anything that might lead to closer involvement with any of the men who swarmed around her, eager to experience fallout from her celebrity, dazzled by her sophistication and beauty. She had learned early in the process how to deflect wandering hands and inappropriate assumptions. She was still a virgin, and remnants of her childhood years in the Nile village clung to her spirit and warded off invaders.

But Carl seemed so familiar, and yet so profoundly different from the men she encountered in her modeling life. He was cheeky and impulsive, reminding her of his sister, moving swiftly past her barriers and standing at the door to the apartment with a mournful look in his eyes as he waited for her to unlock the door after taking her home in the early hours of the morning.

"Let me come in," he begged, "please please please …?" his hand light on the small of her back and his breath on her forehead making her shiver as his lips came down on hers. She let him into the living room and turned to sit on the couch, but before she could reach it he took her in his arms and moments later they were tearing at each other's clothing and stumbling, breathless and laughing, toward the bedroom.

"You're so beautiful," Carl whispered, awed, standing back and taking in the full glory of her body, slim and curvaceous, long legs, her green eyes dark with desire and her whole body yearning toward him. Jasmine flushed and hid her face with her elbow as he laid her on the bed, the better to admire this prize she was offering.

"This is my first time," she whispered, reluctantly. He heard, and held back, slowly kissing her face, her breasts, her smooth tawny abdomen, lower and lower, strong and gentle, making his deliberate way to every intimacy, taking her hand and placing it on himself and leaving a trail of heat on her body that grew and expanded until she could bear no more. She dug her fingers into his shoulders and pulled him down on her, but he resisted, gazing deep into her eyes and asking, "Are you sure?" She gasped, unable to speak. He saw her answer in her face and unleashed the full force of his hunger as he entered her.

Later, like two startled refugees from a typhoon, they lay locked in each others' arms, trying to make sense of the moment. It had been earthshaking, but each of them somehow understood that the affection and desire they had for each other would not carry them far enough. They had experienced a magnificent sensual and sexual feast, but no more than that. Because of Drenka, they had paused in their different trajectories and found an extraordinary moment together that each of them would always remember.

"Did it hurt?" Carl asked anxiously.

"Yes," admitted Jasmine, "but only at first. I wanted it so much." She smiled, and stretched lazily, tasting the sensuous delight that filled every cell in her body.

"I leave for LA tomorrow," said Carl, later, "Will you come and visit me?"

Jasmine paused. She wanted to embrace the moment completely, she wanted to feel sure that there would be more for them to experience together, but she also wanted to be honest, and she knew that they would not be able to sustain a long-distance relationship. She knew Drenka, and because she knew Drenka so well, she knew Carl.

"I do hope to, Carl," she said at last. "I'll try, but you know how busy they keep me, here. Of course, I'll let you know if they ever want me to go to LA for a booking and then you could give me a taste of the LA celebrity scene. I'd like that. And," she snuggled closer and looked up at him, "I wouldn't mind a repeat engagement." He chuckled and held her closer. "But realistically," she added, unwanted tears seeping from her closed eyelids, "I think we both know our lives are heading in very different directions. There's only one first time and I could not have wanted it sweeter. But I'm not sure I see a future for either of us in this. I wish I did."

She stroked the broad expanse of his back as she spoke, tracing the muscles with her fingers. She sighed with regret, "We aren't right for each other in the long run, are we?" she said wistfully, "and we both know it. I am so grateful for this time we have had together, and I certainly hope we'll see each other when you next come to visit Drenka?"

She waited for a response, and when none came, she whispered "I have a feeling that you want it this way, too?"

Carl grunted happily and pulled her to him. "You're quite an extraordinary woman, Jasmine," he said. "You've had so little experience of life, and yet you understand so much. I hope you find the man and the life you want." He lifted his head, his hair rumpled, and grinned engagingly down at her.

"Now. Shall we do that again?" he said.

CHAPTER TWENTY-FOUR

1978 New York
THE ROLLING STONE

At first, Jasmine felt lonely with Drenka gone from the apartment. Drenka sounded busy and happy whenever she called, and gradually Jasmine expanded her life to move into the empty spaces in the apartment and in her heart. She visited Drenka once or twice in her neat little cottage perched above the Palisades, but found that Drenka had put her life as a model so thoroughly behind her that there was little left for them to share. She wasn't at all interested in hearing about Jasmine's college courses. She seemed to spend most of her time fussing about her tiny garden, planting a little vegetable garden in one corner and roses in another. She politely faked interest in Jasmine's gossip and stories about the life they had shared, but Jasmine could see that she was completely immersed in the domesticity she had dreamed of. She was always engaged in one project or another, painting the longest wall of the living room a deep rich burgundy, wrestling with a complex new recipe in the kitchen, clearly not missing the broader life she had so recently led and not really interested in hearing about it anymore.

Jasmine missed the camaraderie and the friendship, but between the demands of her college work and her modeling assignments, she was not lonely.

She was sitting at the dining room table one evening, poring over a text book, so tired that the words blurred into a jagged black line and made no sense, when her doorbell rang insistently. Surprised, Jasmine padded to the door in her slippers and peered through the peephole. "Who are you?" she asked, taken aback by the sight of the huge young man with unkempt beard sprouting from an unshaven face who stood uncertainly looking back at her, a large knapsack dangling from one shoulder, his hair in disarray.

"I'm Jason," he said in a deep voice that reverberated in her chest. "Didn't Carl tell you I was coming?"

"Carl?" Said Jasmine, mystified. "Are you a friend of Carl's? I haven't spoken to him in ages."

They stared at each other through the peephole while Jasmine tried to decide what she should do.

"Well, aren't you going to ask me in?" Demanded the man on the other side of the peephole. "I assure you, I'm not in the least dangerous."

He grinned engagingly, and against her better judgment, Jasmine found herself opening the door to let him in. She pointed the way to the living room and went straight to the phone to call Carl in LA, who chuckled and said contritely,

"Sorry, I forgot to call. I knew you guys would get along. That's why I told him to look you up. Jason's an old friend of mine from our school days in New Jersey. He was always a few years ahead of me at school, but I considered him a sort of older brother. He's an interesting guy, just back from two years in Australia, living and working with the aborigines. He's always been foot loose and fancy free, always off on the next adventure."

Jason had already settled himself on the floor near the couch, his knapsack by his side. "Bathroom?" he asked, jumping to his feet as she put the receiver down. "Through there?"

Jasmine nodded. When he reemerged a while later, he had shaved, washed, and combed his hair into a semblance of order. She liked what she saw. He was not what she considered her type, usually tall lean men with sculptured features, cerebral and verbal, carrying themselves with an air of worldly sophistication, treating her like a piece of exquisite china to be valued and displayed.

Until he smiled, Jason looked as if his features had been thrown together haphazardly, jumbled into place, large, rough, and unpolished, but his smile was what knocked her off balance. His smile dug deep clefts on either side of his generous mouth and rearranged his features into an appealing harmony, while his eyes, a twinkling sapphire blue, illuminated the rocky landscape of his face into a place of serenity.

She made them both a cup of coffee, stealing furtive glances at him as she worked in the kitchen, and they sat, warming their hands on mismatched mugs. They were soon talking about themselves and the different worlds they inhabited.

"How long are you here for?" She asked, "And where are you staying?"

"I'm going to drop my stuff off at the Y and then get a bite to eat," he said, "and I thought you might like to join me?"

Jasmine decided to get changed and accompany him, hoping that the walk would clear her mind. She had a test next day.

They set off for the Y, the huge knapsack swinging between them. Jasmine reflected with pleasure that she had a fairly open week ahead. Perhaps she could spend some time with this interesting man. She was intrigued by him, eager to learn more about his work and his travels. As they walked to the Y in the early spring evening, she surprised herself with how comfortable she felt around him. She found herself telling him about her life as a child in the village by the Nile, and about her brother, Ali, who was always struggling with an excess of aggressive energy that got him into trouble again and again.

"I think of him so often," she said with a laugh and a sigh. "I hope that his life has settled neatly into place, as mine has."

Jason listened intently, those startling blue eyes boring into her as his interest seemed to give validity to her musings. In turn, he shared with her something of the passion and restlessness that drove him to explore the interior and exterior worlds around him, and his hopes that his research might one day coalesce and offer important insights for humanity.

"I've always been drawn to distant places and distant cultures," he said,

"and I have tried to unseal some permanent truths out of comparing the ways in which we humans interact with each other and with (or because of) our landscapes. It's a new and different way of exploring our common humanity, and I find it more and more fascinating as I research the customs and beliefs we all share despite different cultures. I have a lot more work to do, of course, but the patterns I hoped to see are slowly coming into focus, and people are getting more and more interested in my findings."

He looked up and grinned to see that Jasmine was deeply interested. She was clearly intelligent as well as gorgeous to look at. He wanted to know much more about her, and about the lands and cultures that had blended into such an unusual person. He smiled.

Jasmine said thoughtfully, "what started you on such a fascinating search? Was it a mentor? Something you read? An incident in your own life?"

He looked at her, disconcerted. He had not expected such a perceptive question from someone his friend Carl had described as "A real looker. She's a famous model and super hot."

He saw that she was waiting patiently for his answer. "I started off on this research," he said, "when my parents died and my brother and I sold the house in New Jersey. Paul, my brother, lives in the South, now, with his wife and family. Interesting about siblings. He rarely moves out of South Carolina, and I rarely stay long in any one place. Like you and your brother, our lives have taken very different paths. I knew I needed a guiding mission that would take me to some interesting places, and the more I thought about where I would like to travel, the more I saw links and patterns emerging where there seemed to be little commonality, and I felt compelled to explore them and to see where they would lead."

"What brings you to New York City this time?" Asked Jasmine.

"I don't actually know anyone in New York, but I'm writing about my Australian findings and I thought I could park myself here for a while to get the book done. Lots to do here when inspiration fails. Lots to see and discover here. Carl is my oldest friend, and he insisted that if I was going to spend time in New York, I should get in touch with you." He grinned. "He said you were a looker, and he got that right."

Jasmine smiled. She glanced at her watch and sighed. "I'd better get back home," she said, surprised to find herself so reluctant to leave.

"Can I call you tomorrow?" Asked Jason, putting a hand on her arm.

"Sure," she said, "I can show you around a little, but not tomorrow. I have a test tomorrow, but I should be relatively free after that except for whatever modeling assignments come up. Whatever free time I have is yours for the next few days." They both smiled happily at the thought.

It was a beautiful early spring in Manhattan. The trees in Central Park were leafing, daily unfurling clusters of new green, almost luminescent against the brown of the branches. Jason and Jasmine arranged to meet again and again between Jasmine's bookings and her classes, grabbing the times when Jason's inspiration needed a break from his work, meandering through golden days, holding hands in Central Park as they stood gazing up in awe at the cherry trees in full flower and took pictures of each other framed in blossom, Jasmine with blossom in her hair, no make-up, her hair pulled back into a pony tail, in her sweats and sneakers. She was so used to being followed by a train of *paparazzi* even when she was on her way to class, that it was a delightful novelty for her to have found a way to navigate her city unrecognized. After each modeling assignment she hurried home to change into a different self before joining Jason.

It amazed and amused her that he seemed unimpressed that she was a model. He had no interest whatsoever in the celebrity scene she inhabited, or the night-life she could show him. He seemed intent on exploring her with the avidity that he brought to his scientific research, and he pushed her to reveal who she was, what she cared about, what her aspirations were, and how she had become herself. He listened to her as assiduously as he had listened to the Australian aborigines.

It was deeply seductive.

Jasmine found herself cancelling engagements and skipping classes that were not essential. When they held hands as they wandered about the city, electric thrills raced through her body, leaving her shaken and unsatisfied. But the most he did was caress her hand, or place his huge warm hand on the small of her back as they walked.

One weekend, a vigorous spring rain sent them dashing back to his small room at the Y, her hair and clothes dripping onto the floors. Jason found a clean towel and watched as she bent her head, rubbing at her hair, sending sparkling drops around the room. She was laughing as she shook out her top, and suddenly he was behind her, helping her out of her wet clothes, and pulling her to the bed as he tore off his jeans and shirt. She caught a glimpse of a taut abdomen and hairy chest before he pushed her down onto the bed and entered her. It was a passionate frantic encounter, his intensity shaking her as she tried to signal that she needed time to catch up, but Jason cried out and rolled off her, sinking back on the bed, panting and happy, his large hand reaching for her breast as she lay beside him wanting more, wanting him with all her being, unsure how to deal with the onslaught of feelings and emotions that had taken over her body and mind.

From that moment on he filled her every waking moment. She lived for the next time she would see him, the next time he would touch her, the next time he would make love to her, the next time he would spirit her away from her everyday self and transport her to a place where there were only the two of them in the world, and where she could capture all of him for as long as it lasted. She was deliriously happy, but also confused. She could not eat, and she was losing weight.

Within two weeks he had suggested leaving the Y and coming to share her apartment, occupying Drenka's old room. She accepted joyfully, and her appetite returned, as she sank with relief into the security of his presence in her home. Now he was hers. Now she had him close. Now he would not disappear as magically as he had appeared in her life.

Malvina, who had not been consulted, was concerned.

"He's a fly-by-night, Jasmine," she said, pragmatic and protective. "Be careful. Be very careful. I don't want to see you hurt. And don't keep turning down the modeling assignments we send your way. You can only turn your back on so many offers of work before they stop coming altogether. You can't drop everything you've achieved for this man. He's not the marrying kind."

Jasmine glared at her, tears in her eyes. She had stopped in at the townhouse for a rare visit, and to tell Malvina and Tim about the changes in her life.

"You don't understand, he's the gentlest of men," she said bitterly as she leapt up from her chair, gathered her belongings, and started for the door, "He's a rare man who really listens. Everything about me interests him, it's not the celebrity model he wants, the one that everyone wants, even you, it's *me*, the *real* me, the Jamila hidden under the Jasmine."

Malvina, shocked, leaped to her feet and started to interrupt, but Jasmine went on, pushing past her,

"I've never met anyone like him," she shouted, flushed and angry, "I can't stop thinking about him when I'm not with him. He's so different from the men I usually meet. I'm no longer that twelve-year-old from a Nile village, wet behind the ears, Malvina, I'm twenty-two years old and I know all about men. How can you be so negative? I've never really fallen in love before, and this is your response to my news? All you can do is criticize? I thought you'd be happy for me," and she turned her back on Malvina and slammed the door behind her as she rushed out into the street. Malvina stared after her, surprised and hurt, more worried than ever that this relationship was heading for disaster.

As Jason continued to thunder into her life with overwhelming intensity, she surrendered herself to his magnetism. All she wanted was to be with him all the time, to disappear into his huge embrace and trace his rugged features with her fingers. She was obsessed. She could not get enough of their love-making. She forced herself out to her work assignments, turning down all but the most important, sliding along the surface of her work, counting it an unwelcome interruption of the insistent passion that flooded her senses.

Jason began to lay down rules. "I can't get this book done," he complained, exasperated. "You surely don't expect me to concentrate on the Australian aborigines when you come creeping into my room to breathe in my ear?" He was laughing, but his laughter hid a growing concern. There was a book deadline to meet, and he had thought that he would find the quiet time he needed to complete the project in a timely fashion.

She tried to focus on her own life, her studies and her work, but everything paled beside the sensual whirlwind that engulfed her, the pull of Jason's company, and the fascination of the tales he had to tell of his world and his experiences. As the severity of the New York winter set in, she hurried home to her apartment every day with eager anticipation, her body hungry for the excitement of his touch, the electricity of his closeness. She spent more time in the apartment, and she could not resist sitting on the edge of the bed in his room watching him type, trying to ignore the fact that he ignored her presence as he worked, clothes and bedclothes strewn all over the floor, until sooner or later the two of them ended in a tangled heap in bed.

"Shall I ask some people over?" She asked one evening, trying to come up with ways to entertain him as she sensed that he was pulling away, his mind on his work.

"For heaven's sake, don't do any such thing," he exclaimed in horror. "Why would we need other people?" You have your work, and I have mine," and with a puzzled glance he shut himself into his room for the rest of the evening. She sat alone in the living room and waited for him to emerge and take her to bed, dreaming of the hungry look in his eyes that would stir her to ecstasy, and of surrendering entirely to the power of his passion.

One of her favorite photographers stared at her in bewilderment after a photo shoot.

"Whatever has happened to you, Jasmine?" he asked, his irritation evident, "I've been photographing you for years, but now when I photograph you I have this bizarre sense that you are somewhere else, barely managing to hold back something monumental. It's as if you are afraid of what I might make you reveal, as if you are only allowing a small part of yourself to be present. I have tried again and again to capture something of this dichotomy in the photos, it could be interesting, but it eludes me."

He shrugged, exasperated, and added "This shoot misses the mark. Sorry about that, but I'm not sure they'll want to use the pictures. You used to give so much in our sessions, but now all I get is containment, and I have no idea what wildness you are holding back." He stopped, staring at her anxiously, waiting for her answer, but Jasmine only turned away.

"What an imagination you have, Tom," was all she said.

When she was not with Jason, she surfed the crest of the wave, waiting only to be sated. Malvina and Tim watched fearfully as she spun through weeks and months, consumed, almost obliterated by her hunger for Jason. They hardly saw her anymore. She seemed bewitched. Unable to step outside the spell that surrounded her.

Meanwhile, despite the diversions and interruptions, the months led the way out of winter, and spring was almost upon them again. Jason's book was coming along. She eyed the printed out pages piling up beside his computer, but he never suggested that she explore them.

"May I read it?" She asked at last, afraid of a rebuff, but anxious to enter this private space of Jason's and claim her part in it.

He turned to look at her and eyed her hesitantly. "I suppose so," he said after a long pause, a flare of anger lighting his eyes, "but Jasmine, I did explain to you when you let me move in that I would need a lot of privacy for my work. I'm puzzled that you always seem to be here, that you have so much free time this winter? I thought the magazines were always clamoring for you? When we first met, you had difficulty finding any time for us to get together, and now I'm having difficulty carving out alone time for the writing."

His voice rose. "I'm starting to feel suffocated," he said suddenly, with barely controlled fury through clenched teeth, and he grabbed his parka and flung out of the apartment. She cried her eyes out, and when he returned he took her in his arms and smoothed her hair back from her face, rocking her back and forth, "Baby," he said again and again, "baby, don't take on so. It's wonderful to have had this time with you, and wonderful of you to share your home with me. I promise I will think of this often and often, when I am no longer here."

But Jasmine never heard the words, she heard only the soothing sound of his voice and saw only the hunger in his eyes as he lifted her up and spun her into the storm of his passion and hers.

At last, Jason's book was done. He had turned it in to his publisher and had received a favorable response. Prepared for celebration, she hurried to join him at their favorite Thai restaurant, a sliver of a restaurant tucked into the upper east side. Jasmine was watching for him to arrive from a table by the window and she waved exuberantly as he came into sight, surprised that he did not wave back. Confused, she noticed that he seemed unusually moody as he strode in and sat down, immediately filling the place with his outsize person and personality as tiny Taiwanese waitresses scurried about to take his order, suppressing soft giggles as they went about their work.

He did not speak for a while, glancing everywhere but at her, until trying to ignore a swelling tide of apprehension, she asked at last, "Is anything the matter?" lacing her arm through his.

Jason looked at her. "Actually," he said slowly, "I need to share some news with you." He looked down at his plate, fiddling with his chopsticks, finding it hard to come up with the words he knew would dim the happiness in her face.

"It has been so amazing, spending these past few months with you, Jasmine," he said at last, "I have loved learning New York at your side. But here's the thing. I've been offered an extraordinary opportunity to join an exploration team leaving for the Arctic. It's the kind of offer I never thought would come my way. Everything I ever dreamed of. All expenses paid, and a stellar team to accompany me. It will feed right into where my research has been taking me. There'll be a major book deal in it. I have to take it. I know you'll understand." He turned the full force of his magnetic blue eyes toward her.

"Be happy for me, Jasmine," he said, his voice low and pleading. He took her hand and smiled at her uncertainly "these have been the most delightful and productive days of my life, but now I need to go where the tide of my life carries me."

Jasmine was bereft of speech.

Eventually she asked in a whisper, "When do you have to go?"

Jason hesitated, then said, " I'll be gone by the end of next week."

Jasmine stared at him, aghast. "But what about us?" she asked, her voice rising, "How long do you plan to be gone? When will you be back?"

She turned toward him, eyes swimming in tears, and he put his arm around her and held her close, staring out over her head.

"Jasmine," Jason said uneasily, "I thought you knew. I thought you understood that I'm a rolling stone. This was never meant to be anything permanent. I don't do permanent. Never have. It has been a privilege to discover you, to know you, and I'll always treasure the memories of this time we've had together, but I must go when opportunity calls. This is how I live my life. This is what my life has been about. I thought I had always been clear about that and that you were on board with it. There is no room in my life for anything that ties me down, or for regret. I will always remember you, but I'll be gone a very long time," he paused and sighed deeply, and then said, his voice barely above a whisper, "and I may never come back."

A cold tsunami of terror and intimations of the pain to come had begun to sweep into Jasmine's heart. Tears did not come. She froze in place and sat in silence, her food untouched on the plate in front of her.

So this was how it would end.

A week later, a week of tears, recriminations, tortured love-making, and despair, she helped Jason to pack in deep silence, and only lost her self control when he gave her a last abstracted hug and closed the door behind himself, setting out without a backward glance, his knapsack dangling from his shoulder, his face alight with excitement in the future. His future. He was gone. Truly gone. She knew they would not correspond or communicate again. She understood that it had ended with surgical finality. She did not have the courage to explore the emptiness he had left behind. She could not bear to think that Malvina had been right. Alone in her apartment, Jasmine cried herself out and eventually fell into a disturbed sleep.

It took many months before she could look back and grasp the fact that she had been engulfed in an obsessive passion and not wrapped tenderly in the love of her life as she had supposed. Jason had changed her. She had grown up, and would never again hurl herself into a relationship with unquestioning abandon and trust. Her heart was bruised, but the bruise would fade, her heart was not broken. Slowly, she began to pick up the threads of the life she had neglected.

Malvina opened her arms, let her cry on her shoulder, and never said a word.

As time moved on, Jasmine struggled to give her life meaning again. She realized that she would soon have completed her studies and armed with a college degree in business, she needed to think seriously about the type of work she might find fulfilling. She was still much in demand, but she was a pragmatic person, and she knew that modeling would gradually cease to fill all her time. Clearly, she would have to find some concept to develop that could benefit from her celebrity as well as from her studies. Years went by, years filled with challenges and successes, achievements and dreams, plans and celebrity, years that swept past in an avalanche of demands and flirtations, disappointments and delight.

Taking stock of her life as her fortieth birthday approached, she realized with sadness that there was no serious relationship to fill her heart and her time. Granted, Malvina, Tim, and the

Michniks were always there to offer support and encouragement. She had a life that would have seemed enviable to so many, but somewhere deep in her heart she felt a disconnect with the life of privilege and luxury she was leading and the wild-haired child full of hope and laughter that she had once been. Nothing connected her to her past. She had lost those who were closest to her, Ali, her parents, her brothers and sisters, the language of her childhood, the beloved river Nile, the village that she felt sure would now have changed beyond recognition. She had recovered from the pain of Jason's departure, but she started every possible flirtation with a wariness that chilled the men she met and warned them off all hope of deeper meaning. She was stronger and lonelier, and more determined than ever to move on to find the key to a happy productive life.

PART III

CHAPTER TWENTY-FIVE

1982 Central Park, New York
FATHERHOOD

"Papa, can we go to see the seals?" the little boy begged, tugging on his father's arm, his voice just shy of a whine, as they walked down the gravel path in Central Park, brief glimpses of Fifth Avenue flashing through leafy trees filtering sunlight on either side of them.

"Are you sure you wouldn't prefer to go and climb on the Alice in Wonderland statue by the lake?" Sol asked, knowing the answer.

"No! The seals! The seals!" Aldo jumped up and down with the fervor of his request.

"Mama told you last week that they were sea lions, not seals," said Sol, smiling, but Aldo shook his head vehemently.

"They're not *lions,* Papa," he said with scorn, " They're *seals.*" He stopped jumping for a moment and stood still a moment, arrested by a thought.

"Papa, lions don't live in the water," he said earnestly, "I want to see the *seals.*"

"We'll have to get there at the right time, then," said his father. He stood stock still near an archway, pointing up at an elaborate clock set on the top. There were dancing bronze animated figures under the clock, a goat, a kangaroo, a penguin, a bear and a hippo, all playing different musical instruments.

"The *seals*," begged Aldo with the uncompromising focus of a four-year-old.

As they stood together, gazing upward, two bronze monkeys on either side of a large bell above the clock began striking the bell as the hands reached twelve, and the animals below started their stately dance. Nursery rhymes sounded out in tinkling cadence as Sol watched, always enchanted by this delightful frivolity on the way to the Central Park zoo.

"See that, Dodo?" said Sol, pointing upward, "Just look at that clock. Listen to the music. It's magical. Those dancing animals and their music are telling us that it's noon. Isn't it fun?" He glanced down to see his son's eyes riveted ahead. The clock held no attraction compared to the sea lions. He laughed.

"Hungry, Dodo? I bet those sea lions are hungry."

The small boy wriggled himself free from his father's hand and raced toward his favorite park entertainment, the central circular pond where he knew the sea lions would now be swimming and leaping for their midday meal. Sol raced after him, dodging cyclists, balloons, baby carriages, and family groups enjoying the fine summer day, happy that he was wearing sneakers and a light T-shirt. Spending time with little Aldo kept him grounded. The volatile world of stocks and shares spun him with centrifugal force through the week days, but Saturday and Sunday were his days to spend as he wanted, and he loved spending them with his family. Although he was fulfilled and energized by his work, he looked forward with an almost painful intensity to the carefree time he could spend with Lara and Aldo. Aldo released in him a kind of childhood he had never known. He relaxed happily into fatherhood and gave himself fully to experiencing and mirroring the joyful energy of his small American son.

Aldo was a vigorous four years old, hazel eyes sparkling in his neat face, freckles dancing across his nose, rust-colored hair unruly atop his head. He was a happy little fellow. His weekday world revolving around pre-school and play dates with friends, and he loved his part-time babysitter, but his favorite days were the ones where he got to go out with his father.

Sol caught up with Aldo and swung him giggling and wig-gling up onto his shoulder, his small feet kicking as he squealed in a mixture of fear and delight. They headed for the edge of the water, where zoo attendants were standing with large smelly buckets of fresh fish, throwing them in the air for the graceful creatures to leap for. Sol swung the small boy off his shoul-der onto the gravel, keeping a firm hold of his hand. No mat-ter how often Aldo saw this spectacle, he was entranced. He pulled away from his father, jumping up and down, clapping his hands and chortling with delight as the sea lions raced their way toward the fish, their dark heads sleek and shining in the sunlight, knifing through the water as they tumbled, plunged, and sped their way around the pool. Sol grabbed the back of his shirt, keeping a close eye on him, making sure he did not get too close to the edge.

The young woman standing on a rock feeding the fish to the sea lions looked up and recognized them. Smiling, she sang out, "Hello, Aldo," and overcome with embarrassment at having been singled out from the crowds gathering around the pond to view the feeding, the little boy ran to his father and buried his head in his lap. Sol tousled his hair and laughed.

Lara often joined them in their walks and their play, but she had been feeling under the weather lately. It had been a rough winter. Looking at her sunken eyes and tired face, Sol said gently "Why don't you stay home today and get some rest? Dodo and I will wear off some energy. We'll bring back all sorts of good stories to tell you, and we'll stop by the deli and bring food." She smiled gratefully. She suspected that she was pregnant, and while she was delighted to think of having another child, she was a little daunted to think of being mother to two small children while coping with the challenges of her demanding scientific career. She was developing quite a reputation as a researcher and had been able to parlay the enthusiasm for her skills into time with her son through a part-time work plan.

She heard the key in the door and hurried to scoop Aldo up in a hug, wincing slightly as he struggled his way out of her arms and ran to his room, shouting happily "I saw the seals! I saw the seals!"

"They're not seals," said his scientist mother as he raced to his room, "They're *sea lions.*"

"He doesn't buy it," said Sol, shrugging his shoulders and grinning at his wife, "he insists that lions don't live in the water. I couldn't disagree."

Lara shook her head. "I just want him to know the correct name," she said, and laughed. "He loves that lion book, so I suppose he wants to make the point that he knows what lions look like."

Lara knew that Sol would be delighted by the prospect of a second child. He had been lonely growing up and had often made it clear that he didn't want the same circumstances for Aldo. Lara loved and admired her glamorous mother-in-law, but Eliane Mizrahi was a driven woman. She maintained her trim figure, immaculate nails, pristine apartment and ran a hugely demanding financial empire without turning a hair, in fact, with elegantly greying hair that was never out of place. Lara had lost her own mother to an early heart attack soon after her marriage to Sol, and she found herself wishing that Eliane could be a little less driven and a little more nurturing.

She knew Eliane loved Aldo, but she had little time for him and expected him to be presented to her, washed, dressed, and charming when she came to visit. Sol had explained to her that when he was Aldo's age, in Egypt, he had a Swiss nanny who took care of him, and who indeed presented him to his parents before they went out for dinner for an hour of play in the evening after his bath, scrubbed, polished, and in his pajamas. Nonetheless, Lara yearned for the grand-mothering her own mother had so looked forward to providing.

Eliane had not experienced the rough and tumble of parenting, and had missed all the fun of it, Sol said consolingly, but Lara missed her mother and had a hard time accepting the grand-parenting her mother-in-law offered.

"Eliane's visits are more like state visits than cuddly moments spent with an adoring grandmother." Lara complained to Sol, in one of her more ungenerous moments.

"She wasn't always like that," he said, melancholy invading his features, "She changed after we left Egypt. We had a horrible couple of years in that dingy Paris hotel. It was a brutal shock for all of us. Remember how I told you that we were unable to come to terms with any of it, and how that time left us in a damaged splintered world? I told you how miserable I was, and how those sad months destroyed my parents' relationship. Remember? We were all desperately unhappy there. We were never able to return to being the family we had been when we left Egypt. I suppose I can't complain, personally, we made it through, and here we are. But I understand that it was indescribably hard on both my parents in different ways. They really loved each other, but leaving Egypt ripped them out of an environment they understood and ripped them from each other as they each tried to survive in their own way."

Lara nodded, feeling a little ashamed of having made the comment. She had a calm, easy nature that balanced her brilliant mind. Little Aldo had inherited her naturally joyful temperament and her springy rust-colored hair that seemed to grow wildly in different directions and defied order. It was part of his charm, as it was part of hers.

"Do you ever miss Egypt?" Lara asked after a pause, watching Sol closely as he started to follow Aldo to his room. "You hardly ever mention it. Nor does Eliane. I often wonder if you ever wish that you had never left? I can't begin to imagine what it must be like to have to leave everything that you knew and loved, and start over in a different place."

He took her in his arms, suffused in well-being, her face buried in his chest, and he stroked her hair, reveling in the warmth radiating from her small body.

"I truly never think about it anymore," he said slowly. "I have everything I could possibly want, right here. I did miss my friends in the beginning, but for me it was never an identity crisis. As soon as we emerged from the horror of the Victoire days, it was as if the sun blazed out from behind a storm cloud.

The world shone. The world seemed mine for the taking. You know how much I like the challenge and excitement of the work I do. I love this country. America has given me so much. The Hotel Victoire does still sometimes force its ugly way into my consciousness, much more so in the early days here, but I can dismiss it quickly. I was often bored and lonely growing up in that big house in Cairo, you know. Much as I miss the Egyptian sunlight particularly in the winter, I kind of broke into a different kind of sunlight here in New York. I can only describe it as a sunlight of the soul."

He stepped back and smiled at her, a little embarrassed, "sounds kind of mystical I know, but I actually mean it. I love my life here. There is nothing I would change."

"I'm glad," said Lara simply, flushing with pleasure. She determined never again to complain about her mother-in-law, who was generous to a fault. She bent down and picked up the bags and boxes of food off the floor and left the room to start setting out the dinner, a spring to her step.

CHAPTER TWENTY-SIX

1988 Egypt
ALI

After many months of dedication to the Brotherhood, Ali had tired of sitting at the feet of the *Imam*. At first, he had conscientiously followed Hamid's plan for him. He had a quick intelligence and soon learned to read and write. He prayed five times a day with true fervor. He missed Hamid's visits which had become scarce, as age and sickness took their toll.

The *Imam* sought him out one day, his gaze liquid with pity. "Ali," he said, "*Ya ibni*, I have received sad news of your friend, Hamid. When we were last together, he confided in me that his time on earth was short. He was very sick. Now I have received word that he has gone to be with Allah. We will not see him again in this life. You must stand on your own. Never forget that Hamid's kindnesses to you have shown you the way to a better life."

Ali felt the sadness seep into his whole body, a wave of intense weakness in his limbs. Hamid had been the one person he had trusted, the one person who had believed in his destiny.

He nodded perfunctorily at the *Imam* and turned away to hide the tears that burned at his eyes.

He realized that it was time for him to move outward, to work and to earn his living, but when he moved out into the city, he was unable to find work. Day after day, month after month he haunted restaurants, talked to shop-keepers, even climbed the marble steps of gracious villas in Giza and Maadi, embassies in Garden City and Zamalek, looking for any job, from *boab* to waiter to cashier to street sweeper, to gardener's assistant, but there were no jobs to be had.

"*Ya Sidi*," he said, pleading, again and again, "Whatever work you have, I will do ..." but the eyes watching him swerved away from his gaunt face again and again, and taking in the silent message, he moved on.

A disaffected populace swept through the streets, barely held at bay by the ruling militia. The streets grew dirtier and more crowded. Shop fronts closed down, hiding peeling paint behind rusting iron fences. Trams still rattled through the neighborhoods, continuing to disgorge bunches of men into streets where nothing awaited them but fear and starvation. Electricity and food had become even more scarce than in his village by the Nile. At least there, nature had provided a modicum of sustenance.

Hungry and desperate, his strength failing, Ali returned to sit beside the mosque day after day, now reduced to begging for alms from passers by who turned their heads from his ragged clothes and distraught face and hurried their pace. A raging fire began to burn in him, fiercer and fiercer as the months wore on. Why was there no help? Why did some people have everything while he had nothing? Why was Jamila in

America, feeding off the power of the infidel while he starved in the land of their birth?

Ali felt the billowing intensity in him turn vicious and the all-consuming anger roar in his ears, closing off all other sounds. He roamed the streets around the mosque, a feral creature, red-eyed, skeletal, desperate, trying to ignore the painful pangs of hunger that stabbed at his insides. He hid from the kindly *Imam,* who had believed in him, and had made him believe that an education was the key to a good life. He did not want Hamid's friend to see what he was becoming.

As he prowled a side street on the outskirts of the center of Cairo one morning, stepping over rotting garbage and watching clouds of dust and scraps of paper float in the air like dead leaves in a ghostly mist, he glanced to the right and saw that a tray of pastries lay by the ancient cash register of a small bookstore he had not noticed before. He leaned forward and looked through the front window. It was dark inside. Everything in the store looked old and dusty, piles of old books on every surface except for where the tray of pastries sat. He was so tired. He was so hungry. The pastries seemed to glow and shimmer, calling insistently to his starving body. He looked around. No-one was in the store. He thought he had noticed a genial fellow gossiping with neighbors a couple of blocks away, a coffee cup in hand, and he decided it must be the owner taking a break. No-one else seemed to be around. Cautiously, he pushed at the door, his mouth watering at the thought of the pastries, and when the door opened at his touch, he crept inside grabbing a handful of pastries off the tray, stuffing them frantically into his mouth, swallowing them down in great gulps with one eye on the door as he reached an eager hand out toward the cash register. A heap of clothing in a dark corner stirred. A bony brown hand clenched down on his. He yelled in shock and turned to see a very old man staring him down with sadness and anger in his faded brown eyes. He tried to run, but his captor was strong in spite of his age. He shouted toward the door, keeping a tight hold on Ali, who squirmed and struggled to no avail as police arrived with truncheons, immediately beating him over the head. He lost consciousness and awoke in a foul-smelling dark cell, blood still seeping from a wound on his head.

He could hear a rustling around him, and he began to distinguish other occupants crowded into the cell, dark forms muttering and shifting about the darkness. A door opened, sending in a shaft of light and a guard dumped a pail of greasy swill inside. Glancing at Ali he said "Got a bowl? No? Here. Take this" and threw a dented metal bowl in his direction. Others were already pushing and shoving to get at the food. He was too weak to join them, but a man with a deep livid scar down the left side of his face glanced his way and reluctantly reached out to him with a full bowl. Ali was too hungry to wonder what it was. He gulped it down.

"Where am I?" he asked.

"Jail," said the man with the scar "*Caracol* with the rest of us they pulled off the streets. Riff raff. There are some political loudmouths here, a couple of journalists, a few thieves like you, and that fellow over there who murdered his mother and father to get at his inheritance. Sometimes they take one of us out of here to torture. You can hear the screams, on and on and on. See that man over there in the corner? He hasn't said a word since they brought him back. They said he was spying for the Israelis. He is half dead already."

He gave a short bitter laugh. "Get used to it. This is where you live now. We are your family. Unless you have someone with pull on the outside, you're probably here for life. No-one cares. Just be thankful if they don't single you out for questioning and torture."

Ali was about to ask what they would be questioning him about when the call to prayer echoed over the city and clawing hands shoved him out of the way to find space to kneel. Some had their own ragged prayer mats. The rest fell to their knees, jammed together on the floor. Ali rolled over and kneeled beside them trying to remember why he was praying and who he was praying to.

Wary of the foul-mouthed dangerous and aggressive prison inmates who surrounded him, Ali kept to himself, fists up, yelling at anyone who jostled him that he knew how to take care of himself, spitting and snarling like a feral cat if anyone came too close. He prayed morning and night that the *Imam* might somehow learn of his plight and use his influence to save him. Day after day he dreamed of ways he could get word to the *Imam*, but he had no money to bribe a guard, and no friend to come to his rescue. He slowly lost his moorings to the outside world, drifting through time, concentrating on survival within the thick stone walls of the prison.

Weeks immersed in this hellish half-life went by, and he had no intimation that there would ever be any end to it. He had lost all hope and hung onto his life by a thread. But at last, the day came when a guard pushed his way into the foul smelling cell, wielding his truncheon right and left, searching about. He grabbed Ali by the neck, and threw him out into the street. Ali lay like a heap of old clothes. He was conscious, but his battered body was too weary to get him to his feet. At last, he stumbled to his knees and then to his feet, swaying, and slowly made his way toward the mosque. Passers by stared in disgust and gave him a wide berth as he walked, and he realized how filthy he looked and how strongly the smell of prison clung to him.

The *Imam* flung his hands to the sky and shouted in horror when he caught sight of him. He ushered him past the few students sitting and studying on the steps of the mosque and hurried him into the cool cavernous interior and then to a nearby *hammam,* paying the attendant to get him deloused and cleaned up, grumbling at him all the way. "How did you let yourself get to this state," he muttered, shaking his head, "you know that the Koran leads the way to cleanliness in all things."

He brought him a clean robe, and a hot meal, and they talked long into the night after evening prayers. The *Imam* had eventually noticed his absence from the neighborhood and had started inquiries that in time led him to the bookstore, and the prison. Distressed that a boy with such promise had foundered so badly, and sad for his old friend Hamid, who had had such faith in the lad and in the *Imam*'s ability to care for him, he managed to cobble together the bribe that made Ali's freedom possible.

Ali swore to his benefactor that he would never steal again, his dark eyes liquid with intensity, but the kindly old man knew well that unless the boy had work, he would certainly end up in the *caracol* again, and this time there would be no rescue. Shaking his head and muttering to himself, he led Ali back into the mosque and set him to work cleaning and scrubbing in return for shelter and bread.

Days went by. The seasons followed one another down the year, and Ali resigned himself to a life regulated by hard physical work with intervals dedicated to meditation and prayer. Little by little, his anger melted away and disappeared. He appreciated the freedom from choice, and found an unexpected peace in the safe certainty that each day would bring nothing new.

One chilly winter day, the *Imam* came toward him accompanied by a man almost as broad as he was tall. He had a wide smile and an easy stride. Ali was on his hands and knees wielding a brush thick with soap and water. He did not look up until he realized that they were both standing beside him, watching him work.

"This is the boy," said the *Imam*, and Ali got to his feet, surprised, looking from one to the other.

The man, short and squat, his spotless white robe undulating around him as he moved, gazed at him with penetrating eyes.

"I work at the big hospital nearby, *ya ibni*," he said at last in a deep rich voice. "I asked the *Imam* if he knew of a reliable young man, strong and willing, who could replace an orderly we lost recently. I need someone to move patients on stretchers from floor to floor and perform many other needed tasks of this nature." Seeing a flicker of interest in Ali's expression he added "the *Imam* has spoken very highly of you. That is why he has brought me here to meet you."

Watching hope give way to doubt in Ali's dark eyes, he added "Do you think you could do such work? It is hard work, but rewarding. The *Imam* says you can also read and write, which would be a great advantage." He looked up at Ali's gaunt face and added, "The job can be yours if you want it."

Ali opened his mouth, but he wanted so badly to accept that the words came out in a garbled rush. He flushed and tried again, as the man from the hospital grinned. "The job is not running away," he said, a twinkle in his eye, "Take your time. I take it you want to accept?"

Trudging along beside Doctor Amir as they headed out of the mosque, the *Imam* watching them go with a satisfied smile, Ali listened carefully as the doctor talked about the work he was doing. The thought crossed Ali's mind that the doctor talked about his work the way Hamid had talked about his, the way the *Imam* talked about the tenets of his faith. There was a quiet passion and dedicated focus about him that caught Ali's attention. He felt eager to learn more of what was to be found at the hospital, and a flutter of excitement was beginning to replace the anxiety that now always accompanied the start of anything new. He glanced down at the doctor's broad face, large features, and thinning hair. He was so afraid that this, too, would not work out for him. He sighed deeply and the doctor looked up and grinned.

"Nearly there, Ali," he said cheerfully. He put an arm companionably up around Ali's shoulders and added, "you need to understand that I'll be keeping an eye on you. The *Imam* himself has vouched for you, so make sure you listen to Hassan, your boss, and do a good job."

"Huh!" spat the sour-faced old man with skin like baked leather, as soon as Amir had left them together in the humming basement of the large building, machines clattering and shaking like a hoard of voracious monsters, as Ali gazed about him, wide-eyed. "What does a doctor know about the work we do down here? What does he know about what we need? They could not do their fancy work without the work that we do for them, but do they recognize it?" He did not wait for Ali to answer, adding bitterly "They do not. They never will."

He eyed the young man towering above him with suspicion. "I suppose you look strong enough," he muttered reluctantly, "better shape up, my boy, or you're out of here." He grunted, pointing to a corner where a door hung on rusty hinges. "Let's get you changed and get you started. There's work to be done. You can wash over there."

Hassan managed the orderlies like his own personal army. He was quick to anger and hard to please, but to his surprise, Ali found that he loved his job at the hospital. They gave him clean white clothing laundered daily in the hospital laundry, new leather sandals, enough money to eat when he was hungry, and the *Imam* let him continue to sleep in a corner of the mosque nearby, after evening prayers.

After a few days of terror as he struggled to understand what was wanted of him, and to adapt to the pressures and frantic demands of each new situation under Hassan's unforgiving glare, he began to respond to the chaos of the ER with efficiency and speed, and he grew adept at finding a good spot to leave the gurney for each patient he wheeled in. He was deeply horrified by the damaged bodies he saw all around him. There had been horrors in the jail, but somehow he had not expected to encounter such devastation and such suffering anywhere else. He could do nothing about the pain, but he discovered that he could relieve the fear and stress of the wounded and the sick by listening, nodding, laying a calming hand on a head or an arm, offering a few words that addressed their humanity.

As the mechanical demands of the job became easier, he allowed himself to take more interest in the welfare of the people he ferried here and there, stopping Doctor Amir and asking about individual patients when he passed him in the halls. When he had a few moments of free time he hurried to the wards to offer words of comfort, and the patients responded to the presence of a man who clearly knew a great deal about the suffering of body and spirit.

Gradually the pain and stress from the months of useless job search, and the horrifying months in prison began to dissipate, giving way to a sense of pride in his work, and possibility in the future. His sense of self grew stronger the more he connected with others at the hospital and realized that many were eager for his friendship. He had also earned their respect. None of the other orderlies knew how to read or write, and their admiration for Ali's skills buttressed his self-esteem. The younger nurses giggled and bantered with him as patients were wheeled to the operating rooms, drawn to his lanky frame and fierce dark eyes. He began to relax, to banter back, and to help them when they needed an extra hand. He was learning cautiously to love life again, and to engage in the world. He was no longer alone, he was a part of a community.

One day, Doctor Amir called him into the small cubicle he called his office.

"You're doing a really good job, Ali," he said, smiling as he gestured him to the rickety metal chair in a corner. "I hear from my colleagues that you have a special way with the patients. They ask for you as their health improves. Everyone has noticed that you do so much more than wheel your stretchers back and forth." He watched Ali for a moment and added "What do you think you want to do with the rest of your life?"

Ali had not dared to think beyond each day as he navigated the days, well-fed, safe, and deeply engaged in the suffering of those around him. He sat very still and thought about Amir's words. Was it possible that he might be able to do more with the patients? He looked up, and Amir nodded as if he were reading his mind.

"You have an unusual sensitivity to the patients' needs," he said. "I have discussed it with my colleagues, and we think you could become a fine nurse, or a good physical therapist, but you would need more schooling. Would you be willing to go to school at night and see if you could manage the work? Or are you happy as you are? I have discussed this also with the hospital administration and we would be willing to fund your studies, on the understanding that you would continue to work here once you are certified. How does that strike you?"

Ali's vision blurred with the intensity of his pleasure. He had found a community that valued him enough to help him toward a better future. He thought of Jamila and wished he could tell her about this defining moment that had finally come to him, just as hers had come to her, and for the first time the thought of her did not engender bitterness. His own path was beckoning at last, inviting him to a finer world than he could ever have imagined. He wondered what Hamid would have thought about it all.

CHAPTER TWENTY-SEVEN

2001 New York
WINDOWS ON THE WORLD

The sky was a crisp limpid blue, starkly outlining the jagged Manhattan skyline outside her window, as Jasmine put the finishing touches to her hair and makeup and hurried downstairs to catch a cab to her power breakfast at Windows on the World. She stopped by the full length mirror in the lobby and looked herself over critically. She was not a morning person and hated early breakfast meetings, but this meeting could be the key to the rest of her life, and the financiers she was meeting were all high-powered type A's, up with the dawn and raring to go. Yes, the dark grey Versace pantsuit with the ruffle at the neck of the cream-colored blouse was just the thing, businesslike, but totally feminine. Her heels were too high for comfort but added elegance to her walk, and her new leather briefcase was classical and understated. The men she was about to meet would see a woman comfortable with her sexuality in a graceful middle age, who knew her way about the worlds of fashion and business. As she stared at herself, her eyes lit up in excitement and the effect was magnetic. She glanced down quickly at the delicate enameled watch pinned to her lapel and gasped. It was 6:30. She would be late if traffic was bad, and that would never do.

She loved the view from the Windows on the World restaurant and was energized by the prospect of carving a new place in the world for herself. She was 44 years old, and while still in demand as a model, she knew that from now on, there would be no runway shows and few assignments, most of them of limited interest. She and Malvina had agreed that the time had come for her to lay the groundwork for a second career.

She had not taken the time to make coffee, and looked forward anxiously to that first shot of caffeine once she had made her entrance. The cab crawled down the FDR toward the tip of Manhattan island, weaving cautiously through heavy traffic, and she tried to relax and focus her mind on the beauty of the East river in early morning sunlight, glittering as if home to millions of scattered diamonds. Not a hint of cloud in the sky. It was early fall, and the September air, fresh and invigorating met her cheeks as she opened the window enough to enjoy it, but not enough to damage her carefully austere hairstyle. It would be important to project the sleek college graduate rather than the celebrity star model from the celebrated Malvina agency. That was then. This was now, and she was counting on now to draw her into the promise of the future.

The elevator in the twin towers shot her up to her destination, leaving her stomach several floors below, and she stepped out to the admiring gaze of the Maitre d' who hovered around her as she made her way to the table, where her prospective investors were already seated. They rose as one to greet her.

"Can I bring you anything, Madame?" asked the Maitre d' solicitously, holding her chair out for her to be seated.

"Cappuccino, please, right away," she said, smiling at him gratefully, as her companions pointed her to the menu, and she added as he turned to leave, "I'll have a poached egg on whole wheat toast and some fruit."

"So pleased you could make it, Jasmine," said Marcel Michnik, beaming, leaning forward to give her a hug, his Russian accent endearingly familiar. The two younger men stared appreciatively at the elegant woman seated with them, looking forward to the opportunity of evaluating her business proposition.

Jasmine pulled out several copies of her business proposal. She had taken her time to settle on something appropriate and exciting to focus her energies on. She had toyed for many months with several different ways to use her celebrity, from a cosmetic line to perfume, to various fashion possibilities, but in the end she had focussed on a line of branded clothing that would take inspiration from her childhood world, where she would use the colors of the desert, the theme of the wide river and the muted green of the vegetation to create deceptively simple leisure clothing for career women plagued by a lack of time. The folder she handed out was emerald green, the color of her eyes, and the men glanced up at her appreciatively as they began to leaf through her 5-year plan and the sheets of design samples that were included. She ate her breakfast, one eye on the reactions she observed as they read.

"Where do you see your market?" the more skeptical of the three asked after a while. "There are already so many brands in the fashion world. How do you see your Dune brand carving out a new market?"

"I believe that this brand will provide a unique combination of style and leisure clothing for women under pressure," she said, smiling, "I know all about that." The men laughed. "And with the emerald green Jasmine brand, and the gorgeous classical logo we have commissioned, it should be of interest to upmarket independent boutiques as well as to upscale department stores, I am aiming for Bergdorf and Bendel for a start. Many more women are working in the business world these days. When they get home, they want to throw on something loose and easy, something less austere than the clothing they wear to work, but nothing frilly or overtly feminine. We will be relying on color and cutting edge design. I'm hoping that the line will be distinctive enough that it might also be carried by organizations such as the Museum of Modern Art, as well as the more obvious markets."

The men were nodding in understanding, and glancing at her watch, Jasmine thought it might be a good moment to leave them to discuss things among themselves. She excused herself and went in search of a rest room. A harried young woman stopped her outside the rest room door.

"So sorry, Miss, but there's been a problem with the water flow in these rest rooms," she said, "I suggest that you take the elevator down a few floors where I know they'll be happy to accommodate you. Please excuse the inconvenience."

Jasmine sighed, annoyed, but seeing an elevator nearby with open doors, she stepped in. She glanced at her watch. It was 8:30 am. Her prospective investors were clearly intrigued and had asked many challenging questions. She reflected that it had gone very well and she wanted to keep the interest growing. She was so deep in thought that she forgot to press the elevator button, and the floor she wanted had gone by without her noticing. I'll get out at the next one, she thought. She stepped out as the elevator stopped and asked a passer-by where to find the rest rooms. She was anxious to return to the meeting. She was regretting having left the men alone. Clearly, they would have had ample time by now to evaluate the situation among themselves and make their individual decisions. She smiled at herself in the mirror. They had seemed very positive and open to her ideas.

She finished refreshing her lipstick and hurried back toward the elevator, when a tremendous crash detonated around her and made her stumble sideways and cry out. She almost fell. She could feel the blast reverberating around her. Her ears shut down and sounds seemed to be coming in from a great distance. The building shuddered, lights flickered, and people around her streamed out of their office cubicles in alarm. It felt like a huge bomb explosion.

"What was that? What happened?" she asked into the confusion milling about her, but no-one wanted to stop, and no-one seemed to know.

"I need to get back upstairs right now, to Windows on the World," she called out in a panic to a uniformed young woman who was rushing by, "how can I get up there? The elevator seems to be out of order." Jasmine was starting to feel alarmed and out of control. The scenario rapidly unfolding around her had a nightmarish unreality to it. The young woman was moving fast, and Jasmine called after her again, "Could you please give them a call and let them know I seem to be stuck here? You could ask for Marcel Michnik."

The young woman she spoke to grabbed impatiently at a nearby phone and dialed.

"That's odd," she called out, looking back at Jasmine, "there's no answer up there. They're not picking up. The stairway is over there, but I warn you, it curves around and it's a long way up to the restaurant."

Jasmine headed for the stairway, but an ominous screaming floated down from above and smoke began to trickle in and swirl about where she was standing. Now thoroughly alarmed and feeling the beginnings of a crippling terror, Jasmine watched as people began to stagger down the narrow stair. "You can't get up there," they shouted, shaking their heads, "best you can do is get yourself out of the building as fast as you can."

Jasmine climbed a few stairs and saw that above, the stairway seemed to have caved in on itself and steady smoke was swirling through the cracks. She took out her cell phone and tried calling Marcel Michnik, but there was no answer, just a horrible crackling noise with what seemed to be faint voices screaming and shouting in the distance. She was starting to feel faint from sheer terror. Grabbing the metal bannister, her heart beating wildly, she turned and began to follow the gathering crowd downward.

It was an endless terrifying descent. People pushed and shoved others out of the way as they tried to move faster down the stairs away from the thickening smoke. Cries of "there's fire up there. Isn't anyone coming to help us?" rang out around her. As she rounded every corner, passing every floor, more and more people stumbled coughing from smoke-filled offices to join the stream of frightened people hurrying down, some of them bleeding from gashes on the head or arms. She had once heard that there were some 200 flights of stairs in each tower of the World Trade Center, and the Windows on the World restaurant was at the top of the North Tower. She had lost count of the flights of stairs. How many were behind her? How many more to go? What was going on up there?

Her heels were a ridiculous impediment and she kicked them off, groaning as her stockinged feet came into contact with the rough concrete stairs. Turning another corner she saw a slight man in his fifties swivel, lose his balance, and slump to the floor, and realizing that the crowd would soon trample him to death, she pushed against the flow, screaming, and elbowing her way toward where he had fallen. She reached out to him.

"Here, hold onto me, let me help you," she cried, grabbing at his arm and using the bannister and what strength she could muster to help him to his feet. Others streaming past were intent on their own flight from a horror they were just starting to comprehend, and no-one stopped to help. He swayed and struggled, unable to get his balance. Despairing of the situation he called out to her "Leave me, I'll manage somehow. You should save yourself."

"We can do it better together," she said, hanging onto him and helping to steady him as they continued on down. Smoke swirled around and distant clatter and clamor laced with shrieks and cries of fear echoed about them. He was covered in plaster dust as was she, and she hooked her arm under his and half carried, half pushed him downward, making sure that they combined their strength and bulk to ward off the panicked crowd that was now bull-dozing its way forward without consideration.

She could hear his labored breathing, unaware that her own breath was coming out in short gasps, "Are you OK?" she asked, afraid he might be in the throes of a heart attack. She saw that he was younger than she had thought at first.

"Coping," he said briefly, trying to save his breath for the trials ahead. "I couldn't get hold of my wife to let her know I'm alive. She must be frantic. It's on the news, you know. Someone said that a plane smashed into the North Tower and everyone up there is dead." He coughed and steadied himself against the bannister.

" My name's Sol Mizrahi, by the way." He tried to smile, "Yours?"

"Jasmine" she said but had no strength to squander on polite introductions. Her mind baulked at the thought that the powerful vital men she had breakfasted with a few moments earlier were possibly dead. How would she break it to Irina, Marcel's wife of forty years. Her mind was so full of other matters that she almost subconsciously elbowed and punched her way through, clutching onto the man she was determined to save. Firemen, bulky with heavy gear, pushed past them on their way up, and with each floor down, new groups of terrified men and women tried to push and shove their way into the downward stream. The cacophony of desperate voices swelled around her. Her companion again lost his footing, and she yelled for help as she tried to maneuver him back on his feet.

"Leave me," he gasped, "Leave me and save yourself. I can't go on like this. I'll only hold you back."

A fireman on his way up reached back without a word and pulled him to his feet before continuing his steady ascent. Sol clutched the bannister and they inched their way down and down and further down, the hellish pandemonium around them requiring all their focus to stay upright and continue steadfastly to descend, step by step, inch by inch, in an unending horror.

When at last they reached the ground, the chaos and confusion spread all around them. Scraped and sore, Jasmine grabbed a fireman and asked, "Where can I get an ambulance? This man needs help."

The fireman glanced at her bleeding feet and pushed past her, waving in the direction of some ambulances parked some distance away. She looked way up and saw violent flames, red bursts surrounded by huge grey clouds of billowing smoke circling the top floors of the North Tower. Then to her horror she saw that the South Tower was starting to crumble. The people beside her began to scream and scream and she realized that what she had taken to be falling debris up high were people jumping out of windows and falling from the inferno all around them. She began to sob hysterically.

Beside her, the man whose life she had saved patted her head. "Don't cry," he said gently, "You are an amazing person. Thank you. I can walk to the ambulance by myself, now. Come with me and we'll get you some help too." He started off and turned to see if she was following, "God bless you, whoever you are," he said, his eyes glistening with unshed tears, "you saved my life. " And he stumbled off toward the crowd surrounding the EMT crews and the open jaws of the medical vans.

Jasmine hobbled after him toward the EMT van, her raw feet bleeding, sending searing pain up her legs now that the adrenaline from the descent was starting to wear off. She was dizzy and nauseous as she was helped into the van beside Sol. Others crowded around, some helping, some being helped.

Moaning and mumbling, they pushed and squeezed their way into the small space. A young man hopped down from the front and closed the back doors of the van. The ambulance started off toward the closest east side hospital. She looked down at her watch. It was 10:25. Her watch was still working.

A sudden deafening roar and a frantic acceleration of the ambulance across bumpy terrain caused her to look back, and the sight that met her eyes strained all credulity. For a moment she thought she had dropped into the set of an apocalyptic movie. Hordes of ghostly dust-covered figures their limbs flailing, heads thrown back and mouths open wide were stumbling and racing toward her, screaming. Behind them huge billowing clouds of black smoke and flying debris reached out to enfold them as the North tower collapsed. She had been there just moments earlier. Her mind refused to accept what her eyes were seeing. Clutching the arm of the horrified young EMT volunteer, she passed out.

The ambulance found packed waiting rooms and unimaginable chaos at the emergency check ins for Bellevue Hospital, and then at Langone, where scurrying nurses and doctors shook their heads and waved them on impatiently. They swerved onto First Avenue and continued on with their load to New York Hospital on the upper east side. The chaos and buzz seemed a little lighter there and the EMT van disgorged its occupants and headed back to the disaster area, the young crew nauseous with exhaustion and the horrors they were witnessing.

Sol and Jasmine stumbled wearily into the brightly lit emergency center, where the noise level had arisen to a reverberating din. Dizzy with fatigue and the barrage of light and sound, they registered with the guard at the door, and eventually found seating in the packed waiting room as they waited for triage nurses to find them and schedule them for care. They were so tired, dazed with shock and fear. Jasmine got to her feet with difficulty, wincing from the pain, and hobbled off to look for a phone, but the first responders, guards, doctors, and nursing staff milling about in a mixture of panic and procedure, pointed to the long line for the one phone that sat on the registration desk and shrugged their shoulders.

"Have to keep lines open," said a nurse as she ran past to catch hold of a man about to fall, whose left leg was open to the bone, and bleeding profusely from hip to ankle. She found him a seat, added him to her triage list and carried on. Sol's cell phone had fallen from his pocket when he had fallen in the stairwell of the North Tower, and Jasmine's needed a recharge. She moved painfully among the seething groaning crowd, trying to ignore the searing pain from her mangled feet, her face white and tight with pain, asking if anyone had a phone or a cord she could use to charge her own. She knew that Malvina must have learned of the tragedy by now. She had known about the meeting, and would be frantic with anxiety. But there seemed to be no way of getting word of her survival to her. A young man bleeding from a jagged gash on his forehead fished about clumsily in his pocket, swaying as he stood, and handed her his cellphone. "Here," he said, "I think there's some charge left in there. But I spoke to my sister, and you should know there's no transportation running anywhere. People are walking uptown in groups all the way from Wall Street and the Bowery. Only first response vehicles are allowed on the streets." He gave a mirthless laugh, glancing down at her swollen bleeding feet, "Anyway, you won't be out of here for a while," he said.

Jasmine punched in Malvina's number, but there was no answer, so she elbowed her way back to Sol with the phone in her hand.

"Here you are," she said, subsiding onto the seat beside him with a sigh of relief as she took the weight off her feet. "You need to give this back to that man" she pointed behind her, "but at least you may be able to let your wife know you're safe, and where she can come to get you."

There was no answer from Sol's home either. He left a brief message and she waved the owner of the phone over to where they were sitting and returned the phone to him, exhaling and groaning as her legs and feet sent shooting pains up her body.

Sol was slumped in his chair, his face grey with pain and exhaustion. Jasmine looked at him and tried to distract him as they waited, knowing that bad as they felt, others were in far worse shape. They would be among the last on the triage list.

"Do you work in the North tower?" she asked, trying to distract him.

Sol shook his head. "I work in finance in midtown," he said, "and I had just left a meeting with an old friend at Cantor Fitzgerald when the entire world blew up around me." He shuddered. "I can't believe this is happening."

Looking at Jasmine who had shaken off some of the dust that had obscured her person, he added "Now that I can see you more clearly, you look sort of familiar. Celebrity familiar. Are you a star in one of the TV soaps?" He smiled at her and she smiled back, shaking her head, and suddenly he said "I know! Aren't you Jasmine, the famous model? I remember seeing you on the cover of Vogue more than once. And now that I think of it, I believe I saw you at my wedding, years ago. You were in the company of my mother's client, Marcel Michnik and ..." to his consternation, Jasmine burst into tears, sobbing as if her heart would break, taking great gulps of air and trying to swallow down her grief. He put his arm around her, upset to see her so distressed. He patted her shoulder gently, making comforting noises until she had regained her composure.

"Marcel's dead," she said at last, her voice breaking. "He was such a good friend to me, he was like a father. He organized a breakfast meeting for me at Windows on the World with some young financiers who were interested in investing in a company I was trying to form. It's because of me that he was there, so it's my fault he died. It's because of me that they all died." She started to weep again. "How will I tell Irina? How will I tell his wife?" she wept.

"Then it *was* you at my wedding at the Pierre, in 1975?" He stared at her thoughtfully.

She nodded and wiped her eyes. "I do very little modeling, now," she said. "I get a few requests now and then, but after I got my college degree, I tried to reinvent myself. The modeling was all very lucrative and exciting, but I wanted out of the celebrity scene. I knew full well that the fashion industry thrives on new young faces. I was lucky. They stuck with me longer than most."

They sat in quiet reflection for a while, and then Sol asked "How did you get into the modeling business in the first place? That's not a New York accent. Where are you from, originally?"

Jasmine hesitated. "I ... I was born in Egypt," she said, "and Malvina, you know, the founder of the famous Malvina agency?

She discovered me when I was twelve and brought me back here to train me as a model."

"Egypt?" Said Sol slowly, in amazement, "How extraordinary. You see, I was born in Egypt, too, in Cairo, by the Nile. I'm Jewish and my family was thrown out of Egypt, at the time of the Suez crisis. Our papers and passport were taken from us. We lost everything, and we went through some fairly rough times in Paris, before we came here." He paused, reflecting. Then he asked, "Are you from Cairo, too? What part of the city?"

"No," said Jasmine, trying to catch the eye of the triage nurse walking by, "I was born in a small village by the Nile, quite a way upriver from Cairo."

"Amazing!" said Sol, color creeping into his face, "What an extraordinary coincidence. We are both children of the Nile." He smiled. "Have you ever gone back to Egypt?"

"Once," said Jasmine, wishing they could change the subject. She hated discussing her personal life. "I have no wish to return."

"Neither have I," said Sol, sighing. "I was fifteen when I left there. It altered the path of my life forever. However, something from Egypt has settled permanently into my heart, like faint footprints in the sand." He smiled ruefully.

"Come to think of it, fifteen is the age of my son Aldo, now," he said.

He wiped his eyes and added "I often tell my son and daughter of the encompassing warmth of the sun and the clean golden beauty of the desert close by. I had a fine childhood, but I have never wanted to go back. I love it here. America has given me everything I value." He continued, reflective, his eyes clouding over, "Still, we did live in a beautiful house surrounded by lawns, and flowers, palm trees, and huge old mango trees." he paused, thinking back to that distant time, and added "you know, a family from one of those upper Nile villages used to come and harvest our mangoes once a year."

Jasmine had only heard part of what he was saying. She was tired and aching, the pain from her feet overwhelming all other thoughts, anxious to figure out how she might be able to get home, trying to focus the attention of the triage nurse who kept hastening past without a glance.

Sighing as she realized that the nurse was gone, she turned back to her companion.

"Did you say something about a family from a Nile village harvesting your mangoes?" She said, "My aunt told me that my mother and her family used to head along the river path to a big house in Cairo to do that for the owners once a year." She added, "They never did it again after 1956."

Sol stared at her, his face flushing, his thoughts in turmoil. " How old are you?" He asked at last, hesitantly. Jasmine was taken aback by the question. "I'm forty-four, way past resale date," she answered, laughing, turning to catch the sleeve of the triage nurse hurrying by. She did not notice that Sol was staring at her with fascination.

"I'm so sad and so tired," she said, the nurse having escaped her grip. She huddled in her seat and bowed her head.

Sol wiped at his eyes. He was having a hard time coming to terms with where his thoughts had taken him. At last he shook his head,

"Do you believe in coincidence?" He asked.

He saw that Jasmine wasn't listening, her attention caught by a scene developing between one of the triage nurses and a hysterical older woman with cuts all over her face, screaming and crying in anguish, hitting out at the guard, the nurse, anyone who approached.

"I have to find Jimmy," she screamed, "Fuck you all! Let me go! I have to go find Jimmy! Let me go!" flailing and weeping until she was wrestled out of triage into the area behind closed doors, where her voice could still be heard, faintly, "Let me go! Fuck you! Fuck you all! I must find Jimmy…"

Sol sighed, shuddered, and slumped back in his chair, his eyes closed.

Two more hours went by. Badly wounded people staggered in and were taken into the inner sanctum immediately by the triage nurses. They waited. Sol dozed, woke with a start, and dozed again. Jasmine limped her way to the water cooler and brought them both back icy cups of water. They washed their faces and hands and she went back for more. She was looking a little better, and some color had crept back into her cheeks. Sol glanced up and was immediately arrested by the intensity of her slanted green eyes as she smiled at him.

A memory surfaced, faint and indistinct, his mother's voice saying something about her grandmother, Elena. He started to give shape to the thought but Jasmine was pulling at his arm and talking. "Our turn has got to come soon," she was saying, close to tears, "The casualties keep pouring in, but there has to be a point where they actually get to us. We've been here for hours. I talked to the guard by the door, and he told me there was another plane that hit the Pentagon, and one that went down in a field somewhere. The word is that it's a terrorist group, Al Qaeda, led by Osama Ben Laden. They've shut down the airports, the bridges, and all access in and out of Manhattan."

Their turn came eventually. Jasmine's feet were attended to first, and she and Sol exchanged phone numbers as she was led into the inner area.

Sol hugged her with a strange intensity. "Jasmine," he said looking into her eyes, "don't hobble out of my life. We need to see each other again."

She smiled back at him and nodded, surprised, as a nurse led her away.

Sol called Jasmine two days later, "They said I have some minor heart problem," he said. "Nothing to worry about. My wife and I would love to get together with you, so that we can thank you properly for your extraordinary help. Is there anything at all that we can do for you? Would you at least come to us for dinner? You saved my life. And besides, there is something important I want to revisit with you."

"I'm so happy that all is well with you," Jasmine said, "I'm happy to have been of help. As for me, I'm slowly getting better, I just can't use my feet for a while." She laughed. "It's nice to lounge about with my feet up being waited on hand and foot. Malvina has been sleeping here and is taking better of care of me than I could possibly deserve. Thanks, Sol, it was really great to get to know you. I was so lucky to have you by my side throughout that dreadful day. Truly, I have no need of anything."

She added "I also hope we meet again, I somehow feel I have always known you, but I'll have to take a rain check for that dinner until my feet are usable again." She hesitated, feeling that she was on the brink of something, but not sure what it was. "You feel like family, Sol," she said at last, "I know we'll get together soon."

"Perhaps we could plan to get together on each anniversary of that day, and observe the remembrance together," said Sol, "after all, we shared a pretty unique moment of horror and of history. We can't pretend to be strangers."

Jasmine laughed. "You're so right," she said, "you certainly don't feel like a stranger. I suppose we could do that."

But time passed and life began to flow again around them, carrying them away from the horror they had survived, filling each of them with its demands, urgencies, successes and disappointments. The unique day that had propelled them into each other's lives receded into the background, and as each anniversary came and went, each gave thanks in silence and solitude for having survived to move on with their lives.

CHAPTER TWENTY-EIGHT

2002 New York
A SURPRISE FOR JASMINE

"Madam, the car and driver are waiting for you," the voice on the intercom announced.

"Coming," said Jasmine, taking the stairs two at a time, "I'm really late today. I overslept." She was in sneakers and shorts, and with no makeup, her hair tied back, she was unrecognizable as the sophisticated beauty she had so often paraded on the runways and magazine covers. She hopped into the car and gave the driver the Chelsea address of the shoot. She smiled to herself, happy that she had an interesting assignment to attend, reflecting that as a top model, even an old one in her forties, the most admired hair stylists and make-up artists still vied for the privilege of transforming her into celebrity mode.

As the car wove its way through heavy traffic, she could see little of her driver except a strong square neck and a head full of dark curls. When they arrived at the Chelsea building where the photographer had his studio, the driver got out and held the door open for her. He was very tall, and aside from broad shoulders, skinny as a whip. She smiled up at him as she thanked him, and the man blanched, gasped, and took a step back.

"Jamila?" he said in a hoarse whisper. "Jamila, is it really you? Jamila, *wallahi*, I never saw anyone else with eyes like yours. It *has* to be you. I would know you anywhere."

Jasmine stood, frozen to the pavement, about to hurry to her appointment at the studio where she was already inexcusably late.

"It can't be," she said at last, staring at him, tidal waves of emotion welling up in her, sending a flush to her cheeks and sudden tears to her eyes, "you can't be…? Walid? My God, what are you doing in America?" She was almost sobbing. He put out an arm to steady her.

"It's a long story," he said, "So much has happened. So much has changed in our lives and in our country. I never imagined for a moment that I would find you, little Jamila, here in New York City. After you vanished into that taxi with the American woman and disappeared, I thought I would never see you again." He paused, wiped his eyes and cleared his throat.

"I … I have to … I'm late …" she looked around frantically, as if the answer to an unexpressed question lay somewhere behind her.

Walid shook his head emphatically, grinning, "Before you disappear on me again, Jamila," he said, "I insist that we make a plan to meet. Could we get together this evening? I'm taking some courses at Hunter College most evenings, but I could meet you near the college later tonight and we could catch up if you like? Lots to talk about." His winning smile and the sparkle in his deep black eyes went straight to her heart and lodged there. Still reeling from the shock, she stammered "Where?"

"I finish at ten. Meet me at the coffee shop around the corner from Hunter, on 67th Street."

She nodded, turned, and raced upstairs to the photo shoot, fighting to regain her equilibrium. Her emotions in a turmoil, she did her best to hold them in check and give the photographer total professional attention to every detail and every suggestion.

"Great session," he said enthusiastically as she headed for the door, "Thanks, Jasmine, you are a pleasure to work with, as always." She smiled and nodded and ran down the stairs, relieved that the years of rigorous training had not let her down despite the momentous happening that had overwhelmed her earlier.

In the apartment, she raced to her closet and tore out garment after garment, casting them aside with an impatient frown. Nothing looked right. Some were too dressy, others too quirky. She had never before had trouble deciding what to wear. What was happening to her? Eventually she pulled out a luminous green Eileen Fisher silk tunic and decided to wear it over black leggings, with strappy gold sandals and gold jewelry.

When she was ready at last, she stared at herself for a long time in the mirror. Walid had known a barefoot girl with wild hair, leaping from boulder to boulder by the Nile with the ease and abandon of a goat. Would he find her again in the woman she had become?

"So tell me how you came to be here," she said some hours later, as they settled down in an alcove banquette in the coffee shop and gave the waiter their order. She had seen his eyes light up and his exclamation of admiration as she walked into the coffee shop where they had arranged to meet.

He sat back, his eyes drinking in the vision of this stunning woman who had once been the girl he had known years ago.

"Where to begin?" He sighed. "We all went through some very hard times. Your brother, Ali, went to work for Hamid and then left for Cairo one day with Hamid, and never came back. There were rumors that he had been in jail, and eventually that he had left the Muslim Brotherhood for more radical Islamists in the desert. No-one could tell me where you were or what had happened to you. It was as if you had fallen off the edge of the earth."

He looked at her, his eyes full of remembered sorrow.

"So much to tell you," he said, "but first I want to hear how it was for you all those years?"

Her eyes alight with memories, she told him about Malvina and Tim, how good they were to her, and how the arduous training she had undergone had enabled her to become a celebrated fashion model, and had opened the door to an education and a wonderful life.

"I have my own company now," she said proudly, "it's called Dune. I based a line of leisure clothing on the themes and colors of the desert, and it seems to have been catching on. I love thinking up new ways to use the brand to help women enjoy their lives."

"Did you marry?" he asked, and gave an audible sigh of relief at her answer.

"Of course there have been men," she added without apology, "but some part of me always held back when they got too close, always, that is, except for once, and he vanished from my life as quickly as he had entered it. I always thought I would marry when the right time came, and I guess it never did. How about you? Are you married?"

"Never had the time," said Walid with a grin, "besides, my heart belonged to a girl with wild hair and green eyes who always stood between me and the woman I was kissing." He laughed.

"It's so amazing that you are sitting here with me. Tell me everything." She laughed joyously, "Don't leave anything out, Walid. Nothing, you hear?"

Caught in the magnetism of the luminous green eyes he remembered so well, Walid leaned across the table and touched her arm. "You remember that my father had this fine job?" He said, "Well, my father lost his job when his boss fell out of favor with the government, and he couldn't find work anywhere. I left our village and went to live with him. We slept in the deserted house he had once worked in, and walked the streets during the day, looking for work, but no-one anywhere was looking for people like us. Everyone we saw was looking for work, too." He shook his head and sighed, remembering the frustration.

"Then one day, our luck changed," he said. "We were crossing the square across from the Cairo Museum, when a sleek black Cadillac pulled up beside us. An elderly woman with blue hair rolled down the back window and beckoned imperiously to my father. He went to the window."

"Mustafa?" She said, "What on earth are you doing here? Is this your boy?"

"My father was amazed that she had recognized him. It turns out she was in need of someone to run her household, and she remembered my father from the old days, from before he worked for Gamal Abdel Nasser's family. She was the widow of Mohammed Pasha, an aristocrat from the old regime. She was enormously wealthy, but she lived quietly in her magnificent house, hoping to evade the attention of the new ruling class."

"Go on," urged Jasmine, as he paused. She was completely engrossed in the tale he was telling. Walid smiled at her.

"Madame Pasha could no longer entertain the elite of politics and the arts, as she once had, but she held on valiantly to a certain standard of life she had known in the times when the great Jewish families and the British and French embassy staff came often to dine with her and admire the superb Impressionist art on her walls. Her husband was from a distinguished old Turkish family from the Ottoman empire, and she herself was half French. " He paused and looked away. "She was a great lady," he added, emotion clouding his voice.

Jasmine nodded, mesmerized by the story, and even more by the intensity of his personality. She still thought of him as the skinny goatherd who had caused flutters in her young heart, and she looked with wonder at the assured sophisticated man who now sat opposite her.

"Go on," she said again, eager to hear more, stirring her cappuccino absent-mindedly.

"To cut a long story short," said Walid, turning his head and grinning the wide joyous grin she remembered so well, "Madame Pasha took us both in that very day. She insisted on sending me to the best schools. She had no children of her own, and her life had dwindled to a kind of half-life, a life in the shadows since the political changes in Egypt. Most of her cosmopolitan friends had been expelled in 1956, and those who had not been forced to leave left of their own accord in the next few years. She had no-one with whom to share her wealth and her culture, so she focused on me. She taught me French, and she taught me the piano, and she insisted on the manners of an elite society that no longer had a place in Egypt."

"So she changed the little village goatherd into the gentleman you are today," said Jasmine, enthralled, "She did for you what Malvina did for me."

Walid nodded, "She urged me to delve into myself and find the best in myself. I did well in my studies at school, and I ended up at the American University in Cairo, with advanced studies in political theory and economics. My father worked for her and took care of her until he died, two years ago. He was happier there than he had been with the Nasser family. He knew that his polished skills were truly appreciated."

"What about your family in the village?" Asked Jasmine, "I went back once a few years ago, but I couldn't find anyone who knew anything about my family. The village itself was so changed. My family were gone, perhaps to Cairo, perhaps to another village, no-one could tell me. I saw your mother, though, but she didn't recognize me and all she could tell me was that you and your father had left and gone to Cairo." She paused, and added sadly, "did you know that she lost her sight?"

Walid shook his head, his eyes sad. "My father and I never went back to the Nile village," he said, sighing and shaking his head. "I knew nothing of what happened to her and to my brothers and sisters. How sad. I heard that the village got built up into a very different place, and there were rumors that a terrorist group had descended on our village one night not so long after you left, and had massacred many who were suspected of belonging to the Muslim Brotherhood. I think they may have targeted your family, because everyone knew that Sadik belonged to the Brotherhood. He liked to boast about it, didn't he? I would not be surprised if they took Hamid, too. Remember how he used to have those secret meetings at night?"

Jasmine nodded. They were silent, remembering. Then Jasmine said tentatively, "So you think they're all dead?" her voice barely above a whisper. She had imagined the life of the village continuing much the same without her, her brothers and sisters growing up, her parents growing old, moving to some other place. She was deeply troubled by what she was learning. Walid was distressed to see the shock in her face. He took her hand in his, his eyes sorrowful.

"You've been gone such a long time," he said with concern, "I'm sorry, Jamila. So much has changed and so much has gone to waste. Over the years, I watched Cairo crumble into a travesty of the wonderful city Madame Pasha so often described to me. Nothing worked any more. People streamed in from villages like ours in search of a better life, but the technological marvels that had drawn them to the urban centers in the first place were collapsing for want of an educated elite to keep them running and power them into a viable future. The sudden loss of a powerful educated infrastructure in the 1950s has left our beautiful country in chaos. Madame Pasha loved Egypt so much. She truly believed it would be possible to return her beloved Egypt to the days of its greatest glory. She made me promise to go to America to complete my education, and then to return and help our Egypt to rebuild."

His eyes watered and he brushed his hand across his face.

"What was she like? Madame Pasha?" Asked Jasmine.

"She had been a famous beauty in her youth," said Walid, smiling, "there were photos and portraits of her all over the house. She had a glorious mane of flowing black hair down to a tiny waist, and a pale patrician face with bright blue eyes. She had such style and elegance. She loved to tell me tales about her youth, and the princes and kings who were madly in love with her. Mohammed Pasha married her despite furious tirades of disapproval from his haughty Turkish mother. She never trusted Madame Pasha and hated it that Madame Pasha was the daughter of a flirty Frenchwoman and a handsome Egyptian without a *piaster* to his name. She never forgave her son for the marriage." He laughed. "Madame Pasha used to say Mohammed Pasha was insanely jealous and couldn't keep his hands off her." He grinned, "At least, that was what she told me. She loved to talk to me about her past, her adventures, her lovers, and her luxurious life as a queen of Cairo society."

He sighed and gazed into the distance.

"But by the time I knew her," he added, "she had become a very large old woman spilling out of her clothes, with faded hair, a kind heart, and a fondness for mounds of sweet pastries from Groppi that she consumed in huge quantities. She used to send me over to the Rue Adly, to Groppi's, two or three times a week, to pick up big boxes of her favorite pastries. The Swiss couple who owned the famous pastry shop had known her in her days of glory. They always asked after her health and topped off their signature boxes with an enormous blue bow. Once she said to me 'So much that gave me pleasure is gone forever. This, I still find pleasurable, and I have the money to indulge myself. If it kills me, so be it.' This she would say with a twinkle in her eye, and she would laugh her deep rich laugh at my consternation. Sometimes she would pop a melting pastry in my mouth and watch my eyes close with ecstasy as I tasted its sweetness.

'You should always take the time to taste pleasures with all your senses,' she would say, laughing, 'never rush a moment of delight.' She raised me like a prince and taught me to think like the poorest beggar on the streets of Cairo. She told me often that unless I could enter their lives fully in my imagination, I would never understand how to save Egypt from herself."

His eyes glinted with unshed tears. "I loved her," he said, his voice breaking," She died last year. She was more than a mother to me, and I will keep my promise to her."

Jasmine sighed deeply. She looked at her watch. The owner of the coffee shop had been hovering around their alcove for some time. No-one else was there. The waiters and other diners had all left. The owner pointedly dimmed the lights.

"Walid, tell me why you were driving for a car service?" She asked as she reluctantly got to her feet "From what you tell me, I would have thought she would have taken care of you."

"Madame Pasha always told me she would leave most of her money to orphanages and schools. She wanted to do some good in the Egypt she had loved so dearly. She made me promise to dedicate myself to helping my country to better times. She used to say, 'I have given you the tools for a good life, Walid, *ya ibni*, now go out into the world and make it all count for something, for my sake as well as your own.'

She did leave me a small legacy, but it would have been very complicated to get the money out of Egypt for my study and living expenses. The money stayed in Egypt. After her death I saw to the selling of the house and the paintings, as I had promised her I would. At auction they brought in quite a fortune and with the proceeds from the auction, I was able to fund the foundation she had wanted to create. When it was all taken care of as she would have wanted, I obtained a student visa to study for a PhD in economics and political science in America. I wanted to earn my way, but I was fortunate enough to be offered a scholarship for my studies, which gets us to the car service.

The balance of my expenses are covered by my car service. See, I love driving, and Madame Pasha often had me drive her around town for hours, up into the Mocattam hills to the Citadel, or over to Mena House and the pyramids and into the golden calm of the desert among the dunes. She used to say that it soothed her spirit. She also liked to sit in the car and watch the Garbage City people at work, collecting and recycling Cairo's garbage."

Jasmine interrupted, curious, "what is this Garbage City? I never heard of it. When I was in Cairo, the entire city seemed to be a garbage city."

Walid laughed. "The coptic *zabbaleen* were a marginalized minority of Coptic Christians fleeing discrimination and the paucity of jobs and agriculture everywhere. They were forcibly relocated by the government in 1969 and they built a community in the foothills of the Mocattam Hills. They developed their own industry, you know, clearing Cairo of its garbage." He laughed. "Did you know that there are seven beautiful cave churches there, carved out of solid rock? Madame Pasha told me that they are amazing, spacious caverns in the rock, with beautiful engravings. I never saw them, myself." He paused, thinking back to those days. Jasmine watched his eyes glow as he spoke.

"So anyway, when I realized that I needed a regular income over here, driving seemed like an obvious solution to my needs, as you can imagine," he said at last.

They walked companionably out into the street, side by side, silent with the weight of memories and old friendship. Around them, Manhattan was still turbulent with vibrant life. A rowdy group of young people much the worse for wear pushed by them, shouting and laughing, high on youth, and life in general. An ambulance screeched its way down the avenue and Jasmine shivered, the trauma of 9/11 surfacing from deep in her psyche. She turned to Walid, seeing the concern on his face, and explained, "I can never hear that sound without terror since the twin towers fell. Nothing has been the same since. I'll tell you all about that, but not now." Walid put an arm protectively around her shoulders, although she was nearly as tall as he, and he helped her into the car with old-fashioned courtesy, dropping her off outside her building, but not before they had arranged to meet again.

They saw each other frequently over the next few weeks. Walid persuaded her to go with him to Brooklyn, where he had discovered a small hole-in-the-wall restaurant, Baladi, run by a young Egyptian couple. They sat on rickety metal chairs, on worn Persian rugs, ate garlicky *meloukhia* and big bowls of *foul maddamas,* crisp *falafel* with a creamy *techina* tucked into delicious fresh-baked pita bread, and other dimly familiar foods from their childhood. Jasmine listened to the chunky nostalgic sound of the Arabic she had almost forgotten as he chatted with the young owners. She followed him into the New York life he was discovering and he followed her into the life she had built. The closeness between them blossomed like a flower whose seeds had always been there, waiting for the sun.

CHAPTER TWENTY-NINE

2002 New York
LOVE

It all seemed so natural and familiar that it almost took Jasmine by surprise when Walid asked if he could come upstairs one night after they had been dancing till quite late at one of the newer clubs opening on Ninth Avenue.

Jasmine looked up at him, uncertain if the words meant more than their actual meaning. His dark eyes laughed down at her, but gave her no clue.

"Of course," she said, and led the way. He looked around and nodded approvingly. "This is a lovely home," he said appreciatively, as he took in the comfortable furniture, the shelves of books, the floor to ceiling windows, the door open to an opulent bedroom with a king size bed and puffed up duvet. He sighed with pleasure, took her in his arms and kissed her. It was gentle at first, and then a hard, passionate, lingering kiss that awakened desires and hungers in Jasmine that she had not realized had been clamoring to be set free. He cradled her head tenderly, as if it were fine china that might break, and she held onto him tightly, as if he might vanish if she let go for one instant, and she wept with joy, recognizing the enormity of the moment.

"Move in with me," she said suddenly, looking up at him as they moved toward the open door to her bedroom, her eyes huge with longing. Her life held so much that was wonderful, but she had always known that she was waiting for something more, something elemental, and now she knew what that was. She wanted him with all her being and she didn't want to waste a minute.

"Should we marry?" he asked, sometime later, lost in a labyrinth between the ways of the old world and the new. "I love you so much. But you already know that. I have always loved you, even when you were twelve years old and I knew that you might become my father's second wife." He grinned as she gasped, "I never told you. I barely told myself. Now, Allah has smiled on me. He has given my Jamila back to me. So, tell me what you would like to do? I want to be with you always and forever."

Jasmine pondered the question. "Are you ready to stay here forever?" she asked, her voice trembling.

"I have another few years of study here," he said, "but after that I hope that you will come home with me to Egypt and we will work together to make our country a better place."

Tears welled in her eyes. She could not form the words she needed to make him understand.

"My home is here, my life is here, Walid," she said at last through her tears, "This is my country. You need to understand that I will never go back to Egypt. The Egypt I knew as a girl is as long gone as is the little Jamila you knew then. Yes, Egypt has left footprints on my heart, but I'm a woman now. I have defined my path, made my own place in the world here, in America. This is where I need to be. This is where I have taken root and flourished." She buried her head in the warmth of his chest and added, her voice breaking, "But I need you, too, I need you more than I can express. It is surely our destiny to be together. Couldn't you make your life here, with me?" She looked up at him, her eyes darkening with anguish.

Walid sighed deeply. "I want you more than life itself," he said somberly, holding her in his arms, "But I made a promise that I must keep. You need to know that there will come a time when I will have to go back and do what I can for our country." He looked into her sorrowful eyes and added "I will need to go, but I promise that I will return. My heart is yours, totally yours. Nothing can change that, and my promises to you are sacred. After I have fulfilled my word to the woman who gave me everything I am, I will be able to come back to you, I am a man of my word. I promise this to you and I will also keep my promise to Madame Pasha. I would not have been here and I would not have found you again had it not been for her."

So there it was. Separation would be inevitable. She heard echoes of Jason in his words and she shuddered at the remembered pain. She would never be able to feel secure in such a relationship. She could not put herself through that again. She would hold back her deepest emotions and enjoy what she could have for the taking, but she mourned what might have been, as they made passionate love that night.

Except that Walid was not Jason. He wanted it all. He loved her entirely, with his heart and his soul, and he held nothing back. He navigated her world with ease and elegance, and he took her with him to meet a large group of other Egyptian expatriates. At first, she was shy and reserved in their company, but gradually she overcame her hesitation and found solace in experiencing the subterranean murmurings of her lost childhood world. There was much concern among the Egyptian expatriates that the events of 9/11 would negatively influence their lives in the US. There had been an Egyptian on the plane that hit the twin towers.

Malvina and Tim learned about Walid from Jasmine with trepidation. Their unspoken fear was that he might be an undercover terrorist, or another Jason worming his way into her life for his own ends, but an evening in his company, experiencing the sincerity of his open temperament and the clear happiness in Jasmine's voice and eyes convinced them well before she had interpreted it for herself, that this was the man for their girl. They grew to like him enormously as they watched his courtship, and saw him wooing her with his joy, determination, and boundless love. They knew he would overcome her hesitations and that he would prevail.

Jasmine slowly began to let down her defenses and began to realize the full extent of the love she could not bring herself to believe. Walid was hers, he was not Jason. He might leave for a while, but he would be back. He had always been hers. Barefoot Jamila had loved the cheerful little goatherd and Jasmine loved the cultured caring man he had become. Everything came together in him, her past, her present, and her hopes for the future. He folded her past into her present as thoroughly as he folded her into his arms, and she knew with absolute certainty that he held her future. Nothing else mattered.

Jasmine had never been so happy. She insisted that Walid transform the second bedroom in the apartment into an office, with an old oak desk and comfortable chair, and he set out his work plan and began seriously to start researching and writing his thesis in the evenings. He still worked as a driver during the day. She often curled on the small couch with a good book in the evenings and watched him work, drinking in his presence whenever their glances met.

"Don't rush it," she said, laughing away some of the earnestness she found so endearing in him, "Take your time with your thesis. You'll have all the time in the world to finish." He grinned and wagged his finger at her, knowing full well that she meant to keep him right where he was, in his chair, at his desk, and by her side.

He corresponded constantly with his friends from the American University in Cairo, and tried to keep a finger on the pulse of what was going on politically in the country as time passed and news of the political situation worsened.

Jasmine had been feeling unwell and made an appointment to see the doctor.

"Shall I come with you?" asked Malvina, concerned.

"It's just a generalized discomfort. Nothing to worry about," said Jasmine. "I'll let you know what the doctor says. He'll probably say I need more exercise and more sleep." She laughed.

But her first call was to Walid, who pulled up his car, jumped out on the pavement, whirled around and around, and shouted with joy. His passenger, an elderly woman, looked on in some consternation until he got back in the car, apologized and said simply "I am going to be a father."

A couple of months later, they married. It was a simple ceremony at City Hall, with Malvina and Tim as witnesses.

Jasmine wore a dramatic white silk dress and stunning pharaonic gold and turquoise jewelry that Walid had given her that morning.

"Grasp your roots, Jamila," he said with solemnity as he fastened the beautiful necklace around her neck, "You have the exquisite beauty of our ancient people. You must never lose who you are. No matter who you have become, you carry the blood of your ancestors forever. We are marrying each other knowing that we each carry Egypt in our blood. Together we must always help each other to treasure our past in our present. Our child must always know and respect his heritage. Make me that gift, embrace our shared heritage for the baby's sake as well as for mine."

She smiled deep into his eyes as she thanked him, thinking that she had married a man of true gentleness and idealism. She took care not to remind him that she was no longer who she had once been. With profound gratitude she embraced what they had between them and swore silently to herself that she would do everything in her power to be true to her self as well as to their marriage and would not allow their differences to overshadow the deep commitment they had to each other.

They went to great lengths to dodge the *paparazzi*. Even though the glory days of her modeling career had passed, Jasmine was still a star. She was three months pregnant, and radiant with joy. She had never been more beautiful. She had been afraid that at the age of forty-five she might be too old to conceive, but the pregnancy surprised and delighted them both.

"Do you want to have a religious ceremony?" Walid had asked her, dubiously, "Are you still a Muslim? Have you taken another religion?"

Jasmine shook her head. "Not a Muslim, and not anything else," she said, laughing. "I'm just me. I know we have to have our relationship formalized for the little one's sake, but that is all it is. We have long been married already in my eyes, and in yours."

Arm in arm with Malvina and Tim, they turned heads as the four of them wandered through the torturous back-ways of China town in their finery, their happiness spilling from them in a golden haze. They found the sumptuous Chinese banqueting hall they had been searching for, hidden behind the squalor, a vision in gold and scarlet, acres of empty tables and chairs stretching beyond the table where they celebrated the marriage with a banquet of esoteric dishes, waited on hand and foot by a phalanx of star-struck waiters. Malvina, who had planned it all, beamed with pleasure to see Jasmine so happy.

They honeymooned in France, tasting the golden warmth of the sun on the Riviera, weaving their way through the crowds on the Croisette, saturating their hearts with the deep blue of the welcoming Mediterranean, and attending designer fashion shows in Paris, where Jasmine was feted and courted like visiting royalty. It was a time out of time and they savored it to the full.

CHAPTER THIRTY

2003 New York
BIRTH

Jasmine had been feeling more and more like a lumbering elephant as the months moved along, although Walid assured her, grinning, that she was not in the least like an elephant, and most certainly not a lumbering one. To her surprise, she had found herself much in demand to model upscale maternity clothes. She could pick and choose and name her own price. Showing off the baby bulge was newly in fashion, and fashion raced to keep up with the demand. Designers rushed to create styles for this new fashion moment. For Jasmine, assignments came in thick and fast. She became the symbol of beautiful motherhood-in-waiting. She enjoyed using all the skills she had relegated to a back burner for several years, and Walid loved seeing his gorgeous wife in the full bloom of middle age gracing the covers of magazines and the gossip pages of newspapers. Malvina and Tim, eager to assume the role of grandparents-elect, filled the time with worry and gifts.

The pregnancy had gone well. After a brief stint with nausea she had never felt better, or happier. She had agreed to an amniocentesis, because of her age. That had been unpleasant, but was a small price to pay for peace of mind. She went to classes for natural childbirth and busied herself decorating the baby's room while Walid focused on his thesis.

"You can see why it might be a good idea to know whether we're having a boy or a girl?" teased Walid as she obsessed about the color of the walls, the design of the furniture and the baby clothes, holding up tiny garments for his approval. He had wanted to know the sex of the baby, but Jasmine had insisted that they let it be a surprise.

"No problem," said Jasmine complacently, I have found the perfect color. I'm choosing this one, it's called *Nile Green*, and it would work for a boy or a girl. Besides, I like the name. What do you think?"

"The Nile wasn't green," said Walid solemnly, shaking his head, "It was a swirling grey, filled with the silt that made our valley fertile." He watched for her reaction, and burst out laughing, holding his hands up in surrender when she ran at him and pummeled his chest. "I do like it very much, Jamila," he said through his laughter. "Mercy! I was only kidding. It's such a lovely delicate color and it will make the perfect backdrop for everything else you may want to do. The room will be beautiful." He had moved his desk and chair to a corner of the living room.

When the contractions began, she felt a moment of panic. She had been ready for weeks, her small case packed and standing by the door, but when she realized that her body was taking control and that her time was upon her whether she wanted it to be or not, she was suddenly overwhelmed with fear of the unknown. Would she know how to do this? Would she know how to be a mother? Then she remembered the ease with which Salwa had birthed her babies with none of the amenities she would be fortunate enough to have around her. She would know how to do this. She would clear her mind, and focus on her breathing, and all would be well. She knew in her bones that all would be well.

She woke Walid just as her waters broke, and both of them eyed with panic the water gushing uncontrollably from her body. Walid pulled clean towels from the linen closet and packed them around her in the soaking bed, his eyes shining with excitement.

"We should time the contractions, I think," he said, and when they realized the contractions were coming in every five minutes, Walid phoned the doctor, his voice shaking.

"Bring her in right away," said the doctor, "and don't worry, first babies take a while to make their entrance."

Jasmine bundled herself up in a loose coat and stood waiting uncomfortably outside the building for a moment, trying to center her energies as Walid stalked a taxi. They would be going to New York Hospital, and she had not set foot there since the shattering experience of 9/11. She would try not to think of that.

This time there was no waiting about when they arrived. No triage nurses. No time to see anything except walls and doors scrolling past as an aide wheeled her rapidly into the elevator in a wheelchair to where the doctor was waiting. Before she knew it, they were on the sixth floor, Walid holding her hand and rubbing her back as the contractions began to slam in thick and fast. It felt to Jasmine as if everything around her had suddenly whirled her into fast forward. She had no time to think, no time to react. Only to feel, and to respond to her body and her baby. She gave in to the feverish acceleration inside her and around her. Nothing mattered anymore except what her body was compelling her to experience. When this was over, she would be a mother. Tears of joy filled her eyes, and Walid, holding her hand, exclaimed anxiously "Are you alright?"

"It's a boy!" the words seeped through the delivery room noise, every metal clink sudden and sharp as a knife, each sound somehow magnifying into a boom.

"Let me see him." Jasmine managed to get the words out although her body had briefly shut down as the baby burst his way into the world. She felt as if her entire being was ringing like a bell, ringing to celebrate the arrival of her baby, ringing that the birth was over. She could feel the ringing in her bones. She could hear it in her ears.

"Are you OK, Jasmine?" The doctor's face hovered anxiously above her. He smiled at her and began to massage her abdomen disturbing her brief moment of all-enveloping calm. When she cried out, he explained "It's the afterbirth, don't you remember? It has to be expelled."

"My baby? Where's my baby?" mumbled Jasmine, her ears gradually registering a rhythmic insistent mewling somewhere in the room. Someone put a warm little body on her abdomen, the tiny chest moving up and down against her bare skin and she sighed with relief and delight. "So here you are, Wally," she whispered, "So pleased to meet you in person." She giggled and the doctor straightened up from his task in astonishment.

A nurse whisked the baby away to be weighed and measured, calling out "He's a fine fellow, Mrs. Mahfouz, well done!"

Everything ached, and nothing ached.

Walid and the doctor were talking in low voices just out of earshot. She strained to focus but all she could hear was a low irregular murmur. She tried to say "Don't forget to call Malvina and Tim," but the words wouldn't form, and only a tiny stream of indistinct sound left her lips. The doctor was washing his hands, and when she heard the water stop she shifted her head, and heard Walid say "She wouldn't let us find out the sex of the baby ahead of time. She kept saying 'best surprise in the world, and you want to spoil it?'"

The doctor was nodding sympathetically, his hands capably stitching a small tear. "She's a lucky woman," he said, "a *prima gravida* at her age can present many complications. All is good here. You're a very lucky man, my friend. She's as healthy as she is beautiful."

Jasmine winced. The euphoria was wearing off. Why, she wondered, were people talking about her as if she couldn't hear? Her eyes closed. The baby was gone. She was drowsy and content. Voices hummed above her as she fell asleep.

CHAPTER THIRTY-ONE

2007 New York
RE-TOOLING HOPE

Jasmine was lost in wonder every day, as her baby grew more alert and stronger every minute. He smiled, he giggled, his cheeks grew round and rosy. She could not believe that she and Walid together had managed to produce this charming creature. She reveled in every minute of early motherhood, and was only excelled in her devotion by Malvina, who embraced the role of grandmother with almost religious fervor. Wally was an easy baby and gave them few of the sleepless nights they had expected.

As time passed, she noticed that Walid's constant communication with his friends from the American University had slowed. He was filled with delight in his small son, and the pleasure of being there to see his first steps and hear his first words transported him into a joy he had never known before. When he was offered a part-time professorship at City College, he accepted with alacrity and began to savor the result of all his hard work. Although they never discussed it any more, both he and Jasmine knew that someday he would return to Egypt to fulfill his promise to Madame Pasha, but as the years passed and Wally became more and more the center of their lives, "someday" moved further and further away.

Malvina and Tim often came over for dinner, and reveled in the happiness of their little family. One evening, Tim and Walid sat talking political theory in the living room, while Wally slept the sleep of an active four-year-old close by. Malvina cornered Jasmine in the kitchen as she was putting food away in the refrigerator.

"What a delicious dinner, Jasmine," she said, appreciatively. "You have become such a great cook."

Jasmine laughed, "I learned it at my American mother's knee," she said, grinning.

"Very funny," said Malvina, laughing with her, adding "I've been wanting to talk to you about some of the things we actually did share. I don't have to tell you that the fashion business is so different now from the way it was when I started the Malvina agency, and even from when you began your training as a model. It has lost much of its personal touch to the internet and the technological tools of the 21st century. It's not nearly as much fun for me as it used to be. I've been giving the matter of the future of the agency some serious thought."

She gave Jasmine a rueful smile. "Truth is, I'm tired, Jasmine, I'm 78 years old. I've done my bit. We own the townhouse outright, Tim's paintings have sold really well, and Tim and I have enough put away for a comfortable retirement. I'd like to step back a little. Would you consider heading up the Malvina agency now that your Dune brand of lounging clothes is off and running? Would you have time to take on something else?"

"Oh, Malvina," said Jasmine, flustered and surprised, "of course you know I'll help you any way I can, and I'll help you to decide what to do. I am so honored that you have asked this of me. I hope you won't be too disappointed, but I won't be able to take full responsibility for it. You see, Walid has been working with me, helping me to think through another idea I have had for some time now. I find I passionately want to do something that will help people through life-changing events in some way.

As you know, Marcel left me the money he was planning to put into my fashion brand, and I still have most of my savings from my modeling career, so I don't need to focus on earning a living. Have you thought of offering Monica and Claire a chance to buy in? They are such terrific bookers, and they've been with you for years."

"Great idea," said Malvina, "I had thought that perhaps the time has come to give the opportunity to Monica and Claire, but I wanted to offer it to you first. What is it that you and Walid are planning?"

"It hasn't fully taken shape yet," said Jasmine. "I've been pretty busy with little Wally, and I don't want to miss a minute of his childhood. Obviously, I won't be having another baby at my age, so I really want to savor every moment of this little guy's life. He's my miracle child. I love being a mother.

But I guess that what I really want to do with the rest of my life, as well as being a full time mom and a now-and-then fashion model, is to establish a secure way for young women to escape abuse and violence and to help them to a fresh start. It's all about giving people opportunity, isn't it? That's what you did for me. That's what Madame Pasha did for Walid. So many people whose lives are touched by tragedy or political circumstance seem to have been able to pick themselves up and move on, but others sink and drown in the aftermath.

I've been spending time while Wally is at school, talking to Matilda Moran, that extraordinary psychologist. I'm sure you know her work. I met her when I was helping out for the Parents Association at Wally's school. Her daughter and Wally are friends. While they've been having playdates with each other, Matilda and I have been doing the same, trying to figure out ways of identifying destructive vulnerabilities in individuals before they take hold. I guess you could say it's playdates for both generations. We're trying to develop a way of intervening in time to put the feet of the vulnerable onto a safe path.

Malvina nodded.

"The more research Matilda and I have done," Jasmine continued, "the more we found young women, many of them aspiring actresses or models, falling through the cracks of society into the dark underbelly of the world they had hoped to find. I want to give them a rope of salvation to grab hold of and save themselves. I'm calling it ReTooling Hope. The plans are not yet fully developed, but I've been working on an interactive website. I mean to take full advantage of the internet and social media. It would be great if we could also develop a system that allows for interventions and a refuge, but that will take major money, and I'm not sure yet how to go about getting grants. I want to offer the project in gratitude to a world that has given me so much."

Malvina hugged her. "I'm so proud of you, Jasmine," she said.

$\mathcal{C}$HAPTER THIRTY-TWO

2008 New York
ENCOUNTERS WITH DESTINY

The summer months had been hot and humid, but this had not been an unbearable summer with heat wave following heat wave. Jasmine and Walid had enjoyed having the open city streets to themselves as Manhattan emptied out on weekends, the young and the not so young shedding work and chores to seek the peace of their summer homes or to join house parties in their shared Long Island getaways, leaving the city to the festivals and parks and to those brave enough to remain.

As the season began to slip into fall, Jasmine felt a familiar unease gnawing at her. September brought intimations of winter ahead. She dreaded the cold. As Labor Day came and went, the faint feeling of dread became a drumbeat of fear. She knew it had nothing to do with the approach of winter. She knew what it was. She knew that the time had come to face it.

As they sat comfortably eased back in their dining room chairs, replete, contemplating the dirty dishes after a fine breakfast and trying to decide who would interrupt the moment of quiet pleasure to put them in the dishwasher, she turned away from the table and faced Walid.

"Tomorrow is September 11th", she said, her voice strained, "Walid, would you come with me to the 9/11 memorial gathering, down at the World Trade Center? I've never actually been down to ground zero since that terrible day, but today, I feel compelled to go. I need to lay it to rest. After all, it's five years later. That's a long time. Besides, I have you, now, and I have Wally. You give me strength, and you have both given me wonderful images to superimpose on the horrific images from that dreadful day. I am starting to realize that I am going to have to confront my demons head on. Irina has been going to the gathering every year, and she insists that it gives her comfort and peace." She looked pleadingly at him. Walid had not understood her continuing distress. She knew that he had not fully understood that the heart of America had been broken beyond repair on that day.

Coming together year after year in mourning and remembrance, Americans everywhere recognized with sorrow that the youth of America was over. The vibrant optimism that had built vast cities from wilderness and given shelter to thousands, had truly lost its innocence forever. Children, grandchildren, and great-grandchildren of those who had fled discrimination and violence from elsewhere in the world had been forced to acknowledge their continuing vulnerability. The chaos their ancestors had fled had crashed inescapably into their American lives and destroyed their hope of peace and their faith in humanity. They would never feel safe again.

Walid glanced at her, disconcerted. They had watched the yearly solemn ceremonies together on television in the past, but Jasmine had never before wanted to go anywhere near the scene of her worst nightmare. Watching the ceremonies on the television screen had only been possible for her because she knew she could walk away from it to regain her equilibrium whenever she wanted. Walid worried that returning to the scene itself might be too much for her.

"I really think that Wally is old enough to come with us," she said. "He's four years old and full of questions. I think I can handle it all, now that I have you both. My life with the two of you has given me distance and perspective, and has brought me happiness greater than I could ever have imagined, five years ago. Of course, I still mourn Marcel and the thousands who died that day, but I know I can't change what happened. I can't deny it. I shall have to learn to move beyond it. I think that actually being there, together with others who share my memories, may help me to come to terms with it at last."

"Of course we'll plan on being there with you, if you're sure that's what you want?" said Walid, eyeing her dubiously, still concerned.

"It is." Jasmine said simply.

"Or we could watch it on television like every other year?" He suggested cautiously, still not convinced that this was a good idea.

"I need to go there, this time," said Jasmine firmly, "I need to be there with others who went through it. I need to see."

They took the subway down, and Wally giggled and jumped about, filling the somber atmosphere with his cheerful chirping as the three of them walked hand in hand to where the open air celebrations were to be held.

"That day was just like this," said Jasmine sadly, looking up into the cloudless blue sky mantling the city. She smiled at her tall husband and fidgety little son, holding Wally's hand tightly so that he wouldn't slip off into the gathering crowd.

As they moved into the crowd and looked around, a deep and mournful drumbeat thudded into their consciousness as it came louder and closer. The police band and wailing bagpipes approached, the bold colors of the flag they carried flapping in a light breeze.

Glancing to the right, Jasmine suddenly gasped.

"Walid," she said, her voice cracking, "I don't believe it! Follow me," and clutching her son's hand, she pushed her way through a forest of churning bodies to where a man stood, bald head bowed, still deeply engrossed in the ceremony. He had aged, and he had not noticed her arrival, but tears spilled from her eyes as she touched him on the shoulder.

"Sol," she said, "Sol, we meet again." He turned, startled, and then gave a shout, his face contorted with emotion as he saw her face.

"My God! Jasmine! This is the first time I have been able to find the courage to come down here," he said, his voice breaking, "How wonderful to find you here, the elusive Jasmine, always too busy to come to dinner." She laughed through her tears as they hugged and wept together. Joy and pain mingling.

At last, Sol turned to the tall young man standing next to him, and then pulled forward the small woman almost hidden beside him.

"My wife, Lara, my son, Aldo, and the tall girl over there with all the flowing clothes and hair is my eighteen-year-old daughter, Rivka."

He added with a grin, "heaven forbid she should be seen standing with her parents."

Turning to the woman beside him and gently nudging her forward, he said, "Lara, I have been wanting you to meet this woman for five years. This gorgeous young woman put her own life in jeopardy to save mine, five years ago. You know who she is. I would have died on that day, if it had not been for Jasmine."

Lara, her rust-colored hair ruffled appealingly by a sudden breeze, put her arms around Jasmine's tall figure and hugged her warmly, tears creeping down her cheeks. "We can never repay you," she said, emotion shaking her voice, "I was so aware throughout the tolling of name after name that if it had not been for you, my husband's name would have been among them. You cannot know what your strength and courage on that day has meant to our family. You cannot know how deeply I thank you. I was so sorry that you never came to our house for dinner, but when you always said no, Sol explained that you were probably too scarred by the experience to want anything that might remind you of it. I am so happy to meet you at last. Your name is a part of our family, and we can never forget what you did for us all."

The tall young man, grinning widely, said "Are you really Jasmine? The celebrity model, Jasmine? Man! What a thrill to meet you face to face, 'off the page' so to speak."

Jasmine by now was giddy with delight. She pulled Walid and Wally into focus. "Mine!" She said proudly. "My husband and son. I never thought we would meet again. This is my first time here, too."

The ceremony was almost over. Jasmine, Sol and their families walked slowly away together, talking and laughing. They found a diner not too far away. They relaxed into a celebration of their own, exchanging news of the intervening years, and enjoying the easy camaraderie that flowed between Sol and Jasmine and so comfortably included each one of them. Walid, a little taken aback by the turn of events, spoke little, but Wally rode happily on the shoulders of the tall son of his mother's friend.

"Look!" he cried, clutching Aldo's head, "I'm taller than all of you."

"Well, will you look at those two," exclaimed Lara, laughing, "they could be brothers. They actually look so much alike, same exact facial bone structure."

Sol glanced around sharply. He waited for Jasmine as they left the area. He seemed about to speak, but Wally pulled her away to look at something and she turned and waved at Sol, laughing, as she was dragged away. They went their separate ways again. He did not quite know what to do with the disquieting thought that had come to him in the emergency room and had never left him since.

Jasmine felt lighter, almost buoyant as they made their way home. She knew she had done the right thing by attending the memorial ceremony. She would not need to return another year. She nudged Walid playfully, "You were very quiet," she said. He pulled her round and kissed her. "It's hard to realize how ephemeral happiness is," he said quietly, "but it's really important."

As the months and seasons followed one another down the years, Walid redoubled his efforts to complete his thesis. He had toyed with the idea of leaving his car service and working on his studies full time, but he also felt it was important to keep his hand in with the real world while he tinkered with a theoretical one in the evenings. It took a long time, but eventually it was done. His thesis had been accepted and he had his PhD. His professorship and his interactions with students gave him immense satisfaction.

But the world had moved on as well.

Tossing and turning in bed one night, he realized that Jasmine was lying awake by his side.

"Walid, talk to me," she said, "whatever is worrying you will feel less threatening if we share it."

"You're right," he said, sighing, "but I wanted to spare you the anxiety. These past weeks I've been hearing from Salim again. He's been telling me about the group of literati and political activists he has put together. He tells me that there is a growing disaffection in Egypt for the Mubarak regime. He tells me that the economy is tanking without hope of rescue and that the hardships faced by all levels of the population increase on a daily basis." He groaned. "I have such a wonderful life here with you and Wally, and my work at the University. I didn't want to listen, or to pay attention."

He rolled over and took her in his arms, burying his face in her hair, whispering, "but then he also told me about our friend, Basri, imprisoned without trial. They can't find out where he is, he must be hidden in some obscure detention facility, Salim thinks. They are pretty sure he is still alive but there are substantiated rumors of prisoners like Basri being subjected to constant torture. His parents come crying to Salim every day. 'do something, *effendi*,' they say, but Salim can do nothing. I can't bear to think about it. Basri was such a cheerful little fellow. Roley poley and with an indestructible good nature. Ate too much and talked too much. He is married and has two small children." He lifted his head, summoned up a bitter smile, and looked into her eyes.

"It's so painful to me to learn about these things and do nothing," he said, his voice breaking. "Here I am, warm as toast in my comfortable apartment, safe in the arms of my love, my son asleep next door. I have everything. I need nothing. I share nothing with them."

Jasmine felt her heart plummet. She had hoped that their life together would mute Walid's plans to return to Egypt as time melded him more and more into the life they built together, but she knew and loved the caring heart of the man she had married. She felt the loss and pain in his words. He would go back sooner or later. She knew it in her bones. She held him tight and kept her thoughts to herself, comforted that he understood her feelings and that she had his promise that if he left to go to Egypt, he would return.

The political situation in Egypt continued to deteriorate and their expatriate friends gathered together over coffee and discussed it every week, shaking their heads in distress over the loss of the Egypt they had lost and left. But it was a distress without pain. They had each found their place in America, and reveled in the comfort they had earned. Only Walid took it so personally. Only Walid had made an inviolable promise to return.

"Things are so bad over there," he said to Jasmine, his voice desperate, his forehead creasing as they sat at dinner with their small son in their apartment. "You cannot imagine. Corruption of every kind is everywhere, in government, in everything the average person faces every day. I've heard recently that attacks on the Muslim Brotherhood are increasing. It's horrifying to think that there are now many more uneducated and unemployed people crammed into the urban centers looking for work than when my father and I were seeking employment all those years ago." He held his head in his hands. "I don't know what would have become of my father and me if we had not been taken in by Madame Pasha," he said, his voice catching, "not a day goes by that I don't think of her and what she did for us." The small boy watched gravely as his father sat, head in hands, his food untouched.

"Can you help me with my homework, Daddy?" he asked at last, offering the only distraction in his power "and will you read me a story when I go to bed?"

"Homework?" Said Walid, laughing, "I didn't know they gave homework to four-year-olds?" He smiled at the earnest little boy and made space at the table for Wally and his requests. He had often referred to his own work on his thesis as 'homework,' and it amused him greatly to see his small son stretching to imitate the father he admired so much.

But as soon as he had read the required bedtime story with all the grunts, squeals, whistles and roars that the story required, he kissed his sleepy son, tucked him in, breathing in the comfort of the damp warmth of his head, and returned to Jasmine in the living room. She looked at him anxiously.

"Shall I turn on the TV?" She asked, seeing him sitting motionless at his desk. He shook his head and turned to look at her.

"We need to talk," he said, his voice catching in his throat, "I cannot bear to sit here in comfort, while my country writhes in torment. The Mubarak regime has to come to an end. The military elite have accumulated unimaginable wealth on the backs of people like you and me. Those people live without hope. The gap is enormous. I hear that the ferment is reaching a point where the politicos and literati may finally join forces and take action sometime this winter. More and more celebrities are lending their names to the movement."

Jasmine's eyes filled with tears as she came to terms with everything he had not said. There was so much love between them and so much unspoken pain. She could sense his soul leaning further and further toward the country of their birth. She took his hand, "Walid," she said at last, her voice breaking, "I don't want to lose you, but I know that if I try to keep you here, I'll lose you anyway. Make your plans. Go and be with your friends. Go and fight for Egypt's future. Go and keep your promise. Wally and I will be here waiting for you when you can return, and then you will return to us for good."

He nodded. "Thank you for saying that, Jasmine," he said, "I know how hard that was for you to say, and maybe it will not happen quite yet." But he had tears in his eyes and the days that followed were heavy with gloom.

In January 2011, Walid, despondent and emotional, said goodbye to everything he held dear and returned to Cairo as he had promised. Distant tremors and stirrings of change and uprising in Egypt had percolated into the international press, and they both knew that he needed to be a part of whatever was about to happen.

"I'll be back soon," he promised fervently, pale and inarticulate with the pain of parting, "Keep yourself and the boy safe until I get back. "

"Be careful," Jasmine said. "My love, be careful. Things are not as they used to be. There will be much danger in the changes you wish to bring about. Don't forget that I need you. Our son needs you. Come back to us, safe and sound."

Walid nodded, afraid to speak and release the hot flood of tears, and was gone.

CHAPTER THIRTY-THREE

2011 Cairo, Egypt
WALID

Walid stepped off the plane in Cairo into harsh sunlight and the cacophony of many voices. He had reserved a car and driver to take him to his hotel. He had chosen a small hotel off the beaten track, conveniently close to Tahrir Square. He had known of the place in his Madame Pasha days. It was also within walking distance of his friend Salim's apartment. As the car bumped along neglected roadways into the center of town he reflected that it was strange to be coming home to a place where there was no-one to welcome him with shrieks of delight, delicacies set out for his pleasure, and hugs tight enough to take his breath away. He suddenly felt crushed by the deep losses of his father, and of Madame Pasha. How lucky he had been to find Jamila. He recognized that destiny had twice intervened to change the course of his life for the better, once when Madame Pasha had given him a home, and then again when he had found the love of his life in New York City. His home, he knew, was now with Jamila and little Walid. He had no fear. He was confident that nothing would keep him from returning to them as soon as he could.

His few good friends from his days at the University had finally urged him not to postpone his return to Cairo, letting him know as clearly as they could, relying on code words and innuendos, that the political unrest was coming to an imminent head, and sharing with him the details of where he could join them to march with them into the history books, as they had so often planned on doing in their University days. Walid would keep his promise to Madame Pasha.

The car dropped him in front of the hotel. Walid looked up anxiously at the blinking neon light with its missing letters. There was no porter to help with his bag, so he carried it into the dim lighting of the lobby, noticing that the place looked painfully decrepit. The unshaven individual at the front desk of the hotel glared at him suspiciously and handed him a key as he registered his passport. The elevator was out of order again, he muttered with a sneer, a pungent smell of garlic following Walid as he climbed the stairs to his room at the top of the building, happy that he had only brought one small suitcase. He was out of breath when he reached his room, and he sighed, and shook his head. This was not a very good beginning.

He looked around the room, registering peeling wallpaper on the walls and a faint sheen of dust on every surface, including on the chest of drawers standing across from the bed. He didn't want to think what the drawers might be like inside. He would have to leave his clothes in his case, he decided, wrinkling his nose in dismay. The bed itself looked clean enough, a black metal frame with a thin mattress covered by worn white sheets. He glanced longingly at it. He yearned to sink into bed to sleep off his weariness, but he knew that he must find his friends as soon as possible in order to participate in whatever they were planning for the next day. His head was starting to ache.

Becoming gradually aware of a rising tumult outside his window, he decided it would be wise to leave his laptop and his papers hidden. He searched the room for a suitable spot, but could find nothing that could be locked, until he discovered a squeaky floorboard that he could pry up from the floor. Just the thing, he thought. His passport and identity papers would be safer hidden under the floorboards than in the room or on his person as he walked the streets. He could see that the hotel was sorely dilapidated, and the neighborhood certainly did not inspire confidence. It had been a fairly decent little hotel when he had last seen it, but it had clearly gone way past its better days. He pulled over a small yellow rug that lay beside the bed and covered the area where he had returned the floorboard to its original state. With difficulty, he also managed to squeeze his phone and his laptop into the cavity before pressing the board back down. He would be back to retrieve them in due course.

He and Jamila had discussed the fact that they might have serious communication difficulties when he reached Cairo, and in fact, when he tried his new international cellphone he could not get a dial tone. There was, of course, no landline in his room, and even had there been a phone, it would have been fairly unlikely that it would be working, given the current state of the country's infrastructure. Opening his laptop he discovered that a blackout on all internet and social media had recently been put into effect. He could not even send Jamila an email to let her know that he had arrived safely. He knew she would be watching the news avidly on television and would follow the situation as closely as she could, but he wished with all his heart that he could hear her voice or see her face just once more, before plunging into a situation that was coming more and more into focus as unstable and unpredictable.

As soon as he had settled his possessions, concerned and exhausted from the long plane ride, he gave a last worried glance around the room to make sure that everything of value was hidden, and set out for the designated meeting place to connect with his friends. Excited anticipation had kept him awake for the entire flight from New York, but now that the adrenaline had subsided, he walked along with a heavy heart, enveloped in an invisible cloak of sadness as he observed the subtle signs of disintegration all around him. He had forgotten to what an extent wall after wall smothered in bold graffiti felt like an assault on the eye and on the spirit.

He made his way through a network of small streets, garbage strewn underfoot, smells of rotting vegetables making him nauseous. Women veiled and in black from head to foot glided silently past him, shadows without faces. He was appalled to see how the city had deteriorated in the few years he had been away in America, or, he reflected, perhaps the contrast now stood out more clearly. If only Jamila could see this, he thought, she might understand how much Egypt needed people like them to bring their education and their skills to help to improve the country.

At last he found Salim's address, an ancient building with handsome ironwork in need of repair, worn stone steps and medieval balconies. In an upstairs room he found several men gathered. They greeted him with roars of eager welcome. He was saddened to see ravages of age heavy in the faces of the young men he had known in his student days, as they all crowded around, hugged him, and thumped him on the back.

"So you really came back to us, Walid," his friend Salim said, eyes shining with patriotic fervor. "I always hoped that you would. Our time has come at last. I knew you would want to be a part of that. Everything is organized. You are just in time. We march tomorrow. People are already pouring into the city from the villages, and our plan is to occupy Tahrir Square and other plazas peacefully, for as long as it takes to obtain the changes we must have. We want to show the entire world the multitudes gathering here in Cairo, clear evidence that our demonstrations and marches can effect change without violence. Thousands, no, *millions* are waiting to join us to demand the overthrow of Hosni Mubarak. I promise you, a new day will dawn." He laughed triumphantly as he glanced around the room, and the others joined in.

Walid listened patiently. "What will you put in power in his place?" he asked, "Is the Brotherhood on board with all this?"

They brushed his questions aside, elated by the strong wind that carried them on the wings of their ideals, convinced that solutions would appear as needed. For the first time, Walid found a sliver of doubt in his heart. It was all very well to have ideals, but without a new structure to replace the old, how could this wounded nation recover?

A boy arrived with overflowing baskets of food and drink. The men tipped him generously, expansive in their exhilaration, and they roared with laughter as he glanced at the money in his hand and backed swiftly out of the room, hurtling quickly down the stairs and out, fearing that they had made a mistake and might demand their money back.

They ate and drank their fill, slapped each other on the back, toasting the revolution to come, going over their plans for the marches they would lead next day. One of them had brought his *oud,* another, a set of drums. They sang deep into the night, clapping, stomping their feet, thumping out rhythms as the music rose in volume and intensity. They harmonized sweet ballads of love and loss and poured the energy of their passion into rousing marches.

Despite the relentless commotion, Walid managed some sleep on a mattress on the floor in a corner of the big room, a rough blanket pulled over his head, jet-lag taking over at last, swallowing up all sounds of merriment into a welcome oblivion. Salim shook him awake early in the morning, and bleary eyed he washed and pulled himself into shape, regretting that he had left his change of clothes at the hotel. Someone lent him a toothbrush and handed him a cup of strong Turkish coffee.

Gathered at the entrance to the building, Walid and his friends watched, awed into silence, as waves of humanity swept endlessly past them, men in *galabeyas* running fast mingling with men running in shirts and suits, men and boys converging from every angle carrying stones and banners, entire families bearing tents, small children, and food. Women of all ages came running, too, their faces intense and tight with purpose under the many colors of their head scarves, all generations united in anger and protest, feeling the power, waving posters in English and Arabic, and shout-

ing slogans, the women surrounded and protected from police and security forces by cordons of male protestors. Walid
and his friends shifted uneasily closer together under the
banner they had prepared the night before.

"If we get separated, we'll regroup here," shouted Salim, his
eyes fierce as they pushed forward. They entered the thickening
accelerating crowd now thousands strong, the forest of human
bodies clustering closer as gesticulating men flowed fast toward
Tahrir Square from every side street, roaring, hurling rocks and
stones, shouting their own slogans, waving posters, unfurling
banners, advancing inexorably like a tsunami toward Cairo's
central square.

As Walid moved closer to the square, he remembered the
Midan Tahrir he had known in his youth. He remembered a
huge space with a statue marking the center, daunting to a boy
accustomed to a small village. The handsome wide open area
was surrounded by elegant buildings, one side now taken up by
a huge forbidding government building housing dozens of civil
servants including the dreaded *Mubahhaz,* where passports and
visas were given or withheld, and where destinies and desires
vanished in a confusion of red tape and petty power. A tumul-
tuous agglomeration of traffic exploded out into the square in
different directions, making it a major hazard for any pedestri-
an to attempt a crossing on foot. It had once been called *Ismail-
ia*, many years before his birth, and had been conceived as an
architectural focal point to the Paris on the Nile that Cairo was
then fast becoming.

Now, as he rounded a corner, Walid was amazed to see
tents and makeshift shelters already dotted about Tahrir

Square. He watched the crowd part with a tremendous roar as men on horses and camels rode furiously into the square, urging their steeds on with shouts and flailing arms among the galloping hordes of human bodies. He was stunned into immobility by the drama and energy exploding all around him. He had expected a supported protest, but nothing like this. Glancing at the banners and posters, he could see that many diverse ideological factions had united in a common cause as elections neared, in sheer terror of a status quo. Disillusion with government had clearly reached a tipping point. Egyptians had suffered enough. They had come to a decision that embraced all their diversity into a powerful unity. The autocratic rule of the military must end. Hosni Mubarak must be brought down.

Looking around, impressed beyond words by the sheer volume and continuous surges of new people into the square, Walid suddenly realized that he had lost sight of his comrades. "Salim," he shouted, but his voice drowned in the overwhelming chaos, "Salim!" He realized that his group had lost track of each other by the time they reached the edge of the milling crowds already in the square. Isolated within the enormous crowd, each watched, appalled, as the peaceful demonstration of their dreams inflated into a war. A pall of tear-gas smoke hung over areas of the enormous square which was fast becoming a wall to wall mass of seething bodies. People were coughing and choking from the tear gas. Some were falling. Black-garbed police wielded truncheons with increasing brutality and fired rubber bullets indiscriminately into the crowd, until defense became attack in the sea of bodies. Men were killed and women raped. Screams, the boom of exploding canisters, and the shriek of ambulances tore the morning apart. Tear-gas smoke draped everything in a grey mist.

As Walid watched in horror, he saw police dragging a battered bleeding corpse to piles of garbage lining the outer edges of the square, and hurling it onto the stinking piles of refuse. Earlier, some of the protesters had dug symbolic graves, signaling their intent to die rather than give up, and the upturned earth sprawled like open wounds here and there, some of the graves already occupied and covered with fresh earth.

More and more motley crowds of protesters surged toward the crowds packed into Tahrir Square, burning police stations and attacking jails along their way, as more and more continued to join them.

Walid and his friends were marching for freedoms, for justice, for economic issues, for an ideal world where there would be no more corruption and no more hunger. Into their ranks pushed looters and rapists, yelling pummeling gangs of violent young men heading for the encampments that flowered in Tahrir Square. Police and security forces met violence with violence. There were beatings and shootings.

Walid ran wildly wherever he could find space to run. He swerved and ducked, pushing his way through packed bodies, looking frantically for a friendly face, but there were none to be found. A pervasive stench of blood and sweat swirled around him. His heart ached with the death of his dreams and an overwhelming premonition that further disaster was at hand. He turned back and began to weave his way toward the edge of the square. He turned as a voice shouted his name, and he failed to see the truncheon that came crashing down on his defenseless body. His last thought was of Jamila. As he lost consciousness he called out her name.

He was among the hundreds that fell and his blood spilled unrecorded into the mud of Egypt, the country he had loved so deeply and had sworn to save.

Jasmine awoke in a cold sweat in the big king-size bed in Manhattan's upper east side, among pillows and billows of soft comfort. She must have had a bad dream. She shivered and stretched out her hand for Walid. Then she remembered that he was in Egypt. There was no way that she could reach him. She had no idea what he was up against, or when he would return.

There had been no word since he had left her, only the horrifying television coverage of the chaos in Tahrir Square and a disturbing sense of the disintegration of the dreams of Arab Spring in Egypt. She had told him to go, knowing he had to go for his own good, just as her mother had once told her. She felt more lonely than she had ever felt in her life. Egypt was no longer a place to her, it was a concept that had stolen her happiness. A deep dark shadow swept over her. She felt in her heart that she would never see her love again.

In the room across from hers, a small boy cried out. She felt heavier than stone, heavier than the earth itself, but she crawled out of bed and went to comfort her son.

The violence and encampments in Tahrir Square continued as day followed day. Two days after the revolution began, the Muslim Brotherhood threw in its support. Mubarak stepped down, his attempt to replace himself foiled. Eight hundred people died and hundreds more were wounded as the revolution ran its course over a period of eighteen days, and still there was no word from Walid. Jasmine remembered their earlier discussions about the likely communications problem and tried to maintain an acceptable level of calm and normality. Walid had left her with the name and contact information for one of his friends, Salim, and she began to think about what she would have to do to reach out to him if the terrible silence continued. Whatever her heart told her, she needed to hear definitively whether he had survived or not. She would not be able to go on living without knowing for sure.

"Where is Daddy now?" Wally asked, sensing the fear and sadness that was casting such a shadow on his mother. "Will he be coming home soon?"

She nodded wordlessly. He adored his father. She knew she could not share her fears with him. She knew in her heart that he would never see him again. She saw her son off to school every day wondering if this would be the day when she would have to destroy his confident little boy world and plunge him into realities so profound that they would change his life forever. Would this be the day she would hear? How would she hear? Who would tell her?

Malvina and Tim came over often to have dinner with her and to watch the television news coverage with her. They exclaimed over the dramatic videos of fierce men brandishing banners, and others wielding truncheons remorselessly, and they argued over which channel could be relied on for the latest most reliable news.

"You do know he's fine, don't you?" Tim said encouragingly, "You're being unreasonable, Jasmine. How can he get in touch with you with all that stuff going on over there? You'll certainly hear from him soon, or he may just turn up."

She tried to summon up smiles and echo the optimistic words they offered her, but the words rang false even to her own ears. She was not eating and she had lost weight. Every day she made an enormous effort to keep going for Wally's sake. She helped him with his homework every evening and pretended to eat dinner with him, pushing the food around on her plate so that he would not notice that she couldn't swallow it.

But she knew Walid was gone. She knew he was dead. She knew he would never hold her in his arms again. His promise to Madame Pasha had stolen him from her. Egypt had stolen him from her.

CHAPTER THIRTY-FOUR

2012 New York
COMING TO TERMS

As the days crawled by with no news of Walid, Jasmine felt herself sinking into a swamp of mental anguish where she sloshed about in her pain, finding no firm foothold and no pathway forward. There was nothing to hold onto, nothing left to give her hope. At first, she had tried to reach Salim at the address Walid had given her, but there was no answer. When he finally answered his phone, his voice was terse, all he could tell her was that he and Walid had got separated and that Walid had never shown up at the meeting place, nor had he been heard from since the events at Tahrir Square. No-one had seen him after the group had entered the square. She had no other way of finding out what had happened. Gradually, other news took the forefront and the events in Egypt became less and less of a news focus on television.

She could barely get out of bed in the mornings to see Wally off to school and the minute he ran out of the door to wait for the school bus, she fell back into bed, sobbing, moaning, and curled into herself with the pain of her loss. There was nothing left for her to do to discover what had happened to him. He had taken his laptop with him, so all of his interactions with his Egyptian friends had vanished with him. Had it not been for Wally, she would have thought that his reappearance in her life five years earlier had been a dream. She had tried to obtain information through the Egyptian consulate, but all they could tell her was that there had been many bodies in Tahrir Square, and unless he was carrying identifying papers, there was no way of telling if his had been one of them.

Tim and Malvina wept with Jasmine in her all-encompassing sorrow, took care of little Wally, and tried to lead Jasmine away from the dark place she was inhabiting. They immediately transformed the top two floors of the brownstone into a charming home for Jasmine and Wally. She could no longer bear to be in the apartment she had shared with Walid, where vanished happiness awaited her around every corner.

Nothing seemed to bring her out of the depression that had overwhelmed her. Jasmine was lost in a shadowy half-world where she stumbled alone in her nightmare, calling and screaming his name into drifting crowds, where no-one heard her voice. Wally grew accustomed to doing his homework at Malvina's kitchen table, where Jasmine had long ago done hers, creeping up to their apartment after a take-out dinner, quietly, so as not to disturb his mother, to go to sleep in his own bed. He was doing well at school, and his robust spirit, cushioned by the abundant love and support he received from Malvina and Tim, carried him through his bewilderment at the changes in his life. Malvina and Tim tried again and again to reach Jasmine and pull her back into life, but they were at their wits' end. They settled for making sure that she had food available and that her son was well taken care of.

One day Malvina climbed the stairs, calling out "I've a surprise for you, Jasmine." As usual, Jasmine was lying in her darkened bedroom, but a large presence swept past Malvina to the windows and pulled back the drapes.

"Ah no! *Mamoushka*," Irina Muchnik roared as Jasmine cowered on the bed, sunlight blasting into her consciousness, her hands up, covering her eyes. "What is going on here? Time for you to move on. Look at me. Marcel was my life, and I lost him, but I did not lose *myself*. You have your life. You have friends who love you. You have a son. Enough of this." As she talked, she moved heavily about the room, opening Jasmine's closet and pulling out a pale blue silk kimono sprayed with delicate blossom. She marched to the side of the bed, pulled Jasmine off it, and headed her to the bathroom. "Shower!" she announced. "Shampoo."

Jasmine could not help laughing helplessly, on the edge of hysteria as Irina marshaled her into shape. Her laughter suddenly turned into uncontrollable waves of hysterical tears, and Irina held her and stroked her back as she wept the enormous pain of her loss, on and on till her voice was hoarse and her sobs lost in whispers.

"Cry, cry, *Mamoushka,*" she said, "There were not enough tears for my sorrow, and there are not enough for yours. But now you have grieved long enough. Now it is time to think of living. It is not enough to be alive. You must live." She pushed Jasmine to her feet.

"Marcel never told me you were a colonel in the Russian army," Jasmine said, somewhere between tears, hiccups, and laughter.

"Backbone!" Pronounced Irina, unamused. "Backbone! I have it, and so do you." She had brought chicken soup and something wrapped in a cloth that smelled wonderful.

"I told her we could order in when I asked her to come over," said Malvina meekly, "but she wouldn't hear of it."

"Order in!" spat Irina with contempt. "This I made with my own two hands. Come, Jasmine, eat."

Caught up irresistibly in the whirlpool of Irina's energy, Jasmine soon found herself sitting at her kitchen table, clean and comfortable in her blue silk kimono, a steaming cup of chicken soup in front of her and her two elderly friends on either side.

"Now," said Irina in a tone that brooked no argument, "Let us talk about the future. Malvina has been telling me about this plan you have, ReTooling Hope? Did you ever develop that website you told her about? How far along are you with your plans?"

"Oh, Irina, I can't think about that now. I haven't thought about it in a while," said Jasmine wearily. "I never quite got it off the ground at the time, and then it didn't seem to matter," Jasmine shook her head between restorative gulps of Irina's fragrant soup.

"Irina, I have never tasted anything as wonderful as this soup," she added, giving Irina an appreciative smile.

Irina folded her arms, leaned back, and threw a triumphant look at Malvina, who was finding it hard to contain her amusement.

"Well I have an idea of my own," continued Irina, leaning forward. "I want to set up a foundation in Marcel's name, and this sounds just the thing to start out with. You will need money, and I will need help. So we have the perfect partnership." She sat back, beaming with satisfaction.

Jasmine sighed, "Oh, you two!" she said. "I can see what you are trying to do, and I confess, I think your plan is so kind. I do know I need to move on, but everything seems too much and too painful without Walid." Her voice broke and she took a moment to recover herself. Irina and Malvina watched anxiously, afraid that they might have pushed too hard, too soon.

But Jasmine continued, "you will have to give me more time. I promise I will not go back to that dark place you hauled me out of." She looked down at her empty cup.

At last, she glanced up at Irina, "You're right," she said, "I know it's time for that project to get off the ground. Young women at risk need help when they need it, and not months later. Walid believed in the project just as much as I did. It will be an appropriate memorial for him, too. Just give me time. It's so hard to accept his death with no body to bury, no stone to record his life, no place I can go to mourn."

Irina and Malvina nodded, their faces filled with sympathy. They looked at each other and wondered why they had not tackled the situation sooner. Jasmine had needed to be pried from her mourning. It was time.

Jasmine looked about her, suddenly conscious of the mess of rumpled clothes strewn about the room, the balled up tissues scattered all around the bed, and the general atmosphere of chaos in her home.

"I'll need to clean up a little first, though, and find my wits again," she said ruefully, "but I promise I'll get in touch with Matilda Moran sometime in the next weeks and set up a meeting."

She added with a grin, "she's going to love you, Irina."

The two older women rose as one and in no time the room reflected the order and grace it had known at a happier time. Irina had brought a huge bunch of sunflowers with the food she had cooked. She had set the cheerful blooms in a ceramic vase on the kitchen table, but now she took the vase and placed it on Jasmine's bedside table. The sunlight poured in through windows released from drapes, and caught the bold beauty of the gold petals contrasting with the black at the center of each. The room was illuminated. Jasmine caught her breath and lifted her face to the sunlight. Her long night of the soul was over. She was still wounded beyond repair, but life had settled back on her shoulders and was steering her toward a place where she might be able to recover.

Irina and Malvina hugged each other, and Jasmine caught the complicit look of delight they shared. Their plan had worked. They had shocked her back into life.

I am so lucky to have these two wonderful women in my life, Jasmine thought, as they heard footsteps outside and the door opened. Wally came in cautiously, and glanced around in disbelief. He stared at Jasmine in her blue silk kimono. "Mom?" he said, "Mom?" He dropped his book bag and clutched her about the waist, as he wept.

"I thought I lost you, too," he said through his tears.

CHAPTER THIRTY-FIVE

2011 New York
SALIM

Some weeks later, Jasmine's intercom gave an indignant squawk. She moved listlessly to the door, wondering who would come calling at such a late hour. She peered at the intercom and saw a small man, fidgeting, gaunt, and scarred, a slim packet in his hand. She had no idea who he was.

"Who are you?" She asked, cautiously opening the door on the chain.

"Salim," he muttered, constantly looking behind him as he spoke, his fear and unease palpable.

Her heart beating so fast she thought she would suffocate, Jasmine unhooked the chain and stepped back to let him in. For a moment, they stood awkwardly staring at each other.

"Salim," she said at last, with wonder, "How is it that are you here?"

"Walid asked me to find you and talk to you if something happened to him," said Salim. "For a long time, we didn't know where he was. We even thought he might have gone home to

New York until I got your phone messages. He had scribbled the name of his hotel on the bill we received for food we ordered the night before the march. I didn't know where he had been staying, but sometime after they released me from prison I found the bill, quite by chance, folded into a small compact square and wedged between the uneven table leg and the floor to keep the table from wobbling. There it was, still in my rooms, like a message from Walid. He had told me that he left hidden papers under a floorboard in his room, and that he had been given a room on the top floor of the hotel where he was staying."

They stared at each other in sorrowful silence. " What happened to you, Salim?" Jasmine said at last, tears in her eyes.

Salim sighed and looked away before answering.

"I was singled out by police that day in Tahrir Square, beaten repeatedly, and I then spent several weeks in jail. They came to fetch me every day and the torture was relentless…" his voice was strained and he muttered "but enough of that. There was nothing I could tell them, no-one I could lead them to. Eventually, they gave up on me and let me out. I was one of the lucky ones. Others fared much worse."

His hand went to his left leg. He pulled at the trouser leg and Jasmine had a glimpse at twisted scarred flesh. She winced and looked away, and he resumed, "It took me a while to recover. I only recently came upon the folded paper, and I had no energy to go and look for his things in the hotel." He looked Jasmine in the eye and said in a low voice "I will not burden you with the details. All I can tell you is that the prison experience was horrible beyond words. I am still trying to move past it. It took some time before I could look anywhere beyond my own recovery."

Salim's eyes clouded over with dark memories. He looked down, and then glanced apologetically at Jasmine. "You are as beautiful as he told us," he said, embarrassed, "I am only sorry I could not bring him back to you." Tears sprang to Jasmine's eyes as she waited for him to continue.

"The man at the hotel reception didn't want to let me in, but a little *baksheesh* did the trick. I insisted, and he gave me a key in the end, grumbling all the way. I didn't find any clothes in the room, so he must have taken them and sold them when Walid didn't come back, but I did find the loose floorboard Walid had told me about, and his laptop was wedged inside, together with his passport and the other papers, intact."

Jasmine gasped and put a hand to her throat. "That's amazing," She said, "how did you get over here, to New York?"

My mother's sister, my Aunt Hanina owns a small clothing store in Brooklyn and is married to an American. It was her dearest wish that I represent my late mother at the 90th birthday celebration her children were planning for her. They all pulled every string in sight, and managed to obtain a brief tourist visa for me to come to New York for the occasion. I thought I would take this opportunity to fulfill my promise to my dear friend, and bring his treasured possessions to his family." He cleared his throat as he held out the package to her.

"These are his things," he said, sadly, hoarse with emotion, "he never went back for them so I am sure he died that day. Having no identifying papers on him, who knows where they buried him. I am so very sorry. Walid was a good friend. I'm only glad that I have been able to get them back to you. He told us about you and about his little boy, and he had every intention of coming home to you both. Walid was the best and the smartest of us all. He saw right away that we had made a crucial political mistake in not having a leader to put in place immediately when the fever of revolution was still high, but by then, it was too late. Our wonderful Arab Spring ended in violence and chaos and we all paid the price."

He glanced up and met the overwhelming sorrow in Jasmine's eyes. He added firmly, "The dream will continue. My aunt's birthday celebration was yesterday and I return to Egypt tomorrow. I will bring together all who remain of our group. We will bring about change, and we will force stability. His death will not have been in vain."

Jasmine reflected that stability would be hard to find anywhere. She saw that he had tears in his eyes. Impulsively she hugged him and ushered him toward the kitchen. "I know how to make a good Turkish coffee," she said. "I have a nice brass *kanaka* that Walid brought with him when he came to America and he taught me how to make it. He hated the American coffee, although he quite liked the occasional double espresso." She smiled sadly. "Would you like a good *ahwa turki* and something to eat?"

He shook his head regretfully. "No, thank you," he said, "My aunt expects me back as soon as possible. We may never see each other again. She is 90, after all." He smiled, somewhat wistfully. "I must go."

She led him to the door. "Realize his dreams for him, Salim," she said impulsively, "and thank you so much for bringing these things to me. It means more than you can imagine."

She clutched the laptop and the envelopes to her as she closed the door behind him. She would have something of his father to give to Wally one day.

CHAPTER THIRTY-SIX

2011 Cairo
ALI

By the morning of January 11th, 2011, Ali, hurrying along the endless corridors of the large hospital, had become increasingly aware of a deluge of tweets and alerts about a huge protest gathering planned for Tahrir Square. He had hesitated as to whether or not he really wanted to get involved. He had worked and studied so hard for so long, always sustained and encouraged by the support of Doctor Amir, and he had finally obtained certification as a male nurse. He loved his work with patients and he enjoyed the status his new job afforded him. He hesitated to do something that he feared might reopen old wounds. He was anxious not to jeopardize the satisfying life he had created for himself. But as he moved about his work he noticed more and more doctors and nurses, groups of hospital workers gathering and whispering together. He realized that something major was afoot. He had seen the dysfunction spreading throughout Egypt up close and personal, as much from his own experiences as from his daily contact with others in distress. He began to feel compelled to publicly express his hope that things might change. So when he saw Hassan and a squad of his orderlies move eagerly toward the street, he threw caution to the winds, joined them, and made his way into the rivers of protesters streaming toward the huge square.

At first, the men from the hospital were a jocular crowd, laughing, singing, slapping each other on the back, behaving like children given an unexpected day off from school, and glad for the chance to be taking part in something so significant. With them, Ali pushed and pulled and elbowed his way deeper and deeper into the square. Hours went by, and Ali became aware that the mood around him had grown somber as it became clear how many people were packing themselves into the square. He had moved ahead of his friends, trying to forge a path into the massed and turbulent crowd. Turning to say something to Hassan, he realized he had completely lost sight of his co-workers. Only strangers seethed around him, faces contorted with rage and passion. A huge man pushed him out of the way and he almost fell, but managed to keep his balance and to keep moving.

More time passed, and he could find no trace of the others from the hospital. At last, he decided that he should get back. The violence and chaos that surrounded him were opening old wounds. He shuddered, feeling an overwhelming weariness of spirit. Realizing that there would be a need for all hands on deck at the hospital he started to head back, observing more and more people along the way, fallen and writhing in agony, legs, backs, collar-bones fractured, more and more becoming victims of brutality from police and roving gangs whose feet relentlessly pounded ahead regardless of bodies on the ground.

As he began to push his way toward a side street leading to the hospital, he glimpsed an oddly familiar figure far ahead of him. The man was fending off people massing around him and edging toward the limit of the square. As Ali stared at him, the man turned and his profile was momentarily outlined against the light. Ali caught his breath and shouted out a name, hoping he was right, and that his voice would carry above the unmodulated din exploding between them. The man instantly turned his head. Before he could respond, Ali roared in fury as he watched a police truncheon crash down. Horrified, painful memories of his own experience with police brutality surfacing with full force, he scratched, shoved, and clawed his way to where he thought his boyhood friend had gone down. Bodies were everywhere underfoot. He picked his way among the dead with terror in his heart. Ali had lost so many and so much. He could not give up the search, and he could not give up the hope that Walid had survived. A man lying on his side without movement was in his way. He almost stepped on him, but stopped just in time and stepped over him. Looking down, he gasped. Kneeling beside the man, he detected a faint pulse. Walid was unconscious, but he was not dead. Waving frantically at a passing ambulance, its siren wailing relentlessly as it slowly made its way through the thick crowds, Ali was relieved to see that it was from his own hospital. He yelled the names of the orderlies, who shouted and waved, directing the ambulance toward where he stood. He helped them to settle Walid on a stretcher and followed him back to the hospital.

The ER was swarming with chaos, blood slick on the floors, people elbowing each other ruthlessly out of the way and shouting at the tops of their voices. It was a terrifying bewildering kaleidoscope of noise and turbulence. Many wounded were being brought in by distraught relatives or friends. Noticing Ali's drawn face, as he stood, one hand on the stretcher, one of the doctors hurried over to him.

"Ali, are you alright? I was looking for you." He glanced down at the motionless figure on the stretcher and up at Ali's face.

" Friend of yours?"

Ali nodded wordlessly and watched as the doctor motioned for the patient to be moved to a quieter area. He bent over the still figure and carried out a careful examination. The man had sustained a powerful blow to the head, and although he was breathing, he was clearly in a deep coma.

Seeing that he seemed to have no identifying papers, the doctor sighed. "Take him to the sixth floor, Ali," he said kindly, "there's a small room off my office. We should get him out of this mess and you can put him there for a few days until we know who he is, or until he wakes up from the coma. He sustained a pretty bad blow to the head. There may be permanent brain damage. You should know that he may not ever regain consciousness." He put a hand compassionately on Ali's shoulder. "Get back quickly," he added, "you are sorely needed down here."

Ali nodded, deeply saddened as he remembered the last time he had seen Walid in his new *galabeya* and leather sandals as he was about to leave the village, heading to Cairo to join his father, his face alight with dreams of an exciting future. Ali had refused to shake his hand, mired in his own stew of jealousy and anger. All he felt now was a profound sense of loss.

"Where were you, Ali?" The small nurse, Mona, whose merry eyes and rounded figure had made him yearn for her friendship, ran after him as he pushed the stretcher toward the elevator.

"Ali, you left earlier without a word," she said, pouting, "and we couldn't find you. Where were you?"

He turned to her and made a helpless gesture, trying to hold back the sour floods of emotion that were sweeping over him.

"Mona," he said, his voice hoarse, "You have no idea how close I once came to being kicked out of life altogether, like a piece of garbage. There was no work for me. There was no hope. There was no future. I thought I might be able to help to change some of those things for others by joining the protest in Tahrir Square. I thought that was where I should be today. I couldn't see anyone to notify here, and a large boisterous group was heading out for Tahrir Square, so I ran after them. You cannot imagine what crowds were gathering there. And in all that mess, I was amazed to catch a glimpse of an old friend I hadn't seen in years. I was about to go to him, but before I could come close, he was bludgeoned by police and left in this state." He stared sadly at the motionless man on the stretcher.

Mona hesitated, and then said sheepishly, flushing, "I covered for you. They were looking for you earlier." She looked down demurely.

"Thanks," said Ali, giving her a half-hearted smile. His mood lifted, however, and he settled Walid into the small room on the sixth floor with Mona helping to hook him up to the IV and the monitors.

Ali visited the room every day, but nothing changed, and the fallout from the events in Tahrir Square had created a huge increase in his workload. Days and weeks passed, and still

Walid said nothing and his eyes remained sealed to the world around him.

The room was always quiet except for electronic chirps and whistles. The blue light from the monitor beside the bed flickered as it registered the vital signs of the man who lay motionless under the sheet, eyes closed, his breathing regular.

A nurse crept into the room, rubber-soled feet squeaking faintly on the tiled floor. She checked the monitor and the patient, and left as silently as she had come.

After she left, a man opened the door and came slowly into the room. He was tall and handsome with a thick black beard. He was dressed in the clean white uniform of the hospital orderlies and nurses, with an ID card around his neck. He stood by the bed for a long time, motionless, staring down at the figure in the bed.

At last, he bent over, muttering "Walid, you have to wake up. They won't let me keep you here forever. I don't know where you live, or who to contact about you. I found you unconscious in Tahrir Square and brought you here to the hospital where I work." He shook his head. "It has now been many weeks, and they do not know what to do about you. I am a nurse here and so far they have allowed me to care for you, but soon they will need to make a decision to let you go, one way or another. Please wake up, Walid. Please?" His voice broke.

There was no movement from the figure in the bed. The eyes remained closed, the breathing regular. Ali straightened up and shook his head. He gave a sigh of exasperation.

"Walid," he said, "You had no identification on you. None of the authorities seem to know who you are. I have no idea who to contact. I have lost contact with everyone in our village.

Please, please wake up. You were wearing fine clothes when I found you. You must have a good life somewhere, people who care about you, people who are wondering where you are?" There was a note of desperation in his voice.

He stood a little longer, watching, hoping, but there was no movement. He sighed and left the room, his heart heavy, his mind unable to offer a solution as to what he should do. The doctors had indicated that they could no longer keep Walid on life-support unless he seemed capable of coming out of the coma, and so far, there had been no sign that this could happen.

In some odd way, Ali felt as if Walid was the last possible link to his own identity. His village had changed beyond recognition and his parents had disappeared. Hamid was long dead. Jamila had vanished years ago from his life. Yet fate had dropped Walid, unconscious, at his feet. He needed to talk to him. He wanted desperately to talk to him. He needed to feel connected to his past.

The room was always hushed, bathed in a uniformly pale light, monitors winking and blinking by the side of the bed where the still form of the tall man lay, his eyes closed, his breathing slow and regular, his soul lost in a nether world of silence and pain.

The night nurse crept in on rubber-soled feet and stood close to the bed, looking thoughtfully at the man. Handsome, she thought to herself.

"I wonder who you are?" she said aloud into the silence. Sighing, she sat beside the bed and took his hand in hers. "Who brought you in?" she whispered, stroking his hand. "Does nobody miss you? You were there, in Tahrir Square, where it was all happening. You must have been one of the protesters. Now you just lie here, week after week. We all know that you are Ali's friend, but soon they will have to make decisions about you. Nobody knows what to do with you."

She had been taught that it was important to talk to coma patients, so she went on with her thoughts spoken aloud. " I wish you would open your eyes and tell me who you are?" She said it with pain, and she kept whispering to him until the matron swept by the open door, hurried into the room, and sent her packing. "There's so much work, and so many hands are needed in the ER," she said sternly. "Off you go. No time to sit there talking to a handsome man."

The matron hurried after her, but turned for a quick glance at the bed. She gasped, and clutched at her heart. The man in the bed had his eyes open and was staring at her.

CHAPTER THIRTY-SEVEN

New York
JASMINE'S MIRACLE

Jasmine headed slowly up the stairs to the top floor of the townhouse. Malvina called to her as she walked past their open door, but she went on climbing, calling back,

"I've an armful of groceries, Malvina, I'll come down for a chat as soon as I get them put away. Is Wally doing his homework in your kitchen?"

As she struggled to open the door, her heavy bags slipping and sliding, she could hear the phone in her apartment ringing and ringing. There was an urgent insistent sound to the ringing. It kept stopping, and then starting up again. Sighing, she kicked the last bag in and pulled the door closed, turning as the ringing stopped again. She gave a sigh of mixed exasperation and relief, but then it started again. Surprised, she went over to it and picked up the receiver, half annoyed already that anyone could be so insistent.

"Jamila," said a deep voice she did not recognize. "Jamila, it's me, it's Ali."

Her vision blurred and she pulled over a chair and tried to stop her body from shaking. At last, her words came out in a whisper, "Ali?" she said " Ali, my brother? Where are you? How is it that you are calling?" There was much crackling and whistling on the line, but she heard words through it that she could hardly believe.

"Jamila, listen to me. I am here in Cairo at the hospital where I work, and I am with your husband, Walid. He wanted me to tell you that he is fine. He was in a coma for weeks after the events at Tahrir Square, but he will be coming home to you as soon as the doctors say he can be moved. My friend, Doctor Amir, says he will make a complete recovery.

Jamila, I have missed you so. Walid tells me you are his wife. Who can believe such a thing? He tells me that the two of you have a son together. Walid is still very weak, but he wants to speak to you himself."

Jasmine was gasping for breath as she listened to the voice she had thought never to hear again,

"Jamila, I love you."

Much later as she sat in Malvina's comfortable living room, Ted and Malvina hanging on her every word, she told them what had happened, tears pouring down her face as she spoke.

"I never thought to hear either of their voices again," she said, weeping. Pulling herself together she added, "I will need to go to Cairo next week to see Ali, and to bring Walid home. Ali is very happy in his life, he says, but there is so much I want to know about him. We need to fill in all those years we have been apart. I wanted him to come back to America with us, but he has no wish to do so, although he promises to come and visit one day, and is anxious to meet his nephew."

She stopped talking and sobbed uncontrollably, and Malvina came over and rocked her in her arms, murmuring soothing sounds through her own tears of happiness. Wally, who had been doing his homework at the kitchen table, stared at them both with huge disbelieving eyes.

"Is Daddy really coming home?" He asked, "he wasn't dead after all? He's really alive? What happened to him?"

The women nodded through their tears.

"Come here, Wally," said his mother, opening her arms to hug him, "let us together enjoy this extraordinary miracle that has happened in our lives," and she began to laugh, a wild joyous sound he had never heard before. He looked up, startled, and then, caught and held by the moment, he began to laugh too, convinced at last that his father was really coming home.

 PILOGUE

2015 New York
THE LETTER

Jasmine celebrated her sixtieth birthday quietly at Le Cirque, with her husband and her son, Wally. The head waiter, deferential, led her to the best table in the house.

"Madame will be comfortable here," he said solicitously, and she smiled her thanks. She was still an arresting beauty with a superb sense of style, and heads still turned as she stepped into the restaurant, but she no longer excited *paparazzi* to a frenzy.

When Walid brought her home after dinner, she found a small brown package waiting for her in the lobby. She took it up to her apartment, found her scissors and cut the string. Inside, she found an envelope with a letter in a handwriting she did not recognize, and an ornate gold frame with the black and white portrait of a woman from another era, a beautiful, majestic woman. Her period clothes, the rows upon rows of large pearls resting on her bosom, her gathered curls and coquettish hair ornament showed off high cheekbones, slanted eyes and an imperious magnetism. The woman looked oddly familiar.

Her heart beating fast, Jasmine opened the envelope and read:

Dear Jasmine,

If you are reading this letter, I have recently died. Lara promised to make sure that it would get to you. She knows what it contains. She opens her heart and her home to you.

You saved my life and gave me years in which to enjoy my family, and now, most recently, my daughter Rivka's baby, my granddaughter, Elena Jasmine. There is no way that I can ever truly thank you for such a gift. Little Elena fills me with such inexpressible joy. She looks at me with the eyes of my great-grandmother, whom I barely knew. Her eyes are a deep sparkling green, like yours.

So I am moved, before the cloak of death obscures everything, to share with you an exquisite moment I experienced in 1956, a few days before my parents and I left Egypt forever. I was fifteen, restless and lonely. It was the time of the annual mango harvest, and a girl from the mango family had somehow made her way into the house. She was utterly delightful. We talked and laughed and looked at books together, and she was fascinated by the portrait you have in your hand, which sat on an abandoned desk in a small room in the large house. I never knew her name, or the name of the village by the Nile her family came from, but we shared a transcendental moment I have never forgotten, and I have come to believe that because of that moment, you were here to save my life in the twin towers.

Look at it this way. A high fashion model born by the banks of the river Nile in Egypt, with eyes as distinctive as those of my great-grandmother, came to my rescue and saved my life during the 9/11 terrorist attack. Why?

Make of this what you will. Destiny moves in mysterious ways. I have no desire to impose on you in any way. Your life is full and successful. I am proud to know you.

I am now an old man and life has taught me that each of us is the sum of the desires and actions of those who came before us. We cannot see the patterns that our lives create in the world, or the ways in which our lives impact others. We carry in our selves the dreams and choices of a myriad voices, and the chorus of their song makes us who we are. We hear from them a faint music, but we cannot separate them from each other and we cannot distinguish meaning.

This much I do know. It has been my privilege and my blessing to have known you, Jasmine, an extraordinary woman who, alone, created a full, rich life for herself. I cannot know why our destinies intersected on that terrible day. I only know that although I was a stranger to you, you refused to let me die. I know that your strength and determination miraculously sustained me throughout that day. I know that I would not have lived past that day had it not been for you. I know that it was meant to be.

I also know that there is nothing you want or need from me. There is nothing I can give you in return for the inestimably unique gift you gave me of my life.

Except, perhaps, I can give you this story about a charmed encounter in Egypt between a lonely fifteen-year-old boy and a beautiful girl from the mango harvest fam-

ily, who came together for a moment, as both their lives were about to change forever.

I need to tell you that I am certain that you are the result of that moment.

And so I pass along to you this portrait of Elena, my great-grandmother. It is the only object my mother brought with her out of Egypt. She urged me to save it, and give it to my oldest child one day. I have cherished this link to my past, as I know you will.

Thank you for saving my life, the life of a wandering Jew from Egypt, and thank you for being who you are.

I leave you my love, my thanks, my pride, and my blessing.

Sol.

Wally looked up from the book he was holding. "What was your birthday gift, Mother?" he asked, taking the gold frame into large hands so like his father's, and examining the portrait as Walid looked on, amused.

"Who is it from?"

Jasmine studied his face and saw what Lara had seen years earlier. She heard Aunt Nadia's voice telling her about Salwa's venture into the big house at the time of the last mango harvest, and she understood.

Her green eyes glistening with unshed tears, Jasmine hesitated, then answered, her voice shaking,

"It's from my father."

The End

GLOSSARY

(Egyptian terms)

aywa ya sit	yes, madam
abaya	long loose overgarment
ashan di	for this
awaz	do you want
abou	father
biziada	enough
boab	guardian gate-keeper
bukra	tomorrow
daya	rural Egyptian midwife
Effendi	title of respect
falouka	sailing vessel on the Nile
falafel	fried bean cakes
ful medames	fava bean soup
galabeya	garment native to Nile valley
gamoosa	water buffalo
habibti	my darling
hookah	water pipe
ya ibni	my son
kanaka	long-handled Turkish coffee pot

molokhia	Egyptian spinach-like soupy greens
madrassa	school
maquagi	ironer
muezzin	calls Muslims to prayer from tower
muski	Egyptian bazaar
oumi	mother
piaster	Egyptian currency
yallah	get on with it
ya agouz	old man
ya bint	my girl
ya sidi	term of endearment (literally: orange blossom)
wallahi	swear and affirmation word

Printed in Great Britain
by Amazon